ECHOES OF THE HEART

Second-Chance Romance Anthology

Includes these stories:

Heather & Mike

Sandy & Rafe

Liz & Nick

Paige & Bill

Note from the Author

Dear Reader,

Thank you for taking a chance on my second chance romance series. When I looked at the stories forming in my heart, so many were second chance romances, I figured why not have a series?

The characters in these stories are not connected, don't necessarily know each other. They are drawn together by the fact that they have a second chance at true love with someone from their past.

When I asked my friends if they have one love they left behind, each nodded and smiled. I guess many of us moved on from men we truly cared about in days gone by. Some days, when life gets tough, we may wonder, "what if?"

These are those "what if" stories. I hope you enjoy them and will read them all. I write them as they come to me, so I have no set number in mind for the series. I'll bring out second chance romance novellas in this series as close together as possible.

Thank you for taking this journey with me.

Best wishes,

Jean Joachim

HEATHER & MIKE
Echoes of the Heart
JEAN C. JOACHIM

Heather & Mike:
The One That Got Away

Jean C. Joachim

Moonlight Books

A MOONLIGHT BOOKS NOVELLA

Sensual Romance

Heather & Mike

The One That Got Away

Echoes of the Heart series

Copyright © 2018 Jean C. Joachim

COVER DESIGN BY DAWNÉ Dominique

Edited by Sherri Good

Proofread by Renee Waring

All cover art and logo copyright © 2017 by Moonlight Books

PUBLISHER

Moonlight Books

Dedication

For Johnny

Chapter One

New York City, Upper East Side of Manhattan
Thrusting his hand into his pocket, Mike Sullivan made sure the little box from the jewelers was there. Of course, Amy might prefer to pick out her own ring, but she'd been hinting around about marriage for so long he guessed any ring would be welcomed.

On his way to the hair salon to pick up his girl, his phone dinged. It was a text saying they had been backed up and she was behind schedule. Already halfway there, he kept going.

His stomach became queasy. Was proposing to Amy a good idea? Good, old reliable Amy. Bill, his buddy, had made a case for her. He'd pointed out how dependable she was, how down-to-earth, rock solid, predictable. She'd never surprise him with something unpleasant, like screwing around. Mike gave a short laugh. Nope, Amy would never cheat on him because he doubted anyone would ask.

It wasn't that she wasn't a beauty, though she put out a lot of effort and came damn close. The woman had no sexual heat, but she was dependable as hell. He knew, when he got home from work, dinner would be on the table fifteen minutes later—every single night. As he waited for a red light to change, Bill's words echoed in his head.

"What do you expect? Marriage is about give and take. You want someone who's gonna be there to raise your kids. Pick 'em up from school every day. Cook dinner. Amy's an excellent cook."

He was right about that. Amy could cook like a gourmet chef. Mike frowned.

"You're not still mooning over that flaky chick from Fire Island, are you?" Bill had asked.

"You mean Heather?"

"Yeah. That's the one. It's fuckin' five years already. You've looked everywhere for her. She's gone, buddy. You need a dependable girl, like Amy. Get married. Have a couple of kids."

"What about happiness?" Mike had asked.

"Much overrated," Bill had said as he shook his head.

Mike wasn't so sure. Still, he'd planned to move into Amy's apartment. In three days men were coming to stuff his belongings into a storage locker. His place was pretty well packed up. He couldn't move in with her without at least the promise of marriage, could he? A lot of men did, but not Mike. He didn't roll that way. Still, marriage meant giving up his dream of Heather. Was he ready to do that? He pushed her out of his mind and crossed the street.

When he arrived, he had about a half hour wait. Her hair had to be perfect. Everything about Amy had to be perfect; her clothes, her house, he hesitated to put down a glass, even on a coaster, on the coffee table. So God damn perfect it made him nervous. That was about to come to an end, once he moved in. "Messy Mike" she'd nicknamed him. He hated it, but she was right.

Heather popped into his mind. Her shoulder-length light brown hair hadn't been perfect. Wind-blown from the ocean breezes, it had whipped around her face before settling on her shoulders in loose, messy curls. She'd worn no makeup that he could see, except a little lipstick. Pages of articles and stories had littered her beach house. There had been nothing perfect about Heather, except that she'd been perfect for him.

Sitting back, he rummaged through the magazines for customers until he found his favorite, *Esquire.* Glancing over the cover, he spied a small headline for an essay inside. It was titled, *The One that Got Away.* And it was written by a best-selling author named Heather

Stone. He searched his brain, but couldn't recall Heather's last name, but he was pretty sure it wasn't Stone.

Heather had been an aspiring writer when he knew her. But this couldn't be her. Still, he thumbed through to the article, just to make sure. He read the opening sentence, and his mouth went dry.

"Mike, where are you?"

His eyes widened. No, this couldn't be, she must be talking about someone else. But he read on anyway.

I'll be darned if I can remember your last name. But you were the love of my life five years ago and I tossed you away like an old pizza box. I've regretted it ever since. I didn't even listen to your explanation. I dumped you like a hot coal. I was wrong. If you're out there, please give me another chance.

He stared into space, remembering that last day, five years ago.

Broken-hearted, Mike had leaned against the railing on the Fire Island ferry, riding back to civilization. Amid a crowd of twenty-somethings, he had struggled to keep his emotions in check. The boat was jammed with bodies making their way back to life in the big city on Labor Day. Summer was over.

He'd met the girl he'd been waiting for, then screwed it up. Listening to Bill, his best friend, was totally stupid. Anger had seethed in Mike when he thought of the idiotic advice his friend had given him.

"She's one chick. It was ten days. Don't be an asshole. Branch out."

Under Bill's guidance, Mike had spent the next weekend with a girl he'd barely known, instead of Heather. After finding out about it, Heather had cried, refused to speak to him, and taken the ferry back two days early.

On the choppy ride across the bay, he'd stood alone, searching for a way to mend the relationship. In a feeble attempt at a fifth apology, he'd called her, but she'd blocked his number.

She'd breezed into his life and seized his heart as if it was her due. And then she was gone because he had been an idiot. He'd been devastated.

Eventually, he'd moved on. But Mike had never forgotten her.

"Ready?" Amy asked.

Mike looked up. Smiling, Amy stood before him, every hair in place.

"I thought we'd go to Romeo's for dinner. Is that okay?" she asked.

Flustered, he tucked the magazine under his arm and struggled to bring his brain back to the present.

"Sure, sure. Romeo's is fine."

He closed his fingers over the tiny box in his jacket pocket and transferred it to his pants. He pushed it all the way down before opening the door for her and heading uptown.

AFTER DINNER, MIKE stowed the magazine in his briefcase. Itching to read the rest of the piece, he couldn't manage to sneak away from Amy long enough. There was no way he could read that article with her in the room. What if it really was Heather? His Heather? He swallowed. It would be too good to be true.

Amy made decaf and served him a cup.

"Have you thought about taking your father's offer?"

"What?" Damn, he had to focus.

"You know. About switching places with Sean?"

"You mean giving up sales director and being president of the company?"

"That was your father's suggestion, wasn't it?"

"It was. Sean would be lousy in sales. And I like my job. I'm comfortable with sales."

"But it takes you away on trips a couple of times a year. Business dinners."

"Ah, yes. I see. My father pointed that out to me, too. Since Sean doesn't have a steady girl, and I do, it might be better for me to be home and for him to travel?"

She nodded.

"Just because my father owns the company doesn't mean he can move Sean and me around like pawns on a chessboard. I doubt Sean would go for it. And I certainly wouldn't."

She frowned and finished her coffee. "I'm tired. I'm going to bed."

Taking the two empty cups, Mike headed for the kitchen. He turned on the faucet.

"Aren't you coming?" Amy asked.

"You said you were tired. I'm not. I'll clean up."

"I can do that."

"It's okay. I don't mind." He hated hiding his reason for wanting to stay up. Not only was he salivating to get at that article, but he had no interest in making love to Amy. She'd pushed him once too often about giving up sales. Turned him off. Maybe everything about Amy was perfect, but not for Mike. And he had no desire to let her smooth out his rough edges.

She shrugged, kissed him and trotted off to the bedroom. Mike finished the cups and saucers in record time. When he heard the click of the door closing, he whipped out the dog-eared publication.

Dimming the lights, he flipped through it until he got to the article. Torn between a desire to read every word or bag it, and skip to the end, he forced himself to slow down. She described their last encounter. For sure, Heather Stone was his Heather. She admitted how she had been wrong to shut it down without giving him a chance to explain.

Damn right you were, woman!

Then came the hook.

So, Mike, if you're out there, and you feel the same way, let's see if the old magic still exists. Let's get together. I will be at Charlie's River-side Café every Sunday from one until three in the afternoon for the next three months. Come find me.

Mike sat back. He could hardly believe it. Here was his chance. He'd find Heather again and have what he'd only dreamed about for the last five years. He grinned. His body tingled, and his nerves jumped to life. Goosebumps erupted on his skin, and he pushed to his feet to pace. Should he go there alone or drag Bill along? Then it hit him. He'd have to break up with Amy.

How could he marry a woman when he felt this way about someone else? Wasn't it the ultimate lie? Mike considered himself an honest man, sometimes too honest. He couldn't do it. Even the idea of getting back with Heather made his blood race, a whole lot more than Amy ever had. Sweat broke out on his forehead. He'd been with Amy for two years. This would kill her. She'd been counting on him, and he'd done nothing to discourage it.

And what if Heather took one look at him and hated him? What if she'd changed, become some authorly snob? He'd be throwing away a woman who cared for him for nothing, a dream, a whim, a ghost. He chewed a nail.

Pressure built. Mike had to talk to someone, and not Amy. Bill, his best friend Bill, who was responsible for this whole mess from the beginning. He picked up the phone.

"Yeah?"

"It's me."

"I got that. What do you want? It's late."

"Oh, yeah, sorry about that. You've gotta meet me for lunch to-morrow."

"I think I have a business lunch."

"Cancel it. Reschedule. I have to see you. It's urgent."

"You're not dying or anything, are you?" Bill yawned.

"No. But it's urgent. Have you ever known me to say that when it wasn't true?"

"Maybe once or twice. Okay, okay. I'll clear my schedule. Eddie's at twelve?"

"Yes, Eddie's at twelve."

Mike hung up. He sighed. This was good. Bill, who hated Heather for some reason Mike couldn't fathom, would play devil's advocate. If breaking up with Amy was certifiable, totally lunatic, Bill would be the one to tell him. Relieved, Mike headed for the bedroom, too excited to sleep, but too exhausted not to.

ACROSS TOWN, RIVERSIDE Drive

"Did you get your passport today?" Ian asked, coming up behind the brunette.

"Not yet. There's time."

"Heather, angel, we are leaving for Amsterdam in two months," he said, wrapping his arms around her from behind.

"You're leaving. I'm still not sure I can get away. I might have to wait another month or so," she said, stepping out of his embrace.

"Darling, don't you want to come with me?"

She turned and gazed into his gray eyes. His dark blond hair, combed back, his crisp white shirt tailored to his slim frame, he looked and smelled good. A native Dutchman, Ian Slager worked in finance. He was wealthy, cultured, and adored her. Why couldn't she commit to him? She'd been seeing him for a year. He'd met every item on her list of the perfect man—with one exception. He wasn't Mike. Mike what's-his-name.

"Of course I do."

"The apartment is beautiful. Much grander than this," he said, holding up a hand to silence her defense of her digs. "Not that this isn't charming. It is. But if we are to have children, it's a wee bit small."

"New Yorkers are used to tight spaces. Besides, it has a backyard. Most places don't."

"True, true. I promise you an office where you can write all day long."

"I know. But here I have the birds and squirrels to keep me company," she said.

"Ach. You just don't love me enough, that's all."

She stepped closer, kissing him with passion. "How can you say that?"

"Ah, yes, in the bedroom, you are fine. But here? Not so much."

She glanced at her watch.

"Are you going on one of your little jaunts?"

She nodded.

"So mysterious. Why won't you tell me where you go and why?"

"A woman has to have some secrets."

"Ah, give it up. I make enough money for us to live in style. Marry me. Come to Amsterdam. Think of the beautiful children we could make."

Ian's offer tempted her. What a relief it would be to give up the pressure from her publisher, the money drain of her sister, who was going through a messy divorce, and the book she was stalled on. To hightail it out of town, duck responsibilities, and not return dreaded phone calls might be the answer to her unhappiness.

But not yet. She hadn't given up hope of finding Mike. It hadn't been long enough. She'd waited five years before deciding to write that essay. Her publisher pulled every string she could to get it into his favorite magazine. And yet, nothing. She'd been going, faithfully, every Sunday, with no luck. She'd sit at a table in the corner and look at the men who'd show up.

She'd worn sunglasses and a hat, so they wouldn't recognize her easily. She'd know Mike the second she saw him. Or she hoped she would. He could have put on fifty pounds. Even so, she'd recognize those broad shoulders, the thick brown hair, and his impish grin.

He hadn't shown up—yet. Maybe he hadn't read the article? Or maybe he hated her for dumping him. Or maybe he'd never loved her to begin with. She shook her head. Recalling the way his smile faded, the sadness in his eyes when she shut the door in his face. She shuddered to remember how badly she'd behaved. And now it was too late, or almost too late. Or maybe it really was too late. Maybe he was dead. She sucked in air. *God damn!* She'd never considered that. What a horrible idea! He couldn't be dead. Nope, Mike was too full of life to die before he was thirty-five.

She had kept Ian dangling for months. Fear that he would finally leave in disgust dogged her. Her mother had nagged her to tie the knot with him before "he got away" as she so crudely put it. A sweet man, so buttoned-up, he left nothing to chance. He'd wooed her with the intention of winning. Of course, before she became a best-selling author, a man like Ian probably wouldn't have given her a second glance.

She'd been to press parties, publishing parties, and magazine events until her feet ached and she never wanted to see another glass of white wine, ever. Ironically, she'd met Ian at an Esquire party. Marilyn, her publisher, had introduced them. Ian was just out of a six-month relationship and lonely as hell.

He took her to posh restaurants, bought fine wines, the best chocolates, lingerie from Henri Bendel. And she'd caved. Heart-sick for a sweet lover, she'd climbed in with Ian, and couldn't find her way out.

Where Mike was rough-around-the-edges, Ian was well-mannered perfection. Where Mike was a beer and baseball guy, Ian was a rare wine and symphony guy. Where Mike was an up-and-comer,

Ian had already arrived. Where Mike was a no-nonsense truth-teller, Ian was a smooth-talking manipulator. Her mother and her friends agreed that Mike was all wrong for her. Only her sister supported her. Marissa told her to wait for Mike because marrying the wrong man was worse than being alone.

And Heather languished, caught in the middle. She'd promised herself to give it three more months, then she'd go off to Amsterdam, be a good little wife and, maybe, give up writing in favor of motherhood. She sighed.

Chapter Two

Mike's hand trembled for a moment as he raised his Bloody Mary to his lips. He'd been a nervous wreck all morning, waiting to meet with Bill, who was now three minutes late. Mike stared at the door, willing his friend to enter.

The copy of Esquire he'd snatched from the beauty salon rested on their small table. His gaze went to the picture of Heather on the masthead. It wasn't affected by the curled edges of the ragtag magazine. Her hair looked a little shorter than he remembered, but her hazel eyes and dazzling smile captivated him once more.

He flipped to the brief bio about her in the front. It warmed him to see that she'd pursued her dream. He'd encouraged her to throw off the negativity of family and so-called friends. He'd said they were jealous or frustrated. It pleased him to see she'd listened and succeeded. Wow, a best-selling author! He couldn't be prouder.

He checked his watch, five minutes late. He ordered another drink and thought about his job. Working at the craft wood furniture company his dad had built was a dream come true. Mike had taken Heather's advice. His dad, reluctant to give his second son a chance, had agreed to a six-month trial.

That was all he'd needed. During his trial period, Mike had increased sales from their current shops, and opened up a few tony new stores on the West Coast that were selling well. Within a year, his father had made him Sales Director and moved Sean, Mike's older brother, into production and administration. His brother had thanked him. Sean hated sales. A natural born manager, he took over the day-to-day operations.

Sean had expanded their product line and Mike had sold the shit out of it. His commissions soared, giving him a comfortable mid-six-figure income. Together, the brothers had increased the company profits enough to allow their father to take early retirement.

He'd never have bucked his intimidating dad if it hadn't been for Heather. If nothing else, the least he could do to thank her was take her to a nice dinner at Sans Souci, the toniest restaurant in the Big Apple.

Who was he kidding? He had a lot more in mind than that—a lifetime's worth. Before he could check his watch again, Bill was at his table.

"So what's the fuckin' emergency?" he asked, sitting down.

"The usual, Mr. Compton?" the waitress asked.

Bill nodded, then turned his gaze on Mike.

"This," Mike said, pointing to the magazine.

"Esquire? So what?"

The waitress brought another Bloody Mary. Mike opened to Heather's essay.

"Read," he said, pointing.

Bill shrugged and picked up his drink. After a couple of seconds, he started to choke.

"What the fuck?" Bill asked, putting his drink down and mopping his shirt with a napkin.

"Sorry."

"You should have warned me," Bill said.

"You wouldn't have believed me," Mike replied.

Bill picked up the magazine and continued to read. "Holy shit," he muttered.

"Yep."

"That's her?"

"Yep."

"So you finally found her?"

"Yep. Well, nope. Not really."

"Are you going to go to Charlie's on Sunday?"

"Of course. I have to."

"Then why did you call me? I mean, you already know what you're going to do?"

"Because I think I should break it off with Amy."

Bill had made the mistake of taking another mouthful of his beverage when Mike dropped that bomb. Again, he had to clean his shirt.

"Why don't I just take this off until we finish lunch?"

"I'm sorry."

"You're serious? About Amy?" Bill raised his glass. "Can I drink now?"

Mike nodded. He waited for Bill to swallow before continuing. The waitress returned. The men ordered Philly cheese steaks.

"I'm serious."

"Why would you do that? For what, a dream? A what-might-have-been?"

"It's unfair to Amy. When I saw that article, all I wanted to do was find Heather."

"Let Amy decide what's unfair to her. This is so ridiculous. So absurd. You don't even know if you can find her. And what she'll be like. What if she still hates you?"

"Doesn't sound like it."

Bill shook his head. "For a smart guy, you can be fuckin' stupid sometimes."

"And this is one of those times?" Mike asked, eyeing his sandwich.

"Yep."

The men ate in silence for a while.

"The minute I thought there might be a chance with Heather, I knew I couldn't marry Amy. I don't love her. I don't want to give up my job and be who she wants me to be."

"Give up your job?" Bill cocked an eyebrow.

Mike explained Amy's plan for his life.

"Hell, no. I wouldn't either. But she'll back off on that if you don't budge."

"I don't want to live like that. I want a wife who supports what I do."

"And you're convinced Heather will do that?"

Mike nodded and took another bite.

"Buddy, you haven't seen her in five years. And the time you spent together was only ten days. May I remind you—ten lousy, fuckin' days!"

"I fell in love."

"It was sex. You fell in sex. In lust. Whatever," Bill said, waving his hand and reaching for a French fry.

"How would you know?"

"Hey, do whatever you want. You asked my advice. I'm giving it. You're crazy to give up Amy."

"Maybe so. I might regret it. But I'm definitely going to regret it if I marry her. I can't do it. It's not honest. She deserves better."

"I love the false nobility. At least be honest with yourself. You're not backing out because you're doing her a favor, you're doing it for yourself."

Mike chewed on his food, thinking about Bill's words.

"You're right. I'm selfish. That's true. I don't want to marry her. Heather is just an excuse. I mean, I'm still going to get together with her. But this has made me see that I just don't want to marry Amy. And that's the whole story."

"Thank God. Honesty. Finally!" Bill ordered a second drink.

Mike sighed as relief washed through him.

"Thanks, Bill."

"Frankly, I don't understand why you need a sign-off on this from me. It's your damn life. Screw it up any way you want."

"Why are you so mad? It's not your life."

"Because I hate to see you make mistakes. Letting Amy go is one you will live to regret."

"Yeah? Well, going out on Heather, following your advice, is one I've regretted every day for five years." Mike didn't mean for that to come out so angry. Bill's face colored.

"You're not the only one."

"Not the only one what?" Mike asked.

"I've regretted giving you that advice, too. I don't know why you still listen to me."

"Actually, I don't. I knew you'd tell me to stay with Amy. I just wanted to see what your reasons were. And you didn't have any. So that firmed up my decision."

"Why you S.O.B.," Bill said.

Mike laughed. "Yeah. Dragged you over here just to yank your chain."

"Fuck you. You're paying," Bill said.

"Okay. I owe you."

The men finished their meal. Mike paid the check, and they headed for the door. Once outside, Mike turned to go downtown, but Bill grabbed his arm.

"Look, Mike. I really do want you to be happy. I hope you find Heather and it works out. Big odds, but maybe it will. If you want my help, just call."

"Will you go with me to Charlie's?"

"Do you need me to?"

"Yeah."

"Text me time and date. Gotta go."

"Thanks," Mike said, and he walked down to his office on Thirty-Sixth Street.

CHARLIE'S RIVERSIDE Café

A cool breeze blew off the Hudson River. Mike checked his watch. It was twelve forty-five and Bill wasn't there yet. He paced, then took a seat at the bar and ordered a burger and a mimosa.

"I'll have the same," said a familiar voice behind him.

Mike's head snapped around. He grinned.

"Didn't think you were coming."

"What? Have I ever stood you up?" Bill climbed on a seat. "She here yet?"

Mike shook his head. "The article says she comes from one to three. It's not one yet."

"If she doesn't come, we can get wasted."

"That'll give us a good reason," Mike replied.

"Like we've ever needed a good reason?" Bill chuckled.

"Or any reason," Mike said.

They moved from the bar to a table in the front, facing out. Mike slapped the magazine on the glass top and zipped up his jacket. It was cool for a day in mid-June.

"Where'd you find that?" Bill asked.

"At the place where Amy gets her hair done."

"Speaking of Amy, how did you get out of the house?"

Mike chuckled. "I told her you were upset about something and needed to talk to me alone."

Bill laughed. "I suppose that's not a total lie. I am annoyed you dragged me here on this ridiculous hunch."

"There you go. See. It's the truth," Mike said, grinning.

"Have you thought about what you're going to say when she shows up?"

"Endlessly."

"What did you come up with?"

"Nothing that sounds like anything above a Neanderthal."

Bill laughed.

"Seriously. I've tried explanations of what I was doing with what's-her-name that weekend. I even considered blaming it all on you. I haven't completely discarded that one yet."

Bill cocked an eyebrow.

"If it works, I'm using it."

"Cop out," Bill replied.

"Maybe."

"You might never get to give a long explanation. She might shoot you down the minute you start blaming me, your mother, the weather, or the man in the moon."

"I hadn't thought about any of those options, except you."

"Wonderful. I'm honored."

At one thirty, Mike got up and moved around. No single women had come in to Charlie's.

"Maybe she's late?" Bill suggested.

"Maybe."

"Are you going to wait until three?"

Mike shrugged. "I don't know."

"You've come this far. It's only an hour and a half more. Might as well wait it out," Bill said. He signaled for the waiter. They ordered another round and dessert.

Unusually chatty, Bill rambled on about his latest girlfriend and his problems at the office. Mike listened as best he could, darting his attention to the front door every fifteen seconds. Tension gathered in his shoulders.

Checking his watch, he sighed. "Fifteen more minutes."

"Do you think you can stand it?"

"Guess I have to." Mike rose and paced. He went to the railing and stared at the boats, bobbing in the choppy water. His mind drifted back to the lazy days on Fire Island, the big meals with eight people squeezed into a table for six, the pitchers of ice cold sangria, the long walks on the beach, finding unique shells half buried in the sand, and private lovemaking on the dunes.

He'd never taken a share in a house again after that heart-breaking summer with Heather. He'd been back a couple of times as a guest of a friend, but that was it. When he was there, the place depressed him so much, he could hardly get out of bed.

He wondered if he reconnected with Heather, could they recapture what they'd had there? Could they go back and find the magic? He had no clue. Bill tapped him on the shoulder.

"It's time."

"Okay." Mike paid the check and they headed for the street.

"I figured out why she didn't show," Bill said.

Mike's eyebrows shot up. "Really? Why?"

"Did you even look at the magazine?"

"Yeah."

"No, no, at the cover."

Mike plucked it from his friend's hands.

"The issue date, buddy. The issue date."

There it was. The March issue. She'd come for three months: March, April, and May.

"Her trips here finished last month," Bill pointed out.

"Shit!" Mike threw the magazine on the ground.

"Don't get crazy. Have you called the publication and asked for her contact info?"

"Do you think they'd actually give it to me?"

"Who knows? She was willing to meet strangers at Charlie's?"

"Might as well try. Nothing to lose," he said, his gaze lowered to the ground. He scooped up Esquire and continued on his way home. "I figured out what to say."

"Oh?" Bill stopped.

"Yeah."

"What?"

"I'm sorry. Just, plain, I'm sorry."

Bill nodded, patted his buddy on the shoulder and the two men headed for Broadway.

GOING TO CHARLIE'S on Sunday had become a secret routine with Heather. On this fine day in June, she missed it. The bartender, Pete, always put a "reserved" sign on the outside table that faced the door. Not being an Esquire reader, Ian hadn't seen her essay. She'd considered that a lucky break. Then someone, some mean person, had mailed it to him.

Last night they'd had a terrible argument about it. She'd planned to do one more trip to Charlies, but after Ian discovering what she was doing on Sundays there had been the most horrific row. He had been furious. She had almost laughed at his insane jealousy of a man who might not even exist anymore. She cringed remembering his words.

"And every Sunday, *every* Sunday you've been sneaking out to meet this man. This man you're so madly in love with? More than me? You're sleeping with me, but you're in love with this Mike idiot? That's crazy. Insane. I'm not going to hang around, waiting for you to find him and dump me. I'm going to Amsterdam. Either you come with me or we're finished. Choose between your beloved ghost, Mike, or me. Tonight! If you go tomorrow, we're done."

She had cried and tried to convince him she loved him. But in her heart, she knew she loved Mike more. To further assuage

Ian, she'd promised not to go to Charlie's, but to follow Ian to The Netherlands within three weeks. Then they had make-up sex. Standing in her backyard this morning, waiting for Ian to get up, she chewed a fingernail. Confusion muddled her head.

He was right. She was out of her mind to hold a torch for a man she hadn't seen in five years. A man who'd broken her heart—yet she thought maybe he still loved her. Ridiculous! She had no guarantee. Her mother would kill her, turning away a wealthy, charming man like Ian.

So she'd make her mother and Ian happy, marry him, write for a while, then have kids. She sighed. Such a mundane life. Of course, living in Europe would make it more exciting, but she'd miss New York.

Her cell rang. It was Marissa. Heather answered. She eased down into a comfortable chair, in anticipation of a lengthy conversation.

"You mean Ian found out about Mike?"

"Someone sent him the article," Heather replied.

"That's dirty. Who would do that?"

"Mother."

"Oh, no. Come on. She'd never do that to you."

"I saw the envelope. The postmark was Briarcliff. She wants me to marry him and move to Amsterdam. Then she'd have a European headquarters."

"Do you really think that?"

"That's all she talks about when I call. I've stopped calling."

"She asked me about that."

"Make something up. What's up?"

"I hate to ask you..."

"How much?"

"Five thousand. This should be the last legal fee. Honest. That rat, Neil, is going to have to pay. And as soon as my lawyer finds where he's hidden his assets, I'll collect. Then I can pay you back."

"Don't worry about it, Mari. It's okay."

"Thanks. You're the best."

"Yeah. I know."

"Gotta go. Todd's taking me to breakfast."

"Have fun."

Not even legally divorced yet, and Marissa had moved on. She had a boyfriend. How come Marissa could shed the skin of an old relationship so fast and she, Heather, couldn't? She pondered the question as she headed inside to put up a pot of coffee. It was nine. She thought she heard Ian stirring. She smiled. He was such a creature of habit, he'd awake every day at nine, no matter what time he'd gone to sleep.

Rummaging through the refrigerator, she found a carton of eggs and butter. When someone put hands on her waist, she jumped and bumped her head on the freezer door.

"Ouch!"

"Darling! I'm so sorry," Ian said, kissing her head.

"Don't sneak up on me like that."

"I didn't mean to scare you. Let me take a look," he said, running his palm over her hair. He opened the freezer and plucked out an ice cube, then applied it to the injured area.

"This should keep it from swelling."

"Now that I'm injured, you can make breakfast," she said, handing the eggs over.

He laughed. "A fitting punishment. You sit down, keep that on your head, and I'll put up water for your tea."

As she watched him bustle around the kitchen, she kicked herself mentally. How could she let this man go? She could do a lot worse than marry him. *Why don't Ian and I have that mad, crazy, passionate kind of love?* She'd tried to talk herself into it a dozen times, to no avail. Her heart wouldn't budge.

Her cell rang. It was Marcy from the publisher's office.

"Hi, what's up?"

"I'm sorry to bother you on Sunday. But there's one more guy."

Chapter Three

On Monday, Mike called the magazine's office. Holding the phone, his hand trembled a bit while he waited to talk to the right person. The receptionist answered.

"Hi, I'm Mike Sullivan. I'm responding to that article by Heather Stone in the March issue."

"Mike did you say?"

"Yes."

"Sorry. Ms. Stone's not taking any more Mikes."

"What? What do you mean?"

"You are, hmm, let me take a look here. Yep. Mike number two hundred and fourteen."

"What?"

"We've gotten calls from over two hundred guys saying they are the Mike Ms. Stone is looking for."

"Two hundred?" Mike's eyebrows shot up.

"Yep."

"Wow. Okay. But they were wrong and I'm it. I'm the guy. Mike Sullivan. Can you give me her contact info?"

"Sorry, I'm afraid I can't. Company policy."

"Really? Please. It's been five years."

"That's what they all said. Look, I feel for you, but there's nothing I can do."

"Can I speak to the publisher?"

"He's not going to help you either."

"Well, can I give you my contact information? And if Ms. Stone asks if anyone has inquired, you could give it to her?"

There was a short laugh. "Okay. I'll add yours to the list."

"The list?"

"The list of eighty other guys with the same idea."

Mike frowned.

"Look, I understand your frustration. And you may be right. You may actually be the guy. But this story is old news and I've lost my mind keeping track of all this while doing my job. So, yes, I'm adding you to the list. I'll give it to the publisher's secretary. Maybe you'll get lucky. I think she gives the Mike list to Heather once a week. Good luck. Now, what's your number and address?"

Mike gave her the information and hung up. Gloom settled on him like a rain cloud on the Scottish hills. He had run out of ideas. No work got done. He wasted the rest of the afternoon bouncing between feeling sorry for himself, and desperate to connect with her. She was somewhere in this city. If he had to hire a private detective, he would. Bill had encouraged him to give it up, get engaged to Amy, and get on with his life.

It would be so easy to follow his friend's suggestion. Easy peasy, no sweat, Amy would do everything. All Mike would have to do was turn over his paycheck and live the good life. But it wasn't the good life. He'd end up bamboozled into switching jobs with Sean, making them both unhappy, and Sean ready to kill him.

And before he could get out, Amy would get pregnant. Then he'd be doomed, tied to her forever, raising kids together to be perfect little people doing what they were told. He shivered, the image scared the crap out of him. When he played it out that way, reaching for a giant *maybe* with Heather didn't seem so ridiculous. At least the prospect of happiness was fifty/fifty. If he even managed to find her. But if he did, he had a chance of being happy. That's all he needed, a chance, a possibility—instead of the certainty of misery and a wasted life.

He chuckled to himself. Bill was right about one thing. Mike could justify anything. Any crazy thing he'd wanted to do in his teens and twenties, he'd coughed up a seemingly reasonable scenario for doing it, even if it was the dumbest idea on Earth. Bill admired that about Mike.

They'd grown up together. Whenever they'd get caught breaking rules, he'd looked to Mike to find some cockamamie excuse that sounded almost plausible. And Mike had never let him down. Was he doing it to himself? If he was, so what, it was because he wanted happiness and refused to settle for mediocrity instead.

At the end of the day, he got a text.

Meeting my parents for drinks tonight. You promised to come.

That was it—the icing on the cake, the absolutely last thing he wanted to do. How could he face her parents when he was on the verge of breaking her heart? If he couldn't find Heather right now, at least he could untangle himself from Amy.

No. Can we talk?

Uh oh. That sounds ominous.

I'll be home by six.

Okay.

Fear spiked through him. He'd done it now. The meeting was set and it was time for him and Amy to go their separate ways. His stomach clenched. Giving up a loving relationship for a big fat nothing seemed like the dumbest thing in the world. He knew what Bill would say, it was screaming in his brain, but he refused to listen. It was his life. Whether he found Heather or not, Amy wasn't the right woman for him.

He picked up the phone and dialed.

"Atlas Storage? Yeah. I want to cancel a pick up."

"SO WHAT'S THIS ABOUT one more guy, Marcy?"

"Some guy who obviously can't tell one month from another called today. Says he's the real Mike."

"Yeah, yeah, they're all the real Mike." Heather rolled her eyes.

"Do you want his info?"

"Send it at the end of the week, with your regular email."

"Okay. What if he is the real deal?"

"Yeah? And what if goats could fly?"

Marcy chuckled. "You're probably right. Just wanted to check with you."

"If I meet one more wacko who wants to hook up, I'll scream."

"Told ya not to put a picture in the magazine."

"I needed the picture to show Mike it was me."

"Mike, and the horny-and-lonely crowd, I guess."

"I didn't know it would cause such a commotion."

"I applaud your courage."

"Thanks. Wish it had worked." Heather sighed.

"Me, too. I gotta go. Boss is calling. Have a great week."

"You, too." Heather put down the phone.

"Who was that?" Ian asked.

"Just Marcy from Moonlight Books."

"Oh? Are you going to Charlie's today?"

She stared at him. His lip curled slightly in a derisive grin, his eyes were cold.

"I thought we'd settled that."

"Publishers don't call on Sundays."

"Mine does."

"Not about book business," Ian said, crossing his arms over his chest.

"What does that mean?"

"Magic Mike. Your Magic Mike. This has to stop."

"Some guy called, insisting he was the real deal. I don't care. Make you happy?"

"I should be enough to make you happy," Ian insisted.

"You should, yes, that's right. You should."

"Are you saying you're not happy with me?" Red crept up his neck.

"And what if I am?"

"I will leave anytime you request," he said, his lips compressed into a thin line.

A shudder ran through her while her mother's words played in her head. *Where will a skinny, bookish girl like you find another man like Ian?*

"I didn't say that."

"Maybe it's time for you to choose, this phantom, Mike, or me."

"I thought I had made that choice."

"I thought you had, too. But now, I don't know."

Heather sank down on the sofa, tears pricked at the backs of her eyes. "I don't know, either."

"Perhaps, I'd better go back to Amsterdam now. If you decide to come, fine. If not, well, I'll be sad, but it will be your choice."

Fear spiked through her. If he left, she'd be alone. All the time. Did she want that?

"Since you have no answer, I will pack my things. Think about it. Have an answer when I'm finished," Ian said, brushing by her. The rush of air as he passed cooled her.

Settle or be alone, settle or be alone, settle or be alone...her mind seesawed. She walked out to the garden and watched the birds at her feeder. She admired their freedom.

In fifteen minutes, Ian returned. She joined him in the living room.

"Well? What have you decided?"

"Ian, I—"

"You haven't, have you?"

She shook her head.

"I knew you'd say that. So I've done it for you. I'm off to Amsterdam. I wish you good luck finding this Mike whatever. It's been fun, but we're done." He stood dry-eyed, holding a small valise.

"I'm sorry, Ian," she said, relieved he'd made the decision.

"Not everyone is meant to be," he said crossing the room.

"I wish you happiness."

"Don't worry about me. I will find it. It's you who are chasing dreams, ghosts. It's you who has little chance to get what you want. I'll be fine."

She nodded. He yanked open the door and was gone in a flash. Her eyes watered a bit. She went to the stove and put on the flame under the kettle. A cup of tea would help. As the water heated, she picked up the phone.

"Marcy? Call that guy. The last Mike? Tell him I'll be at Charlie's next Sunday."

"Okay. You're the master."

"And cross your fingers."

MIKE BUZZED AND AMY let him in. "

"I've been meaning to give you a set of keys. I mean now that you're going to be living here, too." She thrust a keyring in his hand. He placed it on the front hall table.

"Amy."

"Whiskey or wine?" she asked.

"Scotch neat. Please."

He plunked down on the sofa. Sweat broke out on his forehead. He pulled a handkerchief out of his back pocket and mopped his face. Terror bolted through him. Crying women gave him stomach cramps. He watched Amy pour his whiskey then a glass of wine for herself. She brought the drinks to the couch and sat next to him.

"Now why aren't we having drinks with my parents?"

"Amy, look. About this living together thing..."

"Did you call the storage people?"

"I did."

"Great," she said, interrupting him again.

He placed his hand on her arm. "Please. Don't talk. Just listen, okay?"

She nodded, but her smile melted.

"About us. I'm not ready to move in with you."

"You're what?"

"Listening? Remember?"

She slapped her hand over her mouth. One glance at her eyes told him waterworks were next.

"We're not right for each other."

"But we've been so happy?"

"You've been so happy."

"You haven't?"

He shook his head. A tear slipped down her cheek.

"I'm sorry. What can I do? I'll do anything you say. Do you want me to wear handcuffs? A blindfold? I love you, Mike. We belong together." She threw her arms around his neck.

"We don't. Trust me. We don't." He peeled her off.

His cell dinged. He glanced at it, didn't recognize the number, and hit "ignore".

Now the flood began.

"How could you do this? Now? I thought we were going to get married."

"I never said anything about marriage."

"Please, Mike. Give me another chance?"

He pushed to his feet. Begging sent him over the edge. Backing down had its appeal; anything to stop the pleading and the tears. He went to the window and looked out. Heather was out there somewhere. Even if he didn't find her, he couldn't marry Amy. They'd only end up divorced.

"You called it, Amy. I'm Messy Mike. We're not suited. You don't really know me."

"Yes, I do. And I love you. Okay, you're a slob. I can live with that."

"But I can't live with Miss Perfect. With you, everything has to be perfect all the time. Perfect hair, perfect house, perfect boyfriend. I'm not perfect. Far from it. And I never will be. You'll only grow to hate me, and we'll be divorced in five years. Maybe sooner."

"What's wrong with striving for perfection?"

"Nothing. It's achieving it all the time that's so damned annoying," he said, rubbing his face.

"So you hate me because I'm perfect?"

"I don't hate you. Hell, do you think I'd be here right now if I hated you? We're oil and water, Amy. For two years we've been pretending. I like you. I like you a lot. I admire how far you've come in your life. But this is not the life I want." Once he said it straight out, relief flooded him.

Amy stood up and slapped him across the face.

"What the hell?" he asked, rubbing his burning cheek.

"You just wanted easy sex. That was it, right? Just knowing you could get laid whenever you wanted. That's what kept you with me?"

"I really liked you, Amy. But after that assault, maybe not so much anymore." Anger pulsed through him. "I was trying to be nice, be straight with you."

"Sure, sure you were. Mr. Nice Guy is written all over you."

"I could have simply stopped calling or seeing you."

"That would have been cowardly and cold."

"Exactly. I wish it had been right for us, but it isn't. And I'm not going to lie and ruin my happiness and yours."

"Really? Thanks. You've already ruined mine."

"I'm sorry. I'm truly sorry. I didn't mean to hurt you."

"Oh yeah? Fuck you. Get out!" She strode over to the door and yanked it open. "Now!"

"Fine. Have a good life."

"Yeah? Rot in fucking Hell," she said as she slammed the door behind him.

His anger faded as he rode down in the elevator. His face still stung, but at least the confrontation was over. He commended himself for his bravery as he hit the sidewalk and headed home. Sure, he'd have to unpack everything, but so what? At least he wasn't locked into a dead-end relationship.

He stopped at the diner on his block for dinner. His cell dinged. It was Bill.

"Did you do it?"

"You're talking to a free man," Mike said, sipping a cup of coffee.

"I don't know whether to pat you on the back for your courage or smack you in the head for being stupid."

"I've already been smacked, so you could do the patting thing."

"She smacked you?"

"Slapped."

"Wow. That's a side of Amy I've never seen."

"Makes two of us."

"So what's your next move?" Bill asked.

"I have no fuckin' clue."

SUNDAY MORNING, EIGHT o'clock

Heather filled the bird feeders in her garden. She hadn't expected to miss Ian much. Wrong. A faint hint of his aftershave lingered in the bathroom. The aroma of his favorite coffee wafted from her cabinet. Two magazines and a book he forgot to take occupied the nightstand. It was almost as if he wanted her to remember him. As if she could forget. She'd had some great times with Ian. He'd been sweet and generous.

But the spark wasn't there. He tried to turn her into what he wanted, a housewife, not a working author. She'd not denied her desire to have a family, but she was just thirty with books in her head waiting to be written. It had taken her five years to reach this level of success. Ian pretended to support her work, promising her a writing space in his home. She knew it was temporary. He needed to be in charge, and Heather was a bucking bronco, not willing to be controlled by anyone.

Ian had compartmentalized his life, but Heather had never fit in any compartment, not completely. She doubted that would change because Ian commanded it. And in the bedroom, he never lit her fire much. Ever since Mike, she had refused to settle for ho-hum lovers. She knew the fireworks a skilled lover created and taking less would guarantee a life of frustration and need.

But life without Ian was lonely. She missed the dinners at tony eateries but not the harping about cleaning up her apartment and improving her housekeeping skills. Fuck housekeeping. She'd never liked it, never excelled at it, and never would. She shrugged. Being alone was her choice, so she might as well get used to it. And as her mother would say, "For God's sake, stop whining!"

She showered and picked up a book, but her stomach growled. A sudden desire for Charlie's eggs benedict woke up her taste buds. She'd promised to be at Charlie's one more Sunday. Ugh. Schlepping down there in the September heat didn't appeal, but the memory of the delicious dish drove her to throw on a sundress, sandals, and a straw hat and hit the street.

"Haven't seen you in an age," Pete the bartender said. "Your regular?"

She nodded. "On the rocks, please."

"Mimosa rocks, coming up. Where've you been?"

"I've run out of Mike's, Pete."

"How about me, then?"

"I could do a lot worse," she said, smiling at him. His black hair and blue eyes had tempted her before, but she resisted. Pete flirted with every female in the joint. It was all about the tips. A girl couldn't take him too seriously.

He laughed.

"I'll have the eggs benedict, Pete. Could you place the order, please?"

"Sure thing. Your usual table?"

She nodded, taking her drink, and easing into the chair that faced the entrance. It was one thirty. Maybe she'd missed the Mike Marcy had called. Hell's bells, if he couldn't wait half an hour, fuck 'im. She didn't care.

Within fifteen minutes her food arrived, warm and inviting. She dug in, hungry as if she hadn't eaten in days. The hot air smelled sweet. Birdsongs competed with snatches of conversations from couples at other tables. Being a writer, people-watching was in her wheelhouse. She shifted her chair so she could see the others in the restaurant. Charlie's. Most of the customers occupied tables under the overhang in the shade.

She loved to guess which partner loved the other partner more. She'd observe their body language, watching for signs, like one person taking the other's hand, or leaning in for a kiss, or sharing food. And then she'd delight in the response from the other. Sometimes the couples feuded or one turned a cold shoulder to the other.

Her favorites were the ones who reciprocated the affection of their significant other. Heather sighed, always a sucker for a love story with a happy ending.

She sat back and sank into a daydream. Would Mike be fat and bald? Not in five years, she guessed. Would he be married? She frowned. That was a scary possibility. Did he still live in New York or had he moved to California or England or Hawaii? She had a bazillion questions that only the handsome, sweet, mysterious, missing man could answer.

DEPRESSION SETTLED over Mike like fog in a valley. He hadn't expected to feel so alone and empty. He knew he didn't love Amy, but she had filled up his life. Now, his phone never rang, there were no texts, and he had no place to go after work. Maybe he'd made a mistake.

It was too late. Mutual friends had told Bill that Amy hated Mike and was trashing him everywhere she went. Maybe that was for the best. If it helped her pride to make him out to be a monster, he'd let it be. There was no going back.

Sunday morning was steamy for early September. Having no place to go, Mike slept in. Bill had invited him to brunch with him and his girlfriend, but Mike declined. Being the third wheel sucked.

Mike pledged that, until he found Heather, and decided about her one way or the other, he'd not get involved with anyone else. Breaking up with Amy had been too hideous. The last thing he needed was a repeat. He vowed to call a private detective on Monday. In the meantime, he needed to give attractive, single women a wide berth.

He'd been thinking about getting a dog, so he headed for Riverside Park. Not having owned one, he had no idea what breed would be good for him. Maybe a trip to the dog run would give him some clarity. At least then he wouldn't be alone.

By two o'clock, the dog run was full of canines of all shapes, sizes, and temperament. Some were digging holes, others were chasing each other, and some hid in the shade under benches. People were friendly, offering him tons of advice. A few single women looked interested. He steered clear of them and headed out toward a cooling breeze off the Hudson.

After finding a bench facing the river, Mike whipped out his cell. He remembered there had been a call in the middle of his break-up with Amy. He'd ignored it, but maybe there was a message?

He searched his voicemail until he found it. Probably some pitch for a credit card, a loan, or a used car. Hell, it wasn't like he had anything to do, so he might as well listen. Maybe it was something good? He scoffed at his own optimism. When had anything good come from a number he didn't recognize? He shrugged and played it anyway.

> *This message is for Mike Sullivan. Heather Stone said she'd be at*
> *Charlie's this Sunday, from one to three, if you're still interested.*

His breath stopped. His heartbeat doubled. Heather was at Charlie's! He checked the time. Holy shit, it was two thirty! Mike jumped up and broke into a run. He was only about a dozen blocks from the restaurant.

He raced up the sidewalk. Heat closed in on him, but he kept drawing in air through his nose and expelling it through his mouth. He had to get there. Being late was not an option. After two blocks, his legs protested, but he ignored them. While he ran, he yanked his T-shirt up over his head and fisted it.

As Mike pushed his body to go faster, he caught a glimpse of Charlie's awning. It grew closer. He hit the steps down to the restaurant, gasping. Bent over to facilitate getting air into his lungs, his breathing soon returned to normal, though his pulse stayed in high gear. Afraid to stand up straight because he might see her, or worse, he might not see her, he remained facing the ground.

"Fool," he muttered to himself and straightened up. He needed to know, one way or the other. Either she was going to be the love of his life or he needed to let her go. Despite the heat, his body shivered once as he scanned the outside tables. His breath hitched, his muscles tensed. There, sitting alone, was a woman under a large straw hat. Her legs were crossed. He remembered the pose. Unless his eyes were playing tricks on him, it was Heather.

Frozen to the spot, Mike couldn't move. Then he glanced down at the crumpled T-shirt in his hand and his damp arms. *Shit!* He was a sweaty mess! Slipping the shirt over his head, he tried to smooth out the wrinkles with no success. Keeping his eyes glued to the woman, he wiped his face on his sleeve. All he needed was her to see him do that. Sure, he was grubby, but he prayed she'd be happy to see him anyway. The real Heather wouldn't give a rat's ass how grubby he was, he assured himself.

Slowly, he walked down the stairs. He'd made it with fifteen minutes to spare. The woman under the hat checked her watch and uncrossed her legs. Breathing deep, he approached her table, slowly, as if she were a bird who'd fly away the second she saw him.

"Heather?" he asked, his voice tentative and soft.

She whipped around to face him and removed the hat. It was her. She stood, her hand gripping the table, her gaze connecting with his.

"I'm sorry," they both said at the same time.

Chapter Four

Her heart thudded so loudly she couldn't hear anything else. When her gaze met Mike's, she uttered the two words she'd waited five years to say then froze. He'd filled out a little and looked even more handsome than she had remembered. Tears clouded her eyes as emotion choked her.

He was there. Actually there, standing in front of her. He'd read her essay, sought her out, called, and showed up. Her mouth hung open. He smiled, as his words mirrored hers, and moved closer. Before her brain could process thought, she flung herself into his arms, weeping, sobbing against his chest.

He'd closed his arms around her, his breath warm on her ear.

"It's okay. It's going to be okay. It's all right, baby. It's all right. I'm here."

When she caught her breath, she spoke, "I thought I'd never see you again."

"Me, too."

"I just broke up with someone because, because I believed you were still out there."

"You were right."

She stepped back and looked up. "Are you married?"

"No."

"Seeing anyone?"

"Nope. Just ended that, too. Same reason."

"You did?" Her question came out as a squeak.

He nodded.

Heather's heart skipped a beat. Wrapping her arms around his middle, she snuggled in against his chest and focused on the rapid beat of his heart. *He feels the same. He's here because he still loves me.* He couldn't lie about it because the thudding in his chest would give him away. Joy filled her. She inhaled his scent, laced with a bit of sweat and sweetened with old cologne. He smelled good, damn good.

Happiness flooded her brain and curved her lips into a huge grin as she tightened her arms around him. Closing his hands over her shoulders, he held her away. Before she could speak, his mouth was on hers, kissing her hard, deep, and hungry. She slid her arms around his neck and melted against him.

The kiss aroused her, his scent, intoxicated her. Heather's body jumped to life as he pulled her closer. Stepping back, she ran her hands over his face, through his hair.

"I can't believe it's really you. You're here."

"I love you, Heather," he said, his voice raspy with emotion.

"I love you, too, Mike."

The waiter interrupted. "The owner wanted to give you a bottle of champagne and dinner, on-the-house. In honor of your hooking up. I mean, meeting up. Again. Reconnecting."

Pete, the bartender, hopped out, armed with a camera, and took a dozen shots.

"Marcy called, she wants these. She said she had a hunch this guy was the real deal."

"She was right," Heather said, unable to take her eyes off Mike.

The couple sat close together while the waiter popped the champagne and poured.

"To true love," Mike said, raising his glass.

Heather grinned and touched her flute to his. Along with the bubbly, conversation flowed. They raced through sentences, talking a mile a minute, catching up on five years. Heads bent close, they spoke only for each other.

"I'm so proud of what you've done," he said. "A best-selling author. Famous! You did it. You really did it."

"You pushed me. Even when I was angry at you, I never forgot what you said. How I should keep going, keep writing, and not let anyone stop me." She touched his hand. He raised hers to his lips. "Look at you! You did it, too. The head of sales for your dad's company. Awesome."

"Thanks," Mike replied, blushing. "I confronted my dad like you suggested. He gave me six months. That's all I needed. We've got our product lines in stores in fifteen new states. The company has tripled its profits."

"Wow." She touched his cheek, he leaned in to brush her lips with his.

"You don't want me to give that up, do you?"

"Why would I? You're living your dream."

"It takes me away sometimes. I have business dinners and travel a couple of times a year."

"That's part of the job, right?"

"Some women wouldn't like that."

"It's part of who you are. I'd never want to change that."

He took her hand between both of his. "Thank you."

"If we were together, you wouldn't expect me to give up writing to be a housekeeper and cook, would you?"

"After everything you've been through to get where you are? Never. I make enough money. We'll hire help."

She grinned. "Thank you."

"Children?" he asked.

"Absolutely," she replied.

Even in the summer, the sun set. Heather and Mike ate, drank, and talked into the night. At one thirty, Pete came to them.

"Sorry, folks, we're closing."

They stood up. Mike left a big tip.

"You could come back to my place. Only problem is most of my stuff is packed for storage," Mike said.

"Storage? You're not moving, are you?" she asked, a touch of panic in her voice.

"I was. But I changed my mind."

"Oh, thank God. I don't think I could lose you again. We could go to my place."

"Okay."

She straightened up, clapping her hands. "Wait! Wait! I bought a little house on Fire Island. It's called The Duet. Do you remember it?"

"The little two bedroom, on Cranberry Street, facing the ocean?"

"That's the one. Let's go there."

"Perfect," Mike said, taking her hand.

"At this hour, there won't be any traffic," she said.

"Wait. How long will it take you to pack?"

"I have everything there."

"Good, come with me. I have an SUV. I'll throw a few things in a duffle and we'll go."

"Great." She slipped her hand in his as they headed for his apartment.

IN A HALF AN HOUR, they were on the road. The Long Island Expressway was almost empty at that hour.

"You don't mind if I put Carole King on, do you? I've got the songs on my phone."

He laughed. "You still love her stuff?"

"After Mom passed, listening to her favorite music made her seem closer. Does that make sense?"

"It does. Just like old times. Plug it in."

"Some things don't change," she said.

He squeezed her hand and glanced over. "Thank God."

The song *Far Away* came on. Heather blinked back tears. "This reminded me of you. When I got back to New York, after that terrible weekend, I played it constantly."

He put her hand to his lips. "I'm so sorry."

"I missed you so much."

"Me, too," he whispered. "I tried calling you a dozen times."

"I'd blocked your number."

"Figured."

They listened to the song in silence. Slowing a bit, Mike eased the car into the center lane.

"When I thought about you, this song popped into my head. Now you're here," she sighed. "I don't have to sing this anymore."

"Which song would be us now?" he asked.

She fiddled with the cell and *Some Kind of Wonderful* came on.

"They say it better than I ever could," she said.

He laughed. "You're a writer!"

"But the lyrics are so perfect."

Again, they listened in silence, their fingers touching on the console between them. Noticing Mike's big grin, her heart swelled. Was this a dream or reality?

They arrived around four fifteen to find the dock dark. Mike pulled into a space in the weekend parking lot. He'd almost forgotten that he couldn't bring his car over. No cars on Fire Island.

"The ferry starts up at six," she said. "Look, Ma's Diner is open."

Mike checked his watch. "Breakfast?" he asked.

"I'm starved," she said, yawning.

By six thirty, they were standing at the ferry railing, the wind mussing their hair as they approached the island. Mike's hand covered hers, keeping it warm. She moved closer.

"Cold?"

"A little," she said.

He took off his jacket and wrapped it around her. "Better?"

She nodded. Peace flowed through her as she rested her head on his shoulder.

"Sleepy?"

"I'm not used to staying up all night."

"Last time I did was with you. And we weren't in a car," he chuckled. Hugging her closer, he spoke for her ears only. "Lying on the beach, watching the sunrise with you was amazing."

"We were the only two people in the world." She leaned against him.

"It felt like that," he added, snaking his arm around her shoulders.

Jumbled images of their last night together clicked through her memory. They'd vowed to make love in every conceivable location. On the eve of their return to the City, they still had four places left. Through the early morning hours, they stole from spot to clandestine spot, finally falling asleep on the sand.

"That was an incredible night," she sighed.

"Every night with you was incredible," he said.

She hugged his arm.

The boat docked. It only held a handful of people. Mike helped Heather off. He took a deep breath and scanned the view for a moment before they headed to the cottage.

As they'd made their way slowly down the wood path, one thing kept pounding in her brain—it was a miracle they had reconnected. Call it luck, call it serendipity, use any label at all, she'd be grateful forever.

"The fact that your essay worked was a fuckin' miracle," he said, echoing her thoughts.

"I suppose. Maybe it was Fate?" she asked.

"Could be. Whatever it was, I'm grateful," he said, pulling her to him for another kiss.

"Did you come here often after our falling out?"

"This is my first time back, since that weekend. I went to Ocean Bay Park a couple of times, but never here."

"Really?"

"You didn't come back, did you?" he asked.

She shook her head. "Not until last year. After that weekend, I took a job in Cleveland. Left before October."

"I didn't think you'd be back. Somebody told me you'd left town. Don't remember who."

"I took a job working for a small publisher there. It's where I started serious writing."

He nodded.

"Why didn't you come back?" she asked.

"Wouldn't be the same without you. After you left, I hung around for another couple of days. It was terrible."

She touched his shoulder. "I know what you mean. I only bought the house last year. After I got the idea for the essay."

"You thought that would bring me back?"

"I hoped. Then we'd have the house. If you felt the same—"

"If?" He laughed. "Did you doubt that?"

"After our last words, uh, yeah?"

"Of course, of course. Sorry." He held her hand.

"Do you feel the same?" Her heart leapt into her throat.

"You don't know?" he asked, his eyebrows rising.

"I thought. But, no, that's why I'm asking."

"I haven't been this happy, since our time together here."

She grinned and stopped. Mike took Heather in his arms and kissed her. She inhaled deeply, excited by his unique scent. Terrified to be so deliriously happy, she pushed her worries down deep inside.

When they reached the cottage, Heather retrieved the key from under the mat. Mike plopped his backpack on the floor next to the sofa.

"Last one undressed is a rotten egg," he said, ripping his shirt over his head.

Heather laughed. "This way," she said, taking his hand and heading for the bedroom. Daylight added warmth to the lovely room. Heather turned. Mike had attacked his belt and was unzipping his pants. Staring at his chest, well-muscled and still lightly covered with the sexy dark hair, the way she remembered, Heather could hardly catch her breath.

"Well?" He motioned to her clothes.

"Oh, yes." She began to strip.

"Do you need help?" he asked, a lusty light glowing in his dark eyes.

"Maybe," she replied, reaching for him.

He was at her side in an instant. Down to his boxers, he took his time removing her clothing. His hot stare warmed every bit of her he uncovered.

"Still beautiful," he mumbled, pushing her dress off her shoulders. His gaze slid down to her breasts, while he reached around behind her. He unlatched her bra in a second, and it fell to the floor.

Shyness flashed through her. She covered herself with her arms.

"Shy?"

She nodded. He hugged her to him. "It's okay, baby. No rush." His hands glided down to grip her rear, and he buried his face in her neck.

"You're so hot," he said.

Heather clasped his waist, pushing her hips against his.

"Whoa. Okay. Let's go there," he said, slipping his fingers under her panties, shoving them down. Before she could blink, they were naked. He picked her up and carried her to the bed.

"Let me take a quick look, first. It's been so long." He placed her on the mattress.

"Do I look the same?"

"Better," he said, joining her.

Heather's eyes feasted on his body. He was as gorgeous as ever. Heat flew through her veins as need took over.

HIS MIND RACED, TRYING to take in what was happening. Jumbled thoughts and recollections tumbled through his brain in no particular order. He tried to make sense out of the last few hours and to be sure this was *reality* and not a dream.

He couldn't believe she'd done the perfect thing in the car, she put on Carole King music. She'd turned him on to King five years ago, and he'd bought the Tapestry album and memorized it. Every song reminded him of Heather. Amy had been annoyed hearing it in the car all the time, so he'd restricted his listening to when he was alone behind the wheel and could dream about Heather. On the drive out, they shared the music, singing along, because, by now, he knew every lyric to every song. Heather had been impressed.

The need to keep touching her, which cropped up during dinner, wasn't merely an expression of his affection, but a way to allay the wild, irrational fear that if he wasn't holding on to her, she'd disappear. He knew dreams and fantasies rarely came true. Was today his one lucky day or would this interlude turn into something more? Pushing questions and doubts away, he focused on what was happening.

Since he'd last seen her, she'd put a little meat on her bones in all the right places. All evening, he had tried like hell not to stare at her breasts, but he'd been itching to touch them, and controlling himself was almost impossible. As he stared now, he noted they were bigger than he remembered, at least he thought they were. Only fondling the real thing would tell him. Heather had grown into the most beautiful woman, her energy, her drive drew him like a moth to a flame.

He was here, in her house. She was naked, and he sported the biggest hard-on he'd ever had. Grasping for control, he wanted to stretch out lovemaking to enjoy every second. He'd waited so long to relive this precious time between them. Every nerve, every inch of his skin, tingled at the thought of getting between the sheets with Heather again. Would it be as good? Better? Not like he remembered? He had no clue, but he'd find out, and soon.

Waiting slid into the realm of impossible. He eased her down on the bed and took a good look before joining her. Damn! She looked like a goddess.

"Protection?"

"On the pill."

Magic to his ears. He lay down next to her. Yes, her breasts still fit in his hands, maybe a little tighter this time. Hungry for her, he kissed her. She wound a leg around him, pressing her hips against him.

"Hurry," she whispered.

Damn, exactly what he wanted to hear.

"But,"

"No buts. Damn it. I've waited so long," she said, her voice breathy.

"You said it," he replied, entering her.

AFTER A BIG STRETCH, Heather curled into Mike's embrace. Resting her head on his chest, sleep pressed her. It was fast, but oh,

God, she'd reached an enormous climax in record time. She'd never had such satisfaction from Ian. Not to compare, but Ian could never love her like Mike.

She had given up thinking she'd ever have him inside her again, next to her in bed, kissing her, or loving her. As if she had lost her most prized possession, and discovered it again, by accident. Gratitude washed through her. Mike's persistence, her publisher, her sister, so many to thank for this miracle.

The beat of his heart soothed her. The bed dipped slightly.

"That was awesome," he said, rolling to face her and yawning.

"Oh my God. Yes."

She wanted to talk, but the release had relaxed her enough for exhaustion to take over. They had closed the curtains, to keep daylight out. She sank into a deep slumber. At one point, when she rolled over, her hand smacked into Mike's belly.

"Ooph," he said.

He mumbled something and was asleep again in seconds. She ran her hand over him. The tune *Some Kind of Wonderful* played in her head. She smiled and drifted off.

Peace flowed through Heather's veins. She slept on, dreaming, next to Mike. After about six hours, she awoke. The bed was empty.

Mike was probably in the bathroom. She glanced at the door, but it was open and the light was off. She called his name. No response. Panic seized her. Had it been a dream? Had he come for one night and left her again?

Her mouth went dry and her heart pounded in her ears. Adrenaline flowed, increasing her heart rate and respiration, ramping her up into panic mode. *Maybe I can stop him!* Throwing back the covers, she vaulted out of bed, grabbed a large T-shirt, and yanked it over her head. She raced to the living room, but no one was there. She tried the kitchen, empty.

"Mike! Mike! Where are you?" Fear gripped her heart and tears flowed down her cheeks. Gasping for air, she slumped against the archway that led back to the living room.

"Heather?" A familiar voice called her name.

She couldn't catch her breath.

"Heather? Where are you? Are you okay?"

She turned toward the door to the deck. Mike stood there, wearing only boxers. Heather collapsed, sobbing. He was on her in a second, lifting her up, holding her close.

"Baby, what's wrong? What happened?"

When she could catch her breath, she spoke. "I thought you'd gone. Again. Left. Left me."

He chuckled. "Oh, no, honey, that's not going to happen. That's never going to happen again. I was just standing on the deck. I'd forgotten how great the ocean is. The smell of salt, the wind. That's all."

"I rolled over and you were gone."

"Oh, baby. You were sleeping so soundly, I didn't want to wake you."

"Thank God," she said, into his chest. Her palm flattened against his pecs. The warmth of his skin chased away the chill in her body.

"You thought I'd left you?" He rubbed her back.

She nodded.

"Are you kidding? After everything we've been through to find each other?"

"I didn't know. I mean, it happened before."

"I thought I had explained that. I listened to my asshole friend. Thought I needed to try something else out. Bill had convinced me that what we had couldn't be real. And following his dumb idea showed me that what we had, have, was, is—whatever—real!"

She swiped at her face.

"Wait a sec. Be right back," he said, ducking into the bedroom. Heather wandered out on the deck. The afternoon sun shone on the water. Waves crashed. The wind blew her hair back from her face and dried her tears. At the sound of Mike returning, she stepped closer to the rail.

"Here," he said, handing her his handkerchief.

"I need someone to take care of me a little. Publishing is a hard business. I'm not nearly tough enough. Sometimes I get overwhelmed."

"Don't worry, honey. I'm here."

She raised her gaze to his. "And a song title comes to mind."

"Uh-oh," he said, stepping up behind her, winding his arms around her middle. He kissed her neck. "Carole King?"

"Who else?"

"Shoot."

"*Will You Still Love Me Tomorrow?*"

"I knew it," he said, turning her to him. "Of course, I will. And all the tomorrows to come. I love you, Heather. Really. Honestly. You have to believe that."

"I want to."

"Do you think I'd have gone through this crazy chase if I didn't?"

"I just want to be sure."

"One way to be sure?" he said, dropping to one knee. "Marry me."

"What?"

"You heard me." He took the small box from his palm and opened it, revealing a large diamond ring.

Heather's hand flew to her mouth, her eyes widened.

"There! Does that make you feel better?"

"Yes."

"So, will you?" His face, so adorably hopeful, his dark eyes pleading, his brows raised.

"Of course. Yes. Yes!"

Mike slipped the ring on her finger, then sprang up, grabbed her, and swung her around, laughing. She clung to him, the warmth of love filling her heart.

"Let's seal the deal," he said, picking her up.

"Great idea," she piped up, giggling.

He carried her into the bedroom. They took their time, exploring each other as if they were new. Mike thrust into her slowly, keeping eye contact. Heather let go, giving herself while taking him at the same time. As the pressure of desire grew, a bond joined them. When they could hold back no longer, the heat of shared pleasure whipped through their bodies.

After they made love, Mike tucked her under his shoulder.

"Happy?" he asked.

"Delirious," she replied.

"Have a King song for this, too?"

"Of course."

"Fire away."

"*You Make Me Feel Like a Natural Woman*," she said and kissed him.

Epilogue

Heather and Mike had set a date for the wedding. It was to be a small affair, family and a handful of close friends. Mike had to decide about Bill. He'd skirted the best man issue by giving the job to his brother.

Uneasy about including his old buddy because of his attitude regarding Heather, but hard pressed to leave him out, Mike faced the problem head on. He invited Bill for a drink at Charlie's after work. Mike needed support. With Pete the bartender in the background, Mike didn't feel alone. Besides, they had tables outside, where others couldn't easily overhear conversations.

Oddly, Bill was on time. Mike took that as a sign of respect, a good move on his friend's part. They ordered drinks and Mike straightened in his seat.

"You know the wedding's coming up," Mike said.

Bill nodded. The waiter delivered their beverages.

"I'm having a problem knowing where you fit into all this, Bill."

"Look, before you go on, I know. I admit it. I was wrong about Heather. You knew what you wanted. I should have respected that."

"What?"

"I mean. Well, you'll find out eventually. I told Cherry where you were and with who that weekend."

"Cherry? Heather's house-mate?"

"I'm not proud of it. I didn't know she'd run to Heather."

"Come on, Bill. Be honest. You had to figure the information would get to Heather."

"I suppose I did," Bill said, staring at his hands.

"So you were responsible for our break-up?"

"Not really. The fact that she didn't give you a chance to explain. The fact that you went with that girl in the first place. I mean that was your decision."

"Don't weasel out of this. You tried to break us up and you succeeded."

"Yeah. I'm so sorry. I was a total asshole."

"Ya think?"

"Okay, so maybe I was jealous. I'd made a play for Heather, but she turned me down flat."

"What? You never told me."

"How could I?"

Mike shook his head.

"Look, I'm sorry, Mike. I made a mistake. You were right about her all along. I should have listened. Should have supported you." Bill took a gulp of his drink.

"At least you came here with me the first time," Mike said.

"I did. I realized then that you were sincere and that you and she had a real connection. I was wrong. But I've been your friend since the Stone Age. I'd hate to lose you now."

"Right. Let me think about it."

"If you don't want me to come to the wedding, I'll understand."

The men finished their drinks and parted. The coolness between them had nothing to do with the air temperature.

Back at his office, Mike put aside work and called Heather.

"You and Bill have been friends for so long, I don't think we should leave him out," she said.

"Invite him to the wedding?"

"Yes."

"Are you sure?" Mike leaned back, resting his feet on the trash can.

"A snub like that would live forever. He'd never forget it. Neither would you. If you decided to forgive him, that would always be in the way."

"I don't know if I can forgive him."

"Fortunately, he didn't succeed, did he," she pointed out.

"Still."

"I'd like our wedding to be happy. No dark clouds overhead. Please try to forgive Bill. I'll add him to the invitation list."

"I'm going to trust you on this."

"Good. Besides, I have something in mind."

"Uh oh. One of your schemes?"

"Of course."

"Lay it on me."

"If he's jealous because of what you and I have, then we should do something to make sure Bill finds his true love, too."

"How?"

"Well, my cousin, Cindy—remember her?"

"No, but go ahead."

"She's just out of a relationship. I promised her I'd keep an eye out for a guy. Bill will be perfect."

"Really?"

"Yep. Let's invite them both to the wedding and let nature take its course."

"The hell with nature. I'm going to tell him about her and make sure he asks her out."

"Works for me."

"Now give me some highlights I can pass along," Mike said.

"Well, she has gorgeous red hair. She's in advertising."

THE END

SANDY & RAFE
Echoes of the Heart
JEAN C JOACHIM

Sandy & Rafe

Second Place Heart

Jean C. Joachim
Moonlight Books

A MOONLIGHT BOOKS NOVELLA

Sensual Romance

Sandy & Rafe

Second Place Heart

Echoes of the Heart series

Copyright © 2018 Jean C. Joachim

Cover design by Dawné Dominique

Edited by Sherri Good

Proofread by Renee Waring

All cover art and logo copyright © 2018 by Moonlight Books

PUBLISHER

Moonlight Books

Dedication

To any and all who've ever come in second.

SANDY & RAFE
SECOND PLACE HEART

Jean C. Joachim

Chapter One

Eleven months ago. Behind the scenes at the reality TV show, Marriage Minded.

"Lyle, Rafe, Lyle, Rafe? Bill, help!" Sandy moaned into the phone.

"Okay, give me the shit on these guys," her brother Bill said.

"Lyle is in real estate. He's funny, nice, and keeps talking about our future. He wants to renovate old buildings in Detroit and start a renaissance there. He said we make a good team."

"Sounds good. And the other guy?"

She sighed. "He's so sweet. He's French Canadian. He's an architect. I think he really loves me."

"Architects don't make crap. Real estate is where the money is."

"But Rafe..."

"You asked my opinion. So, you like this Rafe guy better?"

"I did, until Lyle told me Rafe only went on the show to get his green card."

"What? Fuck that. Easy choice, Sandy. Dump the Rafe guy. That's all you need, a guy who sleeps with you for six months, gets his green card, and takes off."

"He doesn't seem the type."

Bill snorted. "Yeah. Right. Like an asshole like that is gonna show his hand?"

"But he's been so nice."

"Who do you love?"

"Both, I think."

"One more than the other? Come on, Sandy. No one loves two guys exactly the same."

"Guess I'm leaning toward Rafe."

"Mr. Green Card? Forget it. If you think you could do marriage with this Lyle guy, then pick him. The other one looks like a phony."

"Thanks, Bill."

"Hey, what are brothers for?"

At the final ceremony, Sandy said "yes" to Lyle's proposal. It broke her heart to see Rafe cry. He turned away from the cameras and shielded his eyes with his hand. Sandy hugged him and walked him to the limo. Guilt washed over her until she reminded herself that he was simply seeking a green card and not a wife.

Doubts about his reasons for being on *Marriage Minded* nagged at her, but would asking him directly get her the truth? She doubted it. Of course, he'd lie, then act offended she'd questioned his motives, spouting on about his true love and how he only had eyes for her. No man would admit to such low motives on the show—in front of the cameras, anyway.

What a cynic she'd become! She had to do the right thing for her, no matter what.

Lyle would provide a stable future. At least that's what he said, and her brother had agreed. Their arguments swayed her. Why, now that she'd said "yes" and Lyle was prancing around like a prize-winning rooster, did she not share his joy?

After the show ended, Sandy informed Pine Grove Elementary School that she'd be taking a year off. She moved into Lyle's townhouse in Detroit. The four-story building, still under renovation, needed decorating, so Lyle pressed Sandy into service. As an art teacher, she had a knack for picking colors and fabrics. While Lyle worked hard selling real estate, Sandy tackled the house, room-by-room, selecting paint, picking out furniture, and supervising everything.

Lyle set up a ton of personal interviews, telling her they were good for business. Seems as if everyone wanted to talk to the new Detroit "power couple" who met on TV. He'd come home after a day's work recounting the phone calls he'd received from people wanting to know more about his vision for Detroit.

"Gwen is making a list. We have fifty people interested in buying our buildings, once they are renovated. Seems no one wants to do it themselves, but they're ready to move into a finished townhouse."

"That's great!"

"And it's all because you chose me on *Marriage Minded*."

"It's because you're doing something amazing, Lyle."

"That, too," he'd said, wearing a smug smile.

Sandy listened eagerly to his tales of buildings he'd bid on and buyers he'd interviewed. His vision of wealth and power fueled her imaginings of a comfortable lifestyle, a family, and a secure, loving future.

After three months, their relationship developed small cracks. With no more interviews, Lyle dug into the nitty-gritty of the next phase of his plan, arranging bank loans, finding collateral and negotiating with contractors. Blaming business meetings, he started coming home later, missing dinner. Their sex life, never stupendous, though Sandy had assured herself it was only a matter of getting to know each other better, slowed to a crawl. She made excuses. Lyle was tired after a twelve hour day at the office, or preoccupied. She ran out of reasons after three months.

The few times they did manage to heat up the sheets, she found herself envisioning Rafe. Though it filled her with guilt, her recollections of her one night with the experienced and talented Frenchman excited her more than her fiancé.

While Lyle immersed himself in his projects, Sandy worked hard supervising the renovation of the top floors into two floor-through apartments. She and Lyle lived on the first two floors and had the basement, as well. Sandy envisioned a playroom down there for their children. When she brought up the subject, Lyle sloughed it off, saying it was too soon to plan for a family.

Once the second apartment was almost finished, her fiancé cooled. His late nights became the norm. They stopped eating dinner together. Sex slowed down to once a week, if that. When she took his white shirts to the laundry, she detected a faint, but distinct, sweet scent that was not Lyle's aftershave.

Sandy dredged up every justification imaginable. Eventually, she stopped believing her own mantra. Desperate, she called her brother. After rattling off a list of Lyle's offenses, she waited.

"What do you think?" She chewed her lip.

"The guy's definitely fooling around."

"Really?" Her voice dropped.

"I can't hide the truth from you, sis."

"Really?" she asked again, hanging on to one last shred of hope.

"You don't want me to lie, do you?"

"No, no, of course not."

"Do you care?" her brother asked.

"What?"

"Do you love this guy?"

She hesitated. Had she ever loved him or had she simply fallen in love with the picture he'd painted of the future?

"I don't know."

"At least you're being honest. If you don't love him and he's being a douche, leave. You're not married."

"Don't you think we should try to work it out?"

"Why," Bill asked.

"To save our relationship?"

"What relationship? He used you to fix up his house and get him tons of free publicity. If there's a relationship there, I'm a kangaroo."

"But I..."

"You can't be broken-hearted. You don't love the guy."

"It's the smashed dreams. I thought I had a future with Lyle."

"But you don't love him. And from the sound of this conversation, you don't even like him."

"I did. I did. He was different on the show. Attentive, funny, and he painted a picture of the life I want."

"Yeah? Looks like he should try out for *Who's the Biggest Liar*?"

"I guess."

"You're stubborn. I get that. But let this one go."

"Just one more try. I'll talk to him. Tonight."

"Forget this guy. Move on."

"I'm so invested here. I hate to just give up."

"It isn't giving up. It's being realistic."

"Maybe. I gotta try."

"Go ahead. Go down with the ship. But don't say I didn't warn you."

But she didn't do what she said, instead she turned a blind eye to his shenanigans and avoided confrontation. Time ticked by, week after week, month after month and nothing improved. In fact, it got worse. They were ships passing in the night, never dining together or in bed together. Lyle slept on the sofa in the den. He'd used the excuse of coming home late, after she was asleep and not wanting to wake her, but he didn't fool Sandy.

It had been almost a year, the most miserable of her twenty-eight. When she smelled the perfume on his shirt again, her patience cracked. Showdown time.

He came home at one o'clock, almost running into Sandy who had perched by the door, shirt in hand. He stopped.

"Whose perfume is this?"

"Sure as hell ain't yours."

RAFE PELLETIER CONSIDERED himself an attractive man, yet he'd camouflaged himself through life, hiding behind his work, side-stepping entanglements. After having his heart stomped on at the tender age of twenty-one, he'd avoided relationships, focusing his energies on his work.

Career-wise, it had paid off. Rafe had his green card, a stable American architecture practice, U.S. citizenship pending, and his house renovated. Tired of living alone, he wanted a woman, a wife, to come home to. At thirty-six, the time to bid farewell to his bachelorhood had arrived.

His French background, good looks, trim body, and sharp wit made him especially attractive to the ladies. Rafe had never had a problem getting dates. He'd become the bachelor most desired on the upscale party circuit in New York City. His business connections morphed into invitations to exclusive gatherings, peppered with plenty of horny, single women. Although they aroused his libido, those women did not make his heart race. He sought a different kind of woman, one who wanted a home, children, and would be devoted to her family.

He and Charlie, his business partner, had lamented about the difficulty of finding a woman like that. Charlie had lucked out in college. He and Sally had been married for six years. They had tried to fix up Rafe with the right woman, but it never worked.

Due to an outrageous rent hike, Rafe and Charlie moved their business from New York City to Oak Bend, a small town two hours from Manhattan. They'd bought a building, renovated it, and set up shop. He and Charlie Larson carved out beautiful office space with one wall of glass. Keeping their big, New York clients meant traveling into the City about once a month. Rafe figured it was a small price to pay for the tranquility and low cost of living in the country.

But there were not a ton of available women for Rafe. Pursuing a woman in the country needed a whole new set of rules. Ready to give up the search, Rafe focused on building the business and pushed aside thoughts about having a family. Then Martha Mayburn came along.

Martha, an older artist, who rented the cottage on his property urged him to apply to *Marriage Minded*.

"They have this wonderful girl, Rafe. Her name is Sandy. I watched her on the program last season. Foolish man didn't pick her. But she's sweet and talked a lot about wanting a home and family. Said that was her dream. She's a school teacher, an artist, and does a lot of gardening on the side. Sounds like she might be just the ticket for you."

Rafe had laughed at her suggestion, but the more he thought about it, the better it looked. Even Charlie encouraged him.

"Got something better to do?" That's about as positive as Charlie ever got.

Their receptionist, Gloria, also encouraged Rafe to apply to the show.

"Lotsa cute girls there. All lookin' to get married. You could do worse," Gloria said, giving him a nudge in the ribs. Rafe found the fortyish woman embarrassing at times, but she could type like the wind and charmed their clients.

Poised to take the next step—marriage and family—he'd ignored his better judgment and applied to *Marriage Minded*. His partner agreed to run the business for the couple of months Rafe would be away. Of course, he made Rafe promise to return the favor. Rafe didn't mind. If he lost, what else would he have to do but work? And if he won, ah, he'd be cocooning with his bride. The image sent a zing through his body.

The first time he'd laid eyes on Sandy, he'd been smitten. Her dark blonde hair, hazel eyes, lush body, and bright smile stopped him cold. Bumbling through his introduction, tongue-tied, and almost forgetting his own name, embarrassment filled him. How could he get this gorgeous woman to fall in love with him if he couldn't speak properly? She'd simply nodded and cupped his cheek, saying she'd been in the same boat a few months earlier. Her understanding put him at ease.

Shocked that she'd selected him for her first date, he believed she simply felt sorry for that poor bumbling Frenchman—his words, not hers. Figuring he'd probably never get another second alone with her, Rafe trotted out his French-Canadian charm.

Willing himself to remove his gaze from her alluring chest, he'd focused on her words, listening intently and parroting back bits and pieces of what she said, reassuring her he had paid attention. To avoid drooling like an idiot, he'd asked her questions. When he paused, she threw one at him—which artist did he like better, Monet or Renoir?

Astounded she'd picked his favorite art genre, he warmed to their conversation.

"Who do you like better?" she asked.

"I like them both. Do you see a difference?" he parried.

"I like Monet for his *Water Lilies*. But Renoir was able to use impressionism on a person, with his *Girl with a Watering Can*. I think that took more talent, maybe discipline. Something. But I love that painting."

"And Seurat? Talk about hard work," he said, pretending to wipe his brow.

"I think he only did six or eight paintings in his lifetime. Each one took forever, but they're masterpieces," she said.

"I agree," he replied, taking her hand. "And so are you, a masterpiece."

"Oh, stop," she said, blushing.

He pulled her close for a kiss.

Her love of French Impressionist art blew him away. He hadn't expected such thoughtful and observant conversation. The minute she'd shown her intelligence, he'd taken her seriously. As they walked and talked, her sweet nature and their similar goals sealed the deal. Before the program was half over, he'd fallen hard. He had to win her.

The rest was a blur of romance, laughter, and genuine giddiness, a new experience for the reserved Rafe. He wangled time with her at cocktail parties and group dates. Risking criticism, she selected him for more one-on-one dates, and his heart took flight.

Rafe had managed to survive to the final two, which guaranteed one night, all night with her—no cameras. Eager to be alone with Sandy, to touch and kiss her in privacy, hope sprang forth in his heart. They made love, tentatively at first, then with fiery passion. He simply couldn't get enough of her and cursed the sunrise. Resting, tangled up naked with Sandy, peace flowed through him. Love filled his heart.

His hopes rode high as they came to the proposal. More nervous than ever before, he'd gotten down on one knee, flashed the ring, and asked the anticipated question.

Stunned, he'd risen to standing, cloaked in disbelief. Was he that myopic, that blind and stupid that he didn't see her affection for him didn't match his for her? Her refusal broke his heart.

Angry and depressed, on the ride home, he'd tried to haze her, but it didn't work. The more energy he put into despising her, the more he missed her. Never a maudlin, sentimental man, he'd found himself taking long walks, and dreaming about what would never happen. He couldn't stop thinking about the lovely Sandy Landeau and the life with her that now haunted his dreams.

PRESENT DAY, OAK BEND, NY

"Look, Rafe." Charlie, his business partner, pointed to the television.

Rafe glanced up from the project he was working on.

"Some guy's throwing the bitch who broke your heart out on the street." Charlie shook his head.

Rafe's eyes widened as he moved closer to the screen.

"Karma gets 'em every time," Charlie said, laughing.

Color heated Rafe's cheeks. He watched as Lyle tossed Sandy Landeau's possessions out of a townhouse's second story window. A newscaster talked while Sandy raced around, gathering her things. He saw a rectangular object fly to the ground. It opened, and a piece of paper floated down. She scooped it up and dumped the book and paper in a shopping bag.

Rafe's mouth went dry. The newscaster shoved a microphone in Sandy's face. The young woman wiped her tears with her fingers and stuttered, attempting to answer the woman's questions.

"Sandy would you agree that not everyone picks the right partner on *Marriage Minded*. Seems like you and Lyle Wilton are not meant to be. Well, well, now it's clothes..."

The camera panned out to catch Lyle dumping a suitcase full of clothes, including lingerie, on the lawn. Then he threw the valise down, too. An SUV pulled up. A man got out and opened the back. Sandy ran over, flung her stuff in the vehicle, then scooped up everything she could grab.

"What's the matter? You'd better sit down, buddy. You don't look so good," Charlie said, shoving a chair behind his partner.

"How humiliating. That bastard. That lowlife fraud. He's disgusting," Rafe said.

"Don't you think she deserved that?"

"*Zut alors*. Nobody deserves that. Especially not Sandy."

"She shot you down. What the hell do you care?"

"Unlike you, I don't turn my feelings on and off like the kitchen faucet." Rafe pushed to his feet, returning to his computer. "I have to get this design done. The contractor is waiting for it."

Rafe turned his attention back to his screen. After half an hour of pretending to focus, he got a cup of coffee, and moseyed over to the window. Rafe gazed out over the meadow.

Watching the newscast, his sharp eye had picked up the dark red book cover sailing through the air in Detroit. After *Marriage Minded* finished, he'd sent a red-leather-bound edition of *Pride and Prejudice* to Sandy through the show. Jane Austen was her favorite. After his anger subsided, he couldn't part from her without leaving something of himself behind. That's when he came up with the idea of the book. Knowing it would be with her forever eased his mind.

He figured a leather-bound version would endure longer than her relationship with that snake, Lyle. He'd included a personal note, which had floated down with the book. She had snatched it up, too, and stuffed both in a bag. Dare he hope she'd find the note?

Desire to see Sandy's life with Lyle fall apart quickly burned in his heart. As time passed, that fire dimmed, and, six months later, it turned to dust, blown away by a breath. Gossip about Sandy and Lyle on the Internet whispered of glowing happiness. Then today, the news coverage had hit him like a tornado, whirling and spinning away his despair. Tiny seeds of anticipation grew inside him. Possibility burst into life in his heart once more.

He wondered if she'd read the note. Maybe she would now? If she did? No guarantee she'd reach out to him. It was stupid to *keep the torch burning*, as Charlie called it. He couldn't help it. He'd fallen deeply in love with Sandy on *Marriage Minded*. But he'd been the runner-up, "Mr. Second Place", as his partner had so succinctly pointed out.

A glimmer of hope sprouted when he noted that, a year later, she still had the book, and Lyle had exited. He chided himself—one doesn't throw out or give away a leather-bound book, do they? It wasn't about sentiment, was it? He shook his head. Sandy was too practical to throw out something of value.

Perusing the woods, Rafe spied a quick flash of something orange. His gaze followed a fox, hiding behind shrubbery, tiptoeing its way across the meadow, sneaking up on some unsuspecting little mouse or bird. He identified with the fox. Could he slip back into Sandy Landeau's life, as easily as the crafty hunter negotiated the landscape?

Rafe checked his watch. Kelly, his once-a-month weekend date, would arrive on the seven o'clock bus from the city. He'd take her out to eat tonight, then they could pick up supplies and cook in on Saturday. In his frame of mind, Kelly's incessant chatter would only irritate him, but it was too late to cancel now. He ground his teeth. Settling for Kelly instead of Sandy went down hard, especially now that she was free.

Sandy's pain and humiliation at the hands of that Neanderthal hit him in the gut. Could he wipe it away? He wished he had the power, but she'd taken it away when she rejected him. Would she want to put her life back together with Mr. Second Place? He doubted it. A woman like Sandy could have any man she wanted. Why would she want someone she had discarded, like a pair of shoes that pinched her toes?

He had no idea why she'd turned him down, but she had, and it seemed unlikely she'd be second-guessing that decision any time soon. Poor Sandy, broken-hearted, alone, humiliated, and on camera, too. He couldn't help but notice the similarity to his situation when she refused his marriage proposal.

Instead of feeling happy for her discomfort, he sympathized. He'd known exactly how that felt and it wasn't good. She had been kind and sweet about it, as only Sandy would be. But the fact that she'd chosen that asshole over him remained. He'd felt it keenly while he tried to avoid the camera that chased him, broadcasting his misery to millions.

Damn. He wanted to hold her, hug her, utter words of comfort. But that ship had sailed, so he'd have to live, in silence, with the pain of her unhappiness, remaining in the shadows, where she had put him. He sighed.

Chapter Two

Riding in the car with her brother Bill at the wheel, Sandy blew out a breath. Good old Bill, her faithful brother, bailing her out of another horrible situation. Where would she be if he hadn't rescued her over and over again? When she was a kid, he'd been her knight in shining armor. Looks like he still was. She cringed, imagining what her parents were saying. None of it would be good, and some, especially from her father, would contain plenty of four-letter words. Sandy recalled one parting shot from her mother from their brief conversation yesterday.

"We told you not to do that," her mother had said before hanging up.

Then Bill had ridden in on his white horse, or SUV.

After she and Bill had loaded everything into his vehicle, he'd hugged his sister.

"Tomorrow, you're yesterday's news, Sis."

"I suppose."

"Come on. Snap out of it. The guy's a jackass loser. You're well rid of him."

Sandy had paid the woman subletting her place to leave early. She'd had to throw in a month's rent at the local motel to get her apartment back.

Bill had driven down from the University of Michigan, where he attended grad school. Without even one question, he'd picked her up and headed for Pine Grove. Gratitude filled Sandy.

"Thanks for coming to get me."

"Hell, Ann Arbor isn't far. No biggie."

"It *is* a biggie. I appreciate it. I think Santa will pack something extra special for you come Christmas."

He laughed. "That's what little brother's do."

"Not all little brothers." She cast a grateful smile at the man behind the wheel. "Well, how does it feel to have millions of people witness the gruesome end to the biggest mistake of your life?" Bill asked.

"Thank you so much, Bill. That makes me feel tons better." She glared at him.

"Mom and dad are furious. The *I told you so's* are going to be brutal."

"Wonderful. Like I haven't already beaten myself to a bloody pulp mentally?"

He reached across the car and patted his sister. "I'd like to have ten minutes alone with that fuckin' asshole. Just ten minutes."

"Great. Then we could go back on TV from the hospital where Lyle would be on life-support."

Bill grinned. "I love that you have faith in me."

"You're it, Bill. The only one left."

"That can't be true. What about at school?"

"Everyone there told me not to do it. I can't imagine there'll be one person who'll feel sorry for me."

"As long as you don't feel sorry for yourself. What about that other guy? The weird French dude from Canada?"

"Rafe?" She shook her head. "I'm sure he's found someone else by now."

"Refresh my memory, why did you pick Lyle over Rafe?"

"Green card? Remember?"

"Oh, yeah. Right."

"Right after the overnight date, Lyle told me Rafe only wanted to get married to get a green card. He said Rafe had owned up to it in the house. He'd said it was the fastest way. And, like the idiot I am, I believed him."

"And it wasn't true?"

Tears pricked at the backs of her eyes. "I checked. Online. He already has his green card. Got it through work, before he even went on the show."

"Fuck! Lyle lied."

"No surprise. Not his only lie."

"Damn. I'm sorry, Sandy."

"I was hoping for a happy ending. And look what I got."

"Your life isn't exactly over yet."

"Might as well be. I'm a laughing stock. Who'd go out with me now? *Marriage Minded double* reject. Loser. Public loser." A few tears slipped down her cheeks.

"Great. Let's have a pity party. You're the most beautiful girl in Pine Grove. Guys'll be knocking down your door as soon as we get home."

"Yeah, right. I don't think so."

"Why don't you wait before you make up your mind?"

"I'll try to be positive."

"You're the most positive person I know."

"Was, Bill. Was."

"I checked with Laura, and you can get back into the apartment any time you want."

"Good. Let's go, okay? It's lick my wounds and try to figure out where I go from here time."

"You're the boss."

They took turns driving, cutting down the time it took to get to New York from Michigan. They took a motel room for one night and rolled into Laura and Barney's driveway about noon the next day. The couple helped them unload. Sandy couldn't believe how much stuff she'd lugged to Lyle's place over the course of a year.

Bill threw his arms around Sandy. "Chin up. You'll come out of this okay. You always do."

"I don't usually mess up this bad," she replied.

"Nope. You usually leave that to me." He chuckled.

"Now it's my turn to get the heat."

"Aw, the folks will forget it soon enough. Mom'll be asking when you're coming to dinner."

"Maybe."

He stepped back and climbed into his car. Sandy waved as he drove away. As if she'd lost her best friend, pain seared through her as she watched her only supporter drive away. Loneliness engulfed her. The quiet of the sleepy town settled on her. With a sigh, Sandy trudged up the stairs to put her life back together, starting with rearranging her small apartment and finding a place for her stuff.

An envelope appeared under her door. It was an invitation to dine with Laura and Barney, her neighbors and landlord. The last thing she wanted was prying eyes. But Laura was the best cook in the county. She knew the woman meant well and wouldn't gossip about her. Maybe it would be good for her to socialize a little. Besides, Laura mentioned beef stew. Sandy hadn't had a good home-cooked meal in ages.

She fished around in her fridge for an open bottle of Moscato and poured herself a glass. Then she surveyed the mess. A year's worth of stuff to sort through. Crap. Could it really have been that long? Only now could she admit she'd known things were going south with him after three months. One by one, he broke every promise. The dream she'd thought they'd build together fell apart, piece by piece.

Lyle was a real estate broker. He'd said he could work anywhere. He'd move with her back to Pine Grove and ply his trade there. Wrong! Entrenched in Detroit real estate, he'd stated that there was a whole lot more money to be made in Detroit and she'd better think about relocating.

That had been the first step on the downward spiral. By six months, they'd stopped sleeping together, and she didn't miss it. Lyle had grown increasingly cold and self-obsessed. Then there was the other woman, whoever she was.

After a long night of arguing and tears, her tears, they'd agreed to part. But she'd sublet her apartment until the end of the year and had no place to go. So, he'd let her sleep on the couch for three months. That's when he started bringing women home. Even as roommates, the situation had become intolerable. And the women who shared his bed had been rude and nasty.

"What are you still doing here?"

"Don't you know when you're not wanted?"

"Why don't you go home?"

He'd made no comment. The morning of the infamous day of their parting, his most steady girlfriend gave him an ultimatum. It was either Sandy or her. Lyle decided Sandy had to go. And when he'd thrown all of her stuff out the window, then ushered her outside, the girlfriend gave her the finger and bolted the door.

That had been the ugliest scene in her life. Someone had called the media, Sandy didn't know who but had her suspicions. Her parents had refused to get involved.

That was yesterday.

Today, Sandy took a sip of wine and surveyed the disaster in front of her. Seeing her apartment littered with broken suitcases, and bags of clothes and stuff tossed everywhere, she wanted to cry. But that wouldn't help. Soon, it would be summer, her favorite season. She had to return to her job in the fall. Could she bear the humiliation? Did she have a choice?

As Bill had said, she'd be yesterday's news by September, even at school. There'd be a lot of comments in the beginning, then, when someone else landed in the gossip spotlight, the focus on Sandy would die down. She needed the money. Fortunately, she had savings. Careful with money, Sandy often sewed her own dresses for school and hawked sales at the grocery and drug stores.

Bag by bag, items were nestled neatly in drawers or on shelves. Sandy sat cross-legged on the floor and eyed the last shopping bag. Nope, she couldn't finish. Cringing, she peeked in to see the jumbled mess of papers and stuff, including something red. Ah, good, she hadn't lost that red leather-bound version of *Pride and Prejudice*.

Popping up, she threw open a small suitcase, dumped in some basics, grabbed the shopping bag and hurried down the stairs to her car. She needed a road trip. Find a cabin on a lake, read, sleep, run, eat, and forget Lyle and men in general. She smiled as she remembered the red-leather book. Reading Jane Austen could cure anything, couldn't it?

"WELL, AREN'T YOU GOING to do something?" Gloria asked Rafe.

"Do something? Do what?"

"I mean that young woman. Poor thing. Publicly humiliated."

"It's terrible. What can I do? What's done is done." Rafe wandered over to the coffee machine.

"Not very chivalrous of you. I'm surprised, Rafe. I thought you were in love with this girl."

"That's personal."

"Really?" She arched an eyebrow.

Heat blossomed in his cheeks. "Yes. No comment."

"And you're deserting her? In her hour of need?"

Rafe laughed. "You're so dramatic. What hour of need? She's free from that snake. She should consider herself lucky she got out before she married that piece of garbage."

"I'm sure she does. But it must sting a helluva lot. And she's all alone."

Before he filled his mug, Rafe turned to face his assistant. "What makes you think she's alone?"

"When would she have time to find anyone? She's been tied to that lowlife for almost a year."

"She has a list of men who would take a bullet for her. She doesn't need me. Believe me, she can have her choice."

"I repeat. That's not very chivalrous of you." She turned on her heel and walked away.

Rafe poured the hot brew, fixed it the way he liked it—one sugar and cream—then wandered to the window. Gloria had hit a nerve. Though he'd never admit it to her, or Charlie either, the video of Sandy's expulsion from Lyle's house had tugged at his heart.

In fact, his eyes had watered as he watched her stammer and stutter on camera, brushing wetness from her cheeks. Even in tears with no makeup, she looked beautiful, and tragic. He wanted to fold her in his arms, rub her back, and tell her everything would be okay. He wanted to tell her that he'd stand by her side through the worst of it and help her pick up the pieces. But she hadn't asked him. He sighed.

She'd pushed him aside, and he had no idea why. Although it had been a year, the pain in his heart still stung. Never a man to fall in love on a whim, Rafe had surprised himself with the intensity of his feelings. He and Sandy had clicked right away and he'd decided they were soulmates. Unable to stop himself with rational thought, his emotions had blundered ahead into full love and devotion mode.

Then she'd tossed him aside, albeit gently, and he'd been crushed and bewildered. Their relationship had grown so quickly, he'd been convinced she'd accept when he proposed. No man in his right mind would pop the question if he thought the lady would turn him down, right? But she had, with no explanation.

He allowed himself to recall their steamy night in the private suite. The sexual tension that had built over time, doubling with each date, each moment spent together, had to be satisfied. He could hardly contain himself when she'd agreed to spend the night with him. Blood had begun pumping between his legs before they even got to the suite. And she had not disappointed him. Making love to her had been perfect, not in the mechanics, surely. There's always that period of adjustment. But the feeling, the passion they shared had left him speechless.

After a night spent in mutual sexual discovery, Rafe had made up his mind. Sandy was the right woman for him, the only woman for him, and he had to have her again and again—and marry her. A rueful smile crossed his lips at the memory of his cockiness, his confidence bordering on arrogance, about his chances. Surely a woman who had responded to him the way she had couldn't possibly love another man? Right? *Wrong.*

His heart squeezed at the humiliation and disillusionment of her refusal. He'd crept away a broken man, hiding it as best he could. A single, tiny hope that refused to die had spurred him to buy the book and write the note. After he'd sent it, he'd regretted it. Rafe Pelletier was not a man to beg...or was he? It didn't matter because she'd never responded to the note and, as far as he could tell from the television clip, had never even seen it.

He'd surprised himself with his reaction. Charlie had expected Rafe to be happy about Sandy's public break-up. Rafe would have expected it, too. What foolish idiot would be sorry for the woman who broke his heart when she got her comeuppance? Only a man still in love with the woman. Yes, a stupid man, a hopeless romantic, a masochistic moron—he, Rafe.

He certainly wasn't going to embarrass himself further by sending the woman flowers. How dense of Gloria to even suggest such a thing? He took a sip of his brew and smiled. Still, Sandy loved roses. Pink was her favorite. They'd cheer her up, let her know he was thinking of her. He frowned. And let her know she could have another pass at his heart? No way!

He clenched his jaw. Where was his pride? Crawling back to Sandy, asking for another chance, begging her to tell him what went wrong? Just the idea caused his stomach to flip-flop. And what if she said she'd made the mistake of her life, that Rafe was the one she loved after all? Could he trust that? Could he believe her? Not on your life.

As he returned to his desk, he glanced at the calendar on the wall. Only a few weeks left until he'd be leaving for England. He'd been hired to work on a special project and teach a course in London, as a visiting professor from the States. He loved that title. It held respect, something that had been in short supply this past year. When the opportunity came for their firm to participate in this program, Rafe had jumped at the chance. Charlie had no interest in going abroad.

Maybe, in England, he'd finally forget about Sandy Landeau, maybe his heart would heal and he could move on? And maybe trucks could fly.

BY FOUR O'CLOCK, ANGER and frustration at not finding a place to stay wore off and exhaustion set in. Sandy saw a sign for Perkins' Cabins by Willow Lake. Turning off, she found her way to Perkins. Sure enough, they had a "vacancy" sign up. She grinned.

After she'd checked in for a week's stay, she drove around to cabin number six, boasting a small porch facing the lake. She unloaded her few things and the grocery essentials she'd picked up along the way. She grabbed a bottle of wine and a bag of pretzels and perched on the deck, awaiting the sunset.

Bird songs broke the silence of the woods. Sandy's shoulders dropped to their normal position as calm filled her veins. Then she remembered. The Jane Austen book—a great read—the perfect addition to her recovery. She dragged the shopping bag onto the deck, took a healthy sip of her Cabernet, plunked down into a chair, and peered inside. The sturdy plastic held a plethora of assorted items, from a brand-new toothbrush, a half-used bottle of hand lotion, and unopened mail. She spied the book and reached in, her fingers landing on a piece of textured paper.

She peered in. It was folded, like a note. Sandy plucked it out, then retrieved the book. Opening the cover, she read the inscription:

May your days be filled with great literature.

As always,

Rafe Pelletier

She ran her palm over the cover. The smooth leather was cool to the touch. She'd forgotten the book was from him. Her mind wandered back to their one night together. Hmm, great literature by day and hot sex by night? She ran the tip of her tongue over her bottom lip, then hugged the book to her chest.

She put the book on the table. The note drew her eye. Who was it from? She opened it.

Just in case things don't work out or you change your mind, I'll be here. If you need

a shoulder to cry on, or...something else. Please call me.

Rafe

P.S. It's not that I don't wish you well. I do. I hope you're happy and your decision

works out for the best. But as Robert Burns said about "best-laid plans..."

He had included his cell phone number. Her mouth went from moist to dry within seconds. She fingered the note, running her thumb along the smooth, linen-like paper. *Call Rafe. Don't call Rafe.*

Call Rafe. Don't call Rafe. Draining her glass, she sat back and stared at the horizon. The note had been written almost a year ago. She couldn't expect him to still be waiting, could she? She chuckled to herself. *Wouldn't that be neat and pretty, thrown into the arms of the man I truly love by the one I thought I did.*

The threat of humiliation hung in the hair. What if he had someone else? She could hear the conversation now.

"Gee, Sandy, what we had was great, but Matilda and I are engaged and getting married tomorrow. Too bad."

Or:

"Hi, Sandy, you conceited, lying little bitch. What the fuck do you want?"

She swallowed. Or even.

"Hello, Sandy. You? Why no. I don't think so. I'm dating three Victoria's Secret Models and you can't hold a candle to them. Bye bye."

Horrified, she tossed out the idea of calling him. She couldn't deny she'd thought of Rafe hundreds of times in the past three months. As it became clear she'd made the worst mistake of her life, she longed for comfort from the Frenchman. He'd never be so cruel, never use her, the way Lyle did. She hung her head as emotion grew. Men like Rafe Pelletier didn't sit around for a year licking their wounds and pining for women who had given them the axe.

The memory of that awful day, when he'd proposed and she'd turned him down, flashed through her mind. His surprise and humiliation still brought wetness to her eyes. Rafe had declared they'd ride into the sunset together. She hadn't realized that he had no clue he'd get turned down. When she'd laced her fingers with his, his hand had been cold.

His words returned to her.

"But I thought you loved me? You said you did."

"And I do."

"But not enough? Is that it? We had so much together, Sandy."

She'd smiled at him.

"Please tell me this is a joke, a cruel joke."

"I wish I could. I'm so sorry."

"Was I crazy? Didn't we have chemistry?"

"We did. And you're amazing. The kindest, sweetest man."

"I'm such a fool."

Then she had stopped and cupped his cheek, staring into his eyes, wet with tears.

"Don't say that. You were never a fool."

"Then what happened?"

She'd been reluctant to tell him. How could she say, "you were the most wonderful man until I found out you were using me to get a green card"? So she'd lied.

"I don't know. It's not your fault."

But clearly, it was his fault. He'd been a user, a fake, a phony all along—there for all the wrong reasons. Or that's what she'd been told. And she had accepted it, without blinking, instead of confronting him. Why hadn't she asked Bill to check out Rafe on the Internet? Trusting, naïve, stupid Sandy had let Lyle convince her—major mistake.

Anger rose in her chest. The word *chump* came to mind when she thought of that day. How could she have been stupid enough to toss away the most sincere, loving man for the manipulative user? She'd sunk her own boat, taken the wrong path, and thrown away happiness.

To further her pity party, Sandy pictured the life she could be leading today if she had accepted Rafe instead of Lyle.

With a quick shake of her head, she padded into the kitchen and refilled her glass. She made a sandwich and retrieved the book from the table outside. Stretching out on the small sofa, she opened it to page one, munched, and read until she fell asleep.

Chapter Three

Sandy awoke early to a sunny day. Enjoying the quiet surrounding the cabin, she dressed, chowed down a bowl of cereal, and headed for the forest. Hiking had always cleared her head. She did her best thinking in the woods.

As she walked, the idea of returning to her teaching job soured. She needed to work and there was no other job on the horizon, so she had no choice. But she didn't have to remain beyond the school year. She'd take the year to find another job or profession or go back to school or do whatever—change her life. The decision calmed her. She could last one more year among the numb-nuts at Pine Grove Elementary.

Sunlight dappled tree trunks and leaves. The occasional rustle drew her gaze. A bird or squirrel rested before continuing their journey for food. A deep breath brought the scent of fresh pine from tall trees shading her way. Anxiety fell away as she absorbed the peace surrounding her.

As she tromped farther in, Rafe floated across her mind. With a sigh, she focused on their halted relationship. Could she do anything about it? Was rekindling their romance out of the question? Was he already engaged to someone else? Could she check him out on the Internet? An exceedingly private person, Rafe wouldn't have his life spread out for the world to examine on the Net. She'd investigate, maybe even rope Bill into her scheme. She had to know if something with him was still possible or if she'd wrecked that forever when she turned him down.

Her cell phone sounded louder than ever amid the tranquility of the forest. She plopped down on an old tree stump and answered.

"Gram. How are you?"

"Fine. But the question is, how are you?"

"Been better."

"Figured."

"I never expected the public humiliation. TV, interviews, cameras..."

"But that's what you signed on for with that hare-brained program."

"I know. But that was for the show. Not for the rest of my life."

"Sometimes we open a can of worms without knowing."

"Yep."

"What's your plan now?"

Sandy shrugged. "Don't have one."

"Why don't you come for a visit?"

"I will when I have some clue what I'm doing."

"You've been given the chance to begin again, Sandy. Not everyone gets that."

"Begin again?" she snorted. "More like scoop up the pieces and try to fit them back together."

"Nonsense! Move past the pity crap. You can start over. Pick a new career. Find a new man. At your age, life is an adventure."

"An adventure in humiliation."

"Oh, get over yourself. Everyone makes mistakes and does dumb things. You're not the first."

"But not everyone does it in front of millions of people."

"Celebrities do it all the time. And that's what you became on that asinine show."

"I suppose."

"It's the truth. If you spend time wallowing, you might miss the opportunity of a lifetime. Get up off your butt and pull yourself together."

"I'm trying, Gram."

"I don't hear any trying. All I hear is whining and complaining."

Sandy laughed. "Guess you're right about that."

"Stop it. Put together a plan and move ahead with your life," her grandmother said.

"You're right. You're always right."

"I know."

Sandy heard a chuckle at the other end. "Okay, okay. You've made a good point. I'm just wasting time, worrying about what people will think."

"Exactly! Nice to know you listen to your old grandma."

"Kinda hard not to."

"I've got a pie in the oven. Gotta go. Hang in there. You're an amazing woman. You can do anything you set your mind to. Love you."

"Love you, too, Gram. And, thanks."

Sandy shoved her cell back in her pocket. Gram's words reverberated in her head. The older woman was right about one thing, never give up. Sandy agreed that people made their own luck, and she could have what she'd gone on that stupid show to find.

"I can have it all, if I want it bad enough," she said to the chickadee chirping nearby.

The challenge was figuring out what she wanted. An hour later, she returned to the cabin. After making a sandwich, she got comfortable on the deck and pulled out *Pride and Prejudice*. She read and napped away the rest of the day. After dinner at a local diner, Sandy crawled into bed and turned out the light.

Staring at the moon shining in the window, she turned her mind to the question she'd been avoiding. Exactly what did she want? Like a bolt of lightning, the answer struck her as she lay in bed. She wanted a man there. She wanted to make love, to be held, to hike with a partner, to read curled up next to a loving husband. That had been her reason for going on *Marriage Minded.*

So she had picked the wrong guy. So what, right? She had found the right guy and pushed him away. But if he wasn't married or dead, then he was still available. She rolled over, scrunching the pillow under her chest. It was Rafe. She wanted Rafe. She sighed. Having an answer calmed her. Determined to check out early in the morning and follow her heart, Sandy fell asleep.

SUNDAY MORNING, RAFE hit the button on the coffee machine. Always an early riser, he moved about quietly so as not to wake Kelly. He'd down three cups of java before she'd stumble out of the bedroom, yawning and barefoot.

A pretty redhead, Kelly had been his friend with benefits for the past three months. He'd caved when he couldn't stand the celibacy any longer. He had given up finding a replacement in his heart for Sandy and settled for some companionship and decent sex.

As he sipped and watched birds at his backyard feeder, he acknowledged that his leaving for London wouldn't be a big deal with Kelly. She probably didn't give a damn. What a relief not to have an unpleasant scene with her begging to tag along and him resisting.

He brought in the Sunday paper from his front stoop and headed for the sofa. An hour later, Kelly made her appearance. Wearing one of his T-shirts, her hair a train wreck and no makeup, she staggered into the living room.

"Coffee?" she muttered.

"Ready," he said, pointing.

She headed for the kitchen and returned holding a mug with a bear on it. Plopping down next to Rafe, she stared at the paper.

"Nothing but bad news these days," she said between sips.

"Unfortunately. But one must know what's going on in the world."

"Not me. I don't give a rat's ass. When do you leave for London?"

"In a couple of weeks. This is our last weekend, I'm afraid."

"Really? That soon, huh?"

He nodded.

"We'd better make the most of it then," she said with a snicker.

"Good idea." He glanced at her. Her lack of passion sometimes made it hard for him to make the first move. She rarely turned him down, and that had to count for something. Sandy had been inspiring. During their one steamy night together, he couldn't take his hands off her. Desire that had been building over weeks wouldn't be satisfied in one night. It would take a lifetime of lovemaking to satisfy his passion for her.

But Kelly was there, willing, and attractive enough. Why not, right? He took their mugs to the kitchen, then led her back to the bedroom. This would have to last until the moon turned purple or someone else of Sandy's caliber came along. He'd better make it good.

For the first time, Rafe's shaft was slow to the game. Kelly applied her skills, and he responded. Closing his eyes, Rafe replayed his first time with Sandy. The memory of the heat they generated hardened him in seconds. Barely able to contain himself until he was inside her, want took over, possessing him completely.

Images of Sandy arching into him, moaning, and meeting his rhythm rekindled a fire he thought had gone out. He didn't care that the woman beneath him was Kelly. In his mind, it was Sandy. The heat in his body threatened to consume him as he thrust into Kelly harder and faster.

She groaned her orgasm and he followed. Panting, he lowered his face to her shoulder. The sweat, beaded on his forehead, now trickled down.

"*Ew*! Are you getting sweat on me?" she asked, uncoupling quickly and wiping her shoulder with the sheet.

"Sorry." Sandy hadn't minded his sweat. He chided himself to stop comparing the two women. It only made him miss Sandy more.

They showered, separately, and dressed. Rafe drove them to his favorite place for a late brunch. They sipped mimosas and gazed at each other.

"So, this is it, huh?" she asked.

"I'm afraid so."

"Can I come and visit?"

"What's the point?"

"What's the point of coming up here once a month? To get laid and have some fun, right?"

"I suppose," he replied, casting his gaze to his glass.

"Maybe it's better. A clean break. I might meet Prince Charming and be whisked away on a white horse to a storybook wedding."

He grinned. "You might."

"And you might find the girl you're looking for."

"The girl I'm looking for?"

"I've known since the beginning. I'm just a substitute, a place-holder, for some girl."

"Some girl?"

"Stop answering a question with a question," she said.

"Was that a question?"

"There you go. Okay, maybe mine wasn't a question. You use questions to hide behind, when you don't want to admit the truth."

"You've analyzed me quite thoroughly for someone who's only known me a couple of months."

"Sleeping together gives me insight," she said.

He chuckled. "Okay. And what have you learned?"

"Someone broke your heart. Bad. Serious. Major."

The grin fell off his face, but he remained silent.

"It's okay. You don't have to admit it. I'm not offended. Her breaking your heart had nothing to do with me. I'm glad I gave you a diversion."

"A diversion?" he asked.

"Yeah. Sex and someone to talk to."

"It's more than that."

"Is it? I don't think so. You don't even want me to visit you in London. It's okay. It is what it is. I accept that. I have from the start. I'm glad you've been honest enough not to pretend we're having some grand love affair or crap like that."

He had tried to save face, but she had been correct. It had never been more than sex and a bit of companionship. There was no relationship there, no bonding—strictly friends with benefits. Her uttering the truth relieved the need for pretense.

"You're right. I'm ashamed to admit it," he said, wiping his lips with his napkin.

She reached over and squeezed his arm. "Don't be. You've helped me. I'm better for knowing you. Really. I left an abusive relationship. Now I'm ready to find a nice man. A man like you. For something real."

"Thank you."

He wished he could reciprocate, tell her she'd helped him get over Sandy, but it wasn't true. All she'd done was put a pause in his life. After she left, he'd probably return to being the same dismal goon, moping around, working too hard, and taking long walks.

After they finished eating, he drove her to the bus station. They kissed, and she boarded on schedule. He stood on the sidewalk, waving until she was out of sight. With a heavy sigh, he drove home. He refilled the bird feeders and resumed reading the paper, fending off loneliness.

SANDY THREW HER SHOPPING bag and valise in the car and headed back to Pine Grove. She looked up Rafe's office address on her phone and put it in her GPS. She didn't intend to talk to him, just take a gander at his digs.

She played her favorite playlist as she scooted much too fast around the bends in the back roads. Singing along, hope rose like a phoenix from the ashes. Determined to find a new path, first on the list was exploring any possibilities with Rafe Pelletier—if he'd even speak to her. Second was investigating masters' degree programs and unusual jobs on Craig's List.

Her first perusal with her morning coffee had revealed such borderline positions as massage therapist, no experience required, or indie film actress wanted. Yeah, right. Hooker and porn star were not on her list.

As she drove, she ran through possible scenarios with Rafe. She'd expect that he'd be so mad and hurt he wouldn't even speak to her. Could she take it if he slammed the door in her face? He'd never do that. Besides, he'd given her the book and the note. Of course, those were written when the wound was still fresh and feelings still present. So many months later, he might have scabbed over and love had turned to hate or indifference.

Although she had to allow for that possibility, she knew Rafe. He wasn't a hater. Sure, he had a temper—what man didn't? But he didn't have a hating heart. At least she hoped he didn't.

She bit her lip as she careened too close to the right. Rejecting the slam-the-door reaction, she envisioned him hurt, asking her why she'd chosen Lyle. Ugh. The image that conjured up created a crapload more anxiety than the angry vision. Hell, would she tell him? Would he then get mad over what a complete idiot she'd been?

What would she say when he asked her why she didn't come to him for the truth? She swallowed. She'd have to admit what a jerk she'd been, how she hadn't given him a chance. Of course, she'd tell him why, but, still, there would be humiliation—again. She ought to be used to that by now. If she loved him and wanted him, then she'd have to 'fess up.

Things were looking grim. His pain on her refusal had sliced through her. If she could have taken it back, she might have, simply to stop hurting him. Could she bear to see that look in his eyes again? Would she see betrayal, rejection, and sadness there? *Damn.* That would be hard to take. She shuddered to think of facing that again.

Walkin' on Sunshine came on, urging Sandy to turn her thoughts to a happier outcome. Maybe he'd be delighted? Would he take her in his arms, kiss her, and ask her, "What took you so long?" Would he propose again? She laughed and shook her head. Rafe was too sane to do something so impulsive, so crazy. And what if he did propose? What would she say?

Sandy swallowed and slowed, stopping the car for a flock of wild turkeys. What would she say? Would he be setting her up for revenge? Would he ask with the idea of leaving her and breaking her heart? Was Rafe vindictive? Could she trust him? Could she trust herself? There were too many questions and no answers.

A horn honking behind her brought her back to the present. The turkeys had wobbled their last little way to the other side. She stepped on the gas and resumed second-guessing how Rafe would react and what she should say. She doubted Rafe would be vindictive, especially once she explained why she'd turned him down. Her stomach clenched. She had to tell him, no matter how stupid, naïve, and judgmental it made her look. There was no hope of rekindling anything without the truth.

Suddenly, running into him didn't seem like such a good idea. She wasn't ready to face him, so she shut off her GPS and headed straight for home. She needed time and maybe another talk with Gram before she worked up the courage to face Rafe.

Sandy arrived home in the early afternoon. The screen door on the Dailey's house opened and Laura moseyed out.

"You're home! Good. I have something for you."

Sandy left her luggage on the bottom step to her place and followed Laura inside.

"Such a shame. These arrived the day after you left. They've wilted some, but still look good," Laura said, handing a vase of red roses to Sandy.

"Oh my. How beautiful. Was there a card?" Sandy's heart leapt into her throat.

"Darn it. Yes. Sorry. I forgot. Where is it?" Laura nosed around her counter. "Here it is. And I didn't even open it. Though Letty Jenkins said I should." Laura chuckled.

"Thank you so much."

"Silly delivery boy left them on the bottom step."

"Thank you for taking them in," Sandy said, stuffing the card in her back pocket and picking up the vase.

"They're not from that Lyle guy, are they? Did he change his mind? If he did, you just tell him to hit the road! Some nerve, that guy," Laura said, shaking a finger.

Sandy smiled. No way was she going to open that card in front of Laura. While she was a dear lady, and a good friend, Sandy needed to keep her life private from now on.

Hiking the bags up on her shoulder, she managed to haul the flowers and her stuff up the stairs and into the apartment at the same time. Once inside, she put everything down right next to the door and plucked the envelope from her pocket. Tearing it, she yanked the card out. It read, simply,

Love, Rafe

Chapter Four

Rafe arrived at work early. Every day he hawked the Internet, looking for news about Sandy but found none. At least she hadn't reconciled with that ape, Lyle. Rafe wanted to know where she was, what she was doing—but was too proud to get in touch. He'd sent the book and the note. If she was interested that should have been enough.

She must have read it by now, opened the book, seen the inscription, his words—why didn't she call? His jaw tightened. Didn't she even believe in thanking people for gifts? Maybe she wasn't the girl he thought she was?

Taking his second cup of coffee to the window, he struggled to focus on work. When his cell rang, he didn't bother because it was a strange number. Letting out a short snort, he ignored it.

"Some stupid fucking sales pitch," he muttered to himself.

On the third ring, he jumped to attention. Or could it be Sandy? Grabbing the phone, he punched *answer* as fast as he could, praying the caller didn't hang up. Breathless, he spoke.

"Hello?"

"Rafe?"

Shit. Damn. Fuck. Sandy. His heart sped up and his lungs stopped working.

"Rafe? Did I catch you at a bad time? Have you been running?"

"No, no. This is fine."

"I just wanted to thank you for the book and the flowers."

"Flowers?" His brows knitted.

"The dozen red roses you sent. They're beautiful."

"Flowers? I didn't—" He stopped, lowered his hand with the phone, and shouted. "Gloria!"

The older woman turned and flashed guilty eyes at him.

"Just a minute, Sandy," he said, then faced his assistant. "Gloria, what did you do?"

"I sent flowers. I knew you'd never do it and, well, she needed something. I figured she'd be real upset and flowers from you would help."

"And what did you put on the card?" He cringed at the idea of Gloria's overblown prose under his name.

"Nothing. I mean, I know you'd never want me to say much. So I only wrote, 'love, Rafe'. That's okay, right?"

He sighed in relief. At least she didn't pledge his undying love for eternity.

"Fine. You shouldn't have done that."

"That her on the phone?"

He nodded.

A devilish glint replaced her guilty-eyed look. "Guess it wasn't a bad idea. Got her to call you, eh?" With those words, she sashayed out of the room. Again, Rafe was speechless, he lifted the phone to his ear.

"You didn't send the flowers?" Sandy asked.

"My assistant did. Took it upon herself. But you should have known. If I had sent them I would have sent pink roses. I believe those are your favorites, are they not?"

A sob at the other end of the phone paused their conversation.

"Sandy? Sandy? Are you still there?"

"You remembered," she sniffled.

"Of course. I remember everything you told me." He attempted to keep an indignant tone from his voice but failed.

"Rafe, I...I don't know what to say. Are you seeing anyone? Engaged? Married?"

"None of the above."

"Did you see my break-up?"

"I did. And I'm so sorry. He's a pig, an ape."

"Thank you. Are you still speaking to me?"

"Of course I am. After all, I'm here on the phone with you."

"Can we meet?"

"You want to see me?" His eyebrows shot up.

"I do."

"Fine. Yes. I'd like to see you, too. Clear up something that's been bugging me."

"Great. When?"

"Can I take you to lunch?"

"Do you really want to be seen with me?"

He laughed. "Of course."

"I'm kind of a pariah."

"Not to me," he said, his voice low.

They set a date, time, and place.

"I'm glad you called," he said, warmth traveling through him.

"The note and the flowers gave me the courage."

"Then I guess I owe Gloria an apology, and thanks."

"I hope you feel that way after we meet."

"I'm sure I will."

He put down the phone and headed for his computer to enter the date in his calendar. Before clicking, Rafe leaned back in his chair, resting his feet on the small wastebasket. He put down his mug, laced his fingers behind his head and shut his eyes.

Images of his dates with Sandy flashed by his inner eye. Running into the waters of a Caribbean beach, candlelit dinner on the stone terrace of an English castle, and horseback riding through the Allegheny mountains in Pennsylvania. There was a cabin at the end of the trail. They had built a fire there and dined on simple fare.

The desire to whisk her into the bedroom and make mad, passionate love to her had risen in his chest, but he had tamped it down. There were cameras everywhere, and there wasn't supposed to be any sex until their overnight date. And he might not get chosen for that. Though none of that had stopped his feelings.

Twined together on the floor in front of the fire, Rafe had been tempted almost beyond control. Sandy had looked so soft and beautiful in the firelight. She'd rested against him, trusting, intimate, and vulnerable. He sighed. That had been the date where he had realized how deeply he loved her. He had wanted to stay like that, protecting her, loving her forever.

The crew had broken up their embrace. There was a storm heading that way and they had to leave. Rafe couldn't hide his disappointment. Being stranded in the cabin with Sandy during a storm would be a dream come true—except, the crew would be there, too. He remembered helping her up, brushing himself off, and climbing into an SUV. He and Sandy had held hands the whole way back. The horses were ushered into a trailer and driven home.

He opened his eyes and clicked on the calendar. Not three weeks away from their lunch date were the big letters, *LEAVING FOR LONDON*. Egad. He'd have only a short time with her. And he didn't even know what had blown them apart or if that barrier still existed.

There was no way he could cancel the trip to England. He had made too many commitments. And asking her to join him? How could he, after she had turned down his proposal? He sighed. Heaviness weighed his shoulders down. He added the lunch date to his calendar and closed the program.

UNABLE TO STAY SEATED, Sandy jumped up from the sofa and paced. She couldn't believe Rafe wasn't seeing anyone. He was available. Could her luck have changed? Drawing her lower lip between her teeth, she pondered the scenario. Did he agree to the lunch so he could yell at her? Humiliate her? Make her feel bad? That didn't seem to be Rafe's style. Besides, he offered to take her to lunch. Not likely he'll berate her then pick up the check, right?

The man who gave her that book and the note didn't hate her. Unless time had caused his emotional wound to fester, he'd not be dumping venom on her at lunch. She sighed. What would she say? What would she wear? To avoid thinking about what to tell Rafe, she attacked her closet. She had to look good, entice him, make him want to get back together with her.

Her cell rang. It was Emily, her best friend.

"Hi. What's up?"

"What are you doing?" Emily asked.

"Trying to find an outfit for a lunch date."

"You're dating? Already?"

"Why not?"

"Five minutes ago, you were engaged."

"So?"

"Shouldn't you at least appear to be sad or sorry the wedding's off?"

"Why? I'm overjoyed the wedding's off. He's a snake. I dodged a bullet, as Bill would say."

"Just sayin'. I mean if you see yourself on the Internet with nasty comments, don't blame me."

"Oh, I won't blame you, Emily. I won't blame you at all. And I don't care what appears there. They can't do me any more harm than has already been done. Frankly, I don't give a flying fuck what other people say."

"You used to."

Sandy stiffened. "Not anymore. Did you want something?"

"I wouldn't be your friend if I didn't point out the possible downside of what you're doing."

"Really? I think a true friend would applaud the fact that I'm not sitting around throwing a pity party. A true friend would support me. Wish me well. And help me pick out the perfect outfit."

"Then I guess I don't qualify. Because I think you're making a mistake."

"Do you? Or do you wish you had someone in your life who wanted to be with you, regardless of how the world saw you?"

Silence.

"Okay then. Bye, Emily. Gotta get back to it."

Sandy clicked the phone off. There goes that one, but did she really lose anything? Obviously, Emily wasn't a real friend, to begin with. Sadness shot through Sandy. She'd hoped she could hang with Emily, from time-to-time, like friends do. That wouldn't be happening now.

Where would it end? How many people would turn their backs on her or disapprove of how she lived her life? If Emily had deserted her, the other teachers at school would, too. Of course, when Sandy had been chosen as a contestant for the first *Marriage Minded*, Emily had been jealous. When Sandy became the star, the green-eyed monster had sliced and diced their friendship.

Sandy chided herself. What did she expect from Emily? Time to think about her own life and what she'd say to Rafe and how she'd say it. She needed to forget naysayers and negative nellies. Sandy would live her life the way she wanted, regardless of the opinion of others. She set her jaw.

Sure, that was easy to say, but when those people were her parents and close colleagues, it wouldn't be so easy to live. She sighed. Being unique wasn't easy. She poked her head in the closet. Where were those black heels? They'd go perfectly with this dress.

Sandy set up the ironing board and filled the steam iron with water. As she pressed the dress she'd wear to lunch with Rafe, she thought about how to tell him the truth. She got that he wanted to know what made her change her mind and pick dumbass Lyle over him. He had a right to know—didn't he?

As she glided the iron along the smooth fabric, she tried out scenarios but always came back to the simple truth. She had been naïve, dumb, and manipulated by Lyle. There was no way around that. She'd have to fess up, admit everything –including the fact that she didn't trust him enough to believe him. She'd already decided, convinced by Lyle, that Rafe wouldn't tell her the truth.

That admission shamed her more than anything. Rafe would see that, too. Would he, could he forgive her lack of faith and be willing to try again? She didn't have the answer. Time to talk to Bill. At least he could give her the man's perspective on the situation. She needed to be prepared for Rafe to reject her, as she had him. A shudder ran through her. Had she lost the best man in the world? Maybe.

ARRIVING EARLY TO WORK on Thursday, so he could take a long lunch, Rafe chuckled. He'd been distracted by Sandy before she called and now even more. Excited to see her, part of him stood back, wary. Would she shoot an arrow straight through his heart –again?

His mood turned optimistic. The Sandy he'd known wasn't like that. She had no reason to reject him now. As far as he knew, she was available. After all, she'd called him, hadn't she?

He hung his navy sports jacket on a hook by his work area and ripped off the green and blue striped tie he'd worn. Le Déjà Vu re-quired a jacket, but not a tie. Still, he wore it in case he wanted it for his lunch date. Button downs without ties always looked awkward to him. Maybe it was his formal upbringing? While he worked, a tie was simply an annoyance. He folded the offending article and stuffed it in the jacket pocket.

"How are the sketches for the new spa coming? We need those okay'd before you leave," Charlie said, leaning against the partition.

"Fine. I'll have them finished today. Do you want to run them over to Ken tonight or tomorrow?"

"Tonight, if possible." Charlie grinned.

"I've got a lunch date today. I'll stay late to make up the time."

"A lunch date? Like with a single woman?" Charlie cocked an eyebrow.

Rafe nodded, turning his attention back to his board.

"Who is she? Isn't it a little late in the game for you to be getting involved with anyone? I mean, you're leaving in less than three weeks."

"I know. The timing's bad. Nothing I can do." Rafe faced his partner.

"She must be pretty hot. Who is she?"

"You wouldn't approve," Rafe said, moving his gaze from Charlie to his work.

"Oh?"

"Let's not go there, okay?"

"Hey, buddy, if you don't want to tell me, don't tell me. None of my business anyway. I'm only your partner and best friend, ya know?"

Rafe sighed. He'd offended him. "Okay. It's Sandy Landeau."

"That bitch from *Marriage Minded?*"

"That's her."

"You've got to be kidding me. You're giving her another chance to shoot you down?"

"She called me."

"What?"

"That's right. She called me."

"Whoa. Wow. That's a surprise."

"Not completely. Gloria sent Sandy a dozen roses and signed my name."

"Why the hell did she do that?"

"Thought she was doing me a favor. I was too chicken to do it myself."

"I've never seen you chicken with women."

"Gloria's idea worked."

"Doubt this babe's going to shoot you down if she called you. But who knows? Maybe she's a sadist and gets off shooting guys down?"

Rafe laughed. "Not likely."

Charlie extended his hand. "I wish you luck, Rafe. Gotta hand it to you. You've stuck by her through all the shit. She's lucky. I hope it works out."

He shook it. "Thanks, Charlie. I hope so, too."

Rafe let out a breath. Having Charlie's blessing relieved his mind. Maybe he was doing the right thing. He'd handle telling her about the trip later. One thing at a time, and patching things up was number one.

He opened the drawings and went to work. Flipping on a classical playlist, Rafe lost himself in his work until twelve.

"Rafe! What are you doing here?"

"What?" He looked up, irritated.

"It's twelve. Your reservation at Le Déjà Vu is for twelve thirty!"

He sat up and blinked. *Shit.* He'd be late for his date. Not a great beginning. Gloria helped him on with his jacket, and he raced out the door. Taking the curves a little faster than he should, Rafe made up a little time on the road. The restaurant was outside of Callicoon. He found a mint in his pocket and popped it in his mouth.

A deer in the road brought him to a screeching halt. He honked, but the animal simply stared at him in doe-eyed wonder. Another honk and the critter ran off into the woods. He glanced at his watch. Yep, another few minutes lost. He stepped on the gas and prayed that turkeys, gophers, groundhogs, deer, and all woodland creatures stayed off the road.

With a sharp turn, he entered the parking lot. Taking a space close to the entrance, he stopped to comb his hair in the rear-view mirror, before turning off his vehicle. He popped out and strode toward the front door. His pulse thumped double time in his ears and sweat broke out on his palms. This was it, wasn't it? Do or die time.

SANDY CLOSED HER CAR door and walked on wobbly high heels to the front of Le Déjà Vu. She pulled her cardigan closer against a breeze. Or was that cold feeling due to nerves? Once inside, she perused the cozy French dining room and didn't see Rafe. Oh, God, he's not coming!

"Do you have a reservation for Rafe Pelletier?" she asked, struggling to keep her voice calm.

"Yes, yes, mademoiselle. We do. Monsieur Pelletier has not arrived yet. May I seat you?"

She nodded and followed the maître'd to an intimate table flanked by two windows. She sat in the chair the man pulled out as he placed two menus on the table.

"Would Mademoiselle care for something to drink?"

"A glass of white wine?"

"Of course."

She smoothed the skirt of her teal blue, sleeveless sheath. Sandy shed her sweater as the table sat partially in the sun. Out the window, she spied bird feeders brimming with seed. The chickadees and goldfinches jockeyed for the perches. The distraction of the pretty birds didn't keep her from glancing at the door. Mindful of the time, her nerves kicked up and her jaw clenched. How long should she wait? If he didn't show up, she'd simply shrivel up and die, right on the spot.

A breathless voice caught her attention.

"A thousand pardons. I'm late. I'm so sorry. I have only work as an excuse."

She looked up and there he was, as handsome as ever, with apology shining in his eyes. He extended his hand to her and she rose from her seat.

"You're as beautiful as ever," he mumbled, folding her into his embrace.

Sandy snaked her arms around his chest and buried her face in his shoulder. The comfort of his closeness melted her control and sobs wracked her body. He tightened his grip, expelling warm breath on her ear.

"It's going to be okay. Believe me. It's going to be all right," he said, stroking her hair.

"Monsieur? Everything all right?" It was the waiter, placing her glass of wine on the table.

Embarrassment filled Sandy. Now she'd caused a scene in the restaurant. Poor Rafe, stuck with such a badly-behaved woman.

"Fine," Rafe said.

"Eh, bien," the man said.

"I'm sorry," she whispered.

Her strength returned, and she stepped back. Rafe offered her his handkerchief as they sat down. He motioned for the waiter and ordered a whiskey and soda.

"You look good, too," she said. The white shirt made his fair complexion, inherited from his mother, look a bit darker. His gray eyes sparkled. He wore his light brown hair a bit longer, more fashionable, than she remembered, and it suited his narrow face.

"I'll wash this and return it to you," she said, indicating the cloth she'd used to wipe her tears.

"Keep it," he responded, closing her fingers around it.

She stared. The jacket emphasized his broad shoulders. Slim and tall, his body held power and grace. A tuft of light brown hair peeked from the neck of his shirt. It reminded her of him naked. The memory of running her fingers through the hair on his chest while they lay undressed sent a shiver up her spine.

He took her hand and raised it to his lips.

"I hoped I'd see you again," he said.

"I've been such an idiot," she moaned.

"Tell me. Tell me what it was. Why didn't you accept my proposal? We never got the chance to talk."

There it was. The big question. And they hadn't even ordered yet. The waiter returned.

"Ready to order, Monsieur?"

Sandy hid behind the menu and took a deep breath. This would only be a temporary diversion. She had to answer.

"I'll have the mushroom and gruyere omelet," she said, handing the menu back to the waiter.

"Boeuf Bourguignon for me," Rafe said.

"Bien. Vin?"

Rafe raised his eyebrows.

"I'm driving. One is fine," Sandy replied.

"None for me."

When the man left, Rafe took her hands in his. "So tell me, my dear. Please. Tell me the truth. I have been bothered ever since. What happened?"

Sandy cleared her throat, swallowed, then met Rafe's gaze.

"I was a fool. I believed Lyle."

"What did he say?"

"He said that you weren't there for the right reasons," she hedged.

"Huh?"

"He said you only wanted to get a green card. You wanted to marry me for a green card."

"What? That is ridiculous! I already had my green card. And you believed this?"

"He was very convincing."

"Oh?"

She sensed color rising to her face. "I shouldn't have believed him."

"You should have come to me. I would have told you the truth."

"That's where the really stupid part comes in. He said you'd deny it. And I agreed. How could you not? I mean if it was a lie, then you'd deny it. But even if it was the truth, you'd have to deny it or get kicked off the show. He said I couldn't believe anything you said."

Rafe dropped her hands and stared at his own. "If you had come to me, I could have shown you my green card. It's in my wallet." He reached into his back pocket and retrieved his billfold. Before he could pull out the document in question, she put her hand over his.

"I know. Afterward, I looked you up online. I knew then that Lyle had lied. But it was too late."

Rafe covered his face with his hands. Sandy slid hers over his arm. "I'm so very, very sorry. You have no idea."

"Oh, yes, I do. Because I am so very sorry, too."

"I know now that you were truthful. The whole time. That you were there for the right reasons."

"I fell in love with you, Sandy. Honestly," he said, uncovering his eyes.

"I know. And I you."

"Did you?" he asked, raising his eyebrows.

She nodded, her eyes filled. "I realized it after about three months."

"Then why didn't you leave him?"

"Embarrassment. Humiliation? Refusal to admit my mistake. I tried to make it work. But it never did."

"Poor baby," Rafe said, taking her hand.

"And I dreamt of you. You, who would never treat me like he did. You, who were kind and loving. It tore me apart."

Again, he brought her hand to his lips. "It tore me apart, too."

"I'm so sorry. I've missed you so much."

"But you could not trust me? You didn't think I would tell you the truth? You believed that ape, Lyle, over me?"

"I was an idiot. I don't know why I believed him."

"It doesn't matter. You did. And we lost what we had."

"Did we? Did we? Can't we get it back?"

"Do you want to?"

"With all my heart."

With that, Sandy pushed to her feet, walked to his side, and slid onto his lap. She took his face in both hands and kissed him for all she was worth. He clasped her back, rubbing up and down her spine as she invaded his mouth.

Passion rose in her; heat traveled to her core. She wanted him, then and there. She wanted to drag him under the table, rip his clothes off, and make love. His hand settled under her breast, his knuckles resting against the underside, making her tingle. She moved back, releasing his lips.

"Wow," he muttered, staring at her with desire.

"We still have it," she said, smiling.

"Your lunch, Mademoiselle?" The waiter spoke, setting a dish by her place.

Sandy eased off him and returned to her seat. A round of applause from the twenty other patrons in the restaurant sent red-hot heat to her cheeks.

"Voilá," the waiter said, bowing and retreating.

Rafe laughed. "Quite a show we've put on."

"I had to show you, how I felt. Words wouldn't do it."

"I agree. But you have left me, uh, wanting more. Is that possible?" He rearranged his napkin.

She chuckled. "It is."

"Where and when?"

"Dinner at my place? Tomorrow night? Six?"

"Perfect. I'll bring the wine."

Chapter Five

Wearing a dopey grin, Rafe stumbled down the hall to his office.

Charlie checked his watch. "Drunk at three o'clock?"

"Drunk on love," he said, then giggled.

"Right. I forgot. Your lunch with that bitch?"

Rafe's smile melted into a frown. "You've got to stop calling her that."

"Sorry. I will. I will. Lunch with...her?"

"Lunch? Heaven."

"She's changed her tune?"

"She has. And she told me what happened. Stupid, fucking Lyle. Dirty dog. Snake," Rafe spat.

"Take it easy. You'll have a heart attack."

"I'm only thirty-six. No heart attacks happening. Except the one launched by Sandy."

"So you taking up with her again?"

"Dinner tomorrow night will tell."

"I see. Okay. I wish you luck. Are you sober enough to finish those drawings?"

"I finished them before lunch. Didn't think I'd be in shape to work on them after."

"Great!"

"Here you go. Deliver them to John with my blessing."

"Thanks," Charlie said, tucking the portfolio under his arm. He took two steps and stopped. "Hey, I mean it about you and this chick. Sandy. Whatever. I hope it works out for you."

"Thanks, Charlie."

Gloria cleared her throat. "Someone owes me a little gratitude."

"Absolutely right," Rafe said. He took a bag off his desk and pulled out a box of candy. "This is for you."

"Oh, my! You didn't have to do that," she said.

"And you didn't have to send the flowers."

Gloria blushed, picked up the box, and returned to the front desk.

"One more thing, not that it's any of my business, but did you tell her you're going to London for a year?" Charlie asked, stopping at the front door.

Rafe rubbed the back of his neck. "No, I didn't."

"Do you really think that's a good idea?"

"Probably not. Just didn't want to throw a wrench in, before we even get started again. Besides, she might take it the wrong way."

"Oh? That you're running away? Maybe that's the right way," Charlie said.

Rafe glared at his partner. "Bull. It's the chance of a lifetime."

"Yeah, yeah, we've been over that."

"I don't want her to think I'm running away from her. And if you think that, so could she."

"Any way you slice it, that's not a great secret to keep."

"I know. I'll tell her. When the time is right."

"When's that? Ten minutes before the plane takes off?"

"Sometimes you can be an annoying bastard," Rafe said.

"Yeah. Especially when I'm right. Look, it's your funeral. Handle it any way you want. I gotta get these to John. See you tomorrow." Charlie headed for the parking lot.

Rafe sat back, thinking about what his partner had said. What would happen when he told her about London? Would she ask him to stay? As nice as that sounded, he'd decided to go, no matter what. No way would he miss out on his chance to teach. Besides, too much planning had gone into this to deep-six it now. Would she understand? Would she be mad? All he could do was guess. The sooner he told her the better, or he'd never get any sleep.

Leaving on the early side, he stopped at the wine store and picked out an expensive bottle of white and one of red. Whatever food she'd planned, he'd be prepared. Food was the last thing on his mind. He hoped she'd be serving up herself.

At home, he reheated leftovers and ate while watching the news. He tried to read a new mystery but couldn't concentrate. He tried television, then radio, but nothing could distract him or settle his stomach.

Tomorrow, he'd know how Sandy felt about him and his year in London. At eleven he crawled into bed and stared at the ceiling. She hadn't trusted him enough to come clean about his green card. What would happen to her trust when she found out about London and that he delayed telling her? Then his mind switched gears.

A vision of Sandy, nude, walking across the bedroom in their suite, kissed by the morning sun danced across his brain. His fingertips tingled with the tactile memory of her skin. She was a goddess. He smiled, rolled over, and hugged a pillow. They had made love until they dropped. Then they dozed, peacefully, tangled together. He smiled at the memory of the best night of his life. His breathing evened out and muscles relaxed as more images of Sandy floated through his mind. Rafe drifted off to a restful sleep.

ON THE WAY HOME FROM lunch, Sandy made a detour to the grocery store. She'd take her time choosing the right items to woo

Rafe's stomach while she planned other methods to take care of the rest of him. Even though she'd been spurred on by his warmth, she'd detected a wariness in his eyes. After what she'd done, he'd be a fool to trust her.

Friday morning, she awoke smiling. Pushing up out of bed, she headed to the kitchen to start preparations for her dinner. Beef stew in the crockpot all day. Homemade apple pie, using Laura Dailey's secret recipe, and a tangy Caesar salad.

As she prepared the dough for the pie crust, Sandy confronted her biggest obstacle, winning Rafe's trust. She had to convince him that he was the one. Chiding herself one more time, she admitted that he'd been the one all along and she'd been an idiot not to see it.

Sandy sat with her morning coffee and peeled apples. Birds clustered at the feeder outside her window. Tonight, she'd have her chance, to make it up to him, to convince him he was her choice. What could she say to make him believe? She chewed her lip as she piled up apple skins.

After shoving the pie in the oven, she padded to the bathroom to check on supplies. She had to look and smell terrific. Seduction, high on the menu, couldn't be achieved if everything wasn't perfect.

Next, she changed the sheets, opened the windows to air out the room, and returned to the kitchen. Time had come to fill the slow cooker. Afterward, Sandy threw on jeans and a T-shirt and headed out for a long walk. Moseying down the country lane, she recalled her time with the sexy architect.

Their first date had started with awkward conversation until their first kiss. He'd leaned over during the first course at dinner.

"I like to get the kiss out of the way early. Reduces nerves," he'd said, as his lips met hers.

What started out sweet went on and on, morphing into passion before it ended. He'd stolen her breath. Sandy could hardly speak. The heat between her thighs conspired with the slamming of her heart in her chest to strip away her control. His eyes had flamed with desire. That's when she knew something special existed with him. Like an electrical current, or a lightning bolt, their chemistry approached tangible.

Because he'd been on the quiet side, she'd not expected a skilled kisser. He'd surprised her. When she slid her hand across the dinner table, he'd picked up on her cue and covered it with his. The romantic setting on the terrace of a glamorous New York City apartment with the lights of the city spread out before them, heightened her feelings.

Intrigued, she'd invited Rafe on a date first—much to the surprise of the producers. She'd selected him because she was curious and planned to eliminate the quiet, more intellectual gentleman from the group quickly.

Drinking in the smell of fresh pine, Sandy wended her way down a deserted road, lost in thought. That first date had confused her. The sexual desire emanating from Rafe seduced her, drove everything from her mind except him. When he'd pulled her into the shadows to kiss her goodnight, she'd wanted more. Silently she begged him to touch her, run his hand up her chest, but he didn't. Almost panting when he let her go, she had smoothed down her skirt and clenched her thighs to quiet the throbbing. But it didn't help.

Even the memory sent a shiver up her spine as she ambled along. Rafe had become unforgettable. Even after dates with other attractive, smart men, she couldn't get Rafe out of her mind. So she went out with him again, wondering if the chemistry remained. It grew stronger. As they got to know each other, common ground added to the sexual tension sparking between them. They liked the same foods, the same kind of art, and the same people.

By then, Lyle had moved in. Also sexually skilled, he'd crossed over the line once or twice when they were hidden from the cameras. Her body had been so charged up, the moment his hand hit her breast, she'd have surrendered. Fortunately, he'd come to his senses and pulled back. Lyle never seemed to get as carried away as she did. Now she understood. Hindsight enlightened her. It had been a game he needed to win. Going all the way would ruin his chances and get him kicked off the show.

Shame colored her face. How foolish she'd been. And all the time, Rafe, the gentleman, stood in the background, building slowly on their relationship and igniting her insides at every opportunity.

By the time she'd narrowed it down and the overnight date had arrived, Sandy had become so horny she could barely string words together in an intelligible sentence. The moment the doors closed, Sandy and Rafe embraced. Tight in a clinch, he'd walked her backward into the bedroom as he'd worked her mouth with his.

Gooseflesh broke out on her arms as she conjured up the sensation of his touch. As she closed her eyes, her breathing increased. Remembering how he had excited her, then satisfied her time and again during the night made her body hum in anticipation. Tonight, they'd get a chance to replay their passion, in total privacy. Sandy could hardly wait. Checking her watch, it was time to return. She had much to do before Rafe arrived.

RAFE LEFT WORK EARLY. He showered and shaved, then stood before his closet, a towel wrapped around his hips. What to wear? Something easy to take off but not too informal would be the ticket. He stroked his smooth chin and rummaged through his wardrobe. Tie or no tie? No tie, too much to remove in the heat of the moment. Settling on a blue short-sleeved sports shirt, and gray slacks, he laid the clothing on the bed.

His newest bottle of cologne caught his attention. With a title like *Midnight Seduction,* how could he go wrong? Not that tonight was going to be challenging. After that kiss at lunch, he knew exactly which side of the bed Sandy stood on. Sex would be on the menu and he'd be ready.

The thought charged his batteries. He shoved a fistful of condoms in his pants pocket. Grabbing the bag containing the wine, Rafe headed for his car, his nerves cranked into third gear.

He flipped on the radio in time to hear his favorite country music song. It was all about love and so was Rafe. Pumped, hitting all cylinders, he grinned and sang along. A chuckle came to his lips as he recalled Sandy's surprise to find out the country genre was his favorite, too.

"Country music? You like country? I mean, you're French. Aren't you supposed to love Edith Piaf or something?"

Her naiveté had been endearing.

"There are many more modern French singers, Sandy. Besides, country music is so American. I never listened to it when I was growing up. I'm making up for lost time. Great beat. Do you like country?"

"I love country music." She had beamed at him as if he had hit the game-winning home run. Maybe he had.

He turned up the sound and sang along as he negotiated the winding road. He'd pushed all thoughts about his trip out of his mind. Tonight was about Sandy and him. He pulled into her driveway and parked.

Still humming the chorus, he climbed the staircase and pressed the bell. The scent of something wonderful drifted to his nose. When Sandy opened the door, she looked like a dream, a fantasy, wearing a filmy, floor-length gown in light aqua and yellow. The top crisscrossed her chest, making it obvious she wasn't wearing a bra. His breath caught in his throat as his gaze traveled down her luscious body. No panty lines, damn! She was stark naked under the flowing dress. Talk about not wasting time getting undressed, hell, she had him beat by a mile.

"Darling," he muttered as he stepped inside and drew her into his arms. As they kissed, he nudged the door closed with his heel. She was warm, soft, and smelled like a dream. Stepping back, she broke the embrace.

He sniffed the air. "What smells so good?"

"Could be beef stew and homemade apple pie," she said.

"You made an apple pie for me?"

She nodded.

"Oh my God. You're amazing. Oh, this is for you. For us." He handed her the bag.

"Thank you." She took it and headed for the kitchen.

Us. He'd waited a year to have the right to use that word. Glancing around the sparse apartment, thoughts of moving Sandy into his spacious place popped up. Too soon, much too soon. Sandy returned with the bottle of red that Rafe had brought and a corkscrew.

"Will you do the honors?"

"Of course," he said, taking the wine and implement. She disappeared into the tiny kitchen again and returned with glasses in one hand and a tray of hors d'oeuvres in the other.

"I remembered you like celery hearts and olives," she said setting the small platter down on the coffee table.

"I also like beautiful women."

Rafe popped the cork and poured. They clinked glasses and drank. Rafe couldn't take his gaze from her. She looked a bit slimmer, with a subtle sadness in her eyes. Otherwise, she appeared to be the same woman he loved.

"You haven't changed."

"It's only been a year," she said.

"Seems like a lifetime."

"Are you still mad at me?"

He shook his head. "Never really got mad. Sad, maybe. Heartbroken, for sure. But never mad."

"That's good," she said, putting her hand on his forearm. "I'm so sorry I hurt you."

He clasped her fingers with his and planted a kiss there. "You're lovelier than ever," he whispered. When he looked up, he spied her staring at his lips. Lifting her chin, he kissed her. She steadied herself by placing her hand on his shoulder. The pressure of her fingers ignited his fire.

"Dinner. Dinner first," she said, catching her breath and pushing to her feet.

"Can I help?" He rose with her.

"Nope. You sit there. I'll be right back," she said.

Rafe sat in his assigned seat and put on his napkin. It was cloth, not paper, and that pleased him. Sandy entered carrying a steaming casserole filled with delectable stew. Next, she brought a plate of French bread, and a salad bowl.

The dishes were nondescript, as were the furnishings.

"Is this your stuff or do you rent furnished?" he asked, eyeing the mouth-watering food.

"It's furnished."

"I see," he said, nodding and ladling some stew into his bowl. The shabbiness of the apartment didn't reflect her lack of taste or money. She'd been a school teacher, probably didn't have much. Her finances didn't matter. Rafe had enough money for both of them.

"Are you going back to your old job?"

"I only took a year's sabbatical. They expect me back."

"This stew is delicious. What magic ingredient did you use?"

She shrugged. "Just an old family stew recipe."

"Are you looking forward to going back to work? Seeing old colleagues again?" he asked.

She shuddered. "Not really. I'm dreading it, actually. I'm sure they'll reiterate how I never should have gone on that stupid program. And how I got my comeuppance for being such a dope."

"They wouldn't really say that, would they?"

She nodded. "Some will. Others will think it but never come out and say it. I'll know anyway."

"Must you go back?" he asked.

"I have to. Or give notice. And I've no other job."

"I see." His mind wrapped around her situation. She might be able to cut her ties, but would he be her choice? "Any plans for the future?"

"Just getting through each day as it comes."

Rafe fought back words of love, of commitment. Who was he to commit? He was leaving soon. Besides, she'd turned him down before, would she do the same again?

SANDY COULD HARDLY believe she was sitting at her table with Rafe, eating dinner, like nothing had ever happened, like she hadn't broken his heart, like they hadn't missed their chance for happily ever after.

Hadn't they—missed it? Or was it still possible? His eyes held warmth. The air in the apartment thickened. Yearning filled her. Would she be destined to always want and never have? Though her appetite had dwindled, Sandy turned her focus back to her food. She pushed a piece of the tasty stew around with her fork.

"Time to heat the pie," she said, rising from her chair.

Rafe's hand on her arm stopped her. "Don't. Let's wait. Can we? I'm stuffed."

She smiled and took the dishes off the table. Rafe picked up the half-empty casserole and followed her. He put the dish down and came up behind her. His presence gave her gooseflesh. When he wrapped his fingers around her shoulders, her resistance crumbled.

"My girl," he whispered. "Are you still?"

"Yes," she whispered, leaning her head on his shoulder.

Rafe bent to kiss her neck. He slid his hands down to pin her arms to her sides. Sandy melted, resting against his sturdy frame. His hands moved down to cover her breasts. His touch tentative. She moaned. God, she'd been dreaming of this.

He eased one hand down to her belly. Flattening his palm, he pulled her flush against his hips. The fingers of his other hand found her peak and rolled it. Fire flashed through her.

Sandy could barely stand. His hardening shaft nudged her rear. No more dreaming. It was time for the real thing. Wanting more, she whirled around. Rafe embraced her and his mouth sought hers for a hungry kiss. Sandy snaked her arms around his neck, molding her body to his.

He moved his hands down to her bottom, squeezed, then drew her to him. He was erect now. Her heart rate increased as anticipation turned her breathing ragged. She pushed back, stared into his eyes, and took his hand.

"This is much easier lying down," she said, leading him to her bedroom.

She unbuttoned his shirt and ran her hands over his chest. Closing her eyes, she gave in to her passion. Rafe bent down, grasped the hem of her dress, and lifted it over her head. She'd forsaken underwear. It made getting naked easy.

A sharp intake of breath drew her attention. His gaze raked her body.

"So beautiful. So ripe," he muttered.

She pushed his shirt off his shoulders, then attacked his belt. Rafe gave a hand and soon he was also bare and ready for action. He bent down and reached into the pocket of his pants.

The condoms he withdrew reminded her she'd given up the pill after she and Lyle stopped sleeping together. Why take medication she didn't need? Thank God Rafe was responsible.

"Not that I don't want to make babies with you. I do. But maybe not today?"

She giggled and climbed on the bed. He joined her.

"Can we slow this down a little? Can I look at you for a moment?"

"I don't know. I've waited a long time," she responded.

He grinned. "Me, too. Okay then. We'll take the second one slow."

"Works for me."

She inched closer. He pulled her up tight, squishing her breasts into his firm chest. The hair tickled. Her nipples hardened. Rafe stretched his legs, sliding one between hers. She reached around and grabbed his small but firm butt, then glided her hand up his back. Her fingertips dipped into his muscles. Rafe's physical strength stoked her passion. Want grew in her, becoming need in the blink of an eye.

He eased her back and made his way down her chest, dropping small kisses along the way.

"These are great," he said, stopping to admire her breasts.

His fingertips skimmed over her skin, sending a tingle through her. His touch almost tickled. Sandy wrapped one leg around his waist. He picked up on her not-so-subtle hint and ran his hand down to her core. The moment he touched her hot flesh, desire ratcheted up and her hips rose. He followed his stroking with a gentle massage from his tongue.

"God, Rafe. Please."

"Impatient?"

"It's been months," she muttered.

"Months?" His eyebrows rose.

"Please. Don't talk now. Take me. Do it. I want you," she breathed, her eyes drifting shut. The next thing she heard was a ripping sound, then the crinkle of latex as he covered himself. Peeking through lowered lashes, she watched him get ready. The sight of his shaft ready for action dialed up her heat. If she got any wetter, they'd need a towel.

"Ready, darling?"

"Yes."

He rolled onto his knees and eased into her. God, it had been longer than she'd remembered.

"You're tight. Amazing," he said, pushing slowly.

As he filled her, every nerve ending jumped to life. She gasped once, clinging to his shoulders as fire consumed her. Damn! He buried his face in her neck and muttered something she couldn't understand. The scent of his aftershave mixed with his skin stoked her passion. She licked his shoulder...he even tasted good.

Heat flew through her veins as he pumped into her. His mouth came down hard and demanding on hers, as he took her in every way. His tongue sought hers and they danced as he thrust in and pulled out, faster and harder. She arched her back, raising her knee to her chest as the intensity spiraled higher and higher.

"God! Rafe!" A powerful orgasm washed over her, and her muscles clenched as she clung to him. Sweat gathered between their chests as he continued for another minute before groaning loudly and collapsing. She ran her tongue along the juncture of his neck and shoulder, tasting the saltiness of his sweat.

"I love you," popped out of her mouth before she could edit it.

"I love you, too. Sweet, lady. All mine," he said.

Oh, yes, she was all his. He kissed the side of her head, then pushed up to support his weight.

"You're amazing. As always," he said.

"Me? You're the master."

"It's as good as it was that night."

"Better. Oh, so much better." She kissed his shoulder.

He pushed up, his gaze seeking hers. "Better? Why?"

"Because there's nothing to worry about. No one else to consider."

"You mean, just us?"

"Exactly!"

"Us. Isn't that a wonderful word?" he asked, pushing her hair back gently.

She hugged him and smiled. "It is."

After planting a sweet kiss on her lips, Rafe headed for the bathroom. Sandy stretched her arms and legs and sighed. Rafe held the title as best lover ever. Refusing to think about tomorrow or next week or next month, Sandy basked in the afterglow of their love.

Rafe returned. "Come here." He tucked her under his arm. She snaked hers across his middle and bent her knees.

"Hold me, please. Just hold me."

"You've had it rough, haven't you?"

She nodded. With control over her emotions wiped away in the aftermath of her release, tears threatened. He had no idea how rough.

"On top of everything, I thought I'd blown it forever with you."

"What changed your mind?"

"The book. The note. Both, I guess. Oh, and the flowers helped."

He chuckled. "Gloria."

"But the others were from you."

"I couldn't let go." An attractive blush stole through his cheeks as he averted his eyes.

"Thank God," she said, running her fingers through his hair, then kissing his chest.

Rafe shifted, piling pillows up and resting against them, his torso uncovered. He motioned for her to get closer. She scooted up but drew the sheet over her chest.

"Why do you cover up?"

"Shy."

"Really? After sleeping with me, more than once?"

She nodded.

He laughed. "You are full of surprises."

Resting her cheek against his pecs, she had to ask. "So where do we go from here?"

Chapter Six

Uh-oh. Rafe pushed up. He hadn't told her he was leaving. Was making love to her even though she didn't know legit? Was he taking advantage? He wanted to take her with him, but could he trust that she wouldn't back out at the last minute? Would she be willing to leave her life behind and start a new one with him in London? That was a pretty big step. They didn't exactly have months of living together to guarantee things between them would work out.

There were no guarantees. Plenty of people live together and still break up. He swallowed hard. Was now the time to tell her? Maybe over pie? If he told her now, would she throw the pie at him? They couldn't be happy unless they had truth between them.

"Well," he began.

She shifted, raising her gaze to his. "Well? Is that the best you can do?"

"No, no, of course not."

"Okay, then. Where do we go from here?"

"There's something I have to tell you." Sweat broke out on his forehead.

"Uh-oh. That doesn't sound good. Is there someone else?" Her eyes filled.

He hugged her, kissing her head. "No, no. There's no one. You. Only you."

"Thank God. I don't think I could take it."

"Sweetheart, if there was someone else, I wouldn't be in bed with you. What kind of man do you think I am?"

"I'm sorry. Of course. No. I don't think you'd do that."

"I wouldn't. But I'm leaving."

"Leaving?" She bolted upright. "Leaving me?"

"Leaving the country."

"What?"

"Yes. In a couple of weeks."

"And you were going to tell me, when?" she asked, cocking an eyebrow.

"Soon. Today. Yesterday. I needed to wait. To see if we were still, uh, good?"

"You waited to sleep with me," she said.

"I suppose that's true. That's part of it."

"And if I didn't have sex with you? What then? You wouldn't tell me?"

"I knew you would."

"Oh, so I'm easy?"

"No, no." He raked his hand through his hair. "This is getting out of hand."

"You can say that again," she said, pushing to her feet and heading for the closet. She yanked a robe off a hook and put it on.

"Darling. It's not like that. I would have told you regardless. It's not about sex."

"Then what is it?"

He got out of bed, slipped on his boxers, and put his hands on her arms. She shoved them off, turning full eyes to him. "You bastard."

"Please, Sandy! Wait!" he said, forcing her against him. He rubbed her back, and she relaxed into his arms. A sob shook through her. "Darling. Don't cry. It's not what you think. I love you. I would never hurt you like that. Please, can we sit down and discuss it?"

She sniffled, reaching into her robe pocket and drawing out a tissue. She wiped her nose and eyes, then nodded. "Okay."

"Good. Let's have some of that apple pie you worked so hard to make." He draped his arm over her shoulders and guided her to the kitchen. She plopped the pie in the oven and turned on the heat. While Rafe tackled her coffeemaker and brewed a fresh pot, he explained about his year in London.

"Did I drive you to this?" Sandy asked, pulling down plates.

He stopped. Had she? Maybe she had, but he didn't want to admit it. He hesitated. She faced him. "Well? Did I?" She stood still, her gaze locked on his. "Ah, yes. I can see that I did."

"Not you per se."

She crossed her arms over her chest.

"Okay, well, maybe, yes. You did. Your rejection did."

"I see. I'm so sorry. I guess I'm going to pay for that bad decision, again."

Her eyes watered. He drew her to him. "No, no. Not necessarily."

"What does that mean?"

"Pie? Coffee's ready."

She served generous slices while he filled mugs with steaming hot java. Once seated at the table, he took a bite.

"This is the best apple pie I've ever had."

"Is it your first?"

"Apple is my favorite."

"Okay, now shoot. What exactly did you mean by not necessarily?"

He took another bite, then a sip of his coffee. Could he chance it? Was one more lovemaking session enough to decide an entire life?

"I had to know how you felt. Even now, I'm not sure. It's been so weird." He paused to take another forkful.

"And...don't keep me in suspense, here."

"I figured if we still felt the same. Once I knew why you'd picked Lyle instead of me. If it was okay. Sort of. If I understood." He sipped his coffee.

"You are making me crazy. Spit it out, Rafe. I can take it. I think." She raised her mug.

"I thought I'd ask you to come with me."

Sandy spit coffee onto her plate. "What?"

"That's it. Come with me."

"Just turn my back on my life and take off?"

"That's it, precisely."

She wiped herself off with her napkin. Now it was his turn to sweat. What would she say?

"I don't know."

"You have about two weeks to think it over," he said.

"Two weeks?"

"I'm leaving in three."

"And this is a done deal? No changing? No backing out?"

"It's done. I've made commitments, to the project, to the school. I'm going. Think about it. Life would be so much better if you were with me."

He slid his hand over hers.

"The school is expecting me back. Then there are my parents. Bill..."

"Look, you don't have to come. We can wait another year. Maybe when I get back, if I come back...we can pick this up again?" He hated the idea and wanted to kick himself for even mentioning it. Yet, if she didn't want to be with him, it wouldn't be good to have her join him.

"Don't you want me to come with you?"

"Didn't I just invite you? You're the one who's waffling here, not me. I gave a definite invitation. I'll pay for your plane ticket."

"And what if it doesn't work out? So few of these do."

"If you don't have faith, don't try, don't compromise, it's doomed. You have to want it, Sandy."

"Do you?"

"With all my heart."

"But, worst case scenario. We break up and I'm stuck in London with no money and no way to get home."

"How about this? I'll give you a round-trip ticket. You can leave any time you want."

"You'd do that?"

"Of course."

"But you don't want to get married?" Sandy swallowed.

"Guess I'm a bit shy about asking that question of the woman who has already turned me down once."

She smiled. "I get it. Okay."

"But if you want to get married, I'm there."

"Not exactly the type of proposal I was looking for."

He laughed. "I suppose you're right."

"Can I think about it?"

"Please do."

They finished eating and cleaned up together. Rafe put on his shirt and pants.

"You're leaving?"

"I was hoping to spend the weekend with you, but maybe that's not a good idea."

Sandy turned to face him. "If you're not comfortable, then—"

"It's you I'm worried about. Do you want me to stay?"

Sandy burst into tears. "I do. Please. How will I know if I should go with you if we don't spend more time together?"

He cuddled her close. "Good point. I was hoping you'd say that."

She sighed. He tightened his grip as if his arms could keep her heart his. Sandy yawned.

"Ready for bed?" he asked.

He led her into the bedroom, undressed, and joined her.

"Can I sleep in your arms?" she asked, her voice quiet.

"I wish you would," he chuckled.

Snuggling up, she rested her palm on his chest. Rafe kissed her head and closed his eyes. Being so close to her, his dick had its own plans. Her hard nipples poked his side and chest, her legs closed around his. Her dampness on his thigh spiked his libido. No way could he sleep with her up against him.

"Darling, do you want to make love?" he whispered.

"I thought you'd never ask," she replied, rolling on her back.

He bent over and took her mouth before he possessed the rest.

TWO WEEKS PASSED IN a flash. Sandy and Rafe were inseparable. They spent every night together, mostly in his beautiful, restored Victorian home. As the time for a decision drew near, she explored all possibilities.

"No more sabbatical time," her principal said.

"But Mr. Josephs. Teachers can take two full-year sabbaticals back-to-back. It's been done before."

"Not under my watch. Look, either you're a teacher here or you're not. Make up your mind, Sandy. You can't have it both ways."

"But..."

He glanced at his watch. "I've already given you more time than I can manage today. Either teach or quit. Those are your options. I have to go to a meeting." He pushed to his feet and strode out of the room.

Sandy sucked her lip between her teeth as she drove home. She hated making decisions, especially big ones, where there were consequences. If she went with Rafe and things didn't work out, she'd have no job to come home to. At home, she put up the kettle for tea and called Bill. After explaining the situation to her brother, she asked for his advice.

"I don't see what's stopping you," he said. "It's a once in a lifetime opportunity."

"But my life here?"

"What life?"

"You. Our parents."

"Forget our parents. They've actually said you should take a year away. Even said things'd calm down while you're gone. And when you get back, next year, all will be forgotten."

"You mean the fact that I humiliated them, you, and myself."

"Something like that."

"Lovely."

"Hey, they are what they are. You took a chance they'd never take. They don't get it. I do. I think you're awesome, Sandy. Even if things didn't go your way. You still went for it."

"Thanks, Bill. That means a lot."

"Don't get mushy on me."

"I'm not. Just don't have a whole lotta friends right now."

"Go to London. You love this guy, right?"

"Yeah. I do."

"So what's the hesitation?"

"To be honest? It'd be different if we were engaged or something. But with nothing, I could get dumped with no money in the middle of a foreign country. That scares the crap out of me."

There was silence.

"If that happened, I'd come and get you. Or wire you money."

"Yeah? What money?"

"Don't worry. That's not going to happen, right? This guy said so, right?"

"Said he'd give me a return ticket. But I haven't seen it yet."

"Okay. I get how scared you are. Just don't screw it up being too cautious."

"It's not like cautious is my middle name, Bill."

He laughed. "You're right. You have my wisdom. Good luck."

"Love you."

"Love you, too," Bill said.

Sandy took a long walk and went over the pros and cons again. She met Rafe at Cowbells, a favorite restaurant, for dinner. He'd arrived early. His brows furrowed, his mouth drawn into a frown.

"What's the matter?" she asked, after his greeting kiss.

"Plans have changed."

"Oh?" she asked, drawing her eyebrows up.

"I have to be there day after tomorrow. I'm leaving on a late-night flight tomorrow."

"Oh my God! I thought we had another week before your flight."

"We did. Not anymore. I need your decision right now, Sandy."

Her heart rose to her throat. She hadn't decided yet. But now he was leaving and while she didn't want him to go, she wasn't ready to go with him.

"I don't know."

His frown deepened.

"I love you, but I'm not ready to throw my life away and follow you," she said.

After they placed their orders, the air grew heavy. When the food came, Sandy couldn't eat. Rafe paid the check and they headed for the parking lot.

"I bet you have a million things to do tonight. I think I should go home."

"You're right. I do. And one of them is to make love to you. Please stay with me. It's our last night until who knows when."

She flew into his arms, sobbing. "I love you so much. But I don't know what to do."

"Let's go home. We'll figure it out."

After a restless night, Sandy helped him get ready. Rafe's parents were arriving in a few days to stay in his house and travel around the

United States. Sandy took a last look at the old Victorian before she threw the car into gear and headed for the highway.

She drove Rafe to the airport and waited in the security line with him until the last second. Unable to hold back tears, she cried softly against his sports jacket as he held her. Regret pricked her heart.

"It's all right, Sandy. We'll find a way. It's all right," he repeated, gripping her tight. After they parted, cool air replaced his frame against her body. She found a seat by the window and stayed there until his plane taxied to the runway.

Heaviness in her chest weighed her down. She got back in her car and made her way home. The apartment seemed so empty without Rafe's quiet, commanding presence. Sandy flung herself across her bed and sobbed. Self-pity ruled. What was the matter with her? She couldn't seem to make the right decision, even when it smacked her in the face.

Epilogue

One month later

Up at six, Sandy showered, dressed and got on her way to school. Along with the new year came the bad jokes by her fellow teachers, at Sandy's expense. Everyone had an opinion on her *Marriage Minded* fiasco. One or two supported her effort, but the rest ridiculed her for her mistakes. None of the negativity had taken her by surprise. She'd expected a wave of unpleasantness when she returned. She gritted her teeth and tried to slough off the insensitive comments as coming from ignorant people who simply didn't know how to behave.

Nights were different. She missed Rafe. Her family told her she'd get over him, but she didn't. The longing didn't lessen but only grew stronger. He'd emailed her several funny messages about his misadventures renting a house and driving on the left side of the street.

Every night, her first move was to open her email. She dared not do that at school, where the principal monitored all email and internet usage. She had to wait until she arrived home. Each time she went online, there was a new message. Some shorter than others, but all loving and most hilarious. She wished she could be there with him.

Once the plane had taken off, Sandy figured Rafe was out of her life. She'd moped around the house until she'd received his first email. Then it became clear he'd keep up the relationship. Nights were the hardest. Sleeping without his warm body next to hers proved difficult.

She sighed. Friday, a welcome end to another brutal week being the butt of stupid jokes, but the beginning of another weekend without Rafe. She drove to school, wondering how she'd pass the time on the two days she was off work.

At lunch, she was called into the office. A short woman sat opposite Principal Josephs' desk.

"This woman has a package for you. She insisted it needed to be hand-delivered. Seems it's insured for a couple thousand dollars or something, and she can only turn it over to you."

"Gloria?"

"Howdy, Miss Landeau. Would you sign here, please?"

Sandy did as requested, and Gloria handed her a box about twelve inches by six.

"Thank you," the older woman said with a gleam in her eye.

"What is this?"

"It's from Rafe," Gloria whispered behind her hand.

"Rafe? What?"

"You'll see. Bye," she said, stopping to give Sandy a hug before she headed for the door.

Sandy took the package and headed for her car. She locked the package in the glove compartment and returned to her duties until three.

Curiosity gnawed at her all day. She couldn't wait to see what Rafe had sent. Driving home, her foot weighed a little heavier than usual on the gas pedal. Finally, she shrugged off her coat and sat at the kitchen table with the box. She grabbed a small, sharp knife and ripped it open. Inside were three items. A DVD, a smaller box, and an envelope.

A post-it on the DVD instructed her to put it in her computer before she touched anything else. She poured a glass of wine and gulped. Being dumped by DVD was a new one on her. She popped the disc into her laptop and waited.

Rafe's smiling face appeared.

"I hope you're not frowning. This is not a bad news video, sweetheart. It's just me, being a nerdy guy, late to the game as always."

He turned around and picked up a bouquet of flowers.

"These are for you," he said. "Aren't they beautiful? Not nearly as pretty as you though. So, let's see. Where to begin. Oh, yes. This month has been hellish torture without you. I miss you more than I thought possible. So, I've come to a decision."

He got down on one knee. "Please pick up the small box. Open it when I tell you. Where was I? Oh, yes. A bad month. As much as we're both afraid of history repeating itself, I've decided it's rubbish and we're being foolish. Open the box, please."

She did as directed. Inside was a stunning three-carat diamond ring.

"Yes, that's right. It's a diamond. And from my own pocket, not from the show. I hate being apart. I love you with all my heart. So, Sandy darling, please, please marry me. If you say "yes", slip the ring on your finger and pack your bag."

Her eyes watered as she picked up the ring and slid it on.

"I hope it fits. Now open the envelope."

Again, she did as told.

"There is a round-trip ticket to London. The plane leaves in two days. I know I didn't give you much time, but hell, we've been apart long enough. I can't stand it. So pack up, tell that old windbag, asshole, principal of yours that you're leaving and fly here to me. I love you and miss you. It's time we tied the knot, don't you think?"

"Yes, I do," she said to the screen.

"Good. I knew you'd agree. I'll meet you at the airport, sweetheart. I can hardly wait."

The screen went blank. Sandy popped up, dried her eyes, blew her nose, and got busy. She typed up her letter of resignation, told

Laura Dailey she'd be moving out, called her brother, and packed two suitcases.

After dropping the letter at school, Sandy returned home to finish up last minute details. She dusted off her passport, overjoyed to find it was still good. She got a haircut, then a good night's sleep.

She paid her parents a visit to say goodbye, then hopped into a limo, and headed for the airport. After two free drinks in first class, Sandy hadn't calmed down. She had emailed "yes" to Rafe before her whirlwind of activity. Now she hoped he'd be there. The stewardess asked her about the stunning ring she wore. Sandy couldn't stop staring at it.

Once he'd made the commitment, she'd shed her old life like a snake does a skin that doesn't fit anymore. She read, dozed, and ate during the long flight. Rereading the *Pride and Prejudice* in the red leather book brought her closer to Rafe.

When the plane landed, the stewardess held back the others and let Sandy off first. Not knowing where to look, she turned at the sound of a whistle. There was Rafe, waving like a madman and looking better than ever. Sandy ran through the gate and into the arms of the man she loved.

** THE END**

LIZ & NICK
Echoes of the Heart
JEAN C. JOACHIM

LIZ & NICK

NO REGRETS

Jean C. Joachim
Moonlight Books

A MOONLIGHT BOOKS NOVELLA

Dedication

To my readers everywhere. I love you all.

LIZ & NICK
NO REGRETS

Jean C. Joachim

Chapter One

Pine Grove, NY, the Senior Prom, ten years ago

Nick and Lizzie clung to each other even after the music stopped.

He whispered in her ear. "Let's go."

"But it's not the last dance."

"Don't be a dork. Break the rules. Just this once," he said, furrowing his brow.

"Okay, okay. Let's go."

They threaded their way through the crowded floor. Slipping out of the gym into the hall, they made a beeline for a side door. Once outside, they leaned against it. Liz took a deep breath.

"Free!" Nick said and laughed.

Liz chuckled and fell into his embrace. The sweet scent of June blossoms lay heavy on the warm spring air.

"Come on," he said, leading her to the parking lot. They hopped into his jalopy and headed for Cedar Lake. Nick pulled the old car into a shadowy lane and parked. Grinning at her, he reached into the back seat and grabbed two towels.

Liz opened the door. Pulling up her long, emerald green gown, she swung her legs out and pushed to her feet. Her spiked heels sank into the soft earth, making her trek slow.

"Those damn shoes. Thought you didn't believe in that fancy-ass shit?"

"It's prom, Nick. Prom."

"Once a girl, always a girl," he said, shaking his head.

"Would you rather I was a guy?" she asked, swiping at him.

"Hell no!"

"This is too slow," he said, picking her up in his arms. Nick Jameson, star defenseman of the Pine Grove Eagles, had arms of steel. He tossed her in the air, then caught her as if she were a piece of balsa wood.

Elizabeth Wenner, five-four and slender, giggled as Nick strode down to the water. When she leaned against his chest, the polyester fabric of his tuxedo rubbed her cheek. The smell of Nick's piney aftershave, mixed with his raw, masculine, slightly sweaty scent created a powerful aphrodisiac that hardened her nipples.

The sound of his heavy footfall on the weathered wood mixed with the soft song of crickets. When he put her down, Liz toed off her shoes. Hiking up her skirt, she peeled off her pantyhose and heaved a sigh.

"You girls wear too many clothes," Nick said.

"Oh, and that stupid cummerbund and those little thingies instead of buttons make sense?"

"Okay. We're even. Last one naked is a rotten egg."

Nick stripped off his complicated suit in record time.

"No fair! You have more experience getting naked," Liz objected.

"Tough. I win. I get to throw you in." He approached her.

She squealed in mock fear. Nick unzipped the back of her dress, and she shed the green jersey, while he unhooked her strapless bra. Liz slid her panties down and kicked them off. He scooped her up, ran to the edge, and tossed her in, then jumped in after.

The night water cooled her body. She surfaced, looking for Nick. Like a whale breaching, he popped up, shaking water off his head. Moonlight kissed his hair, turning it silver. Lizzie treaded water, waiting for him to meet her.

Nick had been on the swim team. His lazy, expert crawl strokes sliced neatly into the surface. Watching Nick do anything athletic was like being at the ballet. For a big guy, he had grace and style. He glided through the water with little splash and wiped his face with his hand when he reached her.

"I didn't think you'd do it."

"You don't know everything about me," she said, jutting her chin out.

He laughed. "Uh, yes, I do. I've known you for over two years. Ain't no secrets."

"Oh yeah?"

"Yeah."

"Bet you didn't know I like Brussel Sprouts?"

"Figures."

"Why?"

"'Cause I don't. You're a veggie lover anyway. I woulda guessed." She splashed his face.

"You startin' something?" he asked, cocking an eyebrow.

Her lips formed an "o", as she feigned fear.

"You're gonna regret that," he said, grabbing her arm.

"Nick!"

Laughing, he pulled her tight to his chest and lowered his mouth to hers. Trapped, unable to tread, she sank. Panic seized her. She clung to his middle, kicking her legs. He rolled onto his back, bringing her above the surface. She let out a breath and gasped.

"You okay?"

She nodded. "Don't do that again."

"Sorry. You know I'd never let you go under."

She did the breaststroke out to the float and clutched the ladder. Nick joined her.

"Did I scare you?"

"For a second."

"I'm sorry, baby," he said, his voice soft. He latched a thick arm around her waist and the other around a rung of the ladder.

She drifted up against him, her breasts teasing his skin. He covered one with a massive hand.

"These are good," he said, giving her a gentle squeeze.

Lizzie pumped her legs slowly. Nick lowered his hand down her belly to the juncture of her thighs and slid one thick digit between her folds. A slow hiss escaped her lips as he slipped a gentle finger inside. Then he eased his leg between hers and brought it up against her sex. He'd started her motor.

"Let's do it here," he whispered, his lips sucking the tender skin of her neck.

"Okay." Lizzie closed her arms around him. His shaft hard and close poked her.

"In the water or out?" he asked.

"Either."

"I can slip right in," he said, pushing his dick toward her. Lizzie brought her knees up and spread them, inviting him. He closed his fingers around her hip and pointed himself at her entrance. He thrust into her while he steadied her with one hand.

Lizzie shut her eyes and gasped as he entered.

"Okay?" he asked.

"Fine," she muttered.

God, it felt good to have him inside her. Nick had turned her on to sex about three weeks after they met. She'd been his tutor for English. They met every day after school. One afternoon, while her parents were working, Nick made love to her.

Lizzie had been curious and ready for sex for some time before Nick came along. But nerds like her never hung out with the cool guys, the ones who knew how to do it. The only guys who paid her any attention were the science nerds. And they knew squat about sex. Just say the word and watch them turn bright red.

But Nick? God, Nick was sex on legs. The first time he showed up at her door, all embarrassed that he needed a tutor, and pissed off about missing video game time, he'd rendered her speechless.

He was gorgeous. Tall, broad-shouldered, so masculine, she could smell it. His presence turned her on. She could hardly string words together. Struggling to focus and stop staring at his chest, she set to teaching him how to diagram a sentence.

It was the hardest thing she'd ever done, keeping her attention on English when all she wanted to do was kiss and touch him. As he caught on to the work, something sparked between them. She remembered what he'd said.

"I thought smart girls were ugly. Nasty. But you're kinda cute."

She had blushed and lowered her eyes. That's when he kissed her, and the rest was history. They'd been together ever since.

"Oh, Lizzie, baby. You feel so damn good. Fuck. I love you," he rasped out, while he slid her up and down.

She raised her chin and he took the hint. His hungry mouth consumed hers while he took her. Slow at first, then he picked up the pace. She got into the rhythm and before long, the tension inside her burst forth.

Crying out his name, she focused on the warm pleasure rocketing through her. Muscles clenching and releasing all around him, Nick followed her, giving his typical grunt, and snuggling his face into her neck. When he raised his head, she cupped his rough cheek. White-hot feelings roiled in her, gaining strength, consuming her, tumbling her emotions round and round, like a tornado. Her heart, full to busting, brought tears to her eyes.

"I love you," she said.

"Me, too." He stroked her head with his palm.

In the moonlight, his clear blue eyes stared at her, warming her skin, despite the coolness of the water. A lump of emotion rose in her throat, almost choking her.

After they uncoupled and swam to shore, Nick tossed her a towel then wrapped one around his waist. She fastened hers at her chest, like a sarong. They padded out to the end of the dock and sat, legs dangling into the water. The moon threw shadows everywhere and gleamed off the still surface of the lake. Lizzie huddled closer. Nick put his arm around her shoulders, and she smiled.

That was her favorite thing, when he drew her close. It was like he threw a protective cape, blanket, or shield around her. She couldn't fathom why that was important. Lizzie had nothing to be afraid of, except two annoying bullies at school. Still, when she was under Nick's wing, all was right with the world, and she wasn't an odd duck who didn't fit in, awkward, and uncomfortable.

She snaked her arm around his waist.

"You did it," he said.

"What?"

"College. You got me into college."

"No, I didn't. You did it yourself."

"If I couldn't pass English with a decent grade, I never would have gotten into Nebraska."

"Ridiculous."

"It's true," he said, facing her. "Why don't you just accept it and say thank you."

"Thank you. Happy?" she quirked an eyebrow.

He hugged her and kissed her head. "You're cute, for a squirt."

"You keep saying that. I'm not a squirt."

"You're not a two-hundred-pound linebacker, either."

"You wouldn't love me if I was."

Lizzie rested her hand on his thigh, feeling the power of his muscle. He reached over, pushing aside terry cloth to fondle her breast. "I'm gonna miss these."

"You'll have a new pair at your disposal within five minutes."

"Hey, hey. We weren't going to talk about that tonight, remember."

"Oh. Yeah. Sorry."

She couldn't help but talk about it. For two weeks, she'd been suppressing thoughts about his leaving for Nebraska the day after prom. He had to be there early for football training. Until he got the letter, they had thought they'd have all summer to hang out and say goodbye.

She took a deep shuddering breath.

"You're gonna be around all those brains. Those Yale guys. All wanting to get laid."

"Hey, now you're doing it."

"I know. It's just that I've been thinking about it all week. It sucks."

"Yep."

"I get why you can't come to Nebraska with me. Sort of."

"We've been over this," she said.

"I know, I know."

"Graduating from Yale is as big a deal in the writing world as you graduating from Nebraska is in pro football. You'll be playing with the best of the best. And I'll be competing with the best of the best."

"I get it. Don't have to like it though."

"Besides, our parents would kill us."

"We're eighteen. We can do what we want."

"My parents would never pay the tuition at Nebraska."

"If we got married, maybe you could get a scholarship, too," he said.

"Nick. I love you. I'd marry you in a heartbeat. But I don't want to go to Nebraska. All my life I've been working my butt off to get into Yale. And I made it."

"It's great. I know. But, well," he sighed, then shrugged, "You know."

"Yeah. I know."

They clung together, sharing body heat and moonlight until almost daybreak.

AT NOON, HIS PARENTS loaded up the family car. Lizzie cried and hugged Nick goodbye.

"See you at Thanksgiving," he said.

"Right. Remember what we agreed?"

"We're free to date anyone we want. We're officially broken up. It's over for four years, or at least the first summer break."

"What?"

"I just added that."

She gave him a playful slap. "We agreed we'd have no ties on each other when we left for college. And no regrets, right?"

"Right. No regrets. Free to date. No regrets," he repeated. His eyes watered. "Damn it, Wenner. Now you made me cry. Defensemen don't cry."

She hugged him. "No one can see."

"I don't want to let you go," he whispered.

"Neither do I. This is so hard," she said, fighting tears.

After another minute, Nick's father tapped him on the shoulder. Nick got in the vehicle, closed the door, and turned to watch Lizzie out the back window. She cried until she couldn't see him anymore.

"No regrets," she muttered, ignoring the pain in her heart. Thanksgiving might as well be light years away.

But it wasn't to be. Lizzie's parents sold their house to pay for her tuition and moved to an apartment in New Hampshire before Thanksgiving.

Lizzie and Nick never saw each other again.

Chapter Two

Ten years later. Java the Hut Coffee Shop, New Haven, Ct

Friday afternoon at two, Dr. Elizabeth Wenner plopped down in the only empty booth. She took off her sunglasses, rubbed her temples, then plucked a folder out of her briefcase. Unlike most professors who hung out at the café grading student papers, Lizzie pulled out a book proposal she'd been writing.

As an assistant professor of American Literature at Yale University, Dr. Wenner spent hour after hour meeting with students in her office. From the exhilaration of working with gifted students to the frustration of working with the lazy ones, Liz devoted a ton of after-class time to teaching. Today, she'd escaped early to grab a couple of hours for herself.

She slapped a paperback on how to write a book proposal on the small table and paged through to where she had left off. As she read, she stopped from time-to-time to sip her coffee and make notes. Liz twirled a hank of her short, dark hair while she read over the marketing section for the third time.

"Lizzie? Lizzie Wenner?"

The deep, masculine voice repeating her name cut through her concentration. She raised her gaze to meet pale blue eyes in a familiar face.

"Nick Jameson?" Her brows knitted.

"Lizzie!" The handsome face broke into a huge grin.

It couldn't be him. He was a successful pro football player. What was he doing here? It must be a mistake. He strode over to her table.

"May I join you?" he asked, not waiting for an answer and sliding into the seat opposite.

"Nick?"

"Lizzie." He took her left hand and raised it to his lips.

Tears burned her eyes. There he was, more gorgeous than ever in an expensive suit, with the perfect haircut, and just the right amount of scruff. He turned her hand to kiss her palm, which she felt to her toes.

"Not married or engaged?" he asked.

For the moment words failed her, she shook her head.

"Me neither."

Anger brought her voice back. "Really? With all those models you date, you couldn't find one to marry?" she blurted out, then clamped her lips together,

"None of them are as smart as you," he said quietly.

She drew in a breath. "What are you doing here?" she asked, changing the subject.

"We're playing a charity game with the Bulldogs."

"They're just college boys, you'll crush them."

"Nah, we'll be gentle. It's a fundraiser."

"I heard about it. But I never. Oh, my God. Nick—"

She gripped his hand and the aloof, professorial demeanor she'd worked years to cultivate cracked like thin ice and melted away. For a moment, she was little misfit, Lizzie Wenner, clinging to her popular boyfriend. Tears leaked down her face as a heaviness settled in her chest.

He whipped a handkerchief from his back pocket and dabbed her cheeks.

"Professor? Is this man bothering you?" The barista had come from behind the counter to stand next to their table, arms folded across his chest.

"Me?" Nick asked.

"Yes, you. She's crying."

"No, Tony. It's okay. I'm fine. Nick is...Nick is an old friend. I'm just surprised to see him."

"As long as you're okay, Dr. Wenner. Because if he bothers you, just raise your hand and I'll throw him out," Tony said, darting a hostile glare in Nick's direction.

The footballer chuckled. "Yeah? You and who else?"

"Nick, please," Lizzie said, putting her hand on his arm.

"Okay, okay. I'll be good."

Tony wiped his hands on his apron and went back to work. Lizzie sighed. Leaning back in her chair, she took a long look at Nick. God damn, he looked good.

"Looks like you have fans everywhere," Nick said.

"Fans?" she shook her head. "Nah. I'm a regular here. That's all."

"It's easy to feel protective toward you, babe," he said, his gaze meeting hers.

Her breath caught. He'd been her protector in high school. Nick Jameson kept everything bad away from her, even the crap that had been happening at home—well almost everything. Before he could speak again, a man poked his head in the door.

"Nick?"

"Yeah?" he said, turning.

"It's time," the man said.

"Okay, Trunk. Give me a sec."

The man Nick called "Trunk" nodded and left.

"I gotta go. Can I call you? Do you want to do dinner?" He rose.

"Perfect," she said, fishing around in her purse. She plucked out a business card and scribbled on the back. "Here. That's my cell."

"Great. You're okay with me calling?"

"Of course. Why not?"

"I mean, you don't have some brainiac waiting or anything, do you?"

"I'm dating someone, but it's not serious."

"Nick!" Trunk called from the door.

Nick leaned over and brushed her cheek with his lips. He slipped her card in his breast pocket and disappeared before she could speak.

"YOU PICKIN' UP CHICKS in a coffee shop now?" Trunk Mahoney, fellow defenseman for the Connecticut Kings asked.

The men walked toward their cars.

"An old, uh, friend."

"Friend?" Trunk raised his eyebrows.

"Okay, okay. Girlfriend."

"What's she doing here?"

"She's a professor at Yale. A doctor. Geez. She's got her doctorate. Damn."

"You're stepping up."

"Not really. She's way out of my league. Always was. And now? Fuck, she's out of my solar system!"

"She's hot," Trunk said.

"Don't get any ideas."

"Hey! I've got my own woman. And she's the hottest ever."

"I don't know about that. Lizzie is steamin'."

"So? Go get her."

They reached their vehicles.

"Me? Nah. I told you, she's way out of my league."

"Yeah? Doesn't look like that to me."

Nick laughed. "You think?"

Trunk slapped him on the back. "It's worth a try, buddy. See you over there."

Nick fastened his seatbelt and started the engine. As he drove to the Yale Bowl, his thoughts dialed back to his old girlfriend. What a punch in the gut to run into Lizzie. He'd wondered what had happened to her. A wry grin stretched his lips. He'd thought about her often but never had the balls to look for her. When he'd arrived home from school and learned that her family had moved, he'd been heartbroken.

Sure, there were chicks to console him in college. Plenty of chicks. But at his first Thanksgiving vacation, he'd counted the hours until he could get home and see her again. Coming back to find her gone with no forwarding address, he'd called, but she'd changed her number.

His mom tried to soothe him by convincing him it wasn't meant to be. He knew better. Late one night during the break, when he couldn't sleep, he went to the kitchen for a glass of milk and overheard his parents talking in the living room.

"Lizzie Wenner? Crap, Martha. She's too smart for our boy. Don't get me wrong. He's no dummy. But the girl's going to Yale. Yale! She's way out of his league. She's probably got a dozen boys with the highest I.Q.'s in the country after her. Sooner or later, she's gonna figure out that Nick can't compete."

"Nick's better than those boys. Stuck up know-it-alls," his mom muttered.

"Maybe so. Still. I doubt she'd marry someone beneath her."

"She'd be damn lucky to marry Nick. He'll make a fine husband. And father, too."

"Dream on, Martha. Nothing against Nick. What you say is true, but Lizzie's gone. Probably a good thing. He'll get over her and move on to find a girl more his speed."

"I still say she'd be lucky to end up with Nick."

Nick had downed his drink and tiptoed upstairs. Back in bed, he stared at the ceiling. It shocked him to hear his father echo his own thoughts and feelings. Lizzie Wenner was simply too damn smart for him. She'd never choose him over some brainiac Yale asshole. No way. Why would she, when she could have any genius she wanted?

That night, he'd made up his mind not to pursue her. Why set himself up to get shot down? By now, she probably had at least three guys after her. How could he compete? A dumb jock? What could he offer her? He had no money, no certain future, and no brains. Well, not outstanding brains, anyway.

A heaviness had grown in his chest. He'd buried his face in his pillow and cried for the first time since he was seven—except when he said goodbye to Lizzie. He'd had plans. Sure, he'd agreed to her "no regrets" bullshit, but only to please her. He'd had no intention of moving on, no plan to walk away. Lizzie Wenner was the girl for him, the only girl.

Even after a couple of months in Nebraska, where he had no problem finding females to warm his bed, Lizzie still held his heart. He figured they'd both screw around in college, then get married after graduation. He'd settle in a plum position on a top NFL team, and she'd get a job until they had kids. Then she'd stay at home. It had been his plan all along, but he'd never told her.

Now his dream was dead, and the pain of that death seared through him like a white-hot spear. His beloved Lizzie would reject him. After a couple of weeks at Yale, she'd probably turn her nose up at the dumb jock from Nebraska. He'd lost her.

Nick moped around for the rest of vacation. His parents thought he was sick. Sick at heart, maybe, but he never confided that to them.

When he returned to school, he did everything he could to forget Lizzie. Had it worked? He thought so. He'd brought girls home for holidays, and Martha Jameson fussed over them, only to have each one replaced by a new female for the next celebration. His mother kept asking him why he didn't settle down and get married.

When he hit the NFL, Nick had convinced himself he'd put Lizzie Wenner behind him, left her in the dust, gotten over her, whatever you want to call it. He dated top models and actresses. He'd made headlines with gorgeous women on his arm. Sure, they weren't as smart as Liz Wenner, but they made the news.

His father appeared envious of his son's lifestyle, while his mother kept asking why he didn't marry one of those sought-after women. He didn't have an answer. There was something about a smart woman that still appealed to him. And he'd yet to meet one who was as smart as Lizzie.

He'd finally convinced himself he'd gotten her out of his blood. Until today. He couldn't believe his eyes. There she sat, prim as usual, sipping coffee and reading, just like old times, except more beautiful than he'd ever seen her. The skinny girl he remembered from high school had put a little meat on her bones and in all the right places.

His heart jumped to life, beating faster, pumping blood to various parts of his body as his gaze stole over her. Hadn't he forgotten her? He thought he had, but he'd simply cemented over his feelings. In one second, the hardened covering had fallen away, crumbling into a million bits.

She was a professor with a Ph. D, teaching at Yale. This was a hundred times worse than her simply attending that esteemed university. He groped for a phrase that surpassed 'out of my league' but couldn't find one. He grinned. Lizzie would probably have four, in seconds, that described their disparity.

Helpless to control his emotions, Nick wanted her all over again and laughed, as if he even stood a sliver of a chance. If, by some miracle, he had a shot, losing her this time would be a whole lot more painful.

LIZZIE SIGHED AS SHE watched Nick Jameson leave. He moved with even more grace than he had when they were in high school. In a few moments, the man had swirled back into her life, like a whirling dervish, turning everything upside down.

She chuckled to herself. He wore a new aftershave and had finally figured out how much, or how little, to use. He'd gotten it just right. The scent lingered, and she took a breath.

Could this be happening? She'd tried calling him during college, but he'd never returned her calls. By junior year, she'd given up. After all, they'd agreed, 'no regrets', right? She had to let him go but prayed he'd return. He never did. She'd kept track of him on the internet, where his dating exploits were mapped out in more detail than his football success.

After a year or two, news of his latest girlfriend had stopped stabbing her through the heart. She read about it for amusement, she'd told herself. Yeah, right—and pigs can fly. About two years ago, she'd stopped checking and ceased to care what happened to him. Or so she thought. He'd achieved serious success in his sport and was happy, she presumed. No need to worry about Nick Jameson, a man who could take care of himself.

> Lying to herself had become a habit. She'd moved on, or
> so she'd told her parents. They

had uttered a sigh of relief that the big man could no longer break their daughter's heart. Her mother and Lizzie's father, before he passed on, had often told her that Nick would never be faithful to a girl, like her, when he had so many models panting after him. Lizzie got the message—plainer girls, like her, didn't deserve the love of handsome, rich footballers. He was out of her league. Funny, but she had agreed and given up. His silence, his refusal to return her calls or answer emails, supported her parents' theory. Obviously, they were right. Weren't they?

Then he blew into her life, stirring up more than dust. Leaner than the last time she saw him, he looked fantastic. The way he smiled at her, she could almost believe he still cared. That couldn't be true. If it was, why had he disappeared for so many years?

Pulling a compact out of her purse, Lizzie fixed her face. She didn't wear much makeup, a bit of blush, eyeliner, and lipstick, but she didn't want anything running down her cheeks. She powdered over her shiny nose and reapplied lip color. One glance told her she looked better than the scrawny, plain, nerdy smart girl she'd been at Pine Grove High. Still, she'd never measure up to the women Nick hung with now.

Instead, she had brains. In high school, he'd seemed truly impressed by her grades. Nick had always respected her intelligence. Some men, many in fact, were threatened by her superior mind. Not Nick. He'd learned from her, asked her questions, and listened. Sometimes, he'd called her "Brainiac". She'd respond by calling him "Superman." It was their little joke.

But most of all, in a mean and unforgiving world, he'd made her feel safe. Compared to the nerds in school, the only ones who'd hang out with her, Nick was her superhero.

If the mean girls were teasing her because she didn't have their curvy figures, snappy clothes, or good looks, the nerds would urge her to move along. Not Nick. He'd speak up on her behalf. He'd faced down many a bully for Lizzie. Damn, Nick wasn't afraid of anything or anyone. She swore his power rubbed off on her. Whenever she was with Nick, she'd be invincible, could do anything, face anything, survive anything. He'd been her rock.

As she put the last touch on her face, she choked up. God, one minute with Nick and she was a basket case, falling all over herself with desire for the big guy, just like in high school.

"You okay?" a familiar voice asked.

She looked up, taking a breath to compose herself before answering. "I'm fine, Frank."

"Tony told me you were crying. Some incredible hulk was at your table, and..." he began, sitting in the vacant seat facing her.

She put her hand on his forearm. "I'm fine."

"Who was it?"

"An old, uh, friend. Someone I used to know."

"Let me know if he bothers you again. I'll call the police."

Wrong answer. Nick would have said, "Let me know if he bothers you again, and I'll punch his lights out." Not that she condoned violence, but the way he said it, she knew he was in charge and nothing bad could happen.

"Don't worry. It's fine."

"Okay then. What are you working on?" he asked, sipping his cup of coffee.

"My book proposal."

He made a face. "Why waste your time?"

"You call yourself my boyfriend?"

"I wouldn't use that antiquated term, Elizabeth," he said.

She shrugged. "Forget it. I've gotta go." She pushed to her feet.

"Can you wait? I'd like to finish this. Walking with coffee, well, I might spill."

Frank was such a sissy sometimes. She sat back down. The minute she was in the booth again, he launched into a monologue about a difficult student and the hassle with the paper he wanted to publish. He complained that no one cared about geology anymore.

Lizzie bit her tongue to keep from saying that she didn't give two damns about it either. The thought of his reaction if she'd said that brought a smile to her lips.

"This isn't funny," he said, his brows furrowed.

"I'm sorry. I know it isn't." What a liar she'd become, because she wasn't sorry at all, and yes, it was totally hilarious.

"Dinner tonight?"

"Not tonight. I need to do some reading," she said, sidestepping his invitation.

"Oh, okay," he replied.

That was her go-to excuse to avoid Frank. Most of the time they got along fine, but sometimes she simply had to get away from his controlling, pedantic attitude. So, she'd use reading as her excuse. Dating Frank was better than staying home. But not by much.

As for sex? No one could hold a candle to Nick. She giggled at her mental comparison of him to a candle. More like a cannon. Frank tried, but he didn't have much experience and was sensitive to suggestions, which he took as criticism. She put up with it. Fortunately, by the time he made his move, which wasn't more than once a week, she was so horny, she came quickly without much foreplay necessary.

All in all, she led the exemplary, boring life. Her mother totally approved of everything, including Frank. She got along okay with her colleagues in the English department. And the students liked her. What more could she want?

Nick, that's what, exciting, unpredictable Nick Jameson. What would she do when he called? She'd go out with him, no question about it. Her palms sweated at the idea of being with him again.

And if he propositioned her? She'd fall into bed in a nanosecond. One look at him, and she knew she'd forget everything and be his again. And when he moved on, like she expected he would, she'd pick up the pieces but have no regrets.

The way he'd greeted her piqued her curiosity. He hadn't made any reference to why he never contacted her again. Though he seemed happy to see her. The lusty light in his eyes made her libido kick up. She remembered that look. And he had it all over him. So why didn't he ever get in touch? Was it only 'no regrets' or was it something else?

"Okay. I'm done. We can go."

"Sure?" she asked.

He nodded. She pushed to her feet and headed for her apartment. Frank followed.

"Can I come over? A little nookie, maybe?"

"Not today."

"That time of the month?" he asked.

Apparently, he assumed having her period would be the only reason she didn't want to sleep with him. His attitude annoyed her.

"Nope. Just not today. Okay?" she snapped.

"Okay, okay. Sorry." He raised his hands. "I'll be in my office. In case you change your mind."

"I won't."

She picked up the pace, anxious to get home, in case Nick called. Was Nick the same? Why hadn't he returned her calls? Why wasn't he married? Was he dating anyone? Would he ever have tried to find her, if he hadn't bumped into her? As always, she had a million questions. "The Inquisitor" was Frank's nickname for her. Maybe he was right.

As she made tracks, the nerve endings in her skin jumped to life. The slight September breeze caressed her, giving her gooseflesh. Was it the breeze, or was it Nick Jameson?

WHEN SHE GOT HOME, Lizzie toed off her shoes and poured a glass of wine. She padded over to her bookcase and pulled out her one and only scrapbook. Before she could open it, her doorbell rang. It was her best friend and neighbor, Carly Craddock.

"Hi, doing anything? Wanna go for ice cream?" Carly asked, tossing her head, bouncing her brunette waves against her shoulders.

"Get in here. I need to talk to you," Lizzie said, yanking her friend's arm.

She explained to Carly about Nick.

"You and a football player? I don't believe it."

"Come here," Lizzie said, pouring another glass of wine. Carly took it and plopped down on the sofa.

Lizzie opened the scrapbook. "Take a look at these."

They thumbed through page after page. Lizzie pointed out who the people were and dropped in choice anecdotes to kick up interest in this trek through her high school history.

"He's adorable. Football, huh? Which team?"

"The Connecticut Kings. Here's a team picture," Lizzie said, grabbing her laptop and clicking on one of the many shots of Nick she kept in her picture file.

Carly practically spit out her wine. "Holy hell! This guy is gorgeous."

"Yep. And he was mine, once, years ago."

"What the hell happened? How did you let him get away?"

"I don't know. We moved away, but I tried to get in touch. He wouldn't answer the phone or call me back. I guess he didn't feel the same. He moved on fast."

"And what now?"

Lizzie shrugged.

"You're going to go out with him, aren't you?" Carly asked.

"Are you kidding? Who could say *no* to that?" she said, pointing to his smiling picture.

"Have a good time. Please, don't fall for him again," Carly said. She finished her wine, then returned to her apartment.

Lizzie didn't voice her objection to her friend's caution. What would be wrong with having an affair with Nick? Was it a horrible idea? Would she get hurt once more? She paused. The real question Lizzie struggled with was could she keep from loving him with every ounce of her being again? Could she keep it light? Knowing Nick, and her own heart, that was doubtful.

At five, Lizzie's phone rang.

"Nick?"

"It's me. Can you do dinner tonight?"

"Sure."

"Can you make a reservation at the best place in town for six thirty?"

"I can. It's called The Silver Spoon. On Grove Street."

"Perfect. Can I meet you there?"

"Of course." At least in separate cars she could make a quick getaway, and so could he. Maybe that was a good thing.

"Can't wait," he said, before hanging up.

Lost in thoughts of Nick, Lizzie sighed, then turned on the tap to run a bath. Sinking into the hot water relaxed her tight muscles. Tense? Nick Jameson knew exactly how to make her tense. Simply kissing her palm while his clear blues gazed into her eyes ratcheted her tension level up about five hundred percent. She smiled at the thought of how Nick would relax her, too.

He hadn't lost his charm, and there was something even more attractive about him. He'd lost the boyish blubber. His body was lean, his face had angles. No more baby-faced boy, Nick Jameson was all man now, probably with muscles hard as rocks. The idea made her shiver. He was sex on a stick and capable of breaking her heart a second time, in the blink of an eye.

Common sense told her to cancel the date or just not show up. Protect herself. She knew there was no way she could do that. Her appetite for Nick had grown over time. As much as she denied it to her family and herself, once he reappeared, the truth grabbed her and wouldn't let go. Nick held her heart in the palm of his hand now, just as he had ten years ago.

Lizzie dipped the washcloth in the steamy water. As she scrubbed herself, she parroted words she imagined her mother would say.

"Pro athlete? They only marry beautiful girls. Models, actresses, not college professors."

"He's not smart enough for you. What's wrong with Frank? Nice scientist. More your speed."

No, actually, Nick was more her speed. Nick brought a bit of recklessness, abandon, rule-breaking, originality to her life. Frank would have given her a hundred reasons not to go skinny-dipping in the lake after dark on the night of the prom. Not Nick. He had simply stripped down, jumped in, and expected her to do the same.

Nick got her. He understood her—at least he had in high school. No one else had, not even her parents. The staid professor wasn't so demure on the inside. He brought out her wild side, whether she wanted him to or not. Would tonight's date be more of the same? She licked her lips in anticipation.

She slipped on a dark pink sheath. The color added cheer to her pale complexion, dark hair and gray eyes.

Carly knocked and called through the door. "It's me!"

Lizzie opened.

"Here. Wear these. Says he's six-four. You need the height." Her friend shoved a pair of strappy, black patent leather sandals into her hands.

"Thanks."

"You look great. Have fun and be yourself," Carly said, padding down the hallway in her bare feet.

Lizzie grinned. She had every intention of being herself. Besides, she couldn't fool Nick for one second. He'd see through anything that wasn't the truth. She loved that about him.

THE GAME HADN'T QUITE been a slam dunk. Trunk warned Nick to be careful.

"Hell, this is a bogus game. Doesn't count for shit. Don't take any chances. You don't want to get hurt and have your career fucked for some Mickey Mouse little college game."

Nick smiled. Good advice—like always from his mentor. The defensemen took it easy in the first half. But when the Bulldogs scored a second time, the Kings' defense worked out a strategy and put muscle behind it. No way were they going to let guys who were probably still virgins show up the Kings. They had their reputation to protect.

It didn't take much to pull the game together and take over the lead. Trunk and Nick intimidated the younger men, running circles around them. On the third Bulldog quarterback sack, they took it easy. No sense damaging a guy for no reason. The college kids played their hearts out. The Kings tightened their game, fine-tuning plays, and running around the Bulldogs. Of course, the pros won, four touchdowns to the Bulldogs two.

In the locker room after the game, Nick scrubbed himself down in the shower, his mind on Lizzie. Fear mixed with lust in his veins. He'd dreamed of making love to her so many times over the years. Lizzie popped back into his head every time he was between women. He had to talk to someone.

Toweling off, Nick spied Trunk Mahoney at his locker, combing his hair.

"Hey, Trunk. Got a sec?"

The big man turned. "Sure, kid. What's up?"

"It's kinda personal."

"Come back to The Savage Beast with me. We can talk there."

"Okay."

Nick dressed and met Trunk at The Beast. He didn't have a lot of time before he had to meet Lizzie in New Haven. Trunk's wife, Carla, the barkeep and owner, made Nick a Carla Special, a nonalcoholic drink, and the two men took a table in the corner.

"So what's up?" Trunk leaned back.

Nick explained about his relationship with Lizzie and how he'd disappeared for ten years.

"Ten years?" Trunk raised his eyebrows.

"I don't know what to do."

"You want to be with this chick?"

"Yeah. I do. But I messed up. Not returning her calls and shit. And she's so smart. I mean, why would she want to be with me? She's probably got a genius boyfriend who's up for the Nobel Prize or something. What would she want with a bum like me?"

"Who told you you're a bum? You're not a bum. You're a successful pro football player. The envy of a shitload of guys."

"Yeah? But none of them graduated from Yale."

"Hell, you don't think some of those kids we played today want to be where you are?"

Nick shrugged. "Maybe."

"You're not dumb."

"I'm smart enough to know I'm not as smart as she is."

"In some things, maybe. But you're probably smarter in other shit. I saw you change your own oil. And didn't you fix one of the tables here?"

"So what? Manual labor. Lots of guys can do that."

"She's not the only Ph.D. in the world, either."

"Frankly, I don't know what she ever saw in me in the first place."

Trunk snickered. "You her first?"

"Yep."

"I'm bettin' that had something to do with it."

"You think those brainiacs don't know how to make love to a woman?"

"Not like we do. Why don't you ask her?"

"Ask her what she saw in me?"

Trunk nodded. "Carla says men are stupid about talking. Communication and that shit. She says we don't express ourselves."

Nick nodded.

"Hell, I express myself between the sheets," Trunk said.

Nick laughed, then checked his watch. "I'd better go."

"Whatever you do, don't be late. Chicks hate that."

"Right. Thanks for the advice, Trunk."

"Anytime, Nick."

The men rose, shook hands, and Nick headed for the door. He set his GPS and took a backroad shortcut to New Haven. To show Lizzie he was serious, he had to be on time. Trunk's advice swirled through his brain. Dare he take a chance and ask Lizzie what the hell she saw in him? Might as well. Sure beat guessing. Maybe he could build on it, win her back, show her he meant business this time. Would she buy it? He had no clue.

Chapter Three

At six, she headed for the street, hopped in her fire engine red Jetta, and drove to the restaurant. She made a good salary, a hundred grand a year, but it was chump change compared to what Nick made. She smiled when she remembered how some of the kids had talked behind his back. The nerds said he'd never amount to much. They claimed he'd play football for one season, get arrested, and become a bum. It warmed her heart that he had proven them wrong.

Lizzie sashayed in about ten minutes early. Nick had not arrived. The maître d' showed her to three different tables before she found the perfect spot. The one she selected was by a window with a view of the gardens. The cozy table had a dark teal blue cloth, with a white one laid on top diagonally and two white candles in glass holders.

She ordered a Cosmo on the sweet side, stared out the window, and tapped her well-shod foot under the table. At the stroke of six thirty, the big man marched to the back of the restaurant. His presence dwarfed the room.

"Hi. You look beautiful," the smooth, deep voice said.

She glanced up. His icy-blue eyes held warmth. Was that lust, love, or simply happiness at seeing an old friend? Hadn't she always been able to read him? This time, she didn't know. Maybe ten years had eroded her knowledge.

"Thank you."

He sat down and took her hand, raising it to his lips. "You've changed your perfume."

She smiled. "You noticed."

"I notice everything about you. Your hair's different, nails the same, smile, too."

She put her hand over his, warming her freezing fingers on his skin.

"Wow, is it that cold in here? Should I ask them to turn down the AC?" he asked.

"It's me. Nerves."

"Nervous with me? Old Nick? Really?"

"Aren't you? Just a little?"

"Excited maybe, but not nervous."

"Of course. You weren't the one whose calls were ignored."

"Ouch." He grimaced.

"Why, Nick?" Lizzie drew her lip over her bottom teeth. She swore to herself she wasn't going to say that. But it simply popped out of her mouth.

"Can I get a drink first?"

"Sure."

He ordered cranberry juice and ginger ale. "Game tomorrow."

She nodded. Discipline. He always had it when it came to football. But for his English studies? It was like pulling teeth.

They were quiet, staring at each other, waiting for his beverage. Nick had aged a tiny bit, but it looked good on him. His slimmer face had a more chiseled appearance. Damn, he could be a model. His hair, cropped short, as always, was medium brown, but she swore there were a few grays in there, too. Nick Jameson would age well. She sighed.

The waiter put down the glass. "Ready to order?"

Nick glanced at Lizzie. "Not quite. Lizzie? An appetizer?"

"No, thanks. Give me a few minutes."

"Of course. No rush," the waiter said and left.

"Okay. You have your drink." Never as brave on the inside as she seemed on the outside, she cringed, dreading what he would say. "Please, tell me the truth. The absolute truth. I'm an adult. I can handle it."

He sighed and dropped his gaze to his drink. "Same old, same old."

"Me?" her eyebrows rose.

He grinned. "Yep. The absolute truth lady. One of the many things I love about you."

"Don't toss that word around."

"And the word lady, too." He laughed.

Anger grew inside her. "Don't say that. Don't use the word 'love' when you refer to me in any way, shape, or form." Tears stung. She panicked. No, no crying, no humiliating tears.

He took a sip, then closed his large hands around hers. "But I have to. It's what I feel and you want the truth. You taught me to respect words."

She ripped from his grasp. "It isn't what you feel. I tried, for two years, to get in touch with you. I called and called. Left message after message. Emails. None of them were returned. So don't use *love* when you talk about me."

He sat back as if she'd slapped him. "I forgot about that. We said no regrets, right?"

"Bull shit, Nick. Be straight with me."

"Okay." He took a deep breath, another slug of juice and lifted his gaze to hers. "You're too smart for me."

"What?"

"That's right. My parents said it. They were right. You're too smart to settle for a dumbass jock like me. I bet you've got at least three certified geniuses after your ass at Yale right now."

Her eyes widened, and she laughed. "Really? You mean that? That's why you didn't call?"

He nodded.

"You broke my heart over that crap?"

"It's not crap. I always knew you were too smart for me. In Pine Grove, it was a privilege. But once you went to Yale, well, hell, I couldn't compete," he said. "I overheard my parents talking. They didn't say anything I hadn't said to myself a thousand times. It's one thing at Pine Grove High. Hell, you didn't have much to choose from. The smart guys there couldn't find their dicks in the dark. But at Yale? Gimme a break. Everybody and I mean *everybody* has an I.Q. three times mine."

She slid her hand over his. Even rapid blinking couldn't stop the tears. Pain seared through her. She couldn't imagine how horrible it must have been to think he wasn't smart enough for her. "You schmuck. I can't believe you thought that. Do you still feel that way? It's crap. BS. Garbage. You have more heart, more love to give than all the boys in Pine Grove High and Yale wrapped up together."

Struggling to control her emotions, she stopped speaking. Nick produced a handkerchief and slid it across the table.

"You can't tell me your parents wanted you to marry a dumb jock like me."

She laughed. "Actually, my parents didn't think I was good enough, pretty enough to be your wife. They said bigtime football players marry models or actresses. And you sure have gone out with plenty. They'd nod and say, 'See. I told you. He's not going to end up with you.'"

Color rose in his neck and flowed to his cheeks. Anger sparked in his eyes.

"That's the biggest crock of shit I've ever heard. Those babes can't compete with you."

"Yeah, right."

He smacked his palm on the table. The silverware and candles jumped. So did Lizzie.

"Sorry. Sometimes I don't know my own strength."

"What are you saying?" she asked, cocking an eyebrow.

"I'm saying, the models and actresses aren't as smart as you. Who wants a dummy for a wife? Not me. I want a smart woman. But what intelligent woman would settle for me?"

"Settle for you?" Lizzie burst out laughing.

"What's funny about that?" The red returned to his cheeks, and his eyes grew cold.

Lizzie wrapped her fingers around his forearm. "No, no. I didn't mean it like that. I wasn't laughing at you. It's just funny that you think I'm so much better than you and my mother thinks you're so much better than I. Or, at least your model friends are. Don't you see the irony?"

He cupped her cheek. "I don't think that's funny at all."

The waiter returned. Nick dropped his hand and focused on the menu.

"Order whatever you want. Sky's the limit," Nick said.

He ordered the scallop appetizer and lobster. Lizzie ordered the asparagus vinaigrette appetizer and the lobster. The waiter brought a basket of warm rolls. Nick ripped one open and buttered it.

"Where were we?" he asked.

"Irony," she said.

"Oh, yeah. I think it's a fuckin' shame that your parents and my parents turned us away from each other."

She sighed. As usual, Nick summed things up perfectly in a simple sentence.

"But it wasn't just them. We bought into it, too," he continued.

"You keep saying how you're not smart, but you just summed up our entire situation in one, short, succinct sentence. I think that's pretty smart."

He smiled. "Maybe. I learned that from you. Let's see if I remember the lesson. Hmm. 'don't use two words when one will do'—that's it right?"

"Right." She smiled.

"I did have the highest grade in English of anyone on the team at Nebraska," he said.

"I'm not surprised."

The waiter brought their appetizers. They seized on the break to change the subject. They ate and chatted about the news and their jobs, avoiding emotionally charged topics. It wasn't until dessert that Lizzie dared to bring up their relationship again.

"Where do we go from here?" she asked.

"I'd say to my apartment, right now. Directly to the bedroom. But that's me."

She laughed.

"Oh, you mean beyond that?" he asked.

"Uh, yeah. Not that I wouldn't go back to your place, I would. I will. I mean if you want me to. I..." she stuttered until he placed a finger over her lips.

"I'm sorry. I didn't mean to skip to this level. Look, I'm interested in you. I want to get back together. I mean, if we can. If you want to. If too much time hasn't gone by. I'm not the crazy guy I used to be. I've changed. I'd guess you have, too. But I'd like to try. You?"

Her eyes filled. She nodded.

"Sure?"

She nodded more vigorously. Nick pushed up, put his arms under hers, and lifted her onto his lap. He closed them around her. Lizzie let the tears flow. He smelled good. And there it was again, that amazing feeling that everything was going to be all right. A little cooing sound escaped from her throat as she curled into his shoulder.

"Ah. Yeah. When I hear that, I know you're okay," he whispered.

NICK HAD NEVER WANTED to make love to a woman as much as he wanted to with Lizzie at dinner. He gazed into her clear eyes throughout the meal, getting lost in their beauty. Her smile warmed his soul. Whatever had changed about Lizzie Wenner, and he was sure there was plenty, her sweetness remained.

Her laugh, her small, delicate hands with unpolished nails—so real, so feminine—inspired him to make contact at every opportunity. Touching her occupied his mind. Those thoughts progressed, luring him, stoking his libido until envisioning her between the sheets filled his mind.

An old wish rose like a phoenix from the ashes. What would it be like to spend the night together, in the same bed? During high school, they never had the chance. He'd imagined waking up to her would be a dream come true. Would she smell as good after a full night's sleep? Maybe even better.

If they could mend fences, if they could try again, maybe he'd get his wish. Would he be able to hold a conversation with her now? Was she so extra smart and learned that he couldn't even talk to her? A quick fear shot through him. If that was true, then she wasn't his Lizzie anymore, and there was no point in his pursuit.

Willing himself to listen to her words and respond appropriately required supreme control. All he wanted was to kiss her. When she said she'd go back to his place, he grinned. He couldn't believe his luck. However, he wouldn't rush things. He couldn't will away the fact that it had been ten years since they'd been together. They needed to get to know each other again before they heated up the boudoir.

Had she given him the green light? He thought so. Happiness he hadn't known in years flooded Nick's heart. He'd talk out his concerns and make it up to her for not calling back. If they could find common ground, maybe they could recapture the love they had shared, back when they were too young and stupid to know how precious a gift they possessed.

The waiter brought the check. Lizzie returned from the ladies' room while Nick paid.

"Maybe if we started dating again?" she asked.

"Perfect." He stuffed his wallet in his back pocket. They walked out hand-in-hand.

"Exclusive. It has to be exclusive," she said.

"I agree."

"So peel off the hordes of gorgeous models clinging to you and let's make a date."

"And you have to dump whoever you're seeing, too."

"I will."

"Joke's on you, though. I'm not dating anyone now," he said, his eyes glittering with mischief. "Can you say the same?"

"Pretty sneaky way of finding out. No, but I have no problem breaking up with him."

"Good. So when's our first date? We're playing at home this week."

"Are you hanging with the team after the game tomorrow?"

"I don't have to."

"Okay. Why don't you come to dinner?"

"What time?"

"Six?" she scribbled something on the back of a scrap of paper. "My address."

"I'll be there."

"Great."

"Do you want to come to the game?"

"I'd love a chance to see you play again," she said.

"I'll leave a ticket in your name at the box office."

"Thank you. We can go straight to my place from there."

"Works for me," he said.

They reached her car. He dawdled, toying with her windshield wiper before stepping closer. Lizzie sighed. He took her in his arms for a long, deep kiss.

"What took you so long?" she whispered.

She melted against him, sliding her hands up around his neck. Nick's erection pressed her belly, getting her juices flowing. His restraint impressed her. If he could wait, so could she. They parted. Lust shone in his eyes, but his brow furrowed.

"Do you still feel the same?" he asked, his voice quiet.

"Yes, do you?"

"Same. I thought it might be gone. Looks like we're going to get a second chance."

"Thank God," she said, stepping into his arms again.

When they parted, he opened her door, then locked and closed it. The little things he did to keep her safe warmed her.

Once at home, she toed off her shoes and sprawled on her back on the bed. Was tonight a dream or was Nick Jameson really back? Would he stay?

Lizzie bolted upright. Damn! He was coming for dinner tomorrow, and she had no clue what to make? She hung up her dress and plopped down at her computer to find the perfect menu.

NICK DROVE TO THE SAVAGE Beast. He needed to talk to Trunk, get guidance from an impartial source. Trunk noticed him at the bar and ambled over.

"How'd the dinner go?"

"Great. Better than I expected. Do you have a minute?" Nick asked.

Trunk leaned on the bar. "Sure. What's up?"

"More advice."

"Shoot," Trunk said, popping open a can of Coke and placing it in front of Nick.

Between gulps, Nick recounted a short version of the evening.

"What do you think? Should I go ahead?"

"Of course."

"But what if—"

Trunk put his hand on Nick's arm. "Life is full of fuckin' 'what if's'. If you start doing that, you'll never get out of bed. Go for it. This chick means a lot to you. Pursue it. What have you got to lose?"

"I don't wanna get hurt."

"No guarantees, Nick. Do you want to be with her?"

"Yeah. She's amazing.

"Then what's holding you back?"

"I don't know. What if—?"

"There you go again. How about this? What if it works out? What if you get married? How about that 'what if'?" Trunk shifted his weight.

Nick nodded. "You're right. That would be fantastic."

"You have my blessing to date this chick. I hope it works out, buddy," Trunk said, slapping Nick on the shoulder.

"Thanks. Me, too."

Nick finished his drink and drove home. Sure, he'd be taking a chance. What if she was simply pissed at him for not calling her back and was setting out to break his heart? He shook his head. Lizzie would never do that. She wasn't the type to waste her time with a shitload of negative energy. She was a truth-teller. Hey, she'd been hostile when she asked him about his silence, hadn't she? If she didn't want him, or think they should try again, she'd have been up front about it. Peace flowed through him

He sighed as he pulled into his garage. He couldn't believe his dumb luck, running into her at the coffee place. Damn, he should give a donation to Yale just to thank them for keeping her there.

When he got inside, he trotted up the steps to his bedroom and got undressed. After opening the closet, he surveyed his clothes. He needed to dress great for his date.

He took out his charcoal gray suit and put it on the side, along with a white shirt and his dark turquoise tie. That was his magic combination, what he wore when seduction was top of mind. It had become his lucky suit. No babe had been able to resist him dressed like that. He hoped it would work on Lizzie.

He laughed. Liz Wenner could never be mistaken for a typical anything, let alone girlfriend. Nothing about her could be found in books or on dating websites. She was an original, thank God. After washing up, he slid into bed, laced his fingers behind his head, and stared out the skylight at the moon.

Tomorrow night wouldn't be about seduction. He suspected Lizzie was willing, but what she said and the way her eyes looked at him... God, the heat she generated simply sitting next to him. Turn up the fan!

The chemistry still churned with Liz. Nick couldn't wait to make love to her again. He chuckled remembering what amateurs they had been in high school. Lizzie had thought him experienced. Hah! So he'd screwed a couple of girls, that only meant he knew where to put his dick, not necessarily what to do with it. Over the last ten years, he'd spent most of his time away from football perfecting his bedroom moves. Proud of his prowess and knowledge—and remembering some of the compliments he'd received—he looked forward to taking Lizzie to the moon. And himself, too.

Once his libido calmed down, he tapped into that feeling he had when he was with her. He felt more intelligent around Liz. There was something about them together that he couldn't put his finger on. The woman made him feel like a million bucks. When Lizzie was by his side, he was a hero, strong, invincible, and smart.

Tomorrow night couldn't come soon enough. First, he'd have to focus on his game against the Columbus Bobcats, then he'd move on to the real challenge—making Lizzie fall in love with him again.

Chapter Four

Lizzie awoke early. Various recipes she'd printed out the night before littered her tiny kitchen table. There was so much to do before her date. Grocery shopping, food preparation, dressing to kill, straightening up, and it was already eight. The game started at two. Since she expected Nick right after the game—there wouldn't be much time to do any of those things.

By ten, Liz had returned from the grocery store and had the meat for her casserole cooking. She shredded lettuce for salad as she hummed along to the radio. After mixing Greek yogurt and sour cream, she added onion soup mix. She took the beef out to cool and fired up the pot for noodles.

Working away, she got the dinner assembled so that all she had to do was plunk it in the microwave and nuke it. Cream puffs from Chez Pierre's bakery rested in their box in the fridge. No wine necessary as Nick didn't drink before a game. Instead, she'd picked up some craft brewery root beer. She even had vanilla ice cream if he wanted a float.

By eleven, she'd taken a bath and lain down for a short nap. Too excited to sleep, she let her thoughts drift to Nick. As she closed her eyes, the disturbing memory of a scary day when she was seventeen came rushing back.

Her parents had been at work. Being home alone had never bothered Lizzie. She'd do her schoolwork, then curl up in a favorite chair and escape into a book. The day had been unusually hot for mid-May. Lizzie wore denim shorts and a halter top. She'd unfolded a lounge chair on the front lawn. The tiny Wenner house rested on the edge of a dusty road, seldom traveled, that abutted a wood.

Nick had begged off on his lesson that day. She'd finish her work later. After pouring a glass of lemonade, she grabbed her book and stretched out on the chair. A buzzing noise had broken the quiet. It grew louder and louder. Annoyed at the interruption, Lizzie sat up and faced the road, ready to give a piece of her mind to the motorcyclist who needed a muffler.

The bike screeched to a halt at the edge of her lawn. The man on the vehicle got off and stood, staring at her. Even now, so many years later, her nerves kicked up at the memory and the hair on her forearms rose. The guy wasn't some nice neighbor, some polite country guy about to apologize for disturbing her. No way. His scraggy beard and dirty jeans drew her eye.

The nastiness of his sneering expression shot fear through her. Brutal, cold, dark eyes like a snake bored into her, then raked over her body. Feeling naked, she folded her arms across her chest. He seemed to have x-ray vision, and she swore he could see under her clothing.

She pushed up and backed toward the house. Her cell phone was on the other side of the chair, out of reach. The man wasn't big, but he was larger than she. He pushed down the kickstand and let go of the handlebars.

"Hey, little lady. Whatcha doin'?" he asked, strolling toward her.

Although the words appeared friendly, his dark stare threatened.

She kept backing up, glancing at the street, wishing with all her heart for a car to come by.

"Where you goin'?" He moved closer.

Almost at the back steps, Lizzie planned her escape. Trembling, she continued to inch toward the house. Keeping her eye on him and feeling behind her to find the stair railing, she tripped over a rock and fell on her butt. He laughed.

"Now that's mighty convenient, having you on the ground," he said, picking up his pace.

"Nope. That's not convenient at all. Stop, asshole! Get away from her!"

Nick appeared from around the other side of the house. He stood a head taller than the biker.

"You heard me. Get on that bike and get outta here before I punch your face in. And don't ever come back."

"Who do you think you're talkin' to?" the biker asked, pulling himself up to his full height but stepping toward his vehicle. Lizzie knew Nick had him. The biker's bravado couldn't hide his fear. Nick balled his hand into a fist and charged. The man jumped on his bike, hit the starter, and wobbled a few feet away. Nick raised his arms and hollered. The man took off, leaving a cloud of dust in his wake.

Even now, Lizzie's heart raced as fear shot through her once more. She shook her head while the rest of the scene played out in her mind.

"What the hell are you doing out here dressed like that?" Nick had hollered. He'd continued dressing her down for being careless and provocative. She'd burst into tears.

"If you hadn't canceled your session, this wouldn't've happened," she'd said, blubbering into a tissue.

"That's true. I'm sorry. I changed my mind. Decided to come." His tone softened as he touched her shoulder.

"Video game stop working?" she asked, cocking an eyebrow and throwing a sour glance his way.

"I decided not to play." He cupped her cheek. "You gotta take better care of yourself. Don't be out here sunbathin' when you're alone. You're inviting trouble. Come here, sweetheart," he said, enveloping her in his arms. His bear hug calmed her.

"So you're all alone?" he asked.

"Yep. Dad's at work. Mom went to New York to meet with a publisher."

"Hmm. Let's go inside," Nick said.

They'd spent the next hour making love, then they got to his lessons. When she arrived at school the next day and told her nerdy friends about the biker, their advice was to run. None of them had the moxie to stand up to the nasty man with evil intentions. Her nerdy buddies were too scared, too ignorant about self-defense, and not committed to their friendship with her to come to her rescue. At least that's how it came across to Lizzie.

That day she'd fallen deeply in love with Nick. She knew what she wanted, what she needed. Ten years later that had not changed.

LIZZIE DOZED UNTIL twelve. She dressed and put some finishing touches on the meal. She pulled on new slinky jeans, a low-cut dark pink sweater, and a denim jacket. September days could be cool. Before she could slip on her flats, the doorbell rang. She glanced through the peephole. Frank waited outside. Damn.

"Wow, you look great." He stepped in.

"Frank. I think you'd better sit down."

"Didn't we make a date to go to lunch today?"

"Not that I remember. I have some news."

He sat on the sofa. "I hope it isn't bad. You're not pregnant, are you?"

She shook her head.

"Oh, good. Not that that would be bad. I mean, I think I'd make a good father. And we could get married. Not that I'm rushing you, but if you're pregnant..."

She ground her teeth. "You're not listening, Frank. I said I'm not pregnant. It's about us."

"We don't have to get married. I'm happy with the way things are."

"Would you be quiet?" she raised her voice.

"Sorry." He closed his mouth.

"I think it's time we parted company."

"What?"

"I want to break up."

"You're breaking up with me?"

"Didn't you hear me? Yes. I'm breaking up with you."

"Why? Is there someone else?"

"It doesn't matter. We're not suited."

"There is someone else. That Neanderthal? That gorilla from the coffee shop?"

"He's not a Neanderthal. And, if you must know, yes, it's him." She'd hoped not to hurt Frank any more than necessary. But he'd pushed and now the truth was out.

"Oh, I see. A big bruiser. Does he have a brain or just a dick?"

She stifled the urge to slap him. Clamping her lips into a tight line, she stared at him.

"Did I say something wrong? The truth hurts. But maybe you prefer a dick to a brain."

"I think you should leave before I say something I'll regret."

"Really? Go ahead. Say it. Say whatever you want. I question the intelligence of any woman who would pick that ape over someone like me, who can think, reason, and talk."

That was it. She slapped him, drawing her hand back in shock after.

"I'm sorry, Frank."

"You should be," he said, his face red and his cheek redder.

"You shouldn't talk like that about Nick."

"Nick? Rhymes with dick. We're done."

"Exactly. You can leave now."

"I was just going," he replied.

She slammed the door behind him, sure that steam flowed from her ears. His words had inflamed her. *Is that what Nick was talking about? Is that the way the world will see us? My mother? His father?* Tears pricked at the backs of her eyes. It hit home that Frank had said what most people would think. Her colleagues would probably snigger behind her back about Nick and the disparity between them. How awful, how terrible!

Frank's words are exactly what Nick had chosen to avoid from the world when he didn't return her messages. She couldn't believe people would be that superficial, that stupid and insensitive. If that's the way the world would look at them, well too damn bad. She chose Nick and was proud of it. Now, she understood his point of view, though. If he still wanted her, she'd be his and live the rest of her life surrounded by his love. World be damned. Liz loved Nick.

She put on her jacket and headed for her car. As she drove, Frank's words fell away and Nick's returned. *"But it looks like we're going to get a second chance."* Lizzie couldn't stop smiling. Yesterday, everything had looked drab, gray, dreary. Life had been dull. Now, Nick had roared into town, and her world blazed in full color.

She spied two of her colleagues in the parking lot. John Woolsey and Martha Stokes taught English Literature, John taught poetry and Martha did the classes on Shakespeare. They joined her on her trek to the box office.

"Where's Frank?" Martha asked.

"Oh, we're not seeing each other anymore."

Martha raised an eyebrow. "Something bad happen?"

Lizzie shook her head. "It's fine. It was destined to end anyway."

"Didn't know you liked football. Martha and I have season tickets. Haven't seen you here before." John said.

Lizzie laughed. "I became a fan in high school."

"Why do I think there's more to this story than football?" Martha said, narrowing her eyes.

"Nothing to discuss," Liz said, taking her ticket. They compared seats.

"Wow. You're sitting in the friends and family section," John noted.

Mary raised her eyebrows. "Don't tell me there's nothing to discuss."

"You're not going out with one of those gorillas on the Kings, are you?" John asked.

"Gorillas? Excuse me?" Lizzie trained a frosty stare on him.

"I'm just sayin'"

"Whatever you're saying, John, please don't. Okay?"

"You can't be serious about this guy. Just a fling, right?" John asked.

"What business is that of yours?" Anger crept through her chest.

"He's not your equal," Martha said.

"I suggest you drop this right now. You don't know Nick. He's my choice, and I don't need your approval. Okay?

"Sorry, sorry. I didn't realize it was such a touchy subject," John responded.

His words infuriated her. "It's not a touchy subject. In fact, it's not a subject at all. It's my life and my choice."

"You're right. As long as you're happy, I'm good," Martha said, patting Lizzie's arm.

She took a deep breath. Was this going to happen everywhere?

"Martha's right. I'm sorry. I apologize. I don't know this guy. If you like him, that's good enough for me."

"Thanks, John." Lizzie gave him a small smile. Whew, she dodged that bullet. She glanced at her watch. The game would start in five minutes.

"Better get to my seat," she said.

They parted company. Lizzie found her row. She smiled as she had a perfect view of the forty-yard line. The announcer came on the loudspeaker and introduced the team. Lizzie stood up and cheered with the Kings' fans. Searching the men in uniform, she spied Nick and committed his number, 58, to memory. He waved and blew a kiss. The crowd cheered. Lizzie laughed, sensing her face turning red.

"Lucky girl. Nick's one of the nicest guys," said the woman sitting next to her. "Hi, I'm Stormy, Devon Drake's wife." The woman held out her hand.

Lizzie shook it. "Thank you. Nice to meet you."

"Same. This is going to be a tough game."

Lizzie gave one nod and turned her attention back to the field. Peace washed over her as she got comfortable being exactly where she belonged.

THE BOBCATS PUSHED Nick to his limit. Play got rough and he took a couple of hard hits, which meant pain in his future. He needed to soak, cold, then hot. But not tonight because Lizzie was waiting for him.

"Nick gets first shower," Trunk called.

The linebacker couldn't believe his buddy did that. Avoiding the chuckles from his teammates, Nick lowered his gaze and stepped under the warm spray. Bullhorn Brodsky broadcast to the whole team about Nick's dinner date with Liz. Hell, what are teammates for, right? Nick toweled himself off, wrapped it around his waist, and headed for his locker.

He took time dressing, even though it was six already. He wanted to look good, smell good, and boost his odds of winning Liz's trust and affection. He combed his hair five times.

"It's not getting any prettier, Jameson. Aren't you keepin' the lady waiting?" Trunk asked.

"Shit," Nick muttered when he checked his watch. Loping out to the parking lot, he snuck up behind her. At the touch of his hand on her shoulder, she jumped. He cleared his throat.

"You scared me," she said.

"Sorry," he replied.

She eyed him closely. "Are you okay? That was a rough game."

"I'll pay for it later. But I'm okay now."

"Sure made me nervous. A couple of times, I didn't know if you'd get up."

"Really? That shit happens all the time. Especially with the Bobcats."

"I'm glad you're not hurt."

"Me, too. Ready?"

She nodded.

"I'll follow you. I've got my car here."

She nodded. When they got to her place, he nabbed the bottle of wine in the back seat and reached her door as she was unlocking.

"This is for you," he croaked out, handing her the bottle.

"Thanks."

Nick stepped into the spacious apartment, decorated in country French in blue and white. His favorite colors. A small table, set for two, sported charming dishes trimmed in a small flower pattern. A candle sat, ready to be lit. Romantic, huh?

Lizzie bustled around, shoving something in the oven, bringing out a tray of cheese and crackers, and then tossed the corkscrew to him.

"Can you have a glass?" she asked.

"Not after a game, but you go ahead," he said, uncorking the bottle with ease.

Within a few minutes, a mouth-watering aroma filled the air.

"What's cooking?"

"A special dish my mother used to make. She called it her Stroganoff casserole."

"Smells great."

"I have ginger ale, Coke, Dr. Pepper. What would you like?"

"You have Dr. Pepper? I haven't had that since Nebraska."

"Coming right up. Take off your jacket. Get comfortable. Dinner's ready in ten minutes."

"Can I help?" he asked, more out of good manners than any desire to do anything. He was a bit tired after the game. He needed to refuel so he could rev up for the bedroom—if that was on the menu.

"Nope."

First, she brought the casserole to the table. Then the salad came next. A small basket with hot biscuits tempted him. Nick pulled out her chair, then sat down himself. She passed the hot dish, and he took a hefty helping. Everything looked and smelled damn good.

"When did you learn to cook?"

"When Daddy got sick."

"Your father got sick?"

"He got cancer. Lasted about two years."

"Oh, God. Lizzie, I'm so sorry. I didn't know." He took her hand.

"That's okay. It's been a while now."

"How's your mom?"

"She's bearing up. A year after Dad passed, she moved back with her sister in Arizona."

"Really?" Nick took a forkful of the most tender beef he had ever eaten.

"When Dad got sick, Mom had to earn the living. I'd drive down once a month and cook up a bunch of food for them for the freezer. I've become a pretty good cook."

"I'll say. Everything's delicious," he said, helping himself to a second roll.

"Thanks."

"Since we'd moved for Dad's job, there was no reason for her to stay in New Hampshire. Might as well be with relatives."

"Makes sense."

"Your folks still in Pine Grove?"

"Yeah. Dad is working fewer hours, but they're both pretty busy. And my sister and brother got places there, too."

"You're lucky to have sibs. I was it for my mom. Sometimes, it was a lot of pressure. With work and stuff."

"I bet."

"I didn't mind visiting her. Kind of miss her now that she's so far away."

"Do you ever think about us? What happened?"

"Of course. Not so much in recent years. I guess your silence put me off. I figured you'd had enough of this nerdy girl and had moved on to greener pastures."

He took her hand again. "There are no greener pastures. I was an idiot. I should have talked to you."

"Maybe it's not so bad. With so many years apart, we've had time to date others and know what we want."

"There you go, putting it in just the right words." He chuckled.

Liz pushed up from the table and stacked the dishes. Nick joined her.

"Can I help?"

"Not much to do. Cream puffs for dessert. They're in a box in the fridge. Can you grab that for me?"

"Sure," he said, retrieving the cardboard container.

"Coffee?"

"Just water. Thanks," he said.

When they were seated again, Nick looked at the confection on his plate and simply couldn't eat anymore.

"I'm stuffed. Can we save these for later?"

"Of course." Together, they put the dessert away and cleaned up the kitchen. As she dried the last dish, Nick came up behind her, placed his hands on her waist, and nuzzled her neck.

"Lizzie, baby. I want you back."

She turned to face him. "You sure?"

"I'm sorry I didn't find you sooner. Regret not calling you back. Yeah, I know you're a shitload smarter than me. So what? I like being with you. I want to have kids with a smart woman, not some dumbass with big tits."

"Mine aren't big enough?" she asked, stifling a grin.

"Stop. You know they are. You know what I mean. I never loved anyone the way I love you. You're the best, Lizzie. And I want the best."

"Nick," she muttered, leaning into him. He pulled her into his embrace and closed his lips over hers. Desire rose in him, blotting out everything else. She melted against him, her body molding to his. Lizzie tasted as good, felt as good and kissed even better than she had in high school. He wanted her with every fiber of his being.

He tightened his grip, holding her close. Breaking from her, he moved his lips to her shoulder then traveled north. He'd always loved her long, slender neck. Kissing his way up, he slid his hand over her breast. He'd swear it was bigger than it had been in high school. She didn't object, only moaned softly in his ear. He smiled. Looked like dessert would be served in the bedroom.

WHEN NICK'S HAND FOUND her breast, Lizzie's eyes drifted shut. Passion flamed up inside her, and old feelings resurfaced. He lowered his lips to hers again. Lord, the man had learned a crapload about kissing! Before she recouped her senses, his fingers dipped under her shirt.

She squirmed under the warmth and pressure of his fingertips on her bare flesh. Pressure gathered between her thighs. Lizzie wanted him bad, so bad. She doubted they'd make it to the bedroom. She loosened his tie, unbuttoned two shirt buttons, and slid her hand inside, flattening it against his rock-hard chest.

His flesh, warm to her cool hand, revved up her heat. Imagining the feel of his skin on different parts of her body sent a shiver up her spine?

"Cold?" he asked.

She shook her head, burying her face against his shoulder. He sloughed off his shirt and she locked her lips on a tender spot near his neck. God, he smelled good, and tasted, wow, like heaven. Curious to see him, she stepped back, giving him a chance to remove her shirt and bra. She smiled at his abrupt intake of breath as his gaze caressed her.

"More beautiful undressed, Lizzie. Like always."

"So are you," she replied.

He'd been a hunk in high school, but his body today dwarfed the past. The ache between her legs grew. She needed him inside her soon, like now.

He eased her down on the sofa.

"Please, Nick."

His brows rose.

"I don't want to wait. I'm sure you're an expert at foreplay, but, well, I mean..." Blood rushed to her face.

"I get it. You want me like I want you. You're right. Why wait?"

"I'm on the pill," she said.

"Fantastic," he said, pushing to his feet. While she lay there watching, he unbuckled his belt and shed his pants. What a sight he was, like an Adonis from a sculpture garden.

"Your turn. I'll help." He chuckled and unsnapped her jeans, making quick work of them along with her red panties.

A blush rose in his chest as he stared at her. Surprised, she squirmed under his scrutiny, covering herself with her arms.

"Are you shy? With me? It's Nick. Remember? Skinny-dipping in the lake, playing naked tag at midnight? Wearing away the material in the backseat of my dad's car?"

She laughed. Nick's sense of humor tickled her.

"Baby, I've waited a long time for this." She stretched out on the sofa, parting her legs. Nick lowered himself down between them. She wrapped her fingers around his erection, delighting in its power.

"Oh, God, baby. When you touch me. Shit."

He moaned, then closed his hands around her thighs and slid them up, meeting at her center. Now it was her turn to groan. She shut her eyes and let him explore her wetness. The pressure of his touch, the movement of his fingers dazed her. Paralyzed by excruciating desire, she let him ratchet up her fire with his hands, then his tongue.

"Nick! Oh, God. I'm gonna come."

"Go ahead. Do it," he said.

She tried to hold back, but he wouldn't stop until she went over the edge. Right before she fell off, he slid a finger inside her. Lizzie bucked her hips and gripped his shoulders hard.

"Nick," she blurted.

As if he read her mind, he was on top of her, then inside her. Oh, God, nothing had ever felt so good. They were still a perfect fit. Lizzie squeezed her eyes shut, focusing on the scent of him, the feel of him, the weight of him. He surrounded her, bringing intense pleasure with each thrust. Her body rocked with his.

"Baby, baby. Shit. Lizzie," he moaned into her hair. His hands braced his body while his lips nuzzled her ear, and his hips drilled his dick in and out. Every nerve in her body buzzed as electricity passed through her. Feelings put on ice, stuffed deep inside burst forth, spreading all the way to her toes, like melted chocolate.

"I can't hold it, honey," he whispered.

She chuckled. "Do it."

He tensed, thrust once more, then stopped. A low groan, ending in her name vibrated against her chest squished up against his. A lightness flowed through her. Could she fly? Float to the ceiling? Love filled her heart.

"Oh, God, Nick."

A grin spread her lips. Sensations she hadn't experienced in ten years warmed her. He kissed her neck, then her lips before pushing up. Sitting back on his haunches, his gaze swept over her.

"Beard burn," he said, shaking his head. "I'm sorry."

"Where?"

He gently touched her cheek then her chest.

"Doesn't hurt."

"It's all red," he said.

"Kiss it and make it better," she replied, shooting a seductive glance his way.

He shook his head, "You're such a flirt." He lowered his head and brushed his lips ever so softly against her chafed skin.

Nick rolled to the side, scooping her into his arms. "We've still got it."

"Thank God," she muttered as she snuggled up to him.

They lay in easy silence. She sighed. Their old comfort level returned, keeping her in lazy repose. Lizzie pushed up on her elbow to face Nick.

"Will you stay the night?"

"I have practice but not until one. I was hoping you'd ask."

She fell back against his pecs and hummed a favorite song.

"How about those cream puffs? Think they're still good?" he asked.

Chapter Five

Nick got his wish, to spend the night with Lizzie. They made love again that night and in the morning. Fresh from the best night's sleep he'd had in forever, Nick kicked butt at practice. He took Lizzie to dinner that night. From then on, they were together. Seesawing from one abode to the other, Nick and Lizzie drew closer.

Separated only when he was on the road, Nick woke up every morning thanking the Fates for bringing him to the coffee shop at the perfect time.

When he was home, sometimes Lizzie cooked, other times they had take-out, or Nick treated her to a restaurant meal. In all his years on his own, he'd never learned to cook.

If his relationship with Liz lasted, he'd learn to cook. He called his mom.

"Cooking lessons?" she asked.

"I'm dating Lizzie Wenner, Ma. She's a damn good cook. I'm gonna have to learn, too. Can't keep going out all the time."

He didn't mention to his mother that staying in meant more time in bed with Liz, but that plan had occurred to him. Why waste time driving to a restaurant and back? If he prepared something at home, they'd be right there for his kind of dessert, the one between the sheets.

"If you come home, I can teach you a few of our favorites. Otherwise, I could send you a book. *The Joy of Cooking* is a good place to start."

"Okay. Let me write that down." Nick punched the title into his phone. "I'll order it online, Ma."

"Okay. How are you?"

"Great."

"Things with Lizzie are okay?"

"Yeah, Ma. She doesn't care that I'm not as smart as her."

"Just be careful, Nick."

His jaw clenched. There it was, the same old crap. Setting his mouth in a frown, he opted for hanging up instead of arguing. "Gotta go, Ma. Take care. Say hi to Dad."

"Will do."

He ordered the book and tried to forget his mother tiptoeing into dangerous territory. Nick hated fighting with his parents, but they'd rarely admit they were wrong, especially to him.

This time, they were out of line. He refused to allow them to trash his relationship with Lizzie. After pushing negative thoughts out of his head, he took a deep breath. He'd never been this happy, and if his observations were correct, she appeared to feel the same.

Still, the disapproval of his parents lingered in the back of his mind. It would only cast a shadow on his relationship if he let it. When he was on the road, away from Lizzie for a few days, doubt crept in. As soon as he returned to her warm embrace, bad thoughts disintegrated into fine dust and blew away.

He'd never been a true partner with a woman—not the way he was with Lizzie. His life, which had always been about football and getting laid, morphed into football and Lizzie. Talking to her, listening to her, opened up his world. Every day he learned something new, picked up some tidbit of knowledge he hadn't had the day before. Sure, he could read the newspaper or books and learn, but how much more satisfying it was to stare into the clear gray eyes of a beautiful woman and let her words wash over him.

Nick spent time with Trunk and Carla. Being around a happy couple gave him hope. Lizzie seemed to like them, too, though they weren't exactly Rhodes scholars. Curiosity about her take on his life gnawed at him. His favorite places to talk were over the dinner table and in bed.

He rolled over, pushing up on his elbow. Lizzie lay on her back, her fingers closed around his upper arm.

"Do you like Trunk and Carla?" he asked, holding his breath.

"Hmm. Trunk and Carla. They're all right."

"Just okay?"

"I mean, they're your friends, you know?" She turned to face him. "I feel kind of stupid around them. I don't know much about football. They know the game inside and out. Sometimes when Trunk analyzes stuff—I don't have a clue."

"That's new for you, right? Not many things you don't know about. Right?"

She laughed. "You give me too much credit. There's plenty I don't know about. Like astrophysics."

"Astrophysics?" he asked.

"Yeah. And football."

"Football is easy. I can teach you."

"Would you?"

"Sure, baby. I can't imagine you feeling stupid about anything."

"I am about football. What's the difference between a pass play and a catch-and-run play?"

"Nothing. Just the words."

"Thank God. I thought I was losing it," she said.

"You'll never lose it, Lizzie."

"Why do they call him a running back when you have a wide receiver who runs, too?"

Nick chuckled. She didn't know crap about the game. Pride filled him. Finally, a subject he knew better.

"I've always wanted to teach you something. Now I can."

"Oh," she said, her voice dipping lower, "you've taught me a lot of things."

"Yeah?"

"How to make love," she cooed, inching closer, pressing her breasts against his chest. He grabbed her and slung his leg over her hips.

"Okay, lady. Time for another lesson," he said.

She sat up. "Wait. I think I need to practice my blow job."

"Go right ahead," he said, lying back, lacing his fingers behind his head.

LIZZIE FASTENED HER lips to his neck and kissed her way down his body. She lingered on his chest, flattening her palm against his pecs as she poked her tongue out and licked down the center.

Continuing her journey, she stopped at his shaft, which was hardening beneath her hand. She slipped it into her mouth. He rubbed her back while she sucked. With her free hand, she explored his balls.

Nick sighed. "You're getting damn good at this."

She picked up the pace a bit and increased the suction. His moans of pleasure penetrated to her bones. Liz couldn't keep her hands off his body. She touched him all the time. From hand holding to snuggling up in bed, physical contact with Nick Jameson jump-started her. His hands were warm and dry. When he touched her, his fingers sent warm tingles to her spine and below.

Settling for her less-than-mediocre physical response to Frank had been a mistake. She'd let habit take over, accepting substandard sex, affection, and love, instead of finding someone who could give her what she needed. Chagrined, she vowed never to accept anything less than the pleasure she got from Nick.

"Whoa. Stop, Lizzie." Nick eased her up.

"Ready?"

He chuckled. "You have to ask? What about you?" he asked, reaching between her legs. Nick took control, treating her body as if it belonged to him, which it did. He nudged her legs open and reached in farther. He slipped a finger inside her.

"Damn. Feels good. But you could be wetter," he said. He twirled her around until she was lying across the bed with her legs dangling off the side. He slid down to the floor on his knees and pulled her to him. Raising her legs to rest on his shoulders, he grasped her thighs and positioned her sex almost on the edge of the bed.

"That's better," he said, burying his face in her.

Lizzie cried out. "Nick! Damn, Nick. Jesus. Amazing."

His tongue swirled over her flesh while his thumbs held her open. He stuck it inside her, and she bucked. Running his fingers down her slit, he nodded.

"Yep. You're ready."

Since Lizzie had gone on the pill, he didn't need to bother with condoms. He pushed to his feet and gripped her hips, raising her just enough. Holding her steady with one hand, he used the other to point his dick right at her entrance. He eased in slowly. Lizzie closed her eyes to focus on the sensations he created. God, when he entered her, it was heaven. Only Nick could put out the fire inside her.

He pushed in all the way, holding her hips flush against his.

"Oh, baby. Damn. Lizzie," he moaned, stopping for a moment.

"Nick. Don't stop. Don't stop," she groaned.

He got into a rhythm, ratcheting her tension higher and higher, until an orgasm burst through her. Nick thrust a few more times, then reached his release. He held her to him for a few moments. Grateful to have their connection continue, Lizzie moaned.

Finally, he pulled out and loped to the bathroom. Lizzie straightened out, sliding under the sheet and turning on her side. She sighed and couldn't stop grinning. When Nick returned, he folded her in his embrace, resting her head on his chest.

"You're amazing, Lizzie," he said.

"No, you are."

"No, you."

"You," she said, poking his chest with her forefinger. "Will you give me football lessons?"

"Yeah. You're smart. You'll get it easy."

"No one is smart in everything. I'm a dummy in lots of things," she said, caressing his chest.

"Like what?"

"Like football."

"Okay. Name something else. And don't say astrophysics. That doesn't count."

"All right. I'm a dummy at standing up for myself."

"That's not a subject."

"Maybe not. But it's important. You can do it. Not me."

"We'll work on that. What else?"

"Don't know jack about geology. Can't tell an igneous rock from a sedimentary one."

"Okay. That's one. Name something else."

"Why are you doing this?"

"Because you're smart at everything, and I'm only smart at football," he said.

"You're smart at a lot more things. Does it matter? I mean, is book-learning that important?"

"It is to some people," he said.

"Not to me."

"Yeah? Then why were you dating some brainiac?"

She sat up. "You're way smarter than he is."

"Me?" His eyebrows shot up.

"You."

"Name one thing. One thing I'm smarter at than him. And don't say 'sex.'"

"You read my mind." She paused, raising her gaze to the ceiling. "You're smarter at life."

"What?"

"You heard me. Life. Getting along with people, being the best at what you do. Making good decisions. Making friends. Managing money. Everything. You're way better at that than I am or Frank, either."

He got quiet, his eyes serious. "You're not just saying that?"

"Have I ever lied to you?"

"You're a bad liar, I'll give you that. I wasn't smart about leaving you."

"That's a different story. That's the past. We've moved on."

"You really think I'm smarter about life?"

She nodded and yawned.

He laughed, kissed her head, and pulled up the blanket. "Thanks. Time for sleep. I got a game tomorrow."

Lizzie turned out the light, and sleep came quickly as she cuddled into his warmth.

BY SEPTEMBER, NICK and Lizzie had settled into a routine. On the road, Nick hung with Trunk and some of the other married guys. He didn't want to be lured into a strip club. After dinner, he'd hang around the hotel bar, or go to a local bar that had pool or darts. He didn't drink but went for the companionship.

He couldn't believe how quickly Lizzie had become a fixture in his life. After away games, he couldn't wait to get home. She'd be there, cooking, looking like Harriet Housewife and his heart flipped.

Life was a jigsaw puzzle with moving pieces. She worked during the week and he on weekends. She worked nights, correcting papers, he watched game films in his den. They even shared meal responsibility. Nick tore into *The Joy of Cooking* and attempted a new dish once a week. Sometimes he had success, other times she bailed them out by ordering a couple of pizzas.

Even his parents had calmed down. They'd stopped criticizing his relationship. Maybe they'd accepted Lizzie? Nick breathed a sigh of relief. Turning away from his family would be hard, but he'd committed to her. His father substituted his critical comments for the Kings' muffed plays.

The night before a game in Miami, Trunk, Nick, Bullhorn Brodsky, and Devon Drake headed to a movie theater. While they waited for the movie to begin, Trunk faced Nick.

"When the fuck are you gonna get married?"

"Married? Who said anything about marriage?"

"Obviously, not you," Trunk replied.

"Yeah. Propose already. Geez. You got the girl. What's the problem?" Bull asked.

"It's not that simple," Nick said.

"Yes, it is. You ask her. She says yes, and you buy a ring. Bingo," Trunk said.

"We come from two different places."

"So what? So does everyone. That's just an excuse," Devon piped up.

"Are any of you married to a brain? A college professor?"

"No. So what? A family is a family. You have kids. That'll give you a lot in common," Bull put in.

"Kids?" Nick's voice raised an octave.

"Slow down, Bull. This guy hasn't even popped the question yet," Trunk said.

"Don't be an asshole. If you don't ask her, someone else will. She's hot," Devon said.

"Keep your eyes off Lizzie."

"Don't get defensive. It was a compliment. I'm married and faithful," Devon replied.

"Okay, okay. I get it. I'll think about it."

"Think about it soon. You're not getting any younger." Trunk chuckled.

"Marry her before you get a career-ending injury," Bull advised.

The lights dimmed and the movie came on, but Nick couldn't stop thinking about his teammates' advice. What would Lizzie do if he got a career-ending injury? She's the kind that would stick, but still. Things wouldn't be the same. What if she left him? Could he blame her? Worry gathered in his mind. Life without football and Lizzie would be unbearable.

After the movie he'd barely paid attention to, he rushed back to his room and dialed Liz.

"Hi, baby. Whatcha doin'?"

"Reading. You?"

"Went to the movies with the guys. Kinda relaxes us before a game. Listen, I was wondering. I know I shouldn't do this over the phone. But. Well. We get along so great and stuff. And I'm not gettin' any younger." He paused. Sweat gathered on his forehead.

"Yes? What is it?"

"Will you marry me?" came out in a rush. He grabbed a hand towel and wiped his face.

"What?"

"Marry me, Lizzie. I love you, baby. Let's tie the knot."

"You are proposing over the phone?"

"I don't want to waste time."

She laughed. "You are one unpredictable man, Nick Jameson."

"Well? Will you?"

"Not exactly romantic proposal of the year."

"I know. I'm sorry. Still? What do you say?"

"I say, *yes*. Does that make you happy?"

A huge grin broke out on his face. He mopped his brow again. "Yeah. It does. That's the right answer."

"Good. Now you can sleep?"

"How'd you guess?"

She laughed. "You're not exactly hard to read."

"Cause I'm not smart?"

"Stop that! You are smart. No. Because I know you so well."

"Oh. That's okay then."

"I love you, Nick. Take care of yourself. Don't take chances. Come home in one piece."

"I love you, too, Lizzie. I'll be okay."

"Good luck."

"Thanks. Goodnight, pretty lady."

"'Night."

Nick plopped down on the bed. Damn! He was an engaged man. He was getting married. And to the best, the smartest, girl in the world. Holy shit! His lips wouldn't stop smiling. Sweat continued to pour down his cheeks.

He checked the clock. It was ten. Too late to tell the guys. He'd have to break the news at breakfast. His shoulders felt light. He jumped up and twirled around, then peeled off his clothing. He washed up and slid between the sheets. Lizzie Wenner was going to be his wife. She'd be with him for the rest of his life, no matter what.

Relief rocketed through his veins. Now that he had his personal life sewn up, time to get back to thinking about football. He grabbed his phone, pulled up a video of the Miami team, and watched the quarterback and wide receivers until his eyelids got heavy. Turning off his phone, he doused the light and shut his eyes. Damn, an engaged man. He could hardly believe it. Could he get any luckier?

The next morning, after his shower, a shave, and packing his bag, he bounded down to breakfast. A buffet was set up in a private dining room. Two other players were there, eating. Nick filled his plate to overflowing. Bursting with the news, he shifted in his seat, and gobbled down bacon and eggs, waiting for the rest of his teammates.

When everyone was there, he rose, holding a juice glass, and tapping it with his knife. The clinking stopped the chatter among the men. They turned their attention to Nick.

"I have an announcement."

The room quieted.

"Stepping aside from the millions of women hot for this body, I have made a decision. I have proposed to Dr. Liz Wenner and been accepted. Yes, I know. I did it on the phone. I flunk romantic proposals. But I did it for the team. Now I can focus on the game. And I'm now an engaged man."

Trunk, Bull, and Devon stood up, clapping. Then the rest followed. Hoots, salacious comments about Nick's past and his dick filled the air. He couldn't stop smiling. On the way to the bus to the stadium, every teammate patted him on the rump or high-fived.

When the bus stopped, Nick headed for the locker room. Pumped from the happy reception he'd received from his buddies, his spirits soared. He changed into his uniform in two minutes, chomping at the bit to take down the enemy. Energy flowed through him as he ran out on the field, ready to demolish the Miami Sharks.

Chapter Six

Lizzie put down her cell and sank down on the bed. Engaged? Could it be real? Did he mean it? She didn't know whether to whoop for joy or scratch her head. Nick didn't sound drunk. Besides, he didn't drink before a game. Then it was true, wasn't it?

She fanned out the fingers of her left hand and stared. Nope, no ring there.

"You can still be engaged without a ring. We're engaged." Excitement stole up her torso. She grinned and picked up her phone.

"Carly, can you come over?"

"Is something wrong?"

"No, everything is incredibly right."

"Be there in ten."

Lizzie jumped up and paced. So much to do. Tomorrow, the Kings would play the Sharks at four. She'd celebrate at home. A feast with Carly and watching the game. After all, her little grin grew wide, her fiancé would be playing.

"Fiancé. Fiancé. I'd like you to meet Nick Jameson, my fiancé," she said as she ambled past the front window. "This is Nick. He's my fiancé." She giggled.

A knock jolted her out of her fantasy. She tightened the sash on her robe and glanced at the clock. Almost ten thirty, she should be in bed. Sleep? No way, she'd be up all night. After all, how many times do you get engaged in your lifetime? Oh, sure, some did it four or five times, but this was the first and would be the last for Lizzie.

"Coming," she called out. She swung the door open so fast and hard it banged against the wall. Putting her hand over her mouth, she stifled a giggle.

Carly's eyes widened. "What's up? Are you okay? You scared me to death."

"I think I just got engaged. I had to tell someone. I'm sorry if you were in bed."

"Engaged? To Nick?"

Lizzie nodded.

"That's awesome! Where's the ring? Where is he, in the bathroom? Or did he faint?"

"He's in Miami."

"Miami?"

"He asked me over the phone."

"Really?" Carly's eyebrows shot up.

"Yes, I know. It's not the most romantic proposal. For some reason, he was in a hurry. It had to be tonight. I'll find out when he gets home."

"Whatever. That doesn't matter. He proposed and you said yes?"

"Yep."

"Wow. That's fantastic. Congratulations," Carly said, hugging Lizzie.

"Thanks. I think. I just hope I didn't dream it."

"Call him back. Ask."

"He's probably asleep. Game tomorrow. Will you watch with me? It's at four. I'll supply food and drink."

"I'd love to. Can I bring Sam?"

"New boyfriend?"

Carly nodded.

"Please do. I'd love to meet him." Lizzie twirled once. "I can't believe I'll be watching my *fiancé* on television tomorrow."

"Awesome!"

The women giggled.

"I've got to get back," Carly said, glancing at Lizzie's clock.

"Sam there?"

"Yeah."

"You left him in bed, waiting for you?"

"Friends. You know."

Lizzie hugged her. "You're the best. Now get back in there and make his dreams come true."

Carly scurried out, leaving Lizzie alone with her thoughts. She poured a glass of wine and picked up the phone. Time to call home.

"Mom?"

"Liz?"

"Yes. I have news. Good news."

"Oh?"

"I'm going to marry Nick Jameson."

"That big ape? Really, Lizzie. What happened to that nice young man? What was his name?"

"Frank? I dumped him."

"Why? Honestly, I'd think you'd be happy to have such a smart fellow agree to go out with you."

"Mother."

"Oh, I know those football types. Handsome. Sweep you off your feet. Though why he'd marry you when he could have any model or actress he wanted. Still. What happens when the bloom is off the bedroom? He'll be looking for another nest to feather. And what will you talk about? Honestly, Liz. He's not your speed at all."

"I thought you'd be happy for me."

"Happy? To see you make the biggest mistake of your life?"

"I love him. And he loves me."

"That's what he says, *now*. But mark my words. In six months, he'll be tomcatting around."

"Not Nick. Why can't you believe he loves me?"

"Because you have nothing in common. And on the internet, well, you saw who he was dating. How he came to find you again and make this silly gesture is beyond me."

Lizzie's eyes filled.

"Don't worry, Mom. I won't bother you about the wedding."

"Wedding? I doubt it will last long enough for you to get to the altar."

Tears spilled over, running down her cheeks. She took a deep breath. "Oh, it will. We'll get married. Our own way. Without you. Because Nick Jameson and I are meant to be. You'll see."

"I hope you're right dear. I'd hate to see you unhappy. Past my bedtime. Thanks for the call."

Lizzie stood staring at the phone. With a shaking hand, she picked up the glass and downed the liquid. She checked the clock. Eleven. Too late to call Nick.

What her mother said was wrong, right? Nick wouldn't find someone new six months after they married, would he? He really loved her, didn't he?

She washed up and sat on her bed. She hugged the stuffed bear Nick had given her. Lying down, she kept the bear tight to her chest. She believed him and trusted her instincts. Hadn't she done enough second-guessing of their relationship in the past three months? Hadn't she been happier than she ever thought possible?

Words from her grandmother, who'd passed when Lizzie was twenty, came to mind.

"Can't let others steer your path. Take the helm. Carve your own path, your own way. Then don't complain, if things don't work out. But give yourself a pat on the back when things go good."

Lizzie sighed. She picked up the framed picture of her and Nick at the beach. He looked so handsome, tall and strong. She couldn't have looked happier, tucked under his arm, smiling. Yes, that's who they were—no matter what anyone said. Lizzie and Nick, forever.

She switched off the light and lay in the dark, still holding the animal. He was her Nick, and always had been. No matter what anyone said, she'd never love another the way she loved Nick. And she truly believed he felt the same way. Anyway, she hoped he did, with all her heart.

THE KINGS BEAT THE Sharks, fourteen to ten. The defense worked their butts off defending their paltry lead. After the game, Nick was exhausted. The team grabbed dinner, then headed for the airport to fly home.

On the plane, Nick looked at diamond rings online. One of the stewardesses helped him pick out settings and find a reputable jeweler. His teammates offered to take him into town after practice to get the ring.

The bus didn't arrive at the stadium until one thirty in the morning. Nick got home at two and crashed. Practice wasn't until eleven. He rose at nine and picked up a couple of egg sandwiches on the way to the stadium. There hadn't been time to call Lizzie until he took a break in the weight room.

"Hi, baby. I'm back. Can I take you to dinner tonight?"

"Sure. Say, did we really get engaged? Or was I dreaming?"

He laughed. "It was real. And tonight, we'll make it official."

"Okay."

"Seven good?"

"Fine."

"Can you meet me at the Sweet Magnolia?"

"Works for me."

"See you then."

He finished his workout and headed for the stadium. Coach Bass went over the mistakes from yesterday's game. The team practiced a few plays, learned a new trick play, and finished at four.

Nick had to hurry to get to the stores before they closed. Devon Drake, Trunk, and Bull Brodsky shuffled him into Trunk's SUV, and they headed for town. After looking at rings on the plane ride home, Nick had an idea what he wanted. Wham! There it was, the perfect ring for his Lizzie. It had a large round diamond with two smaller ones on either side. The band was platinum with a matching wedding band.

He bought it and tucked the tiny box in his jacket pocket. Driving to the Magnolia, Nick rehearsed what he was going to say. He figured he'd better work it out because he wasn't much of a spontaneous speaker. If emotions ran high, his words would tangle up like the gangly legs of a newborn wild turkey.

He managed to arrive only minutes before Lizzie. He ordered a bottle of champagne and closed his fingers around the velvet box. Sweat broke out on his forehead. He mopped his face as he mumbled the words he'd practiced. Even his palms sweated.

He glanced at the archway, and his mouth went dry. There she was in a pale pink dress that hugged her slim frame. He stood as she approached.

"Lizzie, you look beautiful."

"Thank you."

The waiter poured the champagne.

"Give us about ten minutes, okay?" Nick said to the man.

Nick raised his glass. "To us."

"To us," she said, taking a sip.

Nick cleared his throat and took a gulp of water. It was now or never. Time to man up.

"Lizzie, you were the girl of my dreams when I was seventeen. Then we lost each other. Probably my fault. Whatever. Doesn't matter. But we were lucky enough to find each other again. Not many people have a second chance after they've fucked up the first one."

She chuckled.

"I mean, I've gone out with a lotta girls, but none came close to you. You're classy, beautiful, and smart. And you like me, which helps." He took another drink. "I'm not as dumb as I look—" He stopped and raised his hand when she started to object. "Wait. Hear me out. I mean I've learned some stuff. Learned not to take someone like you for granted. And not to take the chance that I might lose you, again. Maybe forever. I love you, Lizzie, with all my heart. So, please, marry me. Say you'll be my wife, and we can be together forever." When he finished, he slid from the chair to one knee in front of her. With his thumb, he flipped open the little box.

The diamond gleamed in the candlelight from the table. Numbed into silence, his heart racing and his hand trembling, Nick snapped out of it when Lizzie gasped.

"Oh my God, Nick. It's so beautiful."

"Not as beautiful as you," he said. "So, will you?"

"Will I?"

"Be my wife? Pay attention, Lizzie." His tone soft, Nick cupped her cheek and smiled into her eyes.

"Hard to do that when you flash a rock like that at me. Yes, I will. Oh, yes. Nick. I love you so much."

He slipped the ring on her finger. When people in the restaurant applauded, tears flowed down Lizzie's cheeks. Nick slipped her his handkerchief. She studied the ring, splaying her fingers wide and holding it this way and that. A grin stole up on his face. The ring was perfect.

"It's so beautiful. So big! I mean, you shouldn't have. Something smaller would have been fine."

"But fine isn't good enough for you." He kissed the back of her hand.

LIZZIE WENT HOME WITH Nick. Since he didn't have a game the next day, they stayed up until three making love then talking about their future.

"I think we should live here. My house is bigger," Nick said, leaning back against the bed.

"But it's a long way for me to go to school every day."

"You teach every day?"

She nodded, then rested her head against his bare chest again.

"Hmm. How about, August to the end of December, we live here. It's football season. But in January, we move to your place and stay there until June."

"That might work. What about July?"

"We take a vacation. At the end of the month and for a couple of weeks in August, I have training camp. Don't know where it'll be next year."

"You'll be gone?" Lizzie sat up.

"Yep. Just a couple of weeks."

"I don't teach in the summer."

"Maybe you can come with me. I'll ask."

"Good. Not going to like having you gone for weeks," she said, lying back down.

Nick stroked her back, as she snuggled into him.

"Maybe you'll be happy to get rid of me for a while. We're gonna get married. We'll be together, just not every day."

"You go on the road during the season, too, don't you?"

"Yep."

"I've lived alone for a long time. I'll be fine. I can handle you being gone for a few days here and there."

"It's a pretty tight schedule. Lots of practice between games."

"I guess. Never thought about it."

"They don't pay us a shitload of money for nothing. We gotta win. That takes practice."

"It's fine. I have papers to grade, syllabus to prepare. I'll be busy."

"Yeah, and in the spring, you'll be the one leaving me alone in front of the tube while you work."

She smiled. "Guess it works out."

"Don't worry about me. I can always watch porn," he said.

She gave him a playful slap. "Porn? Without me?"

"Maybe we'll make our own movies."

"Me? No way. Uh-uh. Nope." She shook her head.

Nick laughed. "Just teasin'. It's so easy to get you riled."

Lizzie rolled onto her stomach. She gazed into Nick's eyes. They changed color slightly when he was up to mischief. She made a note of that. When they were married, he'd never be able to pull anything over on her. His eyes would give him away.

"How about riling me up in another way?"

"Oh? You read my mind," he said, holding her face while he kissed her.

Lizzie's mind went blank, in a good way, as she let her fiancé work his steamy magic on her body. When they finished, Nick snapped off the lights, and they hunkered down together.

Liz had wondered how long it would take to adjust to having him in bed with her all night. Hah! She didn't need to worry. Within two days, she'd gotten used to Nick's large presence on the other side. His soft breathing soothed her, bringing sleep. He had a better bed, too. Resting close to him, touching him all night long, warmed her heart.

The next morning, after Nick left for practice, Lizzie made the dreaded call to her mother.

"You're really marrying *him*?"

"Yes, Mom. And I'm happy about it."

"At least the guy's got bucks."

"Mom! I'm not marrying him for his money. I do pretty well at Yale, you know."

"Do you? That's good. Save your money. Let him pay. Keep it separate. Then, if he leaves you for a younger woman, you'll have some money to take care of yourself. You can't be too careful."

Lizzie frowned, and her stomach roiled. "Thanks for your vote of confidence."

"I'm a truth-teller. I tell it like I see it. Those models, well, they've got some assets..."

"I get it, Mom."

"You might get one of those sex manuals, too. I'm guessing you might need to learn some stuff. That guy is probably pretty experienced. You're not. That could be a problem."

Lizzie bit her lip. "I've gotta go. I've got a ton of things to do."

"Don't forget to invite me to the wedding."

"Yeah. Right. Bye, Mom."

Damn cell phone. Can't slam them down when you want to. Her mother didn't say a word about wanting to do anything for the wedding or even send her a few dollars toward it. She poured another cup of coffee and sank into a chair in the kitchen. Shame heated her cheeks and tears stung behind her eyes. How could she tell Nick that her mother hadn't offered to help with the wedding? Humiliation filled her.

Fortunately, Lizzie had money saved up. She'd accumulated a little rainy-day fund and it was pouring. No need to invite a lot of people. Nick had a ton of friends, but Lizzie only had a handful from the English department at Yale, Carly and a few other folks. Oh, yes, and her mother. Suddenly, planning a wedding became a burden.

How could she make a go of a marriage when her own flesh-and-blood didn't think she had a chance? Lizzie took a deep breath. She would. She'd fool her mom, just like she had about school. Sipping her drink, she recalled two conversations from years ago.

"Honor society? You'll never make the honor society, Elizabeth. A few good grades aren't enough."

"If you can convince your father to waste fifty bucks applying to Yale, who am I to say you can't get in? But, Yale? Really? A waste. Money down the drain," she'd said, shaking her head.

Every time her mother had tried to discourage her from doing anything, Lizzie had prevailed. She'd shown her up every single time. Liz clenched her teeth. She didn't need her approval. She didn't need anyone's approval. It would have been nice if her father had still been alive. At least he'd have walked her down the aisle.

She narrowed her eyes and tightened her jaw. She'd keep Nick, no doubt about that. Remembering her mother's comment about Lizzie's sexual knowledge, a rueful grin rimmed her lips. If she only knew! She had to laugh at that. Once again, Mom didn't know best.

Pushing up from the table, Liz consoled herself with the fact that she'd found a man who truly loved her and would protect and care for her for the rest of her life. What more could any woman want? She sighed. Her mother's jealousy wasn't going to rain on her parade. She had Nick, Yale, and the life she wanted. What could be better?

Chapter Seven

In the locker room, Nick's teammates gathered around to congratulate him.

"A college professor, damn!" Bull said.

"A brainiac, who'd have suspected that of Nick?" Buddy Carruthers, wide receiver, added.

"Yeah. And she's a doctor, too," Nick said.

"Can she examine my shoulder and tell me why it's sore?" Devon Drake asked.

"She's not examining anything on any of you guys. Quit asking. Besides, she's not that kind of doctor."

With the back-patting finished, the men headed to the field for practice. Nick's energy level hit an all-time high. His running time had improved. He took down every man he aimed for, he was on his game. If being engaged pumped him this much, what would being married do? Whatever it was, he was ready, all set for the whole shebang, except telling his parents.

He had to do it but put it off until he was heading home. He turned into a vacant lot and pulled out his cell phone. With a sigh, he dialed. He had to face it sooner or later.

"Hi, Dad. Guess what? I'm getting married."

"Married? To who, Nick? That Ann model with the big tits."

"To Lizzie Wenner."

"Who?"

"You heard me. Lizzie Wenner."

"Where the hell did you find her?"

Before he could answer, his mother picked up the extension. "Married? That's great, Nick."

"I ran into Lizzie in New Haven a couple of months ago."

"You've been dating?" his mother asked.

"Yeah."

"It's not exactly dating anymore, Martha. Now it's hooking up," his father said with a salacious laugh.

"It's not like that," Nick protested.

"Of course not. I'm glad it's Lizzie. Always liked her. Smart girl. Smart to catch you, too," his mother said.

"She didn't catch me, Ma. We caught each other. She's got a doctorate now. She's a prof at Yale."

"What does she want with you? Must be money," his dad piped up.

"No. It's not about money. Nothing like that. Lizzie's not like that. She does pretty good on her own. It's love, Pop. Hard as that is for you to believe."

"When's the wedding? Ralph, I have to get a new dress. Please keep us in the loop, Nick."

"I don't know shit about a wedding. We're getting married's all. No date set."

"Good luck, son. You'll need it."

"Ralph! What kind of thing is that to say?"

"It's the truth, Martha. Nick's got a couple of good earning years left, if he doesn't get hurt. Then what's he gonna do? You'd better save your money, son. Because when football is done with you, you won't be able to earn shit. Good luck with the girl. Hope it works out. I'll be talkin' to you," his dad said and hung up.

Nick begged off and put down his phone. His shoulders sagged. He had to admit that his father was correct. If Nick got tossed from football, what the hell would he do for a living? What fancy professor from one of the top schools in the country wants to be married to a football has-been who has trouble bending over to tie his shoes?

He grabbed a Coke from the fridge, toed off his Nike's and flopped down on the sofa. He turned on the remote, but nothing caught his eye. What exactly were they gonna do when football was through with Nick? He'd saved and had a tidy nest egg, but was it enough to support them for thirty years? Probably not. And he'd be washed up. Would he be one of those old football players who can't talk about anything but the play he made that saved the game, fifteen years ago? He shivered.

The image clutched at his gut. His stomach flipped. He took a long swig of his drink and rested his head on the sofa arm. Lizzie could do better. Better than him. Even a trash collector belonged to a union, made union wages, and couldn't get fired on a whim or even be too old to do his job when he was forty. Where would Nick be when he was forty? Out of a job and trying to build a new life. And what about Lizzie? They'd probably have a kid or two. She'd be riding the crest of her career while Nick would be washed up on the shore, like a beached whale.

He shut his eyes tight and paid attention to his breathing. Maybe marrying Lizzie was a selfish thing to do? Maybe she should be free to find someone better suited, someone with a more secure future? She could have said no, he argued with himself. She didn't have to say she loved him, she didn't have to accept his proposal. Lizzie was smart enough to know that nothing was secure or safe—at least not forever. She'd picked him. He should be flattered. If he was selfish, so what? He'd do everything he could to give her a good life. He'd make sure she didn't regret marrying him. But he wouldn't walk away, wouldn't give his father the satisfaction, or rob himself of the woman he loved. His father was shit, and that was a fact.

Nick finished the soda and pushed to his feet. He was the luckiest man alive to be marrying Lizzie Wenner. Now he'd better start acting like it. Ending his pity party, Nick bounced back. He went down to the gym in his finished basement and worked out for an hour.

DETERMINED NOT TO BE a wimp, Lizzie tackled the giant grill in Nick's backyard.

"I'm a professor at Yale. I have a doctorate. This is just a stupid grill. I *can* and I *will* figure out how to use the damn thing." She placed a platter with marinated meat on the wooden picnic table a few feet from the grill. She approached the contraption with dread and determination. After a thorough examination, she jumped right in. First she opened the propane tank valve, next she lifted the cover, and third, she turned the handle. Nothing happened. She tried the other handles and reached the correct one on her third try.

Breathing a sigh of relief, she adjusted the flame, turned on the other two and plopped the meat in the center. A smug smile of satisfaction graced her lips. She jumped as a masculine voice broke the silence.

"I see you mastered the grill. Impressive."

She turned to see Nick grinning.

"I did."

"I'm proud of you. That thing's tricky."

"I know! I had to try all three burners before I found the right one."

"Whatcha cookin'?"

"Steak."

"My favorite."

"I know."

They chatted about the events of their day while Lizzie cooked and Nick set the table. Peace flowed through her. Weaving her life with his through shared activities brought her dream into focus. This would be life with Nick. She had never wanted fireworks, except maybe in the bedroom. Lizzie had preferred reliable friends and lovers over exotic ones. Nick was right up that alley.

"How was practice?"

"Must have been Coach's time of the month. He bit everyone's head off."

"That's too bad. He's not usually like that?"

"Nah. He's easy going. Buddy said it's his kid, Butch. Said he's a terrible two and is driving Coach nuts. Coach's wife is pregnant with their second, so a lot of the shit with the first falls on Coach Bass."

"That might be you someday," she said, turning the meat.

Nick cozied up behind her, snaking his arms around her waist. He nuzzled her neck. "Fine with me. In fact, we can practice making a baby after dinner."

"Sounds like a plan," she said as her pulse kicked up.

He let her go to serve the meal. They had skirt steak, potatoes cooked on the grill and salad. Nick held out her chair. As he dug into his food, Lizzie broached a new topic.

"Some of my friends in the department want to have a little engagement party for me."

"Yeah? Nice," he said, between bites.

"It would be small. Maybe ten people?"

"Sounds good."

"So you don't object?"

"Why should I object?"

"They're all Yale staff," she said, cutting off a piece of meat.

"So? Your friends might become my friends, too."

"That's right." She leaned over and kissed him. He had a good attitude, which she hoped he'd keep after being thrust into the college professor environment. Nick was amazing, her friends had to see how much he loved her. She sighed. It would be a pretest before she had to tackle the real one—her mother.

"I talked to my parents. My mom's gonna buy a new dress. We should set a date."

"Good idea. How's your schedule?"

"If we make the playoffs, everything changes. I mean the timing. And then there's the Super Bowl, in February."

"So we can't plan a wedding until after the Super Bowl?"

"That depends. You and I can get married whenever we want. I don't care if my parents come. Or my teammates, either. I mean it would be nice but, well, not necessary. Not for me. The only necessary person is you."

Lizzie put a piece of potato into her mouth. She digested his words as she chewed her food. She hadn't considered a wedding with only the two of them, without her mother or his family. Her brow smoothed, and her shoulders relaxed into their normal position.

"Now that's a great idea," she said.

"I thought so. Takes a lot of the wedding craziness shit out of the picture."

"Sure does. I'd rather get married without my mother."

"Yeah? Good. So we can plan to get married whenever you want. We'll have the honeymoon in February. How's that sound?"

Relief filled her. "That's perfect, Nick. Just perfect."

"I'll wear a tux, if you want me to."

"No, no, be comfortable. Do you have a black suit?"

He nodded.

"That'll work. I'll buy a new dress and a nosegay."

"Nosegay? What the hell is that?"

"It's a small bouquet of flowers."

"Oh. One of those fancy words?"

"Yes, I'm sorry," she said, touching his arm.

"Don't apologize. I just learned a new word. Can't wait to spring it on the guys," he chuckled.

Lizzie smiled.

HER FRIENDS HAD SCHEDULED the engagement party on a Friday night. Nick discovered he had a bye week that week—no game. He picked up his black suit from the cleaner and laid it flat in the trunk of his car. Nick had tossed off the engagement party as if it didn't concern him at all. But now, a few hours before, he sweated bullets.

Trying to make small talk, with people who could think rings around him, tongue-tied Nick. How could he speak when he could barely swallow? He'd asked his Kings' buddies for ideas.

"You can always say, 'how about those Mets?'," Trunk suggested.

"I don't think they know who the Mets are," Nick said.

"Everyone knows the Mets," Buddy said.

"Maybe. Something else. Something else. Come on, guys."

"Ask if they've seen the new exhibit at a museum," Bull said.

"Which museum?"

"Any museum."

"The Metropolitan, maybe?" Griff asked. "It's an art museum."

"Bingo. The Metropolitan. Then I can ask them if they liked it. If they'd recommend it," Nick replied.

"That's the idea. Listen to what they're sayin'. Ask questions. People love to talk about themselves. So ask them questions," Trunk said.

"Perfect. Yes. I'll do that. Not like, 'what's your favorite color?' but other stuff."

"You've got it," Bull said, slapping his buddy on the back.

Confidence washed through Nick after that session. Now that the event was here, it all disappeared, and he was left standing, emotionally naked, in a room full of snobs. He met Lizzie at the faculty lounge, where the event was taking place. Dressed in a navy-blue suit, white shirt, and red tie, Nick fidgeted with the collar. Had he put on weight? Why did it seem so tight?

Looking beautiful in peach-colored chiffon, Lizzie opened the door.

"Nick! You look so handsome. Come in, honey. Come in."

Did a trip to the electric chair feel like this? Lizzie tugged on his arm, leading him into a large room. Not surprised to see the place packed, Nick knew she was well-liked. While that was a good thing, did so many of her faculty friends have to show up? Five people would have been perfect. But thirty-five set his heart rate faster and his mouth to desert dry.

"Oh, you must be Nick?" asked an attractive woman, clutching a drink.

"Emily Carton, this is Nick Jameson," Lizzie said, frowning.

"Oh, Lizzie, this one's a keeper. Such a big, strong man." She extended her hand. Nick shook it. When she held on a little too long, he extracted his from hers as gently and tactfully as he could. Though used to women coming on to him, Nick didn't expect that from this crowd.

"Yes, he is. And all mine, Emily." Lizzie snaked her arm around his waist. Emily smiled and backed away.

"Guess you're not the only educated woman who likes beefy guys."

"Don't get any ideas," Lizzie said, mischief in her eyes.

"Babe, no one could compare to you. Did I tell you how beautiful you look?" He leaned over and placed a kiss on her cheek.

A waiter came by with a tray of champagne. Having a week off gave him an excuse to imbibe some alcohol. After Nick took one, a man tapped on his glass with a knife, drawing everyone's attention. He made a short speech that ended in a toast. The crowd lifted their glasses to the couple. Heat headed for Nick's face. No way to melt into this crowd, especially since he'd been singled out. He took a swig of the bubbly liquid, hoping it would calm his nerves.

Lizzie introduced everyone to Nick. Names flashed by him quicker than he could remember them. People smiled, welcoming him into the group. Astonished at the warmth of the greeting, Nick's stomach muscles relaxed enough for him to eat some hors d'oeuvres.

"You're getting a great lady," one older man said.

"Who's that?" Nick whispered to Liz.

"My boss. The department head. Remember?"

"Nope. Too many people and titles," he replied.

"So, who's going to win the Super Bowl, Nick? I'm a betting man," another older man asked.

"I think the Kings have an excellent chance this year."

Nick fell into a discussion of the teams playing with a man he didn't know. Another came over and joined in. He noticed the women admiring Lizzie's ring. Heads together, they chatted, and Lizzie turned several shades of red. Nick figured the subject was sex. Now there was a topic he could talk about all night. Might give some of the nerdier guys a few tips. He chuckled.

Taking the advice of his teammates, he didn't have more than one glass of champagne. Without a game for two weeks, it would have been okay, but he wanted to be alert and not say or do something stupid because of booze.

The food was great. Waiters passed with trays of bite-sized quiches and figs wrapped in bacon. A food table held artistically displayed crudités, cheese cubes, crackers, olives and bricks of various cheeses. Nick filled a small plate and chowed down. Lizzie strolled up next to him. He picked up a cheese cube with a toothpick and offered it to her. She closed her lips over it, keeping eye contact with him. His temperature shot up. Was that a promise for later?

"These people are pretty nice," Nick said.

"See? I told you they were nothing to be afraid of."

"I wasn't scared. Not exactly."

"You were terrified. Admit it."

"Maybe a little nervous. Intimidated?"

Lizzie laughed, then kissed him on the lips. "You're such a faker."

He held her close. She smelled of spring lilacs, making him wish they were alone.

"Big ape. Sex. That's all you're good for. When Elizabeth gets tired of fucking you, you're history."

Nick's head snapped up. A man stood behind Liz, holding a large glass of champagne.

"Who the fuck are you?"

"Frank. Her boyfriend."

"What?" Nick's eyebrows shot up.

"Frank. What the hell are you doing?" Lizzie turned, shielding Nick.

The room quieted down. People froze.

"I'm calling a spade a spade. He's a Neanderthal. Good for only one thing. When you get tired of that, call me. When you want to have an intelligent conversation, call me."

Anger shot through Nick. He grabbed the smaller man by the lapels and fisted his hand.

"That's right. Beat the shit out of me. That's what Neanderthals do."

Nick released him.

"Can't argue your way out of this, can you? Elizabeth is way out of your league. And you know it. She's so much smarter than you, it makes your head spin. Well, she's not smarter than me. Go ahead. Fuck your brains out. When she's done, she'll come back to me."

Lizzie slapped Frank across the face.

He stepped back. An evil grin spread across his face. "Gotta hide behind her? Have her do your dirty work?"

Like a match to gasoline, Nick ignited. He pushed Lizzie out of the way and grabbed Frank. Dragging him to the door, he said, "You wanna take this outside?"

Lizzie ran after him, pulling on his arm. "Don't. Nick. Leave him. He's a bug. A cockroach."

Nick corralled his temper and stepped back. "You're right. Why let one cockroach ruin such a nice party?" Nick adjusted his suit jacket and straightened his tie.

The dean came over. "Frank, you're drunk. You owe Liz an apology, and her fiancé, too. Please do so, then leave." He opened the door. Frank mumbled something unintelligible, and then staggered out, rubbing his cheek.

The minute the door closed, the crowd buzzed. One-by-one people picked up jackets or sweaters and headed for the parking lot. The party was over. Her friends and colleagues stopped to wish her well on their way out. Some apologized to Nick on behalf of the department. They shook hands with Nick and smiled, but he sensed their discomfort.

Until Frank opened his big mouth, Lizzie's gang had accepted Nick. After Frank's diatribe, no one could meet Nick's gaze. Did they all agree with her ex, and simply hide it well? Angry, sad, and confused, Nick kissed Lizzie and joined the crowd leaving.

"You're going?"

"Yep."

"I hope you didn't let that jerk spoil things for you."

"He didn't exactly make things better. He spoke what was on the mind of some of your colleagues, I'm sure."

"Don't say that. No one said a thing."

Nick stopped to face her. "No, they didn't. Proves how good their manners are. But some of them wondered what you see in me. Frankly, I wonder, too. Look, I need some fresh air. I'm heading out."

"I'll see you at home then?"

Nick waited for the last person to leave. He took her left hand in both of his.

"I don't think this is such a good idea, Lizzie. We could be making a big mistake. I need a little time off to think about things. I'm not going home. Let's talk tomorrow."

"That's crazy. What are you doing? Where are you going?"

But he departed without responding.

Chapter Eight

Lizzie left as quickly as she could without appearing rude. Nick's car was long gone. She drove to his house, but it wasn't there. It wasn't parked near her home, either. She stopped at a café to get a bite of dinner and figure out where Nick went. Frank ambled in and sat opposite her.

"What the hell do you want, Frank? You're such an idiot. You've ruined everything. Such a lovely party Dean Hamilton threw for us. And you wrecked it. Get out. Get away from me."

"Where's your shadow?"

"None of your damn business. Get away or I'll call the waiter."

"Flew the coop, did he? He's probably off licking his wounds. I'm still available, any time, Elizabeth."

She threw her drink at him and pushed up from the table. Once outside, she got in her car but didn't know where to go. Putting her head down on the wheel, Liz cried. She simply couldn't lose Nick again. No way, not today, not ever.

She dried her tears and replayed his last words. He'd said he needed time to think. Hmm, where did Nick go to think? It hit her like a bolt of lightning. Of course! She knew where he'd gone, or at least she thought she did. She put the vehicle in gear and headed for the highway.

As she drove, she thought about the party. It had been a lovely affair. Her friends and colleagues had been sweet and accepting of Nick. She hadn't expected that. She hadn't known what would happen. The party hadn't been her idea. When the dean throws you a party, you attend. She'd worried the staff and friends would look down on Nick. What a pleasant surprise! They had even asked him about football. Her heart had warmed—until Frank went into his act.

He'd ruined the friendly atmosphere. Worst of all, he'd put Nick down in the nastiest way, almost as if Frank knew Nick's weak spot and drove a hot spike right through the center. She'd been furious at Frank. Hitting him relieved some of it, but that simply made things worse. By sticking up for him, she'd wounded Nick's pride. Now he took off, needing time to gather his thoughts and remember why he'd picked Lizzie Wenner to be his bride.

Two and a half hours later, she pulled up at the county access ramp to Cedar Lake in Pine Grove. It was their old, high school stomping ground. Nick had to be here. The day had been unusually warm for September, reaching almost ninety degrees. But the night air had cooled down. She wrapped her arms around herself as she made her way to the dock. Stopping to dip her fingers in, she was delighted to find the water warm.

As she got close to the end, a splash drew her attention. Peering into the darkness, she made out the head of a person, swimming to the floating dock. She recognized the pile of clothes near the bushes.

In a flash, Lizzie stripped off her clothing and dove in. Always a strong swimmer, she stopped halfway to the float. A naked man had climbed the ladder. He perched on the wood square, his wet skin shiny in the moonlight.

Putting her head down, she did the crawl and got to the ladder in record time.

"You still got the best crawl I've ever seen," came a deep voice.

She pulled herself up on the lowest rung. "And you've still got the hottest body."

A chuckle met her ears as she pushed up and plopped her naked butt on the hard surface.

"You figured it out," Nick said.

"Of course. You knew I would."

"Yep. Right."

"Why here, Nick?" She turned to face him, trying to ignore his gaze zeroing in on her breasts.

"Because this is where we fell in love. It all started right here."

"True."

"I needed to touch that. After that asshole, Frank. Ya know? I just needed to remember how much we loved each other, so long ago. At the beginning."

"We did, didn't we?"

"We did. And I still do."

"So do I. Forget Frank. He's an idiot. A jealous loser."

"That's right. He lost you, didn't he?"

"He did. It's you and me, Nick. I thought we both knew that."

"I did. And now that you're here, I see you do, too."

"Always. You and me. Forever."

"To be fair, I don't know where I'll be at forty. Probably not in pro football anymore. Who knows? I might be a bum."

"You could never be a bum."

"I want you to understand, before we tie the knot, what you're getting into. One serious injury could finish my career tomorrow. And if that doesn't happen, by the time I'm forty, I'll probably be done. I don't know what else I can do, Lizzie. It's always been just football for me."

"We'll figure it out."

"I don't want to be a burden. You'll be hitting the top of your career, and I'll be on the way down. Are you sure you want to be tied down with me?" He brushed some damp strands of hair from her face.

"Yes. I do. I told you that. Whatever happens, we'll deal with it. As long as we're together, nothing can defeat us. Have faith, Nick."

"I just want you to see the future. The real future. I don't want to disappoint you."

"You could never disappoint me."

"Yes, I could. I'll try not to, but I'm not perfect."

"You're what I want. Strong, smart, and you take good care of me. You love me."

"Like crazy, lady."

"What else could I ask for?"

"Plenty."

"Oh, shut up and kiss me," she said, staring into his eyes.

He leaned in and did as she'd asked. Lizzie threw her arms around his neck and deepened it. Nick eased her down on her back and went to work on her mouth. She raised a knee and moaned.

The hoot of an owl drew their attention. Nick sat up.

"I got a room at the no-tell motel. Stay with me. The county clerk is open tomorrow morning. I bet he'd bend a few rules about waiting periods for marriage licenses for a pro football player."

Lizzie laughed. "Why don't you tell him we waited ten years? Isn't that long enough?"

He grinned. "Works for me. I have my black suit in the trunk."

"Come to think of it, my dress is still in the box in the trunk of my car, too."

"So let's get married tomorrow. You game?"

"Great idea." She sidled up closer to him. "I love you, Nick. And I always will."

"Me, too, Lizzie. You're my goddess."

THE CONNECTICUT KINGS made the playoffs. The first game was at the King's stadium in Monroe, Connecticut. Lizzie, now Mrs. Jameson, sat in the family section. When Nick came out with his team for the national anthem, he made eye contact with his wife.

She pointed to the left. Nick shrugged, he didn't know what she meant, but she kept pointing. He shifted his gaze and spied a row of her Yale friends and colleagues. They sat together with a banner that read, "Ivy Leaguers for Kings."

Man, wasn't that simply the perfect wedding present?

THE END

PAIGE & BILL

One Fine Day
Jean C. Joachim
Moonlight Books

A MOONLIGHT BOOKS NOVELLA

Sensual Romance

Paige & Bill

One Fine Day

Echoes of the Heart series

Copyright © 2018 Jean C. Joachim

Cover design by Dawné Dominique

Edited by Sherri Good

Proofread by Renee Waring

All cover art and logo copyright © 2018 by Moonlight Books

PUBLISHER

Moonlight Books

Dedication

To my readers.
Thank you for making my dreams come true.

Prologue

Camp High Point, Catskill Mountains, NY

"You're gonna put her in instead of Petey? She's a girl?"

"She hits better than Petey. Paige hits better than you, Snake."

"But she's a girl."

"Do you want to beat Camp Callaway or not?"

"Yeah, yeah," Snake replied.

"So shut up and get out of the way," Billy Landeau said. "Paige!" he called, motioning to the brunette. "You're up."

"No fair!" Petey yelled, throwing down his glove and stalking off.

Paige Overton glanced at Billy. "Me?"

"Just get in there and do what you do, Slugger," he said.

She stepped up to the plate and hit the second pitch deep into the outfield, over the heads of the fielders. It was a stand-up triple, knocking in two runs. Billy smiled.

Camp High Point won, seven to three. With Paige beside him, Billy walked toward the refreshment table.

"Where'd you learn to hit like that?"

"My dad. He always wanted a son but got stuck with me," she said, shoving a ball cap down over her short dark hair.

"He taught you good."

"Thanks, Billy."

"It's Bill. I'm thirteen now. No more little kid stuff."

"Bill," she said, nodding.

"You're the best hitter we've got, except for me."

She grinned. Wearing the High Point softball uniform, she could pass for a boy. He didn't care. He had what he needed, a kid who could hit and put High Point on the map.

That summer, Paige stuck to Bill, mimicking his every move, listening, learning. Naturally comfortable with other kids, while she was not, he taught her how to get along, what to say and not say. When the summer ended, Paige had a new best friend, and Bill learned that not all girls were bossy and annoying like his big sister, Sandy.

The next season, Bill couldn't wait to show Paige his new glove. He didn't notice that she'd grown to be almost as tall as he.

"You're a great hitter, but you don't know shit about fielding. Come on."

"But our counselor wants us to write letters home."

"Do you want to be a star or not?"

She nodded.

"Come on." Bill tugged on her sleeve. She followed. He carried his bat over his shoulder as they trudged through the tall grass to the softball field. Bill placed her at shortstop and hit a few grounders.

"No, no. Not like that. Geez, not like a girl. Don't be afraid of it. Run up to meet it," he said, bending down and scooping up the ball.

"But I am a girl," she protested.

"Yeah, but I'm ignoring that. You want to play on my team?" he asked, cocking an eyebrow.

She swallowed.

"Then shut up and listen. You gotta learn to field like a guy. You can do it. Try again," he said, running back to home plate.

They practiced for an hour until Lisa, Paige's cabin-mate, ran up.

"Paige," she called, huffing, trying to catch her breath.

"Yeah?"

"Come on. You'd better get back. Carol keeps asking where you are. We can't tell her you're in the bathroom anymore. The whole cabin is gonna get demerits if you don't get back."

"Gotta go," Paige said.

"We'll do more tomorrow." He waved and trotted off.

When he got back to his cabin, Snake was waiting.

"Where were you?"

"Teaching Paige to field," Bill said.

"Why are you working out with her instead of me?"

"Because she's better 'an you. She's a natural."

"But I'm your best friend."

"Yeah, yeah, but this is about softball."

"Bill's got a crush on Paige," Tommy said.

"Bullshit! She's the best softball player we got. I'm training her, so we can beat the crap out of Camp Calloway again this year.

"I don't believe it," Snake said, turning away.

"Aw, come on. We're still buddies, Snake."

"Show me."

"Okay. You and me. We'll scare the girls in cabin three tonight."

"Yeah?"

"Yeah."

"No Paige?"

"Nope. Just you and me."

The boys did high fives and headed off to swim class. As they walked, Tommy's words ran through Bill's brain. No way could he have a crush on a twelve-year-old girl. She didn't even have boobs. Still, he liked being with her. She listened, followed his instructions and laughed at his jokes. He sighed. Yep, she was better than every other friend he had, except she was a girl. Relieved to know he wasn't crushing on her, he jumped in the water and did fifty laps.

AT FIRST, THE GIRLS in her cabin teased Paige, then ostracized her. They called her a "boy", a "lesbo", and made a fuss about changing in front of her. While their words hurt, Paige knew it wasn't true. Nope, not at all. She loved Bill Landeau, but she kept it to herself.

"Bet he doesn't dance with you once at the party," Lisa said.

"Yeah. Bill doesn't dance with *boys*."

"He'll be all over Tiffany. She's got boobs," Mary put in, gesturing to her chest.

Paige sensed heat in her face. Dancing even once with Bill would be heaven. The girls got ready. Paige pulled out her one and only dress.

"Oh my God! Paige owns a dress!" Lisa ragged.

Their laughter brought tears to Paige's eyes, but she blinked them back. When they got to the meeting hall, Bill was on the other side of the room with Snake and Tommy. She waved and smiled. He raised his hand and nodded but didn't come over.

The DJ started the music, and Bill disappeared.

"He's probably making out with Tiffany on the tennis court," Mary said.

Anger and jealousy swelled inside Paige. She had to know. Slipping away, she took a hidden path behind the bushes. Sure enough, there he was, sitting cross-legged on the court, playing cards. She stepped out into view.

"Look, it's Paige!" Tommy said. "At least I think it's Paige. She's wearing a dress. Can't be Paige."

Snake laughed. Her eyes filled. She fiddled with the belt on her gingham outfit as she cast her gaze to the ground.

"Shut up," Bill said. "You look real nice, Paige."

"She can't play," Snake growled.

"Sorry. This is a *guys only* game."

"Not unless you want to play strip poker," Tommy piped up.

"She's got nothin' to see anyway," Snake pointed out.

"Shut up, asshole," Bill growled.

That was it. Tears burst forth and Paige took off, running. Halfway down the path, someone grabbed her from behind. She struggled until she realized it was Bill.

"They're idiots. Tools. Forget them. You look nice. It's tradition. Snake, Tommy, and I play cards during the dance every year. I'm sorry, but it's guys only."

She wiped her cheeks with her hand. "It's okay. I don't care about them."

"You shouldn't. You're better at softball than they'll ever be. I'm proud of you. You play great. Don't let their stupid mouths get in the way."

"You're my best friend, Bill."

"Same here," he said, giving her a high-five. "I gotta go. See you tomorrow for practice?"

She nodded. Maybe she didn't get a dance, but he admitted that she was his best friend. And he gave her a high-five. He only did that with his closest buddies. Smiling, she returned to the dance. Standing by herself on the sideline, a song caught her ear.

The tune *One Fine Day* came over the loudspeaker. She listened to the lyrics that told of a girl predicting that the boy she loved would love her, too, one fine day. The idea that someday, Bill would want her for his girlfriend, spoke to Paige. That was it. The song captured her feelings perfectly. Yes, one day he'd realize that he loved her, too. Goosebumps broke out on her flesh. She eased into the clutch of girls from her cabin.

"Who's singing that song?" she asked.

"What song?"

"The one about one fine day?"

"Oh, that one? The Chiffons. But don't get any ideas. That's never gonna be you and Bill Landeau," Lisa said, shaking her head.

Paige raised her chin. "I was thinking of someone else. Not Bill. Bill? You mean Bill Landeau? You're joking, right? We're friends. That's all," she sniffed and walked away. No sense giving the mean girls any more ammunition.

The rest of that summer, Paige hummed that song to herself.

"You sing all the time. What are you singing?" Bill asked during batting practice.

Paige felt her face go red. "Nothing. I'm not singing anything."

"I see your lips moving and sound is coming out."

"Oh, yeah. Nothing. Practicing. I...uh...have to give a speech at school."

"In September? You're practicing now? Girls are crazy," Bill said, shaking his head. "You're up."

Paige let out a breath and stepped up to the plate. She'd have to be more careful. If Bill ever found out how she felt, it would be the end. He'd hate her, humiliate her, and she'd die. A ball whizzed by.

"Strike!" the umpire called.

"Focus, Paige!" Bill yelled.

Paige forced her attention on the ball. She narrowed her eyes and went into "batter mode", as she'd described it to Bill. The pitcher got cocky with the next one, throwing it right down the center. Paige swung and connected driving it into home-run territory.

Bill jumped up and down, throwing his cap in the air. It was the final run and the game was over. When she crossed the plate, he picked her up and swung her around. The whole team danced in victory over Camp Callahan.

"We'll get you next year," Edgy Malone said, shaking his fist at Bill.

"In your dreams!"

As she walked back to her cabin, she hummed the song again as a smile graced her face.

When she returned home from camp, Paige bought the CD and played it until her parents complained. She bought earbuds. Yes, Bill Landeau would be hers, one fine day.

LATE JUNE - TWO YEARS later

At sixteen, a counselor-in-training, or CIT, Bill Landeau had to be early to camp to greet the campers as they arrived. Lifting, hauling, shaking hands, and leading newbies to their cabins grew tiresome. Snake and Tommy were there, too.

Bill wondered when Paige would arrive. He glanced up in time to see her parents silver SUV pull into the parking lot. He ambled over. The back door opened, and a pair of the prettiest legs he'd ever seen appeared.

Paige stood up. Ripping her ballcap off her head, she waved it at Bill. Down tumbled lustrous, long dark hair that fell in soft curls below her shoulders. Bill's gaze eased down her body and stopped at several eye-popping curves. Damn! Where did those come from? She sure as hell didn't have those last year.

A faint touch of pink on her lips emphasized their fullness. Her hips, slender but perfectly formed grabbed his attention. Shit, damn, fuck –Paige Overton was the prettiest girl he'd ever seen. His body reacted –heartbeat doubled, and blood pumped to areas best ignored as she ran over. What the hell? Where was his friend, Slugger, and who was this centerfold?

"Bill! Hi!" she said, stopping a few feet in front of him.

His mouth, lips, and tongue had ceased to work, but his eyes continued to stare. He finally found his voice. "Paige? Is that you?"

"Of course it's me, silly."

"You look...different."

"I'm almost fifteen."

"Wow. Uh, yeah. I guess." Again, words failed him.

"I've been practicing. I'm on the softball team in high school. I'm the best hitter."

"I'm not surprised. Still practicing your fielding?"

"Of course."

"Good." He swallowed.

"Young man. Can you help us with the bags?" Paige's mother called.

"Sure, sure," Bill said, happy to have something to do while he pondered the changes in his best friend. Grabbing two bags, he headed for her cabin, with Paige tagging along beside him.

"Dad gave me a new glove for my birthday," she said, pulling it out of the back pocket of her jeans.

He glanced at it. "Nice."

"Nice? It's a Wilson A2000!"

Bill slipped away from Paige, leaving her with her parents. Snake and Tommy found him.

"Holy shit, did you see Paige?" Snake asked.

"Yeah. So?" Bill replied, bending over the water fountain.

"She's got tits, man. Big ones," Tommy said, placing cupped hands on his chest.

"Shut up," Bill said, wiping water from his chin.

"She's really a girl," Snake put in, shaking his head.

"Guys, get over it. Everybody grows up."

"Not like Paige." Tommy shook his head.

Bill ditched his buddies and went for a walk. He needed time to think. One look at Paige had his heart swelling and his mind going in circles. He couldn't be crushing on Slugger, could he? Nope. It wasn't a crush. He took a deep breath. Crap, it was love. She was the perfect combination, a girl he could play ball with, talk to, and kiss.

He shook his head, but the tingling in his body and the dizziness in his heart remained. Paige Overton, the ideal girl. Who ever would have classified her that way before? As much as he tried to shake off this new feeling, it stuck.

At dinner, he watched her eat. There were two new girls in her cabin. She sat with them, talking and laughing. No longer the shunned tomboy; Paige had grown up. Bill had shot up over time, too. One question bugged him. Could she still hit?

He had to find out. The first softball practice, he pitched to her. A line drive almost took his head off. Paige rounded the bases, making it to second. Hell, yeah, she could still hit. A hot girl, who hit like a boy, threw Bill for a loop.

Paige continued to behave as she always had toward him. Soon they fell into easy banter, as usual. He got caught staring at her chest more than once. But she teased him out of it. He tried, unsuccessfully, not to do it again. How could a guy take his eyes off such a hot girl? Not this guy, and he hoped she'd understand.

Snake and Tommy ragged him about Paige, making suggestive comments until Bill took them out and shut them up the old-fashioned way—with his fists. After that, they gave him a wide berth. While he sensed the loss of their support, he put his friendship with Paige first. After a week, Bill's friends accepted her, much to his relief. He had it all, hottest girl and loyal guys. This would be his best summer yet—right?

WHEN THE MIDSUMMER party popped up, Paige was ready. She put on one of three dresses she'd brought. After Missy, her new friend, applied a bit of makeup to Paige's cheeks and lips, they headed for the main house. Colored lights strung up through the trees hugging the blacktop gave a soft glow to the dance floor. A CD player blasted popular music from the 70s and 80s.

Paige fingered the fringe on her sleeve. Shifting her weight from foot to foot, she glanced around for Bill, before remembering his annual card game with Snake and Tommy.

"Care to dance?" a masculine voice said, interrupting her thoughts.

She looked up to see Bill in front of her, his hand outstretched.

"I thought you played cards?" she asked.

"I thought you were a little kid," he replied.

"But Tiffany..."

"Tiffany? She's got nothing on you. Come on. Dance with me."

She fell into his arms. They danced to every song, fast and slow. Snake and Tommy stood on the sidelines, frowning. The camp director announced "last dance," and the song *One Fine Day* came on.

Bill pulled her close. Resting her head on his shoulder, Paige closed her eyes. Was it a dream? She vowed to remember this moment forever. Over too soon for her liking, she stepped away.

"Can I walk you back?" Bill asked.

She nodded. He took her hand and steered her around to the wooded side of the campus, known as the make-out path. She'd heard about it from other girls. Now she'd have her turn to stroll there with the boy she adored. He slipped his arm around her and stopped.

"Paige. I don't—You're so—" Bill stopped talking, shrugged, and bent down to kiss her.

She tilted her chin up. His lips were warm and soft as they pressed against hers. Bill opened his, coaxing her to do the same and then deepened the kiss. Electricity shot down her body as his tongue connected with hers. They stopped to make out three more times on the way to her cabin. Paige floated home on a cloud of love and sexual heat. Paige and Bill spent the next two weeks playing softball during the day and sneaking out of their cabins to meet and make out at night. It wasn't long before kissing alone didn't cut it. One night, he touched her breast, then stopped.

"John told me you're jailbait," Bill said.

"Jailbait?"

"Yeah. You're too young to go all the way."

"Says who?"

"Says the law. And if you do, the guy who does it to you can be arrested for some kind of rape."

"Even if I want to?"

"It's not about you. It's the law," he said, sitting up straight and moving away from her.

Totally ignorant about sex, Paige only knew she didn't want to stop.

"Damn it!" Paige crossed her arms over her chest.

"That's right. And keep 'em like that. I don't want to go to jail."

"Laws suck," she said, moping.

He laughed. "I care about you, Paige. I don't want to hurt you."

"I know. Still."

"You're a virgin. I'm not."

"You're not?" she asked, her eyebrows rising.

"Nope. Not gonna tell about it, either. But we'd better keep hands off. Avoid trouble."

"Tiffany?" she asked.

"I told you, I'm not going to talk about it." He brushed his pants off and stood up. "I've gotta get you back. Come on."

Slowly, she pushed to her feet. "If you say so."

"I do."

"I love you," she blurted out, then covered her mouth with her hand.

When he didn't laugh, she let out a breath. "I wasn't going to tell you."

"Me, too. I mean, like, I feel the same about you." He stumbled over his words.

Paige grinned. The couple tiptoed back to campus. Bill stopped a few feet from Paige's cabin and kissed her nose. "'Night, Slugger," he whispered.

She undressed and slipped into bed, stopping to say a quick prayer of thanks for Bill and Camp High Point.The next morning, the camp director stopped at her table.

"Paige, can I see you a moment?" he asked, gesturing to his office.

She swallowed. Had John gotten wind of her nightly sessions with Bill? Was she to be reprimanded? Sent home? Was Bill in trouble? As she followed him, she caught Bill's eye. He raised his eyebrows. She shrugged.

John closed the door behind her.

"After breakfast, pack your stuff."

"But, I..."

He held up his hand. "It's nothing you've done. Your mother has been in an accident. You aunt is on her way to take you home. I'm sorry."

"Is she okay?" Fear spiked through her.

"I don't know. If there's anything I can do..." He rose. The door opened and Paige's counselor came in.

"Come on, honey, I'll help you." She put her arm around Paige's shoulder.

Shock slowed her. Tears gathered in her eyes and spilled down her cheeks. She stumbled on the steps. Thoughts of Bill flew from her mind as she struggled to take in the news.

Paige was packed in twenty minutes. She sat by her luggage in the parking lot. After her counselor returned to class, Bill wandered over.

"What happened?" he asked.

"I'm going home."

"I get that. But why? Was it something we did?"

She shook her head. Still stunned by the news, words wouldn't come. She hid her face in her hands. Bill eased her into a hug.

"What is it, Paige?" he whispered.

"My mother," she managed, burying her face in his shoulder, "was in an accident."

"Shit. That sucks. Is she okay?"

"I don't know," she said, clinging to him.

"I'm sorry. So sorry." He kissed her hair and tightened his grip. "Will you come back?"

"I don't know."

"Paige, I..." he began.

"Yeah. I know. Me, too." She raised her head, staring into his eyes.

"Someday. Someday." He bent to kiss her.

John trotted over. He took Bill aside and spoke with him for a few moments. Bill stayed until Paige's aunt arrived. He helped load her things into the SUV, then waved goodbye. She turned in her seat and watched him as her aunt drove away. Paige's mother died three days later.

Next June, she heard that Bill had gone to football camp instead of High Point. Paige's days at High Point were over, too. Her father married the first woman to come along. Paige's new stepmother shipped her off to finishing school in Switzerland.

Chapter One

Twelve years later. New York City.

Bill Landeau paced, stopping only to mop his brow. A man with salt-and-pepper hair came hurrying toward him.

"Where the fuck have you been?" Bill asked.

"You don't say 'fuck' to your boss, or didn't they tell you that in fancy-shmancy grad school?"

"I'm sorry, J.C. But we're presenting in two minutes."

"And I'm here, aren't I?"

"Come on," Bill took his arm and ushered him through the door to the giant office building on Sixth Avenue in New York City. Overton Enterprises was on the seventeenth floor.

His nerves kicked up. Crap, if he sweated any more, they'd have to wring him out like a washcloth. It wasn't just the presenting, but Paige Overton, daughter of Jim Overton, President and CEO of Overton Enterprises, would be sitting in on the presentation. He hadn't seen his old camp girlfriend in forever.

Would she remember him? He remembered her, the curvy little tomboy who played softball like a boy. Was he sexist? He shook his head. He'd nicknamed her "Slugger" and it stuck.

J.C. McDonough patted him on the back.

"Don't be nervous. We've got this."

"No, we don't," Bill replied.

"Have faith. My old prep school buddy, Carter Wentworth, said it was in the bag. He's on the board. Said he'd paved the way. All we have to do is pick up the okay from these clowns, sign up some schools, finalize the architectural plans, and we're in business."

"Nothing's ever that simple," Bill argued.

"This one is."

No matter what his boss said, Bill couldn't relax. As the new marketing manager for Sports Unlimited, he'd written this pitch for bucks for his brand-new idea. Everything rode on getting the money. J.C. had already promised the NFL and the New York City police department, that this new idea for a teen sports summer camp was in the bag.

Now Bill had to sell the decision makers at Overton on the concept, had to make them believe this was the most revolutionary idea today. The sports camp would train underprivileged kids in soccer, football, and baseball. The concept was Bill's brainchild from conception to implementation. His neck was stretched out as far as it could go.

J.C. had loved the idea, pronouncing it "genius." He'd lectured the rest of his tiny company about thinking "outside the box", being original, and coming up with new concepts. At the office, the glares from jealous coworkers made Bill embarrassed to show his face.

"This is the most brilliant idea since sliced bread, Bill. Whatcha worrying about?"

"Glad you feel that way, J.C. I hope the people at Overton agree with you."

"They're just rich. What do they know about building self-esteem among minority youth and teaching them how to work as a team? Not a fucking thing. You're going to make them think they thought of this themselves. Let them own it. And the money will flow."

When Bill had presented the idea at his job interview, J.C. had loved it so much, he'd hired him on the spot. Bill had hoped for a job in sports marketing, his specialty in grad school, but J.C. had bought the summer camp thing and put Bill in the hot seat. His job was on the line. If the launch failed, Bill would have to send out his resume again.

J.C. had approached Overton, without consulting Bill. Too chicken to mention he knew Paige, Bill kept the connection to himself. To make matters worse, when he looked up the company, he saw her listed as a member of the Board. He remembered how they had parted—suddenly, almost lovers.

Then he recalled receiving a letter or was it a postcard from Paige—sent from Europe. He'd been totally preoccupied with his studies, football, and the head cheerleader to even write back. An insensitive, asshole move on his part. *Shit!* If she hated him, then this was all for nothing. Good thing he still had the number of a few headhunters.

After the elevator doors closed, Bill swallowed. His mouth was dry as desert sand. They entered the company's lobby and took a seat.

"This is your part, J.C."

"Yeah? Any part I want to talk about is my part, Bill."

"I'm sorry. Of course. But I mean, I've rehearsed this and this and this. But the whole schtick about the company, damn, nobody can do that like you."

"Stop shooting the bull."

"It's true."

"I know. But you look like an ass-kisser telling me. Jesus, Bill. Just be yourself. Your passion is what sold me at the interview. No phony crap, just you, outlining your idea. You were amazing. Tap into that. Drop all that 'presentation 101' shit and just be yourself."

J.C. echoed what Bill's sister, Sandy, had told him. Bill took a deep breath and exhaled. They were both right. Just be himself. Right. Easy-peasy. Uh, no.

PAIGE OPENED A BOTTLE of water, then swiveled in her chair to face the picture window behind her desk. The view didn't divert her from the dread seeping through her.

Picking up the agenda for the upcoming meeting, she stared at the name again. *Bill Landeau.* How many men could there be with that name? She frowned. Of course, there could be others. She shook her head. Nope. He must be the same one, the guy she'd worshipped at camp. The sixteen-year-old who turned her head and captured her heart.

Stretching her fingers, she stared at the obscenely large diamond on the fourth finger of her left hand. Engaged to fellow board member, Carter Wentworth, Paige couldn't imagine Bill, her first love, and Carter, the man she pledged to marry, in the same meeting—together. She shut her eyes. Damn.

She glanced at the tailor-made purple silk jacket hanging on the coat tree. Paige Overton wasn't the same woman she had been at Camp High Point. "Slugger" had disappeared with the total makeover forced on her by her stepmother.

As she recalled that horrible day when her aunt showed up to bring her home, her eyes filled. The memory of being hustled into the car, her fears unanswered, still squeezed her heart. Her beautiful mother, crazy, unique, creative, and the most loving person, survived long enough to say farewell to her daughter.

She snapped a tissue out of a box in her top drawer to blot her eyes. It wouldn't do to have eye makeup running down her face during this meeting. She took a deep shuddering breath and focused on the self-control she'd learned at finishing school.

After a hasty goodbye to Bill, she'd wheedled his address from the camp director a year later. She wrote, but he never answered. Through the camp grapevine, she discovered he'd gone to football camp the following summer. That was the last she knew of him, until now.

And there he was, in the waiting room. A shiver ran up her spine. She tried to sort out her feelings. Did it matter how she felt about Bill? Not in the least. Maybe Bill had forgotten he even knew her?

After dating for three months, she'd said "yes" to Carter and planned to marry him within the year. That was a done deal. Her father approved of her choice and her stepmother seemed relieved to be rid of her. A win/win, right? Did it matter what Paige thought? They assumed she was on board, after all, she'd accepted his proposal.

If everything was so fucking hunky dory, why was she so close to tears? Oops. She mustn't use that language. That was a "Slugger" word, not one used by a well-bred lady. Crap!

Although she had voting rights on the board, she couldn't vote for Bill's proposal, even if she wanted to. She had to recuse herself because she knew him, and they had had a personal relationship. Damn. She remembered Bill as a good guy—for a while, until he didn't respond to her letter.

She sighed. Her life was set, the course charted. But Bill Landeau making an appearance wasn't in those plans. Paige had done everything she could to please her stepmother and father, to have peace. She'd turned her back on her old life, on "Slugger", and anything pertaining to her tomboy days, including friends, clothes, and language.

But she couldn't control her heart. Emotion forced down her cool-headed business-like attitude. Seeing Bill's name on the agenda for today's meeting had opened a Pandora's Box. Simply reading his name uncovered feelings she'd stuffed away years ago. Could this happen at a worse time? Her lips set in a frown—life was tidy. She didn't need Bill Landeau messing it up.

Maybe he was fat and bald? She chuckled to herself. No way could the athletic young man she'd known have let himself go to pot so fast.

Paige chewed on a pen as her mind wandered back. His was her first kiss, given after they'd won a softball game against Camp Callahan. He'd pushed her messy hair, always hanging in her face, to the side, bent down, and placed his mouth oh so softly on hers. Running her tongue over her bottom lip, Paige smiled. In the world of first kisses, his had been the gold standard.

"Ms. Overton?" Her secretary's crisp voice cut through Paige's reverie.

She looked up and raised her eyebrows.

"The meeting starts in five minutes. Do you want coffee?"

"No, thanks, Ruth. There'll be water in the conference room." Paige stood and stretched. Curiosity consumed her. What had become of Bill Landeau, athlete? And what was he doing pitching a bid for a grant for a nonprofit company to teach sports to underprivileged kids? What did he look like now? And, was he married?

She pushed to her feet and walked to the mirror on the back of her door. After straightening her white silk blouse, plucking at her bangs, and refreshing her lipstick, Paige surveyed her image. The stunning reflection of a well put-together young woman met her gaze. Her short, dark hair cut in the latest style, and her suit by Dolce and Gabbana were central casting's perfect vision of a woman in control, a board member of a large corporation. Not bad for a former tomboy slob still in her twenties.

She laughed. Nothing could be further from the truth. Bossed around by her stepmother and father, Paige had given up control years ago. Anything to leave the boarding school she regarded as a prison. Once she played the game by their rules, she'd be happy.

"Living an orderly life will be good for you," her father had said.

"My mother didn't live an orderly life. She was mercurial, creative, unique," she'd retorted, sticking out her chin, just a bit.

Her father's face had clouded over. Lines creased at the corners of his eyes. The moment the words were out of her mouth, she'd regretted it. He put his hand over his eyes and took a deep breath.

"Your mother was one-of-a-kind. But she's gone. We need to carry on. Avery only wants you to be happy. Please, do as she says."

The look on his face had squeezed Paige's heart. For six months, Jim Overton had mourned in silence, alone. He'd sit in his library for hours, days, even, and do nothing but look at scrapbooks and reread the books her mother had written. Then Avery had come along, first as a secretary to gather up the scattered remnants of his life, then to move in and take her mother's place. Her father had leaned on Avery and, a little at a time, she'd taken over.

Now he depended on her and her word was gospel. After months of her acting out, Jim Overton and Avery had shipped her off to boarding school. Being thrust out of her home wounded her heart and sucked the fight from her.

In fear of losing her father's love, Paige knuckled under to the new lady running her home. After two years in that wretched school, Paige returned to New York, a different girl. Gone were the torn jeans, the grubby T-shirts, the ball caps. Refinement, Avery style, meant skirts, dresses, and suits from the finest, most expensive designers. Now, Paige looked the part—daughter of a wealthy businessman. Her engagement to Carter had simply been the icing on the cake. Glowing at the news she'd be planning the huge, costly, tasteful wedding of her stepdaughter to a man of accomplishment and means, Avery had clapped her hands in glee at her ultimate victory.

Paige sighed and opened her office door. What would Bill think of her now? No man wants a slob for a wife. She wasn't exactly a slob, she dressed boyishly. Maybe Bill already had a wife! Wow, she hadn't considered that possibility. She shrugged and continued her walk to the conference room. Whether or not Bill Landeau was married was not her concern. Why should she give a damn?

The lyrics to the song, *One Fine Day,* came back to her.

BILL STRAIGHTENED THE knot on his tie as he made his way across the conference room to the chairs designated for Sports Unlimited. Thankful to be wearing a jacket since he'd probably sweated through his entire shirt already, he took his seat. His eyes scanned the nine people sitting across the table. Pow! There she was. Was that her? Really? Paige Overton, aka Slugger, dressed like that? Gorgeous was an understatement. She took his breath away.

Jim Overton introduced everyone from his company. J.C. introduced himself and Bill, then gave a brief overview of the project before turning the meeting over to Bill. He swallowed, then rose from his seat and went to the screen. J.C. manned the laptop.

Bill rattled off statistics about violence in poor neighborhoods and the deteriorating relations between teens and police. The plan for the camp included training in soccer, football, and baseball. Coaching would be a team effort, with a retired professional ball player teaming up with a member of the police force.

He outlined the expectations of the program—improved self-esteem of the participants as well as the benefits of learning how to play on a team, be a good winner, and a good loser. Then he explained that the close relationship between the kids and members of the local police force would educate both sides about the challenges each faces every day.

J.C. rose and took the Overton board through the dollars and cents—how much was needed and where it would be spent. When he finished, Bill showed the architectural drawings, explaining how the camp would be set up. A camp in Sullivan County, New York would be their first. If it proved successful, they planned to set up camps in ten cities over the next five to ten years.

When Bill returned to his seat, J.C. rose, stressing how much credit they would give to Overton Enterprises for making this possible. He closed the presentation by asking for the grant. After the question-and-answer period, they took a break for lunch to be set up.

Bill escaped to the men's room. He'd gotten steadily more nauseous as the presentation progressed. His future rode on this project getting off the ground. A grant from Overton would launch his dream. He splashed cold water on his face and leaned against the bathroom wall.

J.C. joined him, clapping him on the shoulder. "That went great. Good job."

"I don't know. That guy Carter didn't like me."

"You think so?"

"He frowned when I was talking."

J.C. waved his hand. "The chick couldn't take her eyes off you. Maybe Carter noticed. They're engaged. Don't worry. The presentation was flawless. This should be in the bag."

Paige is engaged?

"They asked good questions, which shows they're listening, and they're serious."

"Yeah, yeah. Right," Bill said.

He dried off, took a leak, and the men left. A buffet of sandwiches and salads covered the conference table. Bill looked for Paige but didn't see her. He jumped when someone touched his shoulder from behind.

"Sorry. Didn't mean to scare you."

"Paige. How nice to see you again," he said.

She put out her hand and he took it with both of his but didn't let go. Their gazes connected. Was she the same girl he'd known at camp? He wondered if that gutsy "Slugger" still lived inside that beautifully clothed, sexy body.

"Nice to see you, too, Bill." His scent wafted her way. God, he still smelled fantastic. A new aftershave, maybe, but the same old sexy Bill smell. "What did you think of the presentation?" More was on his mind than simply Sports Unlimited, but he focused on business.

"It was well done. You were great. What happened to your pro football career?"

"Went up in smoke when I busted up my knee."

"Sorry to hear that." Paige's brows knitted into a vaguely familiar look. The one she used for little kids when they got hurt playing a game. He grinned.

"I got a Master's in Sports Marketing."

"Sports Unlimited is lucky to have you," she said, subtly withdrawing her hand from his.

When he realized he still held it, heat traveled to his cheeks.

"Thanks. I couldn't believe it when J.C. got on board with this idea."

"Are you married?" she blurted out.

"Huh?" he asked.

"Married?" she repeated, her face turning pink.

"No, no. Still single," he said, raising his palms. "You?"

"Engaged," she replied.

His gaze traveled to the large rock on her left hand. His heart squeezed, and his lips compressed into a frown. "Too bad," he muttered.

"What?"

"I mean congratulations," he said.

Carter called to Paige and she turned to leave. "So nice to see you," she said.

He'd never imagined Slugger would be so polished, so poised, so mature...and so incredibly gorgeous. She was a wet dream on legs. J.C. called to him. Bill refocused on food, making a plate and chatting with the board while they ate. Jim Overton directed his questions to Bill.

"What prompted this idea?" he asked, lifting a ham sandwich to his mouth.

"It was my camp experience."

"Camp?"

"I was in charge of the softball team at my summer camp. Each season, I noticed how much happier and well-adjusted the kids were by the end of camp. Some came from dysfunctional homes. There were scholarship kids there, kids from broken homes. They improved their attitude and outlook after learning to play softball and being part of a team."

"Paige went to summer camp. What do you think about that, Paige?"

She colored, cleared her throat, then spoke. "I agree with Mr. Landeau."

Jim nodded.

J.C. changed the subject. "When do you think you'll have an answer for us?"

"Carter will get back to you within a day or two."

When they'd packed up to go, Jim gave J.C. and Bill hearty handshakes and complimented them on a thorough job. On the way home, Bill couldn't stop smiling. He was counting on Paige's vote.

"Looks like we won that one," J.C. said.

"Yep. A home run, for sure," Bill replied, grinning.

AS BILL WALKED OUT the door, Paige scooted to the ladies' room. She hid in a stall to calm down. Holy Hell! Bill Landeau looked ten times better than he had at sixteen. Jesus H, he was so seductive, she was ready to slide under the conference table and spread 'em. Oops. Slugger language. Seeing him rattled her. She had to meet him, alone, to find out about the letter. Did she dare? A shiver shot up her spine at the thought.

"Ms. Paige?"

"Yes, Ruth."

"They're meeting in the conference room."

"I'll be right there." Paige took a deep breath, straightened her clothing and waltzed out, her head held high. Faking it came naturally to her. After all, she'd been practicing for years.

The Overton Enterprises board reconvened to discuss the Sports Unlimited proposal.

"Why was that marketing guy holding your hand?" Carter asked Paige.

"He wasn't. We just shook hands."

"He didn't let go."

"Cool it, Carter." She avoided his gaze.

"You'd better not be cheating on me."

"Relax."

Jim interrupted. "Let's take a vote. Maybe we don't even need a discussion. I vote yes to setting aside the funds but making no firm commitment until they have real numbers. What do you say, Paige?"

"I have to recuse myself, Dad."

"Recuse? Why?"

"I know Bill Landeau. We went to summer camp together."

"I knew there was something between you," Carter put in.

"There's nothing between us except old friends," Paige lied.

Carter narrowed his eyes and stared at her. "You're lying."

Jim huffed. "Carter, this is no place for a personal discussion."

"Right. Let's take a vote then. Paige is out. I vote 'no,'" he said and glared at the four other people in the room.

"Well, I don't know. I mean, we need more..." one member chimed in.

"That's a *no*, right?" Carter piped up.

He intimidated three others into going along, and they voted down the proposal.

"I can't tell you how disappointed I am in this board. First damn good project that comes along in years and you boneheads can't see the worth. Or you're all afraid to go against Carter. He's soon to be my son-in-law, but I'm still running this company," he said, pushing to his feet. "Stupid asses," he mumbled, under his breath.

Paige covered her mouth with her hand. Crap! The last thing she wanted was for Bill's idea to go down in smoke. Anger crept up her neck all the way to her eyes. She strode over to Carter.

"What the fuck have you done?" she asked, hands on hips.

"Paige!" Carter said.

"What?"

"Language."

"Oh shut up. You've fucked Sports Unlimited's chance to do something good in the world just because you're jealous of Bill Landeau. Asshole!" Fury burned inside her.

"What's this? Swearing like a sailor? I've never seen this side of you."

"Stop changing the subject. Why did you do that?"

Carter sat down and crossed his legs. A smug smile appeared. "I don't want you working with him. That's why."

"What? You're denying these kids a way out because you're jealous?"

"I wouldn't say jealous. Cautious, maybe. I'm not taking any chances with you. You're mine and I want to keep it that way."

"Bad idea," she said, heading for the door.

Carter caught up with her, grabbed her elbow, and spun her around. "Don't get all heroic on me. You want our engagement as much as I do."

She stopped struggling. "Maybe, but not if you're going to be a dick. Carter, get your head out of your ass and look around. Maybe do some good for someone else, for a change."

"I am. I'm promising to take care of you for the rest of your life. I think that's pretty good."

She shrugged. "You don't get it."

"I get you. And I want you. Landeau will find another investment firm. If his idea is so great, he'll have companies begging him to take their money. Just for the publicity."

"That could have been us," she said.

"I like the status quo. We don't need him or his idea. The company is doing great."

"It's all about you, isn't it?" she asked.

He sidled up to her, placing his hands on her shoulders. "Look, Paige. I love you. And I'm not going to let anything get in the way of that. It's you and me. We don't need him. The company doesn't need him. I thought you were committed?"

"I am. To the company."

"And me?"

He looked so pathetic, she simply shrugged. "I'm wearing your ring, aren't I?"

"That's a symbol. You gotta feel it in here," he said, tapping his chest.

"Carter, if you're not sure about us, call it off. But don't mix our relationship into company business, okay?"

"If he comes near you again, he'll be sorry," he muttered, turning away.

Paige frowned. "Tool," she said under her breath, striding across the room and yanking the door closed with a bang.

Chapter Two

J.C. took Bill out to dinner to celebrate. He ordered champagne.

"Win or lose, that was a smokin' presentation. Great job, Bill," J.C. said, raising his flute.

Bill grinned. "The support from you, Wendy, and the architects was crucial. I didn't do it by myself."

"But your delivery," his boss said, grinning and shaking his head. "Can't beat the energy and enthusiasm created by genuine passion."

"I believe in this."

"That's obvious. So even if it isn't Overton Enterprises, I know we'll find funding."

"Why wouldn't it be Overton?" Bill asked, taking a sip.

"I dunno. My old buddy hasn't called me."

"You mean that guy, Carter?"

"Yeah."

"I hope my friend will pull it through for us," Bill said.

"Friend?"

"Yeah, Paige Overton and I went to camp together."

"Did you make it with her at camp?"

"We were kids. Sweethearts. She was underage."

"But I bet it crossed your mind," J.C. snickered.

Bill sensed color rising in his face. "That's not the point. We were friends. I hope that will sway her to our side."

"Me, too."

They ordered dinner and talked about the next steps to make the project a reality. Bill got home late but called his sister anyway. She lived in London, five hours ahead.

"Bill?" came a groggy voice. "Are you all right? Has something happened?"

"No, no. Just had our first presentation."

"Do you know what time it is?"

"Yeah. Uh, maybe four o'clock, your time?"

"That's right. You woke me up," she said. Mutterings in the background drew his attention. "And you woke Rafe, too. What the hell?"

"I'm sorry, Sandy. I just had to tell you." He heard a yawn on the other end. "I'll hang up and you can go back to sleep."

"No, no. I'm up now. Let's have it. The whole story."

"You sure?"

"What's going on?" A masculine voice piped up.

Uh oh. "Rafe?"

"Put it on speaker," Rafe said.

"Go ahead, Bill. We're listening," Sandy said.

"Do you remember Paige Overton from Camp High Point?" he began.

The conversation lasted about half an hour until exhaustion caught up with him. He undressed and slipped into bed. Lacing his hands behind his head, Bill stared at the ceiling. After he wrecked his knee, his dream of a career in football died. Sandy had convinced him to go back to school for a Master's. He remembered how disappointed he'd been at the Michigan job fair when he didn't get any offers from sports teams or even sports publications.

He'd been on the phone to Sandy bitching up one side and down the other about how unfair it was that he didn't get even one single job offer. He swore he'd tear up his graduate degree. What good was it if it didn't bring him a lucrative job in sports? Sandy had bucked him up by offering him a room in her lovely home in London to spend time licking his wounds, before getting his act together. He'd almost bought the plane ticket when he got the call from J.C. to come in for an interview. He couldn't believe his ears—an interview. J.C. offered Bill the job on the spot. Shocked that someone had actually listened and shared his vision, Bill accepted.

Working with J.C. to perfect the concept and the pitch, Bill slaved long hours to get everything right. From the depths of the ocean to a rocket to Mars, Bill's ego soared. His vision, his dream would happen. He had "Slugger" to thank for this once-in-a-lifetime opportunity. If she wasn't engaged, he might have to marry her, just to show his gratitude.

What was that about Paige being engaged, anyway? He had fond memories of her and how the little Slugger became a beautiful girl right before his eyes. He'd been blown away. She'd turned into the prettiest girl in camp—and still the best hitter on the team. Of course, it was too late for them, since she'd already found the love of her life.

As his grandmother used to say, "If she ain't married and she ain't dead, she's still available." Bill chuckled at the memory. His granny was a pistol, and he agreed with her. Guess Bill would have to put on a full court press to win the lady. Did his "Slugger" still live in that luscious body covered by fancy clothes? He sure hoped so.

"ARE YOU GOING TO CALL that J.C. guy?" her father asked.

"I don't know him. You call. You're the president," she replied.

"Since you know that guy Bill whatever, why don't you call him, instead?" Jim said to his daughter, sitting on the other side of his massive desk.

"I'm not calling him. You call him," she countered.

"I'm the president, not you. You have to do what I tell you, not the other way around." He set his chin and glared at her.

"What's the matter, Dad? Chicken?"

"What? How dare you call me that. President's don't make calls like that."

"Well, I'm not doing it," she retorted, rising from her chair. "This is going to kill him, and I'm not going to be the one to wield the fatal blow." She flounced out of the room, shutting the door behind her.

As she headed back to her office, a sick feeling in the pit of her stomach soured her on lunch. Bill Landeau had given a fantastic presentation. There was no sane reason on Earth to turn down his proposal.

Carter stood outside her door.

"Problems with Pops?"

"He hates to be called that," she replied.

"Sorry. Just an affectionate name for my future father-in-law. What's up?"

She explained about Bill.

"I'll call him."

"You?"

"Yes. It should be me since I led the team to turn him down."

"Do you really want to call him?" she asked, cocking an eyebrow at him.

"Of course not. But someone has to do it. You won't, and your father doesn't want to. So I'll do it. It's the least I can do. Was your dad super pissed about it?"

"I wouldn't knock on his door for the next couple of days," she replied.

Carter loosened his tie. "Not fair to keep Sports Unlimited hanging, either."

"That's very considerate of you." She cocked an eyebrow.

"Winners should be considerate of losers, don't you think?" he asked.

"I do, but I didn't know you agreed."

He took her hand and kissed the back. "With you at my side, I can only be bigger and better."

"You think you'll run the company when Dad retires?"

Carter blushed. "I might have entertained that idea."

"Forget it. I'm next in line."

"You? A woman?"

"Don't go there," she warned.

"You'll be busy with our five children," he said, grinning.

She sighed. "Are you really that chauvinistic?"

"No. Just kidding. Of course, you'll take over. But you'll need a right-hand man you can trust. And here I am," he said, with a slight bow.

She laughed. "Sometimes you're so cheesy."

He took her in his arms and kissed her. "Love does that to me."

She stayed in his embrace a moment longer, then entered her office. Carter walked down the hall. Chewing her lip, Paige watched him.

"A problem?" Ruth asked.

"Nope. Just trying to figure Carter out."

"You're engaged. Shouldn't you know him already?" Ruth asked.

"I should. But I'm not sure I do."

She entered her office and glanced at the papers on her desk. Unable to focus on work, she swiveled her chair and stared out the window. Though relieved she didn't have to call Bill, the outcome of the vote still didn't sit easy. Her father had been right. They should have made a deal with Sports Unlimited. It was a great program and the positive publicity would do the company a ton of good. They'd have people lined up to work there—the best and the brightest.

She frowned. Carter squelched Bill's proposal because he was jealous. But what was there to be jealous about? She hadn't seen her camp boyfriend in ages. Although he wasn't married, he might have a girlfriend or be in a relationship.

Shame heated her face. She'd out and out lied to Carter. Bill had held her hand, and she'd liked it. His smile had been so warm, his greeting seemed so genuine. Maybe it was all about the money for his project, but she didn't think so. Bill had always had the ability to make her feel like she was the only person in the room, the only one in the world.

He'd used that on little Paige, an awkward, eleven-year-old tomboy, shipped off to camp for the first time. Only two years older, Bill had taken her under his wing, made her feel important. He'd done more to boost her confidence than her father ever had.

Paige had blossomed at Camp High Point. Fond memories flooded back, putting a smile on her face. Learning to swim, being the best at softball, and even excelling in arts and crafts made summer perfect. But mostly it had been about her growing friendship with Bill. An only child, Paige had been lonely, shut up in a fancy townhouse in Manhattan. She'd loved and admired her doting mom, a beautiful, warm woman who had tons of friends and an active social life, but still managed to have time for her daughter.

Chagrined that Carter picked up on her connection with Bill, Paige couldn't lie to herself. Old feelings resurfaced, like a phoenix rising from the ashes. It had been instantaneous, as if they'd never been apart. She could almost see a bolt of electricity spark between them—and, she guessed, so could Carter.

She'd spent years shedding her old "Slugger" image, turning herself into a "lady." Paige had a responsible position in a large company. Board members didn't don ball caps and hit it out of the park, not if they're girls. Nope. Slugger had to remain dormant, shoved into the background, shrunk down to almost nothing. Even if she wanted to revive that persona, there was no going back. Cultured, proficient in three foreign languages, elegant, beautiful—even sexy, some might say, and, above all, intelligent, Paige had made these choices. She couldn't back out now.

"BILL LANDEAU," HE SAID, answering his work phone.

"Carter Wentworth here. From Overton Enterprises."

"Oh, yes. Carter. How are you?"

"Fine. Look, I'm on a tight schedule today, so let's get right to it."

"Ok."

"The board voted, and we've decided to take a pass on your project. You did a great job presenting, but it's just not in our wheelhouse at the moment. I wish you good luck. Thank you for your time. And please thank J.C., too."

"What? Why?"

"I'm so sorry. I don't have time to go into that now. Best of luck to you," Carter said, then the phone went dead.

Anger turned to fury. It rose through his chest to his face and ears. He pushed up from his desk and hollered.

"What the fuck?"

J.C. poked his head in Bill's office. "What's up?"

"That was that asshole Carter Wentworth. From Overton."

"Yeah?"

"He turned us down. Flat. No explanation. Just said, 'it isn't in our wheelhouse,'" Bill said, imitating Carter's voice. "Bullshit."

"No shit?"

"No shit."

"Damn."

"You can say that again," Bill said, sinking down in his chair.

J.C. entered and patted Bill on the back. "They're not the only money people around. Consider that presentation a dress rehearsal."

"I thought it was a slam dunk."

"Me, too, but, hey, who knows what goes on in a company?"

"I thought Paige liked what we presented. I'd hoped she'd swing things our way."

"Hoping for a favor? This is too much money for that."

"She knows me. How could she let me get shot down?"

"How old is old?"

Bill shrugged. "I was sixteen when I last saw her."

"It's a long time ago. Don't take it personally. It's business. I've got a few irons in the fire. We'll find someone else."

"Maybe the idea is just stupid," Bill said.

"Aw, come on. Did you always give up that easy when you played football?"

"No."

"No quitting now. We've got the presentation nailed. Maybe a few tweaks. And we'll take in on the road. I believe in this idea."

"That makes one of us."

"Damn! If you're quitting, you're not the guy I thought you were. This is something that will make a difference in the world. It's not about money."

"That's what I thought."

"And you're going all quitter on me because this ex of yours sold you down the river? Man up. Don't be an asshole. I need you to be confident."

"I will."

"Take today and tomorrow off. I'll have Wendy set up meetings for us over the next three weeks. Come back with your game face on," J.C. said, exiting the room and shutting the door.

Bill shuffled out of the office and walked home. He took the elevator up to the pre-war apartment on West End Avenue. It was Rafe and his partner, Charlie's, New York City digs. They'd stay there when they had business in the City.

Rafe had turned the keys to the spacious studio over to Bill. He was welcome to live there while he got this business off the ground. Once it was up and running, Bill would find his own place. In the meantime, he kept the apartment from growing dusty.

The tony digs, on the tenth floor, had a lovely view of the Hudson River and New Jersey. The room was large with crown molding and other touches from the past. Rafe had renovated it, so the refinished floor was shiny and the walls sported subtle shades of beige with white molding.

Bill dragged himself to the kitchen table and plopped down his bag of takeout from the deli. With no appetite for the ham sandwich and coffee, he grabbed a beer from the fridge, instead. After twisting off the top and sinking down on a chair, he called Sandy.

"I may lose my job," he began.

"What?"

Bill explained what had happened, then stopped to take a drink.

"That's awful. I'm so sorry."

"Do you remember Paige from camp?"

"The girl you used to call 'slugger'?"

"Yep."

"I remember her. Turned out to be pretty cute, if I recall."

"She shot down the business plan."

"Wow. Really? Bet you didn't see that coming."

"I was totally surprised to see her. I'd forgotten her name was Overton. And she's on the board. Never would have expected that."

"Did she wear a baseball uniform to the meeting?"

"Very funny. Not!"

"Sorry."

"She dressed up all fancy in a pink suit. She looked amazing, but not like the same girl I knew."

"Guess she's changed."

"You could say that."

"What a shame. You guys had sparks."

"How'd you know?"

Sandy laughed. "Everyone in camp knew. It's not like you two making out behind the tennis courts at midnight was a big secret."

Bill sensed heat in his cheeks. "Really?"

"Gossip traveled like wildfire at High Point."

"I never knew."

"We were taking bets on you two going steady by the end of the summer. Then Paige had to leave early."

"Bets?"

Sandy laughed. "I shouldn't have told you."

"We were going steady. I'd given her a necklace."

"Really? That's news. With what money?"

"Tip money from the year before. Unlike some people, I save." He grinned.

"You sneaky guy! Wait a minute. Rafe's talking."

Bill took the lull in conversation as a chance to swig down more beer. After a minute his sister returned.

"Rafe says not to worry about the apartment. Stay there as long as you want. Charlie is swamped in Pine Grove and we're here for another year, so you can stay."

"Tell him thanks."

"I will. And don't worry. I'm sure between this J.C. guy and you, you'll pull a rabbit out of the hat and get the funding you need."

"Thanks."

"Gotta go. It's dinner time."

With Sandy's encouragement, Bill's appetite returned, he wolfed down his sandwich. Since it was still early, he headed out for a walk along the Hudson River. After exiting the building, he turned left toward Riverside Park. There were only a handful of people on the promenade at six o'clock. He ambled along by the water. People with dogs of all shapes and sizes, along with a few folks on rollerblades, passed. A woman holding up a large camera crouched by the railing. Although dressed in jeans and a T-shirt, she looked familiar.

It couldn't be, because Bill didn't know anyone in New York. Wait.

"Paige?" he asked. She lowered the camera and turned. "What are you doing here?"

"Taking pictures," she responded. "Do you live here?"

"A few blocks away."

"Huh. Me, too."

Anger bubbled up in his chest. "Why did you do it?"

"Do what?"

"Sink my project."

"I didn't."

"You voted against it, didn't you?" His brows knitted.

She shook her head. "I recused myself. Because I know you."

"Would your vote have changed the outcome?"

"I can't say. That's confidential," she said, lifting her camera.

Bill pushed her camera down. "I'm talking to you."

"That conversation is over. You got what you wanted."

"No, I didn't. Why did you abstain?"

"I told you," she said, moving away.

He grabbed her arm. "I thought we were friends."

She whirled around to face him. "And I thought we were much more."

His mouth dropped open.

"After I left camp, I wrote to you. You never answered."

"I was a kid. Seventeen. I'm not a letter writer."

"You could have called."

"Are you saying you cried your eyes out because I didn't write?" His stare bored into her.

"Not exactly." She cast her gaze to the ground.

"Are you telling me I broke your heart?"

"I'm saying I don't understand why you disappeared. I thought we had something special."

"Yeah, special for kids. And you're the one who disappeared."

"Did you miss me?"

"Maybe." It was his turn to turn his gaze away.

She narrowed her eyes and peered at him. "You mean you never, ever thought about us? Never wondered if we could have had something, been something...more?"

His lips parted, then froze. How could he tell her she'd always been his gold standard? Every woman he ever dated he'd measured against her—and found wanting. He found out, through his sister, that Paige came from money, big money, translation—way out of his league. That sealed it. He had nothing to offer, hell, he didn't even have a permanent job until a few months ago, so he'd never tried to find her.

"That's what I thought. You just didn't give a damn. I was a good make-out for the summer and that's it." She backed away from him.

He grabbed her arm. "You couldn't be more wrong."

"Then what?"

"Nothing." *I'm not in her league and never will be. She's fancy, expensive. I'm broke, living in a borrowed apartment.*

"Nothing? That's what I thought." She stopped, her tone softened. "Good luck. Your idea is great. I hope you find a backer," she said. For a moment, he saw a glimmer of the old warmth in her eyes. Then it faded.

"Good luck marrying that dickwad Carter," he muttered, turning away.

"What did you say?" she asked, her voice raised.

He faced her again. "You heard me. Go ahead. Marry Carter. You deserve each other."

She slapped his face. He jumped back as his hand flew up to his reddening flesh. "What the hell was that for?"

"How dare you call me a dickwad."

"I didn't say that."

"You said he was and that we deserved each other."

"Well, maybe that was over-the-top. I'm sorry." He rubbed his face.

Paige approached. He retreated. "I'm not going to hit you again."

"Good."

She tugged his hand away and examined his cheek, then placed a gentle kiss there."

"Do you love him?" he asked, in a whisper, cupping her shoulder.

"I've agreed to marry him." She stepped away.

"That's not what I asked."

"Why do you care?"

"Because you're my Slugger," he said, meeting her gaze.

Her eyes watered. "Once, maybe. I haven't been your Slugger for forever. Slugger is gone."

"Hell, you can dress in all the designer shit you want, talk with a fancy accent, flash money around, and turn your nose up at me and all the other have-nots, but inside, you'll always be my slugger," he said, bending down to kiss her.

Chapter Three

Was this a dream? Bill Landeau kissed her, not simply a peck and it wasn't brotherly. As the pressure from his lips increased, her knees weakened. When the tip of his tongue asked for admittance, she opened. Damn, the man could kiss, and even better than when he was a teen.

All thoughts, including Carter Wentworth, flew out of her head. Her senses ruled. Bill pushed the camera, hanging around her neck, to one side before he pulled her closer, pressing his hard chest to her much softer one. Her hands, clutching his shoulders, slid around his neck.

As he deepened the kiss, she melted against him. If he'd wanted to take her right there in the park, she wouldn't have resisted. Pent-up desire leaked through her defenses. She'd dreamt about making love with him for years. As if he could read her mind, knew she hungered for his touch, his hand closed over her breast.

A small moan escaped her mouth when he made contact. She pressed her hips against his and glowed with the knowledge that he was getting hard. He broke first. Cool air replaced his warm body and chilled her.

"I'm sorry. I shouldn't have done that. You're engaged to another man. I should respect that. Even if it is that dick, Carter."

She smiled. How could she disagree when she had called Carter a dick a few times herself?

"Why him? Why?" he asked.

She shrugged. "He asked. You didn't."

He inched closer. "And if I had? Would you have said 'yes'?"

She cast her gaze to her shoes. Her mother always told her that her eyes gave her away. While they stood there, the strains of the song *One Fine Day* danced through her mind. Would today be that day?

He tipped her chin up, making eye contact. Not ready for him to see her true feelings, she closed hers.

"Open up. Come on."

She did, staring into his lust-filled brown eyes. "Happy?"

His eyes widened with wonder. "Damn. You would have, wouldn't you?"

She pushed off his chest. "I've got to go."

Once again, he detained her by grabbing her arm. "Why? Conversation getting too hot for you?

"Maybe. Look, Bill. You can't just show up and expect us to roll back all these years and take up where we left off. I'm not the same person. And neither are you."

"I haven't changed much. And I bet, inside, you're the same, too."

"It's another lifetime for me. Six months after my mother died, my father found a new wife. Everything changed. They sent me away to boarding school in Switzerland to learn to behave the way she wanted. I suffered there for two years until I finally figured it out. Do it her way and I could come home. So, I did. And I became a 'young lady', as my stepmother said." Her voice faltered on the last few words.

Bill drew her to him and held her close. Tears leaked down her cheeks. Damn. Wasn't she over this yet?

"I'm so sorry, Paige."

She snuggled her face into his shoulder. He smelled of piney deodorant, masculinity and a touch of sweat. It was familiar and welcome. Carter's face appeared in her mind's eye. He'd have a fit if he knew. Slowly, she disengaged.

"I really have to go." Paige took two tentative steps back."Can I see you?" he asked, his brows drawn together, his eyes cloudy.

"I don't think that would be a good idea."

"You're not going to marry Carter now, are you? I mean after this?"

"Was this just a ploy to get me to cheat on him?"

"You know me better than that."

"Do I?" she asked. "It's been a long time."

"I've never been a liar. Not gonna start now."

"Look, Bill. You can't simply appear and turn my world upside down, just because you want to. I have a life. Responsibilities. I shouldn't have kissed you."

"The girl I loved is still in there. And I'm not going to stop until she's freed from her jail." He kissed her nose, turned on his heel, and strode away.

She touched her bottom lip. Wasn't this what she'd always wanted? Maybe back then, but now? *I can't control myself. I can't stop.* The only way to keep her life stable would be to stay away from Bill Landeau. Did she want that? Was her life stable or boring, or not her own at all?

Her head hurt. Too many ideas warred in her brain. Her hedonistic self wanted to sleep with Bill. But she belonged to Carter, who would drop her immediately if she crossed the line with Bill. Who did she want, Carter or Bill? Easy answer—Bill. But he didn't have much of a future. They'd live in a studio apartment and eat rice and beans.

But he'd make her laugh and they'd spend their nights making love. Would that be so bad? Paige ambled toward the park exit. So many thoughts tumbled through her brain. When she returned to her townhouse, she stretched out on the couch. Paige closed her eyes, hoping her dreams would solve her dilemma.

BILL AMBLED HOME AND slipped into bed. At two o'clock, he pushed up and turned on the television. No way was he getting to sleep. Paige wanted him. He sensed it in her kiss and the way her body molded to his.

Good thing they hadn't been somewhere private, or they'd have made love. He'd been ready, but then, again, he'd been ready for her for years. What does an honorable man do? Does he respect the fact the lady is engaged to another man and keep hands off? Or does he woo the lady to win her away from the obnoxious, idiot whose ring she wore?

He couldn't call Sandy. Some things a guy doesn't confess to his beloved big sister. How could he tell her Paige had almost cheated on Carter? He envisioned Sandy's frown. He knew what she'd say.

Hell, he couldn't leave her with Carter, doomed to a life of misery with that jerk-off. He popped a beer and took a swig. Nope, he'd have to make a play for her. He'd conduct a rescue mission. That's it, yes! A rescue-Paige-from-the-asshole mission, should he choose to accept it. Which, of course, he would.

Bill remembered how much she liked Chinese food. Picking up his phone, he searched for Chinese restaurants in the neighborhood. After he found one with excellent reviews, he looked up Paige's email. Now he had to think of a clever way to ask her to dinner and get her phone number in the same message.

Sure, Carter could out buy him in the fancy dinner department. Bill didn't deny that. But he'd bet a hundred bucks the phony sleazeball had never taken her out for Chinese. What Bill lacked in financial resources he'd make up for in care, concern, and listening.

Satisfied he'd decided on the right course, he finished his beer and got back into bed. Sleep came quickly, and he passed a restful night.

In the morning, full of energy, as if he'd slept all night instead of worrying for half of it, he showered and dressed. His good spirits drooped as he hit the elevator to the temporary office J.C. had set up. What the hell were they going to do now?

He straightened the knot on his tie as he entered the Sports Unlimited private offices and knocked on J.C.'s door.

"Come in."

"Hi."

"Hey there," J. C. said, looking up from his computer. "Such a sad face!"

"The Overton Enterprises disaster."

"No worries. I have three more presentations lined up."

"You do?" Bill's eyebrows flew up.

"Of course. You don't think I'd have only one iron in the fire, do you? Never do that. Always have a back-up or three in your pocket."

"That's great, J.C. What's the schedule?"

"Here are the three company names. Have Wendy create a dozen presentation folders for each of these."

"When are we presenting."

"The schedule's on the bottom of the page."

"Fantastic." Bill rose to leave the office.

He set to work but remembered to take time out to dig out Paige's office number. At three, he loosened his tie and picked up his cell. He regarded it as a good sign that he made it past her secretary to Paige.

"Hi, babe."

"Hi, yourself. I'm working. What's up?"

"Dinner? Chinese?"

There was silence on the end.

"No fair. You know it's my favorite."

"And that's bad?"

"I suppose not."

"When can you go?"

"Tomorrow."

"Perfect. Shall I pick you up or do you want to meet me at the restaurant??"

"I'll meet you there," she said. "Text me the name and address."

He chuckled. "You got it. See you tomorrow." He put his phone down.Wendy knocked. "Here you go. I have the first two done."

"Great. Thank you. Put them on the credenza."

She nodded, deposited the folders, and left. Paige occupied his mind. He had to get this settled, one way or another. He picked up the phone.

"Sandy?" He rocked back in his chair.

"What's up?"

"I'm taking Paige out to dinner tomorrow night."

"Oh?" He envisioned her eyebrows shooting up.

"Yep. Chinese. Her favorite." He held his breath.

"I thought she was engaged."

"Yeah, to a real tool. Total douche."

"Is that any of your business?"

"It is now."

"I don't like to be critical, Bill, but aren't you butting in where you don't belong?"

"That depends." He put his feet flat on the floor and sat up straight.

"On what?"

"On the way she kissed me yesterday." Okay, okay, so he couldn't keep a secret from his sister.

"Really? You kissed her?"

"It was mutual." He pushed to his feet and walked to the window.

"I see."

"All's fair in love and war, right?"

"You sure about this?"

"Never been more sure of anything in my life." He exaggerated a bit, or maybe a whole lot.

"I just don't want you to get hurt."

"Too late." He rubbed his scruffy chin.

"Crap."

"I have my chance. At least she knows I'm not loaded. She's seen the real me."

"Okay. I suppose that's good."

"And she's going with me anyway." He paced.

"What you lack in funds, you make up for in charm."

"Thank you, dear sister. Can I take that as support?"

"You can. I only want you to be happy."

"And Paige would make me very happy."

"As long as you're sure."

"I think underneath her veneer, she's the same slugger she used to be."

"Fingers crossed."

"Thanks. Say hello to Rafe for me."

"Will do. Love you."

"Love you, too."

He hung up. Sandy's approval was the one missing piece. Now, he had all he needed. Picking up one of the folders, Bill perused it, checking for mistakes. They had to win one of their presentations and do it soon, or he'd be out of a job. Charm alone wouldn't do much for winning Paige if he was unemployed.

"WHY DON'T YOU POP AROUND for dinner tomorrow?" Avery, her stepmother, said.

Paige made a face into the phone. "I'm going out."

"Bring Carter, too. We haven't seen him in ages."

"I'm going with a friend." Paige held her breath.

"A friend? Male or female?"

"It's my business. I have to go, Avery. Business calls."

"Don't you dare hang up on me. Answer the question."

"Gotta go." She hadn't fooled her stepmother. Simply her refusal to answer was the equivalent of an answer. She hated the third degree Avery gave her at every opportunity. Now she'd be on her case like an effing bloodhound. Why was it so important to her that Paige marry Carter? Seemed the more Avery wanted it, the less Paige did.

She turned her cell off and resumed shuffling through the papers on her desk. Losing focus, she put a pen between her lips and stared out the window. What the hell was she doing, having dinner with Bill? If Carter found out, he'd throw a fit.

An hour later, there was a knock on her door. Her father appeared.

"Avery tells me you're stepping out on Carter tonight. Do you think that's wise?"

"I'm not stepping out on him. I'm having dinner with an old friend."

Her dad quirked an eyebrow.

"Okay. So he was an old boyfriend. It's just dinner."

"That guy? The one who made the presentation?"

"So what?"

"As long as it's only dinner and doesn't turn into all night."

"That's my business."

"And Carter's too, I'm afraid." Her father eased down into the chair next to her desk. He took her hand in both of his.

"Paige, do you really want to marry Carter?"

"I agreed to, didn't I?"

"That wasn't my question. Are you happy?"

Paige glanced at her fingernails. "I think so."

"You *think* so?" His eyebrows shot up. "Break it off, before it's too late.""I can't."

"Yes, you can."

"Carter's nice to me. It would be a good life."

"Not if you don't love him. Your mother and I, well, what we had was special. It only comes along once."

"Do you miss her?" Paige made eye contact with her dad.

"Every day, sweetheart. Every day."

"So do I," she said. Her eyes filled. Her father hugged her.

"She'd want you to be happy."

"I know."

"Is this other man the right one?"

"I don't know."

"Well, find out. Quickly."

"What if he doesn't feel the same about me?"

Her dad chuckled. "Paige, what man wouldn't want to marry you?"

"It's not about the money."

"Of course not! You're a beautiful, charming, intelligent young woman. What man wouldn't want you to be his wife?"

"You're prejudiced."

"Damn right." He laughed and stood up. "Don't settle, Paige. I didn't and it's made all the difference."

"How?"

"I have you, sweetheart," he said, giving her a quick hug before exiting her office.

Paige swiveled to face the big window. She sighed. Exactly what did she want? As she looked out at the tall buildings blocking her view of the shoreline, she mulled over life with Carter versus life with Bill. Carter would provide stability, Bill, adventure—and, maybe, love. Not that Carter didn't love her. He did, didn't he? She shrugged. With him, it was hard to tell if he cared for her or if she was simply a trophy to him. Although she respected Carter's business intelligence, her heart belonged to Bill.

She stared at her engagement ring. The diamond flashed back a cold light, more like a shackle than a token of love. What had happened to the independent Paige? Where was "Slugger"? Had she vanished? She slipped the ring off and put it in her top desk drawer. Lighter than before, her hand seemed naked but free.

Paige picked up her phone, took a deep breath, and called Carter. "We need to talk."

"Can it wait? I'm at the airport. We have a crisis in Kansas City. I'll be back in two days, hopefully."

"Okay."

She put down her phone and slid the ring back on. After rummaging around in her drawer, she found the box it came in. She stroked the velvet covering. Keeping the box gave her a place to put the gem when she returned it. She sighed. Kissing security goodbye kicked up her nerves.

Paige decided she needed more time with her old camp boyfriend before she could make a final decision. Bill had always been competitive. Was he serious or just goaded by the challenge? Beating Camp Calloway drove him every summer. She'd admired his desire to win, but was she simply another prize? She had two days to spend time with Bill, chaste time, no sex, to discover if he should replace Carter.

He'd have a fit if he knew what she was doing. But she needed to be sure, completely sure, and the temptation Bill Landeau offered rattled her. If Carter was the right man to marry, why did she crave Bill?

To avoid Avery and her father, and thinking about her life, Paige skipped out and went to the movies. There was a new romance playing about ten blocks away. She took a seat in the middle flanked by a large tub of popcorn on one side and a Coke on the other.

The movie sucked her in. When it finished, she pushed to her feet and took her trash to the garbage can. Was it silly that a movie, which had no relation to her, had solidified her resolve? She needed romance, love, affection, and laughter. Whichever man brought that would be the one to own her heart.

On her way home, she stopped at Franklin's, a high-end boutique, to buy a new dress for her dinner with Bill. She didn't have anything easy breezy for a low-key Chinese restaurant. She went home with a new tunic and a pair of white crop leggings. Hell, if Carter came into Low Chow's, he wouldn't recognize her. She laughed. Maybe putting her hair in pigtails would complete the look?

BILL STEPPED OUT OF the shower and wrapped a towel around his waist. He hummed as he lathered up to shave. Uncertain whether Paige preferred clean-shaven men or men with scruff, he opted for the safe route and took it all off. He flipped on the radio then worked the razor over his face. The song, *One Fine Day,* came on. He stopped to smile. Did that song pertain to him?

He slapped aftershave on and headed for the closet. Perusing his meager wardrobe, he frowned. With grad school to pay for, there had been zero bucks left over for new clothes. All he owned were bargain-basement duds. Frustrated, he went through his shirts, discarding each one. His only decent shirts were dress shirts for work. Those would never do.

He considered a T-shirt but rejected that as too casual. Then it popped out at him. A stupid, loud Hawaiian shirt his sister bought for him as a goof. She came back from her honeymoon cruise with the shirt. They'd had a good laugh about it. The short-sleeved garment had a black background with blue and green palm trees on it.

Having no other choice, Bill sighed and pulled it from the hanger. The Paige he knew and loved would be silly enough, crazy enough to like the ridiculous garment. At least, he hoped so. He shrugged it over his muscular shoulders and donned his only pair of casual pants, khakis.

He took one more gander in the mirror, ran a comb through his hair, and ignored the flutters in his belly. Whistling *One Fine Day*, he hit the street and arrived fifteen minutes early.

The restaurant gave him a free glass of wine, as so many Chinese restaurants do in New York City. He stared at his hands as he pondered what to say to Paige. He needed to catch up on her life since camp but didn't want his questions to sound like an interrogation.

How did she end up with that creep, Carter? He'd broach that topic delicately, so he wouldn't look jealous, even if he was. And he'd refrain from calling the man names, no easy task. As topics whirled through his brain, a voice startled him.

"Bill?"

He looked up. There she stood, wearing a casual short dress with cropped leggings, her dark hair framed her face. She took his breath away.

"Paige!"

"You were expecting someone else?"

His manners returning, he jumped up and grabbed her chair, pulling it out so fast he almost knocked her down. She latched onto his arm to steady herself.

"I'm so sorry," he said, pulling her close to keep her from falling.

She laughed. "No harm done." She eased down onto the chair, and he retook his seat.

A waiter appeared with wine for Paige. They sipped while they discussed what to order. They agreed on the fried dumplings, pepper steak and crispy prawns with walnuts. The first course came quickly. While they munched, Bill took charge of the conversation.

"You've filled me in on a little bit of your life after camp. What about after finishing school? When you came home, did you go right into your father's business?"

Paige gave him the highlights of her years since leaving Switzerland. She then tossed the ball to Bill, who spoke about his early dead-end jobs until he enrolled in graduate school. Dishes magically appeared and disappeared as the couple focused on each other.

"Do you do any sports?" Bill asked, digging into the last piece of pepper steak on his plate.

"I joined a women's softball league. I played for a few years without telling my dad or Avery. I gave it up three years ago. Something about not having anyone in the stands rooting for me kind of took the fun out of it."

Bill squeezed her hand. "That's too bad. I bet you were their best hitter."

"Number two, actually." She smiled at him.

The waiter brought the check. Bill paid and held the door open for Paige. It was twilight in late June. The sky flashed brilliant shades of orange and pink as the sun made its way to bed for the night. The air cooled.

"Where do you live?" he asked.

"One-oh-four, between West End and Riverside."

"Can I walk you home?"

"Sure."

They laced fingers as they strolled up West End Avenue. The perfect date continued. When he reached her door, his brows met.

"I don't see any apartment number. In fact, no apartments at all."

"That's right. I own this townhouse. I rent out the top two floors. My tenants have the combination to the front door," she said, stepping up and punching in a five-digit number.

Bill's mouth hung open for a few seconds. Rich? Way beyond rich—and so out of his league.

"My father bought it for me," she explained, opening the carved oak door.

"I see," Bill said and swallowed. Nobody owned three stories in any building in Manhattan. Nobody he knew—until now.

"Don't get crazy, okay? I pay the taxes and upkeep on the building and oversee the maintenance. Yes, he handed it to me. But he said he'd rather I have it now, while he's alive than after he's dead. I kinda agree."

They entered a small foyer and faced a staircase. Paige led him past the steps and down the hall to another entrance. He gasped as he stepped into the most gorgeous modern living room he'd ever seen.

"What can I say? This is the most beautiful place in all of Manhattan."

Paige dropped her purse on a side table and laughed.

"I mean it," he said, stopping in front of the floor to ceiling windows facing the backyard.

"Want a beer?"

"Sure."

"Inside or out?" she asked, moving to a bar set up on a black lacquer cart.

"Outside?"

"Yeah. I have some chairs and stuff out there."

"Out."

She ambled to the refrigerator. Bill followed. The open kitchen was spacious. She yanked on a stainless steel door and plucked out two bottles.

"This way," she said, moving past a small dining table to a side door. She punched in another code and they went outside. Paige led him along a short, winding stone path to a little clearing with a round wrought iron and glass table. Trees created a canopy, shielding the cozy space from the sun. Matching ice cream chairs had rose-colored seat cushions.

They sat close. A bird feeder caught Bill's eye.

"Can't believe you get birds in this city," he remarked.

Paige put her bottle down. "Cut the crap. Stop stalling. Say what's on your mind."

He took her hand between both of his. "Don't marry Carter."

Chapter Four

She slid her hand away from him. "Don't."

"Why not?"

"I'm committed. We can't do anything. That kiss was a mistake. Not doing that again."

"Why are you with him? He's a dog. Cut him loose. Be with me instead."

"Be with you? Is that an offer?"

"Do I have to get down on bended knee?"

"Uh, yeah. Maybe. We have a lot of catching up to do. Don't propose if you don't mean it. And how could you? We haven't seen each other in years."

"I know, I know. Everything you say makes sense. But we have chemistry. I feel the connection. It's still there."

"Maybe we need to dust it off."

"Exactly!"

"But not as long as I'm engaged to Carter."

"So what are you waiting for? Dump him and give us a chance."

Paige stared at her engagement ring. "And what if it doesn't work out between us? I think you'd better go before we do something stupid."

"Making love with me is stupid?"

"As long as I'm engaged to Carter, it is. Come on, Bill. You know you wouldn't respect me if I cheated on him."

He lowered his head, staring at his feet. "You're right. I wouldn't. You're no cheater."

She pushed to her feet. "Thanks for understanding."

He joined her. "Hey, I can't give you any guarantees. I don't know if we'll make it. But I want to try."

"I get it. Let it go for now." Afraid of what she might do if he stood too close, she stepped away.

"Will you get free?" He rested his hands on her upper arms.

"Carter is out of town. I'll talk with him when he gets back."

"Or I could just bust him in the nose." Bill dropped his hands.

She laughed and moseyed over to the rose bushes. "Right."

"I'm not kidding." His brows knitted.

"You should be," she said, heading for the back door. "You can't bully your way into this."

Heat made its way into his face. "God damn it, Paige! I've wasted all this time trying to find a woman to replace you. No go. Can't you see we're meant to be?" His hand fisted at his side.

"What?" She stared at him.

"Every woman I've dated I've measured against you. Some weren't smart enough, or not pretty enough, or not funny enough, or didn't laugh at my stupid jokes. Some only wanted a secure future. Some...well, you get the picture."

"Really? But we were kids."

"So what? I haven't changed, except maybe I've grown up a little. Let's just say if you sent me that letter now, I'd write back. Call, or something."

"I've changed." She lowered her lashes.

"I doubt that. I bet underneath all this fancy stuff is the same girl I fell for."

"Slugger?"

He nodded.

"I doubt it. She's been gone for such a long time." Paige's eyes filled.

He took her in his arms. Damn, it felt good. Paige rested her head on his shoulder and sniffled.

"Come on. You believe in my idea, right?"

She nodded.

He spoke quietly. "So be with me. Help me. It would be so much easier to launch this crazy thing if you were by my side."

She pushed away. "I can't. No promises. All I can do is talk to Carter."

"What will you say? Hey, let me sleep with Bill so I'll know if I'd rather marry him than you?"

She laughed. "Not exactly."

"Then what?"

"I don't know. I'll figure it out."

Bill leaned in and kissed the tip of her nose. "That's my girl."

She showed him to the front door and raised her hand to signal goodbye as he ambled down the block. She sighed. Bill Landeau, still a hunk, and in love with her. Who'd have guessed that one? The song from camp, *One Fine Day,* played through her mind. Yes, he knew their love was meant to be. And she did, too, didn't she? But what about Carter? Paige knew he'd never agree, never understand what she had with Bill. Was she doing the right thing? Could she make Carter accept it without anger or rancor?

What if it didn't work out with Bill? Wasn't she stepping off the ledge with a leap of faith, believing a childhood crush could be the real thing? She swallowed. If she lost both Carter and Bill, then what? She sighed and mumbled her mantra, "I'll figure it out."

Of course she would—she always did. With a smile, Paige hummed the song as she bid Bill farewell and returned to her sumptuous townhouse.

AS HE UNLOCKED HIS door, his cell rang. It was Sandy. Barely inside the door, he answered.

"You'll never believe this, but Stanley Malone is a big gun at a nonprofit."

"Yeah? So?"

"Present your camp stuff to him."

"Who is he anyway?"

"I met him at camp. Didn't you?"

"I don't remember."

"You only remember camp friends by their bra size?"

"Shut the fuck up."

She chuckled. "Okay, okay. Low blow. Anyway, I called him for you. He wants to see you and J.C."

"Really? When"

"Friday. At ten. Can you do it?"

Bill sank down on the sofa. "Let me check my schedule."

"What a big muck-a-muck you are! Check your schedule."

"We have a presentation in the afternoon, but the morning is free."

"I'll text you his email. Good luck."

"Thanks, Sandy. I owe you one."

"Nah."

"You're the best."

He clicked off then on again and dialed J. C. Their schedule wasn't totally empty, but it wasn't overflowing with companies dying to force millions on Sports Unlimited, either.

J.C. agreed. Bill emailed Stanley Malone and scratched his head, trying to place the name with a face. He headed for the kitchen, opened a beer and shoved a frozen meal in the microwave. Didn't matter who the guy was, he'd agreed to meet with them. That was a good sign.

Bill listened to the news with only half an ear. Paige had looked luscious at dinner, damn, he couldn't get her out of his mind. The way her dress pulled ever so slightly across her breasts drew his eye again and again.

Sure, he hungered to get her into bed, but there was so much more, wasn't there? At dinner, when he finally got his mind off sex, the old feeling of comfort he had with Slugger washed over him. Talking with her, he'd slipped back into easy mode. She laughed at his stupid "horse walked into a bar" joke. When he'd revealed some of his struggles to find the right job, she'd declared the people in charge of hiring deaf, dumb, and blind. She understood him now like she had when he was sixteen. Damn, could that be possible?

Friday morning, time to get his game face on and stop obsessing about Paige. Tonight, he'd know about everything, whether or not they had a chance to get the money for Sports Unlimited from either of the two companies they were meeting with, and about Paige. Would she still be engaged to Carter by Sunday?

He showered, shaved carefully, and dressed in his best suit, newest shirt, and tie. After downing two cups of coffee, he forced himself to eat a bowl of cereal. Hell, there'd be plenty of time for a big meal to celebrate, if things went well.

He met his boss at 666 Fifth Avenue. J.C. straightened his tie.

"So you know this Stanley Malone dude?"

"Sandy does. I can't place him."

"That must have been some camp you went to."

"It was pretty great. But who knew it would change my life so many years later."

The men entered the lobby of American Projects and announced themselves to the receptionist. They settled into comfortable chairs while she contacted Stanley Malone.

Within five minutes, a secretary showed up and led them to the conference room. Five men were waiting there. Bill perused the faces.

"Edgy? Edgy, is that you?"

"It's Stanley now," he said, extending his hand.

"How great to see you," Bill gushed.

"When Sandy called, I couldn't exactly turn her down."

That wasn't the reply he'd been hoping for. Now he remembered. Edgy wasn't from Camp High Point, but their arch rival, Camp Callahan. How many times had his team had beaten Edgy's in softball, volleyball, and swim meets? Bill almost couldn't count that high.

Suspicion entered his mind. Why would Edgy, who always came up the loser, want to help Bill, his nemesis? Didn't make sense. But they were there, so he had to give it all he had. Maybe Edgy had grown up and didn't resent him anymore? Yeah, and maybe moose could fly.

J.C. started the presentation. After fifteen minutes he handed it off to Bill. When he sat down, he made a thumb's up sign, under the table. Bill swallowed, took a sip of water, then rose to his feet and strode over to the screen.

"Some people think nothing can be done to thwart gangs and redirect inner city kids to more positive and productive lives. We don't agree."

He warmed to his subject and the presentation, which he knew by heart. After wrapping it up, he asked for questions.

"Why should I care about these people?" Edgy asked.

Bill's eyes widened. "Because it's the right thing to do."

"We're concerned with science, not unruly teens."

"Have you considered branching out to improving the safety of cities by reducing the gang population?" J.C. put in.

"Isn't that the job of the police department?"

The desire to deck Edgy rose up in Bill. He squelched it.

"If this doesn't resonate with you, then perhaps you shouldn't invest," Bill responded, his patience wearing thin. Frowning, J.C. stared at his partner.

"We'll have to discuss this idea. It's new to us," the president said.

"Ground-breaking, you might say," Bill replied.

The president nodded. "We'll meet this afternoon and let you know." He stood up.

The meeting was over. The triumphant look in Edgy's eyes bugged Bill. He wanted to wipe the smug smile off his old competitor's face. Bill and J.C. shook hands with all the members of the board. As they were leaving, Edgy caught up with him. He whispered, "I might have a proposition for you."

Bill's eyebrows rose. "Really?"

"I'll call you."

"Thanks."

"Don't thank me yet," Stanley "Edgy" Malone said with a snarl in his voice.

PAIGE PACED IN HER apartment. Due any minute, Carter had been bursting to tell her about his successful trip. She bit her lip. He had no idea she'd be hitting him with a major relationship discussion. Was she blindsiding him? Maybe. Definitely. But there was no other option. She wanted to be with Bill and couldn't do that as long as she was engaged to Carter.

She rummaged through her messy kitchen drawer until she found the corkscrew. She uncorked a bottle of Riesling and put two glasses on the coffee table. Before checking her watch, she combed her fingers through her hair and glanced in the mirror. He'd be there in five minutes—Carter was never late.

Her stomach flipped, then squeezed. She searched the medicine cabinet for an antacid. As she popped one into her mouth, the doorbell rang. Quickly chewing the medicine, she hurried to answer it. Peeking through the peephole, she took a breath. There he stood, holding a bouquet of yellow roses, and grinning. Damn! This would be even harder than she'd imagined.

"Hi," she said, lowering her gaze.

Carter lowered his head, but his lips missed hers. He kissed her cheek instead.

"These are for you. Miss me?" he asked, thrusting the flowers at her. She hated yellow.

"Thanks," she said, shutting the door behind him. "I'll just go put these in water." Paige disappeared into the kitchen, but Carter followed.

"You wouldn't believe what happened on the trip," he began, then continued telling her, in detail, about the new manager at the Kansas City office and what a mess she'd made of things there. Paige nodded from time to time, pretending she was listening. She waited for a place to jump in.

"So that was my trip. How's your week been?" he asked, reaching for the Chivas Regal on the counter. "Ice?"

"I opened a bottle of Riesling."

"That's a chick drink. Men drink scotch."

"Okay." She put the extra wine glass back in the cabinet.

"I repeat, 'ice'?"

"Of course," she said, opening the freezer door and pulling out a tray.

They made small talk for a few minutes until both had their beverages. Carter put his on the coffee table and wound his arms around his fiancée.

"Come here. I need some sugar," he said, bending to nuzzle her neck. Paige squirmed out of his grasp.

He frowned. "Okay. What did I do this time?" His brows knitted.

"Nothing. Nothing. It's me."

"That time of the month?"

"No." Shame and guilt morphed into anger. "Why do you say that every time I don't want you all over me?"

"Because a fiancée is supposed to satisfy her man."

"Oh?" She arched an eyebrow. "Really? And where is that written?"

"It's common knowledge. It's the woman's job to please her man. And that means sex on demand. Except, when, well, during that time. You know." His cheeks pinked.

"You mean when I have my period?"

"Yeah, yeah. Then."

She stuck her chin out. "Can't say it?"

"Yeah. It embarrasses me. Never been married, lived with a woman, don't have a sister. I don't know about these things."

"These things? Like natural stuff? Like a woman shedding the lining of her uterus if there's no fertilized egg?"

The color in his cheeks deepened to red. "Do you have to say that? Geez. Can't you be a little more delicate?"

"Oh, I see. So, you can say *shit*, *fuck*, and *dickwad*, and I can't say *uterus*? Or talk honestly about what happens to my body every month?"

"Exactly."

"Well, *fuck* that!"

"Paige!"

His shocked expression made her laugh. "You're such a hypocrite."

"Me? I'm not the one who brought this up. Hell, I just wanted to make love to my fiancée. Is that against the rules?"

"Only when you expect me to feel the same all the time, every time you're horny. Sometimes I don't feel like it."

"Can't you fake it, once in a while?"

Her eyebrows shot up. "You son of a bitch!"

"Language, Paige."

The urge to slap him grew so strong, she bounded toward the sofa and plopped down on her hands to keep from assaulting him.

"Shut the fuck up, dickwad," she replied, the heat of anger rising in her neck.

He grabbed the flowers from the vase and strode to the door. "I'll bring these back when you're in a better mood."

"You mean when I feel like screwing you?"

The shocked look on his face made her grin in satisfaction.

"What's happening here? What's wrong with you?" His hand was on the knob.

"Nothing. Sometimes I don't feel like having sex when you feel like it."

"Call me when you're feeling normal," he said, jerking open the door.

"Like never," she muttered, watching his back as he left, slamming the door. She jumped at the loud sound. Her eyes filled. *What have I done? Picked a fight just to keep from having an honest talk? Yes, exactly. Coward. I'm a coward. Carter may be a selfish, pompous ass sometimes, but he didn't deserve that.*

BILL AND J.C. WENT to a bar after the presentation. They downed a few beers and burgers then went their separate ways. Bill walked to his apartment, hoping to sober up a bit before hitting the sheets. Before he could lock the door, his phone rang.

"Hello?"

"Bill?"

"Yes."

"Stanley. Edgy, to you."

"Oh, hi. What's up? Did you decide?"

"It was a tie. The deciding vote is mine."

Bill frowned. "Is that good or bad?"

"Depends on your point of view. Where I sit, it's wonderful. "

"How so?"

"I'm giving you a test. I want one more chance to beat you."

"What? Beat me? At what?"

"Softball."

"You're kidding." Bill's eyebrows shot up.

"Never been more serious. Here's the deal. Mixed teams, five women, four men. I'll reserve a field in Chelsea Park. I'll give you the date. If you win, the deal is yours. If you lose, well, you lose the deal. And I'll have the final victory. You on board?"

"This is insane. It's been years and years, Edgy. Get over it."

"Fuck that. Not so cocky now, are you? It was one thing with a bunch of camp kids who could hit straight or field. But with adults? It's another ballgame, as they say. Chicken?"

The hair on the back of his neck bristled. "Of course not. I've beat you before, and I can beat you again."

"So, put your ass where your mouth is. Get a team together. This will be the most important game of your life."

"No. This is stupid."

"Fine. Then the answer is no, right now. Goodbye, and good luck getting your dumbass idea off the ground."

Bill pulled his lower lip over his teeth. What about the kids? The ones counting on him to give them a way out? But, could he do it? Pull together and direct a winning team now? It had been ages. Did he still have the spark, the leadership to motivate people? Desire to beat Edgy, to pound him into the ground, grew in his chest. He wanted the grant and he wanted to win. No, he wanted the money, and he wanted to beat the shit out of that dickwad, Edgy.

"Don't hang up!" Bill shouted.

"Oh?" Edgy asked, his voice quiet.

"Okay. Okay. You've got a deal."

"Honest?"

"I give you my word."

"So, you'll meet me on the field, when I choose, and play?"

"Yes. No ringers, though. No pro-softball players. Just regular people. Five women, four men."

"Okay. I agree."

"And if I win. You'll fund the first camp?"

"And if you lose, you'll admit it, in writing, in an ad in the New York Times, and forget ever asking my company for money, a job, or anything again."

"Yes." Bill swallowed.

"You'll go away, quietly. Tail between legs?"

"Yes." Anger burned in Bill's belly.

"Good," came the smug response. "Exactly what I wanted. I'll be in touch."

The phone went dead. Bill, barely able to squelch the urge to fling his phone against the wall, sank down on the sofa. Edgy may be crazy, but at least Bill had a shot. Maybe. His mind raced. Where the hell would he get eight top-notch softball players?

He called J.C.

"In the morning, man. In the morning," his boss said and hung up.

Afraid to fall asleep, Bill knew he'd wake up and think it was all a dream. Could anyone be that insane? Edgy Malone could. With phone in hand, about to dial Sandy, he checked the clock. Two o'clock in New York meant seven in London. She'd be up! He hit speed dial.

"Sandy?"

"What's up?"

"You'll never believe this," he started.

After explaining everything, exhaustion crept in. He headed for the bedroom. Just after stripping off his clothes, the phone rang again.

"Probably Edgy calling to say April Fool." But it wasn't April. Still, Bill expected Edgy but was surprised to hear J.C.'s voice.

"Was I drunk or did you call me?"

"I did. We might have the money. I heard from that creep Malone."

"You did?"

"Yeah. But it's kinda crazy. I mean, you won't believe his terms."

"Terms? Like for repaying? I thought we'd asked for a grant?"

"We did. Not repaying. For getting the grant. Humiliating me is part of the bargain. And if he can't, then we win and get the money."

"I don't understand."

"It's personal with him. I guess he's been holding a grudge against me all these years for beating him in softball."

"You beat the guy once and he's doing this? Is he crazy?"

"No, J.C. I beat him every summer. And more than once a summer, too."

"Oh, okay. Got it."

"We need to get a team together fast. There's you and me."

"I've never played softball."

"Well, you will now."

"Guess so. This is truly bizarre," J.C. said.

"Agreed. But we want the money, don't we?"

"We do. All right, I'll make a few calls."

"Me, too."

"Let's discuss this over lunch tomorrow."

"Fine."

"Good luck. Maybe we'll hear from another company before that stupid friggin' game."

"Maybe."

"In the meantime, we have to try to win," J.C. said. "Don't give up."

"Thanks."

Bill ended the call and went back to bed. He stared at the ceiling, trying to recall everyone he knew who could play ball. The first name that came to mind was the last person who'd agree to play.

Chapter Five

Paige picked up her phone. "You want me to do what?"

"Play ball. Piece of cake. Especially for you," Bill said.

"I haven't picked up a bat in years. What makes you think I can still play?" Paige asked.

"Once a slugger, always a slugger."

"What's going on?" Paige sat back on the sofa and rested her bare feet on the coffee table while Bill explained the deal.

"And so Edgy wants to have the last word," Bill said."And you want the funding?"

"Right. I could give a shit about the stupid ball game. He needs to grow up."

"Ya think?""So? Will you?"

Desire to help Bill in any way she could pushed her to agree. But what would Carter think? He'd have a friggin' fit. Could Bill count on her to come through like she had in the past? Paige chewed her lip. She had no clue."I don't know. Let me talk it over with Carter."

"What's he got to do with it? Didn't you break up with him yet?"

"Not exactly."

"And what does that mean?"

"It means we're still engaged. Sort of. It's just that I know how he feels about you."

"When are you going to break it off?"

"Soon. Soon." She picked at a cuticle.

"Okay. Talk it over with him and let me know. I'm counting on you, Paige."

Bill hung up. Paige drew her lip over her bottom teeth. She called Shelby, her old roommate from Switzerland.

"I don't know what the problem is, Paige. You've got Carter. He's not gorgeous, but he'll do, and he's got money, a fantastic job. And then there's Bill. A real loser. He's got nothing. A dorky maybe kind of job. Hell, he's looking for people to give his company the money to pay him a salary! And what's he doing? Fooling around with some stupid summer camp idea. If you ask, me, he's the one who hasn't grown up."

Although Paige didn't agree, she saw what her friend was talking about. Maybe that's what her father saw, too. And Carter. But that wasn't the way it was. Bill was trying to do something worthwhile, something hard that would make a difference in the world. Something that didn't have anything to do with money—except he needed money to make it happen.

"I don't know, Shelby. Bill likes me for me. He doesn't expect me to dress fancy or stop swearing."

"Hey, I like you for you, too. But you don't want to marry me!"

"You're a girl."

"So what? Bill's hanging on your coattails. Shake him off. And don't play ball on his team. You could hurt yourself."

Paige laughed. "I'm not gonna hurt myself. But I haven't played in a long time."

"That's what I mean. You're out of shape."

"True."

"Look, I've got a date. I gotta go. Don't listen to me. I'm into security. Do the best thing for your heart."

"Thanks." Paige rested her phone on the cushion. Great advice, but what was the best thing for her heart? Before she could decide the cell tweeted again. Carter.

"Are you feeling better?" he asked, his voice tentative and soft.

"Want to come over?" she asked, dodging his question.

"Sure. Now?"

"Yep. As good a time as any."

"I'll pick up some fried chicken and be right over."

"Great. Thanks."

Paige ended the conversation and padded into the bathroom. She turned on the shower. As she scrubbed herself down, she thought about what she was doing—getting ready for sex with Carter. He wasn't bad in bed, but she fantasized that Bill would be better.

Carter had been generous with her, always picking up the dinner check and bringing flowers. They got along fairly well. She didn't feel a ton of passion for him, but she didn't hate him either. He'd been the obvious choice, approved of by her father and stepmother. So she'd given in, figuring she'd have a calm, if uneventful, life with him.

Carter was nothing like Bill. Her camp boyfriend was volatile, passionate, energetic, funny, and affectionate. Would he provide a stable, financially secure life? Maybe, or maybe not. But life with him would never be dull. She'd never be tempted to cheat. She'd be happy, even if she had to turn her back on designer duds and French Riviera vacations.

She turned off the water and dried off. In the bedroom, she eyed her selection of robes and picked a silky, sexy one. Why bother with underwear if she'd be taking it off right after they ate? She slipped the dark red garment over her shoulders. The bell rang. Good. She was hungry, and Carter was always more agreeable after a meal.

She opened the door, and he strode in with a delicious-smelling bag in one hand and his briefcase in the other. He stopped to kiss her, then deposited the bag on the counter in the kitchen.

"You were right," he said, dropping his briefcase next to the dining room table.

"I was?"

"The sex should always be consensual. I mean, the woman should have the right to say no sometimes."

"Glad you see it my way."

"So, how about tonight?" he asked, placing his hands on her waist.

"Food first."

As she pulled down plates, she got a text. It was from Bill

The game is Saturday afternoon. One game. Winner take all. We need you.

Watching Carter uncork the bottle of wine he brought, she sneaked a reply.

I'll get back to you in a few.

While plucking utensils from the drawer, she cleared her throat.

"You wouldn't mind if I played in a softball game, would you?"

"Since when do you play softball? Why are you asking?" He glanced at her as he yanked the cork free.

"Just don't want to blindside you."

"Blindside me? With a ball game?" he asked, filling the two glasses.

"Well, Bill's in a kind of a jam."

"Bill? Did you say, Bill? Him again? Honestly, Paige, when are you going to get over that childish crush?"

"It's not a crush. He's a friend. And since you screwed over his project, he's dug up another possible investor."

Carter arched an eyebrow and sipped his drink.

"Okay. I'll tell you the whole story." She placed Carter's favorite pieces, a breast and thigh, on a plate, added macaroni and potato salads and handed it to him. She served herself and joined him at the table.

"Spit it out. The whole story."

"Okay."

While she ate, Paige doled out bits and pieces of Bill's story. Carter watched her with wary eyes. He refilled her glass, and she took a healthy sip. Would this lead to their break-up?

"So, the game is Saturday afternoon?" he asked.

She nodded.

"That's the fundraiser tennis tournament for the governor. I told you about it. We're scheduled to play mixed doubles."

Paige swallowed. Carter had run that by her months ago. She'd totally forgotten about it.

"Really? Can you check?"

"I don't need to check. I got a reminder about it this afternoon. This is very important for me. I might pursue a political career. Being friendly with the governor could be a big help."

"But this game means everything to Bill."

"And that tennis tournament means everything to me. Whose side are you on?"

She gulped.

"As your fiancé, I could forbid it," he started. "But I won't. I know you'll put me first. I don't need to demand it. You've always been supportive."

He'd boxed her into a corner. Was she sure she didn't want to marry him? *If so, just tell him you're going to the ballgame and that should do it.* She opened her mouth, then closed it again. Words wouldn't come. They'd been engaged only three months. Still, backing away from her commitment didn't come easy.

"Okay."

"Good. Thanks." He cut a piece of chicken and put it in his mouth. His gaze slid down her body. She shivered, chilled by his hungry stare. While no Casanova, Carter was a competent lover. She'd never complained. Suddenly, Bill popped into her thoughts. She recalled him in a bathing suit, standing on the diving board. Just the sight of him had inspired feelings, twinges, aches in new places. And she'd only been fourteen.

Sure, she wanted him, but to throw over Carter and take up with Bill in the blink of an eye? What would her father say? She knew what her stepmother would say.

She excused herself to go to the bathroom and texted Bill.

Carter and I are competing in a charity tennis tournament. I can't let him down at the last minute. I hope you understand. You'll have to do it without me. I'm sorry.

She held her breath, waiting for his reply. When it came, she closed her eyes for a second, dreading what he would say.

I understand. No worries. I hope you win.

Her heart swelled. He cared for her more than he did about winning. She didn't expect that. When she returned to dinner, Carter had finished. He wiped his mouth with a napkin.

"Now for dessert." He rose from his chair and headed for the bedroom. "Coming?"

"I've got to clear the table."

"Leave it."

"No, really. It'll just take a minute," she said, stalling.

Carter stepped over and swept his arm across the table. The dishes crashed to the floor, smashing into bits. Paige jumped back, fear spiraling through her.

"Now, it's cleared," he said. His calm tone of voice didn't reassure her.

"I think you'd better go." Her hands trembled.

"Not until I have dessert. You promised."

"Carter! What's the matter with you? Look at what you've done. You scared the crap out of me. I'm not going to sleep with you now. Go home!"

He grabbed her arm. "You were texting Bill in the bathroom, weren't you?"

"Let go. You're hurting me."

"Weren't you?"

"Yes. He's more of a good sport than you are. He took it well."

"Took what?"

"That I couldn't play on his team."

"I'll bet."

"He did. Now let go."

He released her. "Come on," he said, stopping in the bedroom doorway.

"No. The mood is gone."

"Like hell it is. Bill's here, isn't he?"

"I don't know what you mean."

"Yes, you do. He's standing between us. Before he showed up, you were all gung ho to marry me, sleep with me—the whole thing. Now you're holding back, resisting. It's because of him. You'd better get over him, if you want to marry me."

"Go home. Sleep it off," she said, going into the bedroom and slamming the door. Throwing herself down on the bed, she burst into tears, missing the sound of the front door closing.

PAIGE CHECKED HER WATCH. It was noon. Bill's game time was at two. She looked up and down the street, but no sign of her partner. Damn, they had to get going! Paige ran to one end of the block, nothing. When she turned, there was Carter hurrying down the street.

"Sorry I'm late."

"It's okay. Let's go," she said, sliding behind the wheel.

They had not seen each other since their argument. Paige had promised to play tennis with him, and she'd keep her word. Dressed in an all-white Henley shirt and tennis skirt, she threw the car in gear and pulled out onto Riverside Drive.

"I'm sorry about slamming your door," Carter said.

"So you said on the phone."

"I don't know how, why, we get into these fights. The only thing that's different is that asshole, Bill Landeau!"

"Don't start." She raised a hand.

Carter slumped down in his seat and stared out the window. Paige pressed down on the accelerator. Traffic was light. The Harbor Club in Tarrytown wasn't far. She zipped into the first parking spot she found and let Carter retrieve their tennis gear from the trunk.

"Lunch?" he asked.

"Already ate."

He nodded. Her nerves kicked into high gear. How fast could she play in this stupid tournament and still have time to get to Bill's game?

"I'm going to get a snack. And a drink," Carter said.

"Okay. I'll meet you at the snack bar," she said, heading for the tennis court.

After a brief conversation with the organizer, she stuffed a hundred dollar bill in his breast pocket. Before joining Carter, she stretched her leg muscles. An announcement came over the loudspeaker.

"The order of play has been changed. The Wentworth Overton pair is up first."

She spied Carter spit out some of his drink. As he strode over to her, she imagined steam coming out of his ears.

"What happened? Did you do this?"

"And what if I did? Let's go." She retied her shoes and shifted her weight back and forth like she did on the court. "Ready?"

"We've got to beat the first two to survive."

"I know. I'll do my best."

At the stroke of one o'clock, the foursome was on the court. Carter would serve first. The sun beat down on Paige. The heat, coupled with her nerves, generated sweat. It trickled down between her breasts, annoying and distracting her. She missed an easy shot.

"Focus, Paige!" Carter yelled.

"Sorry," she replied.

Back and forth, back and forth, the ball flew, each team stretching, running and leaping to make the return. Paige ran to the sideline for a moment to towel off her face and glance at the clock. Holy crap! It was already two fifteen. They had tied the first two sets, going to tie-breakers.

"Come on, lady. You're holding up the game," the referee said.

Paige got back on the court.

"We can take them," Carter whispered.

But Paige had other ideas. In fifteen minutes, the softball game would begin. Time was running out. The woman on the other side of the net served. Paige missed. Returning the next serve, Paige smacked it out of bounds. Again and again, Paige flubbed the shot.

Red crept up Carter's neck. Paige refused to acknowledge his anger. There was nothing she could do. She had to get to that softball game. Everything depended on it. The man on the other side fired one at Carter, who returned it to the amazement of his opponent. Damn, Carter was good.

He served, the volley went back and forth until it came to Paige. Again, she hit it out of bounds. Carter threw his racquet down and approached her. His face, bright red, was an inch away.

"I know what you're doing."

"I'm sorry. I'm distracted."

"By that asshole Bill! You're throwing the game so you can go to him, aren't you?"

Lying through her teeth, Paige denied it. Damn, Carter knew her too well.

"I'm gonna call for the other side if you two don't get the game going. No delay of game," the referee called.

Paige had nothing to lose. Carter knew what she was doing, so what the hell? She missed every shot that came her way. Within twenty minutes, the game was over. Carter seethed as he stalked off the court.

She made her way to the parking lot but stopped short when she saw Carter, cooling his heels, leaning against her car.

"Going somewhere?"

She checked her watch. It was three. And it would take her almost an hour to get to the field.

"Get out of the way," she said, taking out her key.

He slammed his palm on the hood of her car, making her jump.

"This is all about Bill, isn't it? If you go to him, go to that game right now, it's over between us," he growled.

Inspired by the smug look on his face, she twisted off her engagement ring and put it in his hand. "If you insist. Yes. It's been fun. But it's over. I gotta go," she said.

"How am I going to get home?" he sputtered.

"Take the train," she shot at him as she yanked open the door.

BILL MOPPED THE SWEAT from his brow with his sleeve. He wiped his hand on the back of his pants. It wasn't the strong sun that brought about such a waterfall of perspiration but the fact they were losing. Yep, that asshole, Edgy Malone had put together a winning team. The score was Edgy six and Bill's team three.

Bill faced the other team's biggest slugger, Fats McGinty.

"You can do it." The encouraging words came from Bill's old camp pal, Snake, at first base. Bill had rustled up as many Camp High Point people as he could find in such a short time. But it didn't matter. Edgy's team had the lead. Things looked grim.

As he dug in the dirt on the mound with his toe, his mind kept going back to Paige. If only she had been there. Yeah, Paige. She'd made a choice, maybe the right one for her. She'd chosen Carter over him. He sighed. Couldn't blame her, could he? What did he have to offer her? Goose egg. Nada. Zip. Zero. Just some crazy idea that would never get funding.

"Come on, Landeau! Pitch!" Edgy hollered.

J.C. had a couple of meetings set up for two months from now, but Bill had lost hope. This game had to do it. They had to win. He took a deep breath and pitched. Fats swung and smacked it hard for a home run. Bill swore under his breath and kicked the dirt.

Next up was Edgy's weakest girl. Easy out. Bill fired one in so close he almost hit her and the ump called a ball.

"What the fuck! Focus, Bill," Snake yelled.

Bill swallowed, shook off the sweat and rifled one right over the plate. The girl took a swing and connected, sort of. The ball bounced right into Snake's hands. That made two outs. Edgy stepped up to the plate.

Hatred for the humiliation he'd been suffering at the hands of his opponent choked Bill's chest. He narrowed his eyes and gritted his teeth. The bastard needed to strike out. Focusing all his energy, Bill zoomed one high but just over the corner. Strike one. Then strike two. And for the third one, Edgy, desperate to get a hit, swung. The ball was way low and would have been called a ball, but the batter took a chance. Strike out! Bill did a fist pump.

"So what? We're still leading. You'll never catch up," Edgy taunted, heading for the pitcher's mound.

It was the last half inning. If Bill's team didn't score, Edgy's team would win. But, if Bill's team scored five runs, then they would win. They were four runs behind. Tension hit an all-time high. It didn't look promising.

"You never know in baseball," Bill said to Snake.

He gave his team a pep talk before Snake hit the batter's box. He walked, and Bill hit a double. Snake ran like the wind and scored all the way from first. Only four more to go. Their next batter bunted and outran the throw to end up on first, bringing Bill to third. Irene, up next whacked a single sending Bill home and the first girl to second. Now the score was seven to five, with two on base. The next batter struck out.

Bill could hardly breathe. Was it possible? Could they win? Could he get his dream?

"Bill! Bill! Wait!" came a woman's voice.

He turned. Paige was racing across the field. His heart almost leapt out of his chest.

"She can't play," Edgy said.

"Substitution," Bill called, ignoring his opponent.

"She's not in uniform," Edgy said.

"There's no rule about that."

"Yes, there is."

Bill took off his jersey and tossed it to Paige.

"It's sweaty and smelly. Sorry about that."

"I don't care," she said, slipping the big shirt over her tennis outfit.

"You're up," Bill said.

"Good try. Too little too late," Edgy said.

"Shut up." Bill slipped his arm around Paige. "I know you can do it. Relax. Focus. Remember who you are," he whispered.

She nodded and picked up the bat. As Paige took her stance, Bill muttered a prayer. Edgy narrowed his eyes. He twitched, licked his hand, and squinted before winding up to pitch.

With fingers crossed, Bill held his breath.

"Ball!" the umpire said.

Bill breathed free. Edgy let go another pitch.

"Strike."

Paige and Edgy ran the count up to three balls and two strikes. Sweat poured down Bill's face. Paige shifted her weight a couple of times, spit on the ground, and raised the bat.

Edgy let fly and Paige swung hard. Bill heard the crack of the bat on the ball, then watched the line drive go right to the shortstop who caught it and fired a shot straight at the first baseman, catching the runner off base, creating a double play.

Paige was out, the runner from first was out, and the game was over. Edgy leaped up in the air, grinning. His team did high fives. Bill's heartbeat slowed, his hearing shut down. As if he was walking underwater, everything happened in slow motion.

Tears streamed down Paige's face as she picked up the bat.

"Loser returns the equipment," Edgy said, extending his hand to Bill.

Bill shook and nodded. "Congratulations."

"How does it feel to be the loser for a change?"

"It sucks."

"I know," Edgy said, unable to keep the glee out of his voice.

Paige helped to gather the bases and balls. "I'm sorry."

"Don't worry about it."

"Guess I'm not the slugger anymore."

He pulled her to him. "You'll always be Slugger to me. You came. And you tried. That's what counts." He kissed the top of her head.

"But you lost. And you lost the funding, too."

He wiped tears from her cheek with his hand. "We did everything we could."

"Game well played," J.C. said, shaking Bill's hand. "We'll regroup on Monday."

Bill nodded. He and Paige carried the equipment to the storage shed.

"Dinner?" he asked.

"Chinese takeout and eat at my place?" she responded.

"Sounds great." He laced his fingers with hers and stopped. He glanced down then up. "No ring?"

"I gave it back to Carter today."

"You're free?" he asked, raising his eyebrows.

"Yep," she said, leading them out of the park to the street.

"Guess that makes me a winner after all."

Chapter Six

Bill pushed concerns about saving his job out of his mind. Tonight, he had to focus on Paige. He couldn't believe she'd ditched that idiot, Carter. His heart swelled. Did Bill have a chance? What did he have to offer? Nothing but total love and devotion. His job might be shaky, he didn't even have his own apartment, but no one could love Paige more than he did. Dumping Carter meant a wide-open field. This could be his green light.

After a trip to the Chinese restaurant, they spread out the food containers on the table outside Paige's townhouse. She listened as he recounted the game, inning by inning, then she told him about the tennis match.

"I threw it."

"You what?"

"I threw the match. I screwed up on purpose."

"Why?"

"So I could get to your game. Duh! You said you needed me. And then I messed up."

Bill took her hand and kissed it. "Win some, lose some. You can't expect your first at bat in a gazillion years to end in a home run."

"I did, though. I did expect that I could win it for you," she said, tears forming. "I wanted to. After the raw deal you got from Carter. I wanted that win so bad."

He kissed her. "That's what matters. That you wanted it. I bet Carter was pissed."

A sly smile crossed her face. "He was so mad! He gave me an ultimatum."

"He did?"

"Yep. He said if I went to your game, then we were through. He didn't know that we were already through. So I gave him his ring back and took off."

Bill laughed. "Poor guy. He lost more than the tennis match."

"I love you," she said, her voice so soft he almost didn't hear her.

"Oh, baby. I've waited a long time to hear that."

She fisted his T-shirt and pulled his mouth to hers. Without breaking the lip-lock, Bill whisked her up out of her chair and onto his lap. She tasted of fortune cookie and beer, a heady combination. Desire grew in his loins. Memories of the hours they'd spent kissing and touching at camp filled his brain. He reached for her breast, and she didn't object. They were fuller than he remembered, and oh so soft.

"Not here," she whispered.

One glance around the walled in yard and he noticed other townhouse windows overlooking her little haven. Color crept into his cheeks. He eased her off, stood up, and shielded his crotch with his bottle of beer.

"Yeah. Inside. Definitely inside."

"It's like a stage, you know?"

He nodded, chuckling. "Well said."

She led him into the house and straight up the stairs. Her bedroom was roomy, housing a queen-size bed with a rose-colored chenille spread, a loveseat in pink, a small coffee table, and a dressing table. Bill perused the gathering of lotions and potions on display. He shook his head.

"You don't need that stuff to look beautiful."

"And you're an expert?" she asked, cocking an eyebrow.

"On beautiful women? I do consider myself somewhat more knowledgeable than the average man. And you, well, you're amazing."

He smiled at her blush. Moving closer, he cupped her cheek. "You've always been beautiful."

"Even in a baseball cap and pigtails?"

"Yep. Even with a bat in your hands. Especially in the batter's box."

She threw her arms around his neck. The force of her embrace toppled them over onto the bed. She giggled as they bounced. He landed on top of her.

Her sweet tones brought him back. When they were teens, he'd enjoyed making her laugh, almost as much as he'd liked touching her. Because she was underage, they never went all the way, but, when they could steal alone time, they'd explored each other.

The warmth of her gaze sent heat through him.

"I want you," he muttered.

"Then take me."

"I've waited a long time," he replied.

"Stop talking and do it," she said.

He'd been dreaming about this day. He prayed he could keep from coming too soon. He mounted her, insinuating his leg between hers, pushing up her little tennis skirt. She raised one leg, her foot flat on the bed. He pressed his knee against her center.

Paige tugged off his baseball jersey and slid her palm across his chest. Her touch stoked his fire. Bill glided his hand down her side and around to the back, dipping his fingers under her tennis panties to squeeze her bare bottom. Then he eased his fingers to the front and down her slit. She moaned and pushed against him.

Rolling on his side, and taking Paige with him, he took her mouth. Her arms wound around his neck, and she arched, keeping her chest against his. She slid the nails of one hand down his spine. He shivered—long nails were invented for lovers.

They broke for air. Bill stared down into her passionate gray eyes.

"Are you sure you want to do this?" he asked, his brows drawing together.

"Are you kidding? I've been waiting for forever," she replied.

He smiled. "Me, too." He yanked her shirt up and off.

"Now this," he said, snapping her bra open with one hand.

"Wow. Experienced."

He pushed to his feet and shed his remaining clothes in one movement. Naked, he eased back down on the bed and slowly stripped Paige bare. She cupped his chin, raising his lips to hers. He kissed her once, then turned his attention to her chest.

"You don't know how much I've wanted to see these in daylight."

She laughed. "It's getting dark."

"But it's not midnight."

He stared for a few seconds before putting his face between her breasts and holding them against his cheeks.

"Oh, man. Oh. Oh," he muttered, his eyes drifting shut. He used his fingertips along her skin instead of his eyes. Memories flooded back. Hurried kisses, quick feels, pressing against each other behind the trunk of an old tree. He took a deep breath, inhaling her sweet scent, and the erotic aroma of sexual arousal suspended in the air.

PAIGE SWALLOWED, TRYING to rein in her desire. She studied his face. Though more care-worn than at camp, his rugged features were still handsome. She brushed her fingertips along his cheek, meeting his gaze with hers. Then he lowered his head. When he captured a nipple, her heart flipped. She combed her fingers through his hair and kissed his forehead.

"Darling, Billy," she whispered, taking a deep breath. His scent brought back memories of warm summer nights and the smell of freshly mowed grass.

He snorted and raised his head. "Billy?"

"It's an affectionate nickname and a helluva lot better than slugger." She leaned forward and licked his neck. He tasted the same, uniquely Bill mixed with a dash of salt. How many times had she had him racing through her mind and senses that last summer? Too many to count.

Bill ignored her reply to his comment and returned to grazing on her left breast a bit before moving to the right. When he closed his hand around her thigh, pressing his fingers into her flesh, her body burned for him. He slid his hand all the way up and raised his head.

"If I remember, you used to like this," he whispered, circling his thumb around her sensitive flesh.

"Oh shit. God. Yes," she muttered, easing her shoulders back into the pillows and thrusting her hips up. Her eyes drifted shut.

When he slipped a finger inside her, tension coiled in her loins.

"Yes, yes. Do it. Oh, God. Bill," she said, opening her eyes.

He was propped up, one leg between hers, his face only inches away. His intense, dark eyes bored into hers, lust darkening their already mahogany color. She saw the light of love, glowing there, too.

"I want you. I've always wanted you, and I always will," he said.

"Then take me. Go ahead. Do it."

"I want you screaming for it," he said, sliding down her body. He clasped her hips tight, holding them still while his tongue made contact.

"Holy Hell," she muttered as the heat in her body climbed.

"Delicious," he murmured before returning to his task.

When he pushed up onto his knees, she reached down and curled her hand round his erection. Damn, he was hard as stone.

He pushed her hand away. "Stop."

Crouching down again, he flattened his tongue against her, circling, driving her mad.

"Bill, if you don't—I'm gonna come, I swear," she moaned.

"You want it? Scream for it. Scream for me," he said.

"Yes! Yes, damn it, yes, yes, yes," she hollered.

He chuckled and sat up. "Protected?"

"I'm on the pill."

"Good."

Bill pushed her knees up, and his hot breath on her cheek almost diverted her from the delicious sensation of his penetration. Paige had waited a long time for this. Clasping his chest to hers, she snaked her arms around him, pushing her fingertips into his back muscles. Was he trying to drive her mad by taking it so slow?

"Faster," she huffed.

"I'm taking my time. Waited forever. Not rushing now," he puffed.

A giggle escaped her throat. He had a point. Bill buried himself balls deep, then snuggled his face into her neck.

"God damn, woman," he gasped before drawing out then thrusting back in.

Fire flew through Paige's veins. She'd never been this turned on, this hot, and totally at his mercy. Stubborn, smart, and independent, Paige couldn't imagine turning the reins of her emotions over to a man. But in lovemaking, Bill held all the cards. Her hips fell in with his rhythm as he picked up the pace.

Struggling to control herself to keep from climaxing, Paige finally gave in. When the tension hit the top and boiled over, she groaned loudly as her hips bucked and her muscles contracted. Everything inside her squeezed.

"Oh, baby," Bill muttered.

She opened her eyes to find him staring at her. Sweat beaded on his forehead, chest, and upper lip, but he kept going, even speeding up. She kissed him hard, then lay back, and watched him find his release. Red crept up his neck as he moaned her name, eyes closed.

He blew out a breath and cupped her cheek.

"That was amazing. Worth the wait."

She nodded. God, lovemaking rose to a new level of intensity. As she relaxed in the afterglow and caught her breath, she stared at Bill. Her camp crush had grown into her heart's desire. Who could have known?

BILL TUCKED PAIGE INTO his shoulder and pulled up the sheet. Peace washed over him, making words unnecessary. Love filled his heart. Absently, his thumb caressed the soft skin of her shoulder. He breathed in her sweet scent. What was it, honey? Lilac? Maybe both?

As she snuggled closer, he wondered how it would be to go to sleep like this every night and wake up to Paige beside him every morning. Before a cloud of reality blew his dream away, he focused on how lucky he was to find her.

"God, Bill. Jesus. That was beyond words."

He grinned. Paige twisted around to look up into his eyes. "Well?"

"What can I say? You said it. That was beyond words."

She laughed and eased her arm around his middle. He checked his watch. Throwing open the covers, he swung his legs over the side.

"It's getting late."

"You're leaving?"

He nodded. "Early day tomorrow."

"I have an early day every day. Stay." She grabbed his thumb and stopped him.

"Really?" he asked, raising his eyebrows.

"Really. Come on, do you want to leave?"

"No, but I'd never assume you want me to stay."

"Well, I'm telling you. Okay?"

He climbed back in bed.

"Where were we before you did something dumb?"

He stared at her bare beauty. "Nice talk. Just being polite."

"And a fuck-and-run is polite? Not in my book."

"Then let's do it your way," he replied, pulling her up against him.

"Again? So soon?"

"You're inspirational."

She laughed.

He stilled, raised his hand to brush her hair off her face, then cupped her cheek. "Get over here," he ordered, sliding her to him.

"Aye, aye, sir." She leaned back. Mischief danced in her eyes, but her lips invited him. He bent over to take her mouth. As his passion grew, Bill let go. His senses ruled as he touched and kissed her in anticipation of another coupling. This would be a night to remember for the rest of his life. As she moaned against him, he took a breath and eased his hand down her side. No reason to rush. The lady was more than willing, and he had all the time in the world.

At sunrise, Bill rolled out of bed. He yawned, stretched, and eased up, not disturbing Paige. Before he hit the bathroom, he stopped to gaze at his woman. So vulnerable, sound asleep, her dark hair mussed from loving, her body relaxed. He slipped the sheet down to peek at her rump. What a sight! He grinned.

So what if she didn't vote for his dream? He understood the pressures on her. She still loved him, and that made up for everything. She sighed and changed position. Bill tiptoed into the bathroom and shut the door quietly.

When he'd cleaned up, gotten out, and was ready to dress for the day, she shifted. Pushing up on her hands, she greeted him with a sleepy smile. He thrust his legs into his pants and pulled them up.

"Is it you and me, now?" he asked, perching on the side of the bed.

Paige hugged him, resting her head on his shoulder. "Yes."

Bill swallowed. "I don't have anything to offer you, Paige. Hell, my job might disappear. Especially with this latest loss. I don't even have my own apartment." He took a deep breath.

"So?"

"So how's a guy going to ask a girl to marry him if he has nothing?"

"Marry you?" Her eyebrows shot up.

Shit! Now he'd blown it. In another minute, she'd be laughing. What would the girl with everything want from the boy with nothing?

"I didn't mean to blurt it out like that."

"What did you mean?"

"I meant this," he said, kneeling on the floor in front of the bed, taking her hand. "No matter what I have to do, scrub floors, drive a cab, anything. I promise to provide a good life for you, to make you happy, and to love you forever. Paige, will you marry me?"

Her eyes filled. Bill cringed. She was going to turn him down flat. Ugh, how'd he get himself into this mess?

"What took you so long?" she whispered, a tear sliding down her cheek.

"What?"

"You heard me."

"Is that a yes?"

"Bill Landeau. Sometimes you can be the densest man. Yes, that's a yes!"

Bill's pulse leaped as adrenaline shot through his body. He jumped on Paige, pinning her to the bed while he rained kisses all over her face.

BILL BUTTONED HIS SHIRT, then leaned down to kiss her.

"Early meeting. Call you later. Okay?"

She nodded and watched him dress. As he turned toward the door. "Wait!"

He shot her a questioning look.

"Are we really engaged?"

"I think so. You agreed. Can't back out now."

"I don't want to back out. Just making sure."

"Don't worry. A ring is coming."

"I don't care. Just as long as I have you."

He eased down on the bed next to her.

"You have me for as long as you want me. Maybe a lifetime." He kissed her.

"Go conquer the world," she said as he headed for the door.

Paige sat up in bed and pondered how her family would take the news of her switching her engagement to Bill instead of Carter. Wasn't it time she struck out on her own? She'd dreamt of escaping the expectations of her father and stepmother and living her life her own way.

Paige hadn't deserted her own judgment. As a single woman, before Carter, she'd slept with her fair share of men. She knew when a guy was simply getting off and when he meant it. And Bill meant it. His marriage proposal washed away any doubts. What would her father think of Bill—as a son-in-law? Not that she needed daddy's approval, but it would be nice to know he backed her up.

"Hi, Dad. Do you have a minute for me this morning?"

"Sure. How's ten?"

"Great."

She headed for the shower, where she did her best thinking. Lathering up her hair, she sorted through strategies. Settling on the plain, unvarnished truth, she breathed a sigh and rinsed off.

She styled her hair in a matter of minutes, then donned one of her best suits in rose with a white shell and black pumps. As she headed for the office, strength flowed through her. Bill had been so on target. It was about time she stood up for herself and got what she wanted.

Walking down the street at a brisk pace, she made up her mind. Today was the perfect day to begin her independence. She let out a breath. Finally, living her life her way. Fearless of the consequences, she pushed open the doors of the office building and headed for the elevator. She had fifteen minutes before her conference with Dad. Just enough time for one cup of courage.

When she reached his door, he stood there, leaning against the jamb. His bushy eyebrows drawn together, he looked daunting.

"Hi, Dad," she flipped off, striding past him into his office. "Please close the door."

"Now what is so all-fired important you have to disrupt my entire morning? What's going on? Better not be bad news," he said, positioning himself in his large chair. He lifted an unlit cigar, one he kept by his desk, he never lit or smoked it. "This better not have anything to do with your engagement to Carter."

"Did you talk to him?" she asked, easing down on his sofa.

"He called. Then stopped by."

"Oh?" She quirked an eyebrow.

"To hand me his resignation."

"His resignation?" She sat up straight.

"Told me you'd know all about it."

"I didn't expect him to resign."

"What's done is done. So you don't know about it?"

"I had no idea he'd leave the company," she said, meeting her father's gaze.

"What does that mean for your engagement? You're not leaving, are you?"

"I don't plan to, but you never know."

"Get to the point. Tell me about your engagement to Carter." He picked up his coffee mug.

"Actually, Dad. It's more about me."

Jim Overton sat in a winged chair next to the sofa. "What is?"

"I broke off my engagement to Carter. I'm now engaged to Bill Landeau."

"Bill who?"

"My old camp boyfriend."

"The guy who came in here pitching for a grant for sports summer camps?"

"That's the one."

"I actually liked that idea. So why don't you tell me about him," Jim said, sitting back.

"Well, it started at camp. I was the best hitter on the softball team," she began.

"You played softball?" he asked, his eyebrows rising.

"Not just played. Was the best, Dad. The best. Next to Bill. He coached the team."

Her father leaned back in his chair. "Your mother would have been proud. She picked that camp. Did you know that?"

She shook her head.

He chuckled. "Go on."

THREE WEEKS LATER. Bill's apartment

"I got it. It's perfect. Thanks, Sandy."

"Good. I was so afraid it would get lost."

"I deposited the money in your account. Did it show up?" he asked.

"Yep. We're all squared away. When are you giving it to her?"

"Don't know yet. I'm supposed to see her tomorrow night."

"Any word on your job?"

"J.C. assured me that they would keep me on for another two months. But if funding doesn't show up by then, they will have to take me off payroll. He said I could work for them part-time as a consultant."

"It's better than nothing."

"It's generous of him." Bill sighed.

"Fingers crossed something comes through soon."

"Gotta go. Love you."

"Love you, too." Sandy replied.

Before Bill could put down his phone, it rang again. The number was unknown.

"You're picking up my daughter tonight?"

"Who's this?"

"Jim Overton."

"Oh. Yes, I am."

"Please stop by my office first. I have a proposition for you."

"Can't you tell me now?"

"No time." The phone went dead.

Bill shrugged and went back to work. J.C. stuck his head in.

"I'm expecting calls from West Industries and Colton and Hemmings tonight. Say a prayer. Cross your fingers. Light a candle. Whatever."

"Will do," Bill said, shooting a grin at his boss.

Bill finished up tinkering with the proposal to submit it to another company. He printed it out and gave it to J.C.'s secretary to copy and put in folders. He combed his hair, put on his suit jacket, and headed for Paige's office.

He stopped in front of Jim's secretary.

"Go right in. He's expecting you."

Bill entered the office. Jim rose from his chair and pasted a smile on his face. The hair on Bill's neck stood up.

"Come in, come in, my boy."

Uh, no, I'm not your boy. But I plan to be your son-in-law.

Bill stepped stiffly toward the desk. "You wanted to see me."

"Sit down. Relax."

Remaining on his feet, Bill checked his watch. "I don't have much time. I'm picking up Paige in ten minutes. What can I do for you?"

"It's more about what I can do for you. I've polled the board. Even with Paige abstaining, they would approve your proposal. There's only one vote undecided."

"Really?" Bill's nerves kicked up.

"Yes. That's mine. You can easily have my vote."

"What's stopping you?" An uncertain smile played at his lips.

"I want something in return."

"Oh? What?"

"Here's my proposition. Walk away from my daughter. Break your engagement. Break it off completely, and you'll have my vote."

As if the air had been sucked out of his lungs, Bill stood, unable to speak.

"That's right. Let her go. She's way above your pay grade. I know you're marrying her for her money. Walk away. You get what you want—the grant. And I get what I want, a daughter free from a leech. I think that's a fair deal."

Anger burst in his chest. "Are you out of your mind?"

"If you don't do this, I'll cut Paige off. I'll fire her from the company. She'll be evicted from the townhouse. She'll have nothing."

"I don't care. I don't want her money. I'll make my own."

"Oh? Really? How many companies are breaking down your door to give you the money you need? And if you don't find one soon, how long will your boss keep you? Not long, I'd guess. Take my offer. Get your dream and leave Paige to have the luxury she's used to."

"You're out of your fucking mind. I'd never agree to that."

"Then you'll end up with a pauper for a girlfriend."

"For a *wife*. I don't care. Keep your grant. Fire your daughter. Turn her out of her house. Show her the mean, controlling bastard you are. We'll get along fine. We don't need you."

Bill turned to walk away and almost knocked Paige over. She stood in the doorway. Her face flushed, her eyes were wet, and her chest heaved.

"Paige!" Bill said, bumping into her but catching her before she toppled over.

"Paige. Honey. I didn't see you," her father said, his face coloring.

"Obviously," she replied.

"Really, sweetheart. He's just a gold-digger. He's just after your money."

"You just heard him say he didn't care. He turned down your disgusting offer. Didn't he?"

"You're making a mistake," Jim said, coming out from behind the desk.

"I don't think so. You're the one making the mistake. The biggest mistake of your life."

"Come on, Paige. We don't have to listen to him," Bill said, taking her hand.

"No, we don't."

She shot her father an icy stare and walked out, gripping Bill's arm.

Epilogue

*T*hree weeks later.

Paige closed the latch on her suitcase and wheeled it to the front door. She wrote a quick note and put it on the kitchen table along with a set of keys. She straightened up and looked around. With a sigh, she scanned the beautiful house. *A gilded cage.* Oh sure, the luxury was nice, but the price she'd paid—handing over her freedom—had been way too high.

She stretched her arms up in the air and took a deep breath. Scared? Sure. But the unknown was always scary. The sound of a horn honking drew her attention. She stuffed a tissue in her pocket, picked up her Prada handbag, and opened the front door.

Paige waved to Bill, who sat behind the wheel at the curb in front of her townhouse. When she approached the vehicle, he popped the trunk, got out, and drew her into his arms. After brushing his lips against the corner of her mouth, he took her bag and placed it next to his. With a flourish, Bill opened the door, and she got in. Butterflies danced in her belly. Could she do this?

"Nervous?" he asked, joining her in the front seat.

"Terrified."

"Don't be. Marry me?"

"I already said yes."

"This makes it official," he said, pulling out a small velvet box.

He opened it to reveal a gorgeous emerald-cut diamond ring, significantly smaller than the one she had returned to Carter. Her heartbeat doubled.

"Can you afford this?"

"I've been employed for a while now and saved my money. But don't ever ask me again if I can afford something I'm giving you." He frowned.

"I'm sorry," she said, as he slipped the ring on her finger.

He kissed her. "You're forgiven."

She pulled him to her and pressed her lips to his.

"Seatbelt," he said, grinning.

"Where are we going?"

"A little place called Pine Grove," he said, putting the car in gear.

"Pine Grove?"

"Yep. Colton and Hemmings came through. We've got the grant. We're scouting for locations upstate. And West Industries is on board for next year, in Michigan. North of Detroit."

"Really?" Her eyes widened.

"J.C. called last night. He said they'd signed the papers. This thing is really happening."

Paige snuggled into her seat, grinning. "Amazing."

"Isn't it?" he asked, turning to face her before getting on the West Side Highway, heading north. "Never stop believing."

"You're right. I promise never to stop believing in you," she replied.

"In us. In *us*, Paige. As long as you're with me, we can do anything. We were meant to be."

"Amen to that."

The song *One Fine Day* played on the radio. She turned up the sound and stared out the window as they wound their way along the Palisades Parkway. For the first time in her life, she was traveling on the right road. Happiness filled her heart.

THE END

If you enjoyed these stories, would you be so kind to leave a brief review? Thank you.

About the Author

Jean Joachim is an award-winning, international best-selling romance fiction author, with books hitting the Amazon Top 100 list since 2012. She writes contemporary romance, which includes sports romance and romantic suspense.

Dangerous Love Lost & Found, First Place winner in the 2015 Oklahoma Romance Writers of America, International Digital Award contest. *The Renovated Heart* won Best Novel of the Year from Love Romances Café. *Lovers & Liars* was a RomCon finalist in 2013. And *The Marriage List* tied for third place as Best Contemporary Romance from the Gulf Coast RWA.

To Love or Not to Love tied for second place in the 2014 New England Chapter of Romance Writers of America Reader's Choice contest.

She was chosen Author of the Year in 2012 by the New York City chapter of RWA.

Married and the mother of two sons, Jean lives in New York City. Early in the morning, you'll find her at her computer, writing, with a cup of tea, and a secret stash of black licorice.

Jean has 44 books, novellas and short stories published. Find it here: http://www.jeanjoachimbooks.com. Chat with Jean in her Facebook group, JJ's Book Buddies. Join here: https://www.facebook.com/groups/489790604419710/

Books by Jean C. Joachim

<u>ECHOES OF THE HEART</u>
HEATHER & MIKE: THE ONE THAT GOT AWAY
SANDY & RAFE: SECOND PLACE HEART
LIZ & NICK: NO REGRETS
<u>BOTTOM OF THE NINTH</u>
DAN ALEXANDER, PITCHER
MATT JACKSON, CATCHER
JAKE LAWRENCE, THIRD BASEMAN
NAT OWEN, FIRST BASE
BOBBY HERNANDEZ, SECOND BASE
SKIP QUINCY, SHORT STOP
EXTRA INNINGS
<u>FIRST & TEN SERIES</u>
GRIFF MONTGOMERY, QUARTERBACK
BUDDY CARRUTHERS, WIDE RECEIVER
PETE SEBASTIAN, COACH
DEVON DRAKE, CORNERBACK
SLY "BULLHORN" BRODSKY, OFFENSIVE LINE
AL "TRUNK" MAHONEY, DEFENSIVE LINE
HARLEY BRENNAN, RUNNING BACK
OVERTIME, THE FINAL TOUCHDOWN
A KING'S CHRISTMAS
<u>THE MANHATTAN DINNER CLUB</u>

RESCUE MY HEART
SEDUCING HIS HEART
SHINE YOUR LOVE ON ME
TO LOVE OR NOT TO LOVE
<u>HOLLYWOOD HEARTS SERIES</u>
IF I LOVED YOU
RED CARPET ROMANCE
MEMORIES OF LOVE
MOVIE LOVERS
LOVE'S LAST CHANCE
LOVERS & LIARS
His Leading Lady (Series Starter)
<u>NOW AND FOREVER SERIES</u>
NOW AND FOREVER 1, A LOVE STORY
NOW AND FOREVER 2, THE BOOK OF DANNY
NOW AND FOREVER 3, BLIND LOVE
NOW AND FOREVER 4, THE RENOVATED HEART
NOW AND FOREVER 5, LOVE'S JOURNEY
NOW AND FOREVER, CALLIE'S STORY (prequel)
<u>MOONLIGHT SERIES</u>
SUNNY DAYS, MOONLIT NIGHTS
APRIL'S KISS IN THE MOONLIGHT
UNDER THE MIDNIGHT MOON
MOONLIGHT & ROSES (prequel)
<u>LOST & FOUND SERIES</u>
LOVE, LOST AND FOUND
DANGEROUS LOVE, LOST AND FOUND
<u>NEW YORK NIGHTS NOVELS</u>
THE MARRIAGE LIST
THE LOVE LIST
THE DATING LIST
<u>SHORT STORIES</u>

SWEET LOVE REMEMBERED
TUFFER'S CHRISTMAS WISH
THE HOUSE-SITTER'S CHRISTMAS

Don't miss out!

Visit the website below and you can sign up to receive emails whenever Jean C. Joachim publishes a new book. There's no charge and no obligation.

https://books2read.com/r/B-A-MDPF-LYSV

BOOKS 2 READ

Connecting independent readers to independent writers.